$= \dfrac{6.80}{\text{cxx}}$

2

BOOKS BY JOSEPH WAMBAUGH

Fiction

The New Centurions
The Blue Knight
The Choirboys
The Black Marble
The Glitter Dome
The Delta Star
The Secrets of Harry Bright
The Golden Orange
Fugitive Nights
Finnegan's Week
Floaters

Nonfiction

The Onion Field
Lines and Shadows
Echoes in the Darkness
The Blooding

JOSEPH WAMBAUGH
FLOATERS

BANTAM BOOKS

NEW YORK   TORONTO   LONDON   SYDNEY   AUCKLAND

FLOATERS

A Bantam Book / June 1996

BOOK DESIGN BY GLEN EDELSTEIN.

Library of Congress Cataloging-in-Publication Data
Wambaugh, Joseph.
Floaters / Joseph Wambaugh.
p.   cm.
ISBN 0-553-10351-2
I. Title.
PS3573.A475F58   1996
813'.54—dc20   95-26625
                                                              CIP

Published simultaneously in the United States and Canada

Bantam Books are published by Bantam Books, a division of Bantam Doubleday Dell Publishing Group, Inc. Its trademark, consisting of the words "Bantam Books" and the portrayal of a rooster, is Registered in U.S. Patent and Trademark Office and in other countries. Marca Registrada. Bantam Books, 1540 Broadway, New York, New York 10036.

PRINTED IN THE UNITED STATES OF AMERICA

BG   0 9 8 7 6 5 4 3 2 1

For the Gants:
Dick, Janene, Loxie, and Holden

ACKNOWLEDGMENTS

As usual, terrific cop talk was arranged by the San Diego Police Department's storytelling impresario, Detective Tony Puente.

SDPD officers included: Russ Bristol, Cheri Curley, Jorge Duran, Antoine El-Assis, Karl Ellison, Christine Gregg, Rick Hansen, Barbara Harrison, Renee Hill, Roy Huntington, Alicia Lampert, Scott Lee, Joe Lehr, Dave Michalek, Bill Montejano, Sharon Newberry, Anne O'Dell, Mike O'Neill, Mike Richardson, Rich Rundberg, Sandra Smullen, Lou Tamagni, and John Tefft.

Wonderful conversation was also provided by officers of the Harbor Police: Jen Borgen, Kathy Fabregas, Gordon Galligan, Dave King, Gary Leeson, and Cynthia Markley.

Team New Zealand anecdotes were offered by grinder Craig Monk, as well as by Dave Pizzini of the Otahuhu Police and John Purkis of the Auckland Police, the team security force.

Jerry La Dow of Team Dennis Conner was extremely helpful in unraveling the intricacies of America's Cup yacht racing.

Tom and Jane Wilson of the San Diego Yacht Club related the fascinating history and captivating lore of the Cup itself.

Other yachtsmen who furnished lively chat and insight were Fred Delaney, John Driscoll, Mike Driscoll, Larry Maio, and Bryan Worthington of the San Diego Yacht Club.

Dr. Tom Cummings and John Urquhart also provided valuable facts.

The author offers a thousand thanks to one and all. There could not have been a book without them.

FLOATERS

PROLOGUE

On December 7, exactly fifty-three years after the day that lives in infamy, a 75-foot boat that cost nearly as much as some of those lost in the Pearl Harbor raid was photographed just after it fell from its cradle fifteen feet above the launching dock. The keel of the boat, like all of the closely guarded, supersecret keels of the America's Cup sailing yachts, was driven up through the deck like a torpedo. It was to have been the maiden launching of this boat, called *France 2* by the French yachting syndicate.

The team members were so beside themselves that one of the sailors actually started screaming, *"Sacré bleu! Sacré bleu!"* causing a man who was snapping pictures to say to his partner, "I thought they only said that in *Pink Panther* movies."

The irony of the boat being trashed on Pearl Harbor day wasn't lost on the partner, who said, "This time around nobody can blame it on the banzai boys. They're too busy with the Kiwis for sneak attacks."

By that he meant that in a sport notorious for espionage, Team Nippon had its hands full with America's Cup racing and Cup politics, confronted as it was by two hot boats in the New Zealand syndicate as well as the Kiwis' accusations that the Japanese had violated the two-boat limit with their added *JPN-30* hull.

Moreover, Team Nippon had to worry about a formidable foe in oneAustralia, although the other Australian challenger didn't scare anybody, nor did the Spanish. Nor any longer did the French, now that they were gawking at Waterloo on Mission Bay.

Suddenly, one of the Frenchmen—a starboard trimmer from Cherbourg who was even ruder than the others—spotted the man snapping the photos. This was the same Frog who threatened to phone the consulate every time he got stopped for ripping around Mission Bay like a Paris cabbie in one of those dopey little Citroëns, fit only for delivery of car bombs by neurotic Arabs. His idea of defensive driving was tooting the horn, and Mission Bay cops referred to him as a marginally rehabilitated Algerian terrorist. They also called him "the crème de la crumbs."

The Froggie scampered across the boatyard to the fence, yelling: "No! You shall not to fo-*toe* le keel!"

The shutterbug's partner could only gape as the 25-ton yacht settled a few more inches, causing the keel to angle up. His comment was "Ooh-la-la. Like a giant hard-on yearning to be free."

The photographer stopped snapping long enough to say, "Let's beat feet to the Photo-Mat. Gotta get these to the press before Carlos the Jackal here phones the mayor, the State Department, and Catherine Deneuve!"

While the furious Frog stormed away, yammering to his team that their secret keel was being compromised, two security guards belatedly tossed a tarp over it. And the crane operator who'd dropped the boat sat in his crane, jaw agape, trying to decide whether to jump into Mission Bay and swim for Catalina or climb down and be torn limb from limb by three dozen raging Frenchies.

Unlike the Kiwis and Aussies, the French were relentlessly arrogant with the cops, infuriating all five members of Mission Bay's San Diego Police Department Harbor Unit. The cops promised a case of beer to the first one who could bust a Frog for DUI or any other law violation on land or water. And that included French syndicate sponsors and their boyfriends, girlfriends, priests, or poodles.

A short time later the photographer and his partner were still grinning like chum-lusting tiger sharks when they boarded their 22-foot Boston Whaler to begin their routine patrol of Mission Bay. But when they cruised past the compound of the French, who were wondering what to do with a $2 million mangled heap of fiber-reinforced composites, the amateur photographer turned on the patrol boat's gumball-blue light and hit them with a few siren yelps.

The Froggies returned fire with rude French gestures as well as with American expressions all ending in "cock-suck-airs!" And the snapshooter turned to his partner, saying, "Sometimes a policeman's lot really *is* a happy one."

His photograph, headlined "French Follies," was soon seen in all parts of the planet where anyone gives a damn about a regatta that last time around had cost the *losing* Italian syndicate more than $100 million, triggering bankruptcy and suicide.

Of course, the happy shutterbug couldn't have known that his picture of a dildo keel would soon inspire a plot leading to murder and ensnare human beings like dolphins in a gill net. For he was just a San Diego cop who drove a boat, not a true man of the sea. Not one who understands in his soul that the actions of people are like the tides that chase the moon but invariably come crashing back, with all manner of thrashing things roiling in their foamy wake.

CHAPTER 1

BLAZE USED TO USE A HENNA RINSE ON HER PUBIC HAIR BEFORE SHE became an outcall masseuse. Of course, she was no more a real masseuse than she'd been a real dancer back in the days when she'd hire out at parties delivering striptease telegrams. Her massage customers didn't care about fiery pubes any more than telegram recipients had cared that she'd been a hopeless singer and dancer, for she had other attributes.

Blaze Duvall was a lustrously muscled but relentlessly female aerobics devotee who diligently practiced every buns-of-steel exercise devised by instructors at the class she took five times a week. But with her thirtieth birthday approaching, Blaze imagined she saw disturbing things in the full-length mirror behind the entry door of her overpriced, one-bedroom Fashion Hills apartment: a tiny dollop of cellulite here, a minuscule sag there, where flesh used to be firm as plastic.

With only two thousand dollars in her bank account and a net worth of no more than twenty thousand—including her yellow Mustang convertible, her modestly priced furniture, and some decent jewelry given by bucks-up clients who appreciated her talents—Blaze's future was tenuous.

Foremost among her talents was an ability to talk to men.

Long before her shoulder-length mane became ferociously red at seventy-five dollars a pop, excluding tip, and long before her name was Blaze Duvall, she'd been able to do that very well. Because she'd *always* been a woman and every man she'd ever known was a child. Secondly, Blaze was a chameleon, able to adjust to any audience.

Blaze examined her naked body in the mirror. Brown pubic hair? Who cared, now that she was no longer stripping in lighted rooms, singing bawdy telegrams off-key?

For this evening she chose a matching set of panties and bra, pink with scalloped bands of lace. Her client, "number eight," liked pink even though it wasn't her best color, not with flaming hair, wide-set, shamrock-green eyes, and a dust of sandy freckles all over. But the customer was always right as long as the customer obeyed her rules.

The doorbell. Blaze checked the time on her gold Rolex and put on her blue terry robe. She squinted through the peeper in gloomy twilight at a spindly blonde, who knew she was being observed.

"Hi, Blaze!" said Dawn Coyote, whose true name was no more Dawn Coyote than hers was Blaze Duvall. The San Diego police and Dawn's mother also knew her as Jane Kelly.

Dawn entered the apartment in her street costume: see-through cobweb of a red blouse, shiny black leather skirt, red spike heels. She was way past lean now, bones knobbing out at the wrists, knees, and ankles. Mournful blue eyes peered out under ragged putty-colored bangs that might as well have been cut with pruning shears.

Blaze was mad. "I told you *don't* come here when you're working! You're gonna bring cops here one of these days. How do you know Vice isn't following you?"

Dawn rushed past her, wobbling on the spikes, heading straight for the tiny kitchen, saying, "They ain't, Blaze. They ain't."

Dawn Coyote had lisped ever since she got her tongue pierced, finding it hard to wrap it around sibilants what with the zircon stud getting in the way. She tore open a bag of M&M's and popped a few in her mouth.

Blaze watched Dawn pulling up the sleeves of the red polyester blouse, examining the tracks where she slammed her speedballs, a mixture of powdered cocaine and Mexican tar heroin.

"Girl, don't you dare shoot up in my home!" Blaze said.

"I ain't, Blaze!" Dawn lisped. "I'm jist putting some vitamins on, is all. Works better than cream. But, like, I gotta put it on right after I shoot up."

The young woman's bony hand trembled as she squeezed liquid from a plastic bottle and dabbed it on her inner forearm. Then she put the bottle away and started scratching. First her ass, then her underarms, then below her tiny tits. Then she backed against the fridge and scratched herself on the chrome door-pull.

Disgusted, Blaze said, "You were better off tweaking. Your color's all leached out. Your beautiful skin is wrecked. You're gonna look forty when you're thirty if you don't get off those speedballs."

"I'm getting off," Dawn promised, as she always did. "Soon as I dump Oliver."

"I'm sick of warning you about that pimp. You better shine him now."

"Kin you loan me a hundred, Blaze? I got me a two-hundred-dollar date Saturday night."

"Why don't you get it from Oliver?"

"He's all pissy these days. Won't give me nothin' hardly. I'm gonna go to L.A., see my sister. Might jist stay there." Then she paused and said, "Got any gum?"

Blaze opened the kitchen cabinet and gave Dawn a pack of Juicy Fruit, saying, "Here, this flavor works best."

"Ever try bubble gum?" Dawn asked, biting open the pack. "Some girls say bubble gum works best."

"What're you gonna do with the baby?"

The sallow, sniffling girl jammed two sticks in her mouth and began chewing painfully.

"My sister'll help me with Billy. She wouldn't if he was Oliver's baby. She goes, 'Long as he ain't half nigger I'll take him.' Lucky for him he ain't."

"Wait here." Blaze disappeared into the bedroom and closed the door. Dawn was her friend, but a junkie's a junkie. She retrieved a roll of bills from inside a knitted ski cap at the top of the closet and counted out five twenties. When she returned, she found Dawn unbuttoning the polyester blouse and displaying her bare torso before the full-length mirror.

"Whadda ya think, Blaze? Oliver says the johns'll pay jist to *look* at this!"

Dawn's little breasts were tattooed with giant spiders whose legs encircled her nipples. A gold alligator clip was clamped onto each nipple, joined by a gold chain that was hooked onto a second chain that disappeared down inside her skirt. Dawn unzipped her leather skirt, peeled it down, and showed Blaze where the second chain went.

"Tit 'n' clit chains. Right now they're only clamped on, but pretty soon I'm gonna get 'em pierced, like when I get used to the pain."

"You dumb shit!" Blaze said. "Take that off!"

"No, wait! It ain't gonna hurt no more once it's done right. Oliver says the johns like to pull on the chain a little bit when they can't get movin' and groovin'. Then I get all, like, I'm in pain big time? And the john gets all feelin' bad? 'Cause me, I'm cryin'! So they give me an extra twenty at least! Oliver goes—"

Interrupting, Blaze said, "Remember that movie *Pretty Woman*? The one you loved so much, about the happy young hooker? Well, they forgot to show *this* fucking part!"

When Dawn's skirt snagged on the clit chain, she whimpered and rezipped it gingerly.

"Tell me, Dawn," Blaze said, "did you nurse your baby when you were shooting up speedballs?"

Shaking her head, "I wouldn't do that, Blaze. I bottle-fed him."

"What kind of fool am I?" Blaze asked rhetorically, but went ahead and handed Dawn the twenties.

Dawn tucked the money inside her panties, took out the gum pack, and shoved yet another stick in her mouth.

When Blaze opened the door, Dawn said, "I don't know? Maybe bubble gum *would* do it better? I jist can't *ever* get the taste a condoms outta my mouth! Kin you?"

•   •   •

Norman G. "Letch" Boggs was one of those middle-aged cops immune to sexual-harassment complaints. Letch was short, bald, lardy at the hips, with the muscle tone of a bruised banana. He smelled worse than a Beastie Boys concert because he consumed more garlic than Sicily. He loved it roasted, fried, sautéed, raw. He ate tomato-mayonnaise-and-raw-garlic sandwiches that made people want to puke just watching him. Convinced that garlic retarded aging and enhanced potency, Letch claimed he'd get garlic withdrawal if ever he missed a day. So he didn't.

Letch's wet grin—more of a leer, which exposed oversized rodent teeth—had a lecherous quality to it, hence his nickname. Moreover, he spent more time watching confiscated porn flicks than any vice cop in the history of the SDPD, so his sobriquet was earned. Though he'd made a pass at nearly every female who'd set foot on the fifth floor of the downtown police headquarters, no one believed that a woman would take him seriously. Still, some had; he was twice divorced.

Letch could get away with amorous suggestions, lascivious whispers, even an occasional pat that'd make his target gasp and retreat the second she caught a whiff, but it never initiated a complaint. That's because sex with the leering debauchee was unthinkable. Letch was like a police dog that humped your leg.

But he was an astoundingly effective vice cop with a memory like an IBM laptop. And Letch had the instincts of a ferret, which was even better for someone in his sordid line of work.

He sat dozing in his unmarked vice car on a street in Fashion Hills, staked out on Dawn Coyote, who was visiting an unknown person in one of those nice little apartments overlooking Mission Valley. He wasn't directly concerned about a junkie hooker like Dawn Coyote, but he knew she worked for Oliver Mantleberry, a pimp long overdue for a serious fall. Having busted Dawn twice when she was a tweak monster on crystal meth, and hearing that she was now heavy into speedballs, Letch figured she was ripe to roll over on her pimp. Especially if Letch could use her little cub as leverage.

They were all alike, junkie whores, their whelps being their last link to a sense of self as human beings. Use their cubs as a twist and they'd drop a dime on their mothers. Or their pimps as the case might be.

Letch Boggs was sleepy because he'd been up late for the third night in a row, peeing on a tree. All because this nutcase little Scottish terrier living next door to him was driving him crazy. The dog started barking the minute his mistress left for work at 8:00 A.M. That was just when the weary night-shift vice cop would be deepest into REM sleep, dreaming about Jacuzzis and pubescent maidens. Letch thought about slipping the bowser some barbiturates but was afraid it might croak. He didn't want an OD'd Scottie on his conscience.

One morning he noticed that each time the buxom mistress took her Scottie for a stroll, the dog got all obsessive-compulsive about peeing on top of any other dog pee he encountered. He particularly favored a pepper tree between the neighbor's house and Letch's duplex apartment in his residential neighborhood on the north side of Ocean Beach.

The Scottie's mistress was a buffed-out Aussie, and after returning from work in the late afternoon she usually wore a wraparound skirt over a leotard and tights while walking the Scottie. In the past, Letch had displayed his hamster leer and tried a "G'day" on her a few times, but she'd just given him a chilly nod. Once when she was only wearing the leotard and tights minus the skirt, he whistled "Tie Me Kangaroo Down, Sport," but she told him to bugger off.

So Letch finally changed tack and confronted her at the curb in front of his duplex. He suggested that maybe her little dog was real unhappy, what with her gone to work six days a week, because the little hairball barked nonstop from 8:00 A.M. till he got hoarse. Letch suggested that she ought to consider giving the dog to the nice family across the street because the only time he'd shut up was when one of the kids came over to play with him and give him treats. He was sure they'd take the dog off her hands in a heartbeat, and the pooch'd have a much happier home.

The Aussie told Letch she doubted that the terrier barked all that much because nobody else had ever complained. And, sure, the dog could come and go through the doggy door in the daytime, but he almost always preferred to stay inside and sit quietly on the back of the sofa by the window. "Gazing quietly and doglike at life on the street outside" was what she said.

Letch told her he was a day sleeper and, trust him, the dog didn't sit quietly on the sofa, and would she please just lock him in when she went to work because at least his yapping would be somewhat muffled.

She said that a dog could not be expected to hold his pee that long, and she wasn't going to risk his hurting his kidneys by making him do it.

In that case, Letch said, he'd have to take the matter into his own hands. She asked him what *that* meant and Letch answered that he didn't know, but maybe a dognapper'd throw the little bastard into a billabong—whatever that was—like the poor old swagman in "Waltzing Matilda."

She answered by threatening to call the police.

That's when Letch devised the scheme to pee on the tree and drive the little bowwow bonkers.

It worked like magic the first time he tried it. Letch got home very late after his Saturday shift, choked down three glasses of water, and crept outside, making just enough noise on the walkway for the terrier to come to the window.

Then Letch whipped out his willie and started to pee on the tree, right through the chain-link fence, lighting up the scene with the beam from his pencil flashlight so the Scottie couldn't miss it.

The dog went ballistic. He barked and clawed the window and whined. Letch shut it off prematurely and tiptoed back inside the apartment to drink more water and wait.

Presently he heard the doggy-door flap open when she raised the slider to let the terrier out. Of course the pooch padded down the steps heading straight for the tree to pee over Letch's.

After the Scottie went back inside, Letch sidled outside and whistled just loud enough for canine ears. When the pooch looked out, Letch headed for the tree and turned on the beam and the stream.

This time the terrier howled like a wolf. Letch sneaked into the laundry room by the back porch and heard the Aussie open the door and yell, "Bloody hell, Nigel! This is the last time!"

The frantic terrier scuttled down the steps, made a beeline for the tree, hardly paused to sniff, and peed over Letch's. Three minutes after the anxious dog scampered back inside, Letch did it again. A few squirts was all he could muster this time, but Nigel peeked out the window and made a *terrible* ruckus. Music to a weary vice cop's ears.

Last night was the third in a row that he'd tormented the compulsive terrier. Letch figured another night or two and the babe would *pay* the kids across the street to adopt the stressed-out pooch. But Letch was dog-tired himself from all the night prowling. Not to mention all the stops and starts that weren't helping his bladder *or* his prostate.

Just then, Dawn Coyote emerged from a doorway on the second floor of the apartment complex and Letch trained his binoculars on the door before it closed. It was nearly obscured by mottled shadows, but he caught a glimpse of the number 2A on the door and made a mental note.

When Dawn got back behind the wheel of Oliver Mantleberry's white Jaguar, Letch followed her at a safe distance to her place of business, a corner on El Cajon Boulevard. Under a streetlight. Like every whore for a hundred years.

•   •   •

While Blaze was rummaging through her crowded closet trying to find something pink for fashion-challenged number eight, she was the subject of a telephone call from number sixty-three.

That telephone call, like all the calls regarding Blaze Duvall, had a life of its own. First the caller would reach a number at an answering service that never picked up. The call would be forwarded after one ring to a seventy-two-year-old former hooker called Serenity Jones, who at one time had had twenty girls working for her before she got busted and sentenced to six months in jail for pandering. Now Serenity Jones contracted with just three girls, who did outcall massages at $200 a visit. Whatever they got over and above that was their business, as long as Serenity got her forty-percent commission on the standard fee. Serenity never tried to chisel her girls and wouldn't stand for it in return.

Nevertheless, Blaze and the other two masseuses would occasionally burn the old madam. When they had a regular client they could trust, they'd sometimes suggest he call a different number listed to a close friend of the masseuse's. That way the masseuse could keep the whole tariff and Serenity would be none the wiser.

Blaze liked Serenity, and she especially liked the first-class clients Serenity sent her way, so she was careful not to cheat the old babe too often. Blaze's pal for the occasional beat-the-madam call was Dawn Coyote, who maintained a separate phone line and answering machine bought and paid for by Blaze Duvall. She also paid Dawn $200 a month for the service.

When Serenity took the call from number sixty-three, she was sprawled in her leather recliner with a Siamese cat on her lap. Dribbles of ice cream splattered her flowered muumuu and the cat licked them from time to time. Serenity's platinum hair was in rollers, but even in the daytime she wore a trowel load of eye shadow, and her crimson acrylic nails were long enough for spearfishing.

Serenity knew from personal experience that without a scanner the cops would have a hard time tracing her if she used a mobile cellular phone. Even so, when she got a suspicious call on her cell phone she was always prepared to say adios and move on down the road to another apartment. People in her business couldn't get sentimental about hearth and home.

That afternoon Serenity was really getting into the panel they had on her favorite trash talk show. Five transsexuals, the smallest of whom weighed more than two hundred and fifty pounds, were telling the audience how it was easier to be a fat babe than a fat dude. Serenity got annoyed when the cell phone rang, but she hit the mute button on her TV remote and answered.

While Blaze Duvall was still trying to figure out how the hell to be pretty in pink, a male voice said to Serenity, "This is number sixty-three. Please tell the lovely redhead that I'd like to see her tomorrow night. Eight-thirty. Same place as last time. Same room number."

Serenity said, "Okay, doll, that's fab. Any special instructions?"

The male voice said, "Warm. I'd like it *warm* this time."

"Fab, doll," Serenity said, hanging up and pressing the mute button just in time to hear the TV host ask one of the transsexuals whether she ever missed her penis. And what did she think when sick persons asked her if she'd pickled and jarred it as a memento?

Serenity tossed the tabby off her tummy and waddled to the fridge for another dish of cookies'n fudge ice cream, wondering how she'd ever coped with life before the freak shows. After she plopped back down in the recliner, she dialed a number, reaching Blaze's voice mail.

Blaze never picked up, but she listened to Serenity say, "Hello, darling. Number sixty-three would like to see your good self tomorrow evening. Eight-thirty. Same place as last time. And, oh yeah, he wants it warm this time. Bye, darling doll."

After looking as good as she could in a horrible pink turtleneck and tight blue jeans, Blaze wrote on a notepad beside the answering machine, "Icy Hot. 63."

She was very glad to hear from number sixty-three. It'd been three months, yet he'd always been a reliable bimonthly client at $200 per. And he'd give her at least a $20 tip if she used any imagination at all.

"Wants it warm" referred to his fetish for Icy Hot or Ben-Gay, cream used to heat up strained muscles and sports injuries. When she'd first started in the business, Blaze made the mistake of accidentally smearing a gob on a client's balls. The john came up off the bed like a Harrier jet and she never made that mistake again.

When she'd told Serenity about the accident, the old pro had just given her a dimpled smile and said, "Stay away from Petey and the twins with that stuff. The johns can get *that* at the ballpark."

"Get what?" Blaze had wanted to know.

Serenity had sung a little learning jingle to her novice masseuse: "Hot nuts! Red-hot nuts! They can get 'em from the pea-nut maaaan!"

CHAPTER 2

APRIL FOOL'S DAY FELL ON A SATURDAY, AND THE KEEPER OF THE CUP was delighted to turn on his TV without fear of encountering the O. J. Simpson legal circus. The trial was especially unfortunate for the America's Cup regatta because TV coverage would draw away attention from the defender and challenger finals that were set to begin on April 10 and 11, televised live on ESPN.

The Keeper of the Cup sat on the rear deck of his hillside house in Point Loma, drinking his morning coffee and enjoying an unobstructed view of San Diego harbor and a white-water view of Coronado. After his sister died he had become the sole heir to his widowed mother's estate, which consisted only of the nondescript sixty-five-year-old house with a leaky roof and termites galore.

But because of the glorious view the place was worth at least $1,250,000. His realtor colleagues thought the land might fetch even more without the ramshackle house on it, but he was one of the few local real-estate agents with faith that the California housing market would rebound. He was determined to live in the house until it happened, or until termites brought it down on his head, which was possible.

The property, his mother had liked to remind him, would provide enough money to see him comfortably through old age—because, in her words, he'd never provided adequately for himself. He was, after all, not even a broker, only an agent. She'd never tired of reminding him that he had been destined for mediocrity from the moment he'd dropped out of college. That was a reckless decision his father had never gotten over, or so his mother had needed to reiterate most of his life.

Long before her death at age eighty-five, he'd given up defending himself against her belittling and her unfavorable comparisons to his sister Sheila's unbearably aggressive husband, Bradley, a big-bucks plastic surgeon. The fact is, his tear ducts hadn't been overworked by the passing of either of the two women in his life. It was no wonder he'd never married, what with a lifetime of trying to outswim those man-eaters.

He considered pouring himself another cup of coffee, hoping the morning overcast would soon burn off. Everyone talked about how the wet winter had seemed endless this year and how it might affect the unpredictable seas off San Diego and the America's Cup regatta.

Then he thought maybe he should go to the office, weekend or not. There'd been quite a bit of walk-in tourist action at the local real-estate offices during the America's Cup challenger trials. Hopefully there'd be a lot more when the finals got under way, but of course most of the tourists were looky-loos. Still, you never knew. People who followed yacht racing didn't need food stamps. In fact, one of his real-estate competitors had sold a $1,350,000 Sunset Cliffs oceanfront home to a walk-in client that very week. You couldn't predict the out-of-town sailing crowd.

There was a big article in the paper that morning about the New Zealand challenger, and as he looked at the headline, it brought a cold lump to his gut, like a bag of wet sand. The New Zealanders were more than good. And their two boats? Seagoing rockets. He hated to even think of the Cup going to Auckland next month.

Everyone said that if the Cup left the San Diego Yacht Club it'd never return, not in his lifetime, perhaps not in the Cup's lifetime. Nobody was going to mount another $65 million campaign under the aegis of the San Diego Yacht Club as Kansas millionaire Bill Koch had done successfully in the Cup regatta of 1992. Since then the blustering Koch felt that he had been badly treated by the yacht club and had made his views all too public. The Keeper of the Cup had to agree that if it went, it would never be won back by a San Diego challenger.

He glanced at the time: 9:10. His Omega Speedmaster gold chronograph reminded him of where it had come from—an Omega company executive had given it to him when he'd accompanied the Cup to the Barcelona Boat Show.

He and the Cup had gone to Spain twice, to Paris three times, and to Monaco, where he'd stood in a receiving line and met Prince Rainier himself. He'd been to England four times, and to Ireland, where the enthusiasm was wonderful.

He'd traveled with it to Hong Kong, and to Tokyo, where the Japanese went wild over it. He'd taken it to Sydney and Toronto and Bern. He and the Cup had gone to one hundred American cities during the seven and a half years since Dennis Conner and his boat, *Stars and Stripes,* had won it back from the Aussies at Fremantle.

What a time *that* was! A DC-10 was almost filled with only America's Cup rooters when it landed back in San Diego on a Saturday afternoon. A parade of convertible cars was hastily formed and were driven with the Cup and the conquerors from the airport to the Broadway Pier, then back to the plane and on to New York to meet Ronald Reagan and two thousand yachting enthusiasts. The Keeper of the Cup nostalgically recalled it all: the pipers, the bands, the yacht club commodores, all waiting for them in New York.

And he resented the yachting world for criticizing San Diego's handling of the Cup. From 1851 to 1983 the Keepers of the Cup at the New York Yacht Club had never shown the Cup to anybody, yet the San Diego Yacht Club had shown it to the world. And he, an unpaid volunteer, just a dedicated club member, had lovingly protected that baroque twenty-seven-inch chunk of silver every-

to five miles an hour, the same speed limit as in the channels and smaller passages all over the water park.

The water cops thought their uniform alone was a plus. Instead of the regular tan SDPD wool blend, the Harbor Unit got to wear comfortable cotton khaki with an embroidered badge that wouldn't rust in the salt spray. And nylon gun belts with a quick-detacher in case they fell overboard. And blue baseball caps, with blue jackets that doubled as flotation devices. They could even wear shorts, weather permitting. Nylon gun belts were issued after it was discovered that in just a few months on the bay, a leather Sam Browne would come to resemble an elephant's ass.

So far, Leeds hadn't come up with an April Fool's Day joke to play on his boss. Two years earlier he'd gone to the trouble of capturing a ground squirrel and putting it in the bottom drawer of the sergeant's desk. Recapturing it after it scared the crap out of the guy had nearly destroyed the entire office.

These days Leeds was preoccupied with politics rather than practical jokes. A hobnailed Republican, he'd dedicated himself to purging the nation of President Clinton, whom he called the dude with the world's worst taste in babes. Anything could bring on a political diatribe. When they cruised past the Youth Camp area on Fiesta Island and a boozy bunch of teenagers playing volleyball on the beach flipped them off, Leeds said, "I wanna retire to a place where everyone waves at cops with *all* their fingers. It's still not too late to turn the country around if the Republicans get the White House."

"Here we go again." Fortney sighed.

Leeds said, "Okay, okay," meaning he wouldn't get started on politics that irritated Fortney, a self-styled Libertarian who believed that *all* politicians were gasbags and that people who belonged to tongs and tribes were better led.

To get Leeds off the subject Fortney pointed to an up-to-the-minute yupster standing on the bow of a 31-foot Chaparral with twin screws and a radar arch. The guy wore one of those banded-collar shirts with trendy sleeves down past his elbows, brand-new chambray shorts, and sockless Top-Siders. He was topped off by a Greg Norman golf hat, and lazily swung a five iron while his bikini-clad girlfriend drove the boat. He'd stop each swing at the top and pose, asking her if his club had passed horizontal.

"He swings like one of Jerry's kids," Fortney said. "Get him a telethon. Tonight he'll be in the cabin with palms up staring at a crystal pyramid and listening to Yanni. I've seen chimps better dressed on the David Letterman show."

Leeds said, "You're just jealous of his boat. *And* his clothes, and especially his girlfriend."

"Well, no shit," said Fortney. "How observant you are."

"Trouble with you is, you're a very archaic person for someone who ain't that old," Leeds said, checking out the babe, who smiled at him.

Fortney said, "In August I'm forty-five. *Then* I'm old."

"You been old for years," Leeds said. "Give the modern world a chance. You probably didn't vote Republican in the last election because our senatorial candidate's wife was a New Age preacher. Am I right?"

Fortney replied, "Okay, name the most nonsensical things in the modern world if it isn't New Age music, decaf coffee, booze-free beer, and Ross Perot."

"You didn't vote for our candidate, did ya?" Leeds persisted. "Even though *lots* of political leaders had crackpot spouses. People like Abe Lincoln, Ferdinand Marcos, Nelson Mandela, Hillary Clinton."

"There you go again," Fortney said. "I happen to think Willie's main squeeze is sexy. If I ever take a third wife I'd like somebody much like Hillary Clinton, only warm-blooded."

"What was wrong with that babe down at the bar the other night?" Leeds wanted to know. "The cuppie with the black hair and slightly gray roots? She doesn't have Hillary's chunky loins, but what the hell."

"What's a cuppie?"

"That's what they call the America's Cup groupies," Leeds said. "Cuppies."

"Nothing's wrong with her except she's older than the regatta."

"She told me she's thirty-eight."

"Sure," Fortney said. "If you ever pull off her panty girdle, just count the rings and report back if she's thirty-eight."

Leeds eyed a leggy babe sprawled on the seat of a 22-foot ski boat. Her boyfriend tried to throttle back to the speed limit as soon as he spotted the cops. "I won't be pulling off panty girdles," he said. "My marriage is as sacred to me as Gramma's underpants."

Fortney didn't reply. He knew that his handsome young partner spent at least two nights a week at the little gin mill on Quivira Way, feasting on Aussie leftovers whenever the professional sailors weren't around to handle roving cuppies.

"Look at this," Fortney said suddenly, turning the Boston Whaler toward a rented Bayliner that had run aground at Crown Point.

There were six black gangbangers on the grounded powerboat, all in colors. Each one wore an oversized tank top or sweatshirt and Jams baggy enough to hold his ass and a case of Colt 45 malt liquor. Two of the bangers had shaved heads, two others wore knit caps; all wore black high-top sneakers, half unlaced. They were *trying* to look bad, but that's pretty hard to do when you're sitting dead in the water and a beach full of white teenagers is hooting and hollering.

The first thing Fortney said when he rafted up to the Bayliner was "Okay, gentlemen, we're here to help, but first thing we do is, we put on these."

Leeds tossed six dumb-looking orange life jackets to the bangers, who said things like "Shee-it, we gotta wear these funky things? We rather drown, man!"

"Gotta be nice and safe when we're doing a heroic rescue," Leeds told them.

The bangers couldn't stop glaring at the teenagers on the beach, who were dissing them louder than ever, and when the cops were finally motoring the jacketed bangers back to the boat rental, Fortney got the bad-eye from the most sullen one, who had a high-top haircut with nubs on top.

So Fortney said, "I know how it is, dude. Awful hard to *style* with those goofy fucking jackets on. Kinda makes you look like the plastic cones they use for roadwork."

•   •   •

Late that Saturday afternoon Serenity Jones received a call on her cell phone while she soaked her bulk in the bathtub, devouring chocolate-chip cookies and the *National Enquirer*.

She picked up the call on the third ring as usual and was surprised to hear the familiar voice of number sixty-three.

"Please tell our redhead to change the location tonight," he told her. "Ask her to meet me at eight o'clock. Corner of Rosecrans and Shelter Island Drive in Point Loma. I'll be parked near the intersection."

"Fab, darling," Serenity said. "I'll see she gets the message. Anything else?"

"No," he said, "nothing else."

Blaze Duvall was also surprised to hear that sixty-three was changing the location. He'd never done that before. He was *very* anal, sixty-three was, rigid and predictable. Once he'd told her that he seldom wore a necktie that he hadn't bought from the same mail-order catalog. He said that some of the ties cost a hundred dollars, but were worth it because they were "utterly reliable." Blaze had wondered at the time what a necktie had to do to be utterly reliable, but she'd let it pass.

Now she was wondering why he'd be meeting her in his car. Apparently, he'd be taking her somewhere. She hoped to hell he wasn't in the mood for a "real date." It happened sometimes with clients his age. Instead of a massage and a quick blowjob in a motel room, they'd get all sentimental about a candlelight dinner. Then

Blaze would have to let them know gently that a massage took far less time than dinner, no matter how pleasant such an evening would be. And that she just didn't have the time, working as she did all day long as a licensed massage therapist in the proper office of a physician who specialized in pain control through massage and acupuncture.

All of which was bullshit. Blaze had learned all she knew about massage from rented videos and a how-to manual she'd read in thirty minutes. But the clients wanted to believe she was legit, that the *extra* things she did was because they had "rapport." That such an obviously intelligent young woman recognized special needs that could never be satisfied by wives or regular girlfriends. Clients were always quick to reassure Blaze that hers was the first "massage of its kind" they'd ever received, and that they had only contacted her in the first place because of recommendations from "a very upscale massage salon" frequented by downtown businessmen.

As if Blaze Duvall gave a shit. Actually, the downtown massage salon wasn't downtown but on El Cajon Boulevard in the vicinity of North Park, where street whores occupied ten blocks of the boulevard, day and night. The salon was operated by an old pal of Serenity Jones's, who referred very promising clients to Serenity when the client wanted "something special" that the salon didn't dare provide because of unannounced visits from vice cops.

Blaze got dressed for the appointment the way number sixty-three preferred women to dress: tailored. That's what he'd told her the first time they'd met. She decided on a plaid linen jacket and long pants of linen and wool, all in neutral shades of beige. Under it she wore a long-sleeved creamy cotton blouse, and with it of course sensible pumps. That'd suit him.

She knew without a doubt he'd be wearing a blue blazer, gray or tan trousers, and loafers. Since it was Saturday night he'd also be wearing a white or blue dress shirt and one of those hundred-dollar neckties that he called "old boy" ties.

Blaze hoped this wasn't going to be one of those let's-have-a-real-date episodes. They could get *so* gooey. She had to think for a minute whether he'd know her yellow Mustang. He was always in the motel room when she arrived, and they'd never left together. Well, that was *his* problem. He was the one who had changed the location to a goddamn street corner.

While driving to Point Loma at dusk, she thought that rather than a lengthy story as to why she couldn't go on a boring dinner date, she'd rather blow him right there in his car. That's what Dawn would do. But the Dawn Coyotes of this world went to jail often and got hurt and even murdered doing their work in cars. Sometimes they got killed by tricks they'd done business with safely on other occasions. There were lots of unsolved prostitute murders in San Diego, like everywhere else.

When Blaze arrived, she spotted him right away, sitting behind the wheel of a ten-year-old red Cadillac Seville, nervously fiddling with his old-boy necktie.

He saw her and waved shyly.

When she drove up beside his car, he mouthed the words "Follow me" and drove off, leading her out toward the naval base, toward a pricy part of Point Loma called La Playa, where she'd never been.

He pulled to the curb on a quiet residential street just off Rosecrans and Blaze pulled in behind him. He leaned out the window and gestured for her to lock her car, so she got out carrying her beach duffel crammed with powder, oils, and other implements.

"I'm taking you home, Blaze," he said, opening the door of the Cadillac. "I have something very important to discuss with you."

"Okay," she said with her sunniest smile, but feeling some apprehension.

As the Cadillac snaked around the narrow streets, climbing ever higher toward the top of the point, he didn't say a word. This was unpredictable, but she felt that sixty-three was harmless, a very shy and polite older gentleman.

It was reassuring for her to recall how, when they'd begun their relationship seven months earlier, she'd told him that it was better for both of them if he never used his name, just a number when he phoned, one he'd remember.

"Sixty-three," he'd replied instantly, not explaining the choice.

She'd jotted it down without comment. But on one occasion when he was in the bathroom showering after his massage, she'd peeked in his wallet to learn his true name and address. In her business you never knew when such information might come in handy.

She'd had to stifle a giggle upon reading his birthdate. Very predictable. He was sixty-three years old.

CHAPTER 3

THE OFFICE WALLS WERE PAINTED YOUR BASIC POLICE-STATION BILIOUS green. Everything else, including desks and file cabinets, was mucous gray. But the "designer" had added a touch that vice officers called "nouvelle cop," a no-nap bile-green carpet that showed every coffee stain and ended up looking like camouflage tarps from the Gulf War. The cops repaired all rips with gray duct tape.

"I don't believe this!" Officer Rita Mason said to her eyebrows when she encountered Letch Boggs that evening. He was all alone in the vice office, feet on a table, doing what he did best.

Letch was watching a confiscated videotape. In the tape a naked woman was writhing on a bed to background music by Madonna. And trying her damnedest to insert a baby boa into her own vagina, tail first.

Letch hadn't heard Rita Mason come in. Engrossed, he was munching on one of those horrible tomato-and-garlic sandwiches he brought from home. She saw a Pepsi bottle beneath the desk, also from home, no doubt. The leering hamster was notoriously cheap and never patronized the drink machines. As usual, he was wearing one of those cheesy Hawaiian shirts, this one covered with the world's ugliest pink flamingos, resembling turtles on stilts.

Finally Letch noticed Rita behind him, all tarted-up for another evening on the john detail: Day-Glo green satin shorts, knee-high green plastic boots with spike heels, a white peekaboo chemise, a sequined jacket on top. Her hair was ratted and teased and she thought she looked disgusting.

Letch thought she was devastating. He *loved* girls this large in the bustle. Displaying his leer, he said, "Gosh, you look smashing, Rita!"

"Why wouldn't I?" she responded. "Sixteen guys teaching me how to become a slut? Only thing this outfit lacks is neon. What're you doing watching that garbage again? Don't you have any shame?" Then she answered herself: "Dumb question."

"I'm only paying close attention to the wallpaper, Rita," Letch said. "I think I know where this was taped. A motel over on Midway Drive."

Rita sneered at the randy vice cop. "Uh-huh. And how about the snake? Recognize *him*?"

"I think he works down in the mayor's office, but I ain't sure." Letch mashed the last of the garlic cloves with those rodentlike teeth of his, saying, "Go, snake! Go!"

"You're sick!" Rita said. "I can't wait to go back to patrol, where I only gotta deal with nice clean stabbings and drive-bys."

Letch sighed and turned off the TV. "Okay, Rita, let's go to work. I watch any more a this, I'll start slapping my slinky."

"You really *are* a revolting old pervert!" Rita said sincerely. Then she took a closer look at the Pepsi bottle on the floor. "Why's that Pepsi yellow?"

To which Letch failed to respond.

"What's *in* that freaking bottle?" Rita demanded. "Is it what I *think* it is?"

"I could find more compassion in a Tijuana bullring," Letch said grumpily, gathering his gun, handcuffs, and flashlight. "I don't have a jelly bean for a prostate. I'm fifty-three years old, for chris-sake. My prostate's bigger'n your left tit, and it's a long walk to the head. And, anyways, I didn't wanna leave at the good part. You know, where the snake looks around with that goofy look on his serpent kisser? Like he's saying, It's *not* the booze, honey. I really do *care* about you. *That* part."

Rita Mason was getting green around the gills. "I'll meet you in the car. Take that bottle and pour it in the goddamn *toilet!*"

While she was stalking down the hall in her spike-heeled boots, she heard Letch muttering something about passing a kidney stone bigger than Alcatraz.

When they were driving out to El Cajon Boulevard in Letch's brown Camaro vice car, preparing to rendezvous with two vice teams who would tune to the transmitter Rita wore under her bra, Letch said, "You know a whore named Dawn Coyote? Junkie? Skinny blonde? Always got the shakes?"

"I've seen a girl like that out there," Rita said. "Why?"

"I been trying to nail her old man. Pimp named Oliver Mantleberry. I hear when she's having domestic problems with Oliver—like when he's kicked the living piss outta her—she takes her baby to the streets with her. And I hear he stomped her ass last night."

"What's she do with the baby?"

"A snitch told me she puts the little whelp in that motel we busted last month. The Dream Scene Motel?"

"How old's the baby?"

"Plenty old enough to take care of himself," Letch said. "About ten months, I think."

"Jesus," Rita said. "Gimme a good stabbing or a drive-by. You can *have* this vice shit."

"Anyways," Letch said, "when you're out there looking oh-so-cute and getting lots a offers from all the horny Harrys, keep an eye out for Dawn. You see her, just talk into the wire. Tell me where she's at, what she's doing. Tell me if you see a black pimp in a white Jag cruising the boulevard."

"Four more weeks." Rita Mason sighed. "Then I'm outta here."

"I used to know a massage-parlor hooker that looked *just* like you," Letch said, working those gray-brown eyebrows that looked like proned-out chipmunks. "She gave me a massage with rubber gloves on before I busted her. Now every time I go to a supermarket and see Playtex Living gloves I get a big woody. You ever consider giving a guy a massage?"

"Sure, Letch," she said. "Long as I can use an oil substitute."

"Saliva?"

"Ground glass."

"Gee, I'll miss you, Rita," Letch said dreamily.

With a curling lip: "Me too, Letch. Just like I'd miss lawyers and vaginal warts. Or a horned toad in my panty hose."

•   •   •

While Officer Rita Mason was getting ready to take offers of sex for money from horny Harrys who'd be swooped up by lurking vice cops, Blaze Duvall was entering the hillside Point Loma home of number sixty-three, the man she'd called "Jeremy" during previous encounters. A man she knew from her surreptitious search of his wallet to be Ambrose Willis Lutterworth, Jr.

"It's not much of a house," he said, turning on the light in the living room and locking the front door behind them.

"Wow!" Blaze was stunned by the breathtaking view through the picture window. At this time of evening the rising moon was hanging over the twinkling high-rise office buildings studding the waterfront, and the sky and glassy harbor were lavender in the vanishing twilight.

Ambrose Lutterworth chuckled nervously. "As they say in real estate: location location location. The house is badly built and worthless, but the land's worth plenty. It's a double lot, actually."

Blaze put her blue duffel on the sofa, pretending to admire the furnishings but reassuring herself there was not someone lurking in one of the spooky little nooks.

"Would you like a drink, Blaze?" he asked. "We've never had the opportunity to raise a glass before, not in those motel rooms."

"Sure. White wine if you have it."

"I've got a bottle in the fridge," he said. "Make yourself comfortable."

After he disappeared into the kitchen, Blaze peeked into the little study just off the living room. The entire house was meticulous. On his desk number-two pencils lay in perfect formation, each the same length.

When she heard the refrigerator door open, she risked taking a few steps down the hall to look into what appeared to be an old lady's bedroom. There was a lace doily on the back of a worn-out reading chair and the lamp table beside it was covered by a lace tablecloth, starched and white. The bed was a double four-poster, like in a moldy movie set.

Blaze hurried back to the tidy living room before he returned, and managed a smile when he handed her the crystal wineglass.

He poured one for himself, then motioned to the leather chesterfield sofa. "Sit down, Blaze. There, where you can enjoy the view. When the city lights all come on it's very beautiful. That's part of the reason I haven't sold. I'd miss the city lights."

Blaze sipped the wine. "Very good. Chardonnay?"

"Right you are, Blaze," he said. "You're obviously a sophisticated girl who appreciates fine things. I've known you were special from the first."

Here it comes. *I want to get to know you better, Blaze. I'm lonely, Blaze. Perhaps we could go on dates. Perhaps . . .*

He stopped her by saying, "I'm going to give you the chance to make some money. *Real* money. I'm going to make you a business offer."

With a cute but seductive smile this time: "As Dumbo would say, I'm all ears."

"First of all," he said, "my name isn't Jeremy. It's Ambrose. Ambrose Lutterworth."

"Well, I can understand the need to be careful."

"I wonder if your real name is Blaze?"

"Yes, it really is."

"Suits you. That lovely flaming hair."

"Thank you . . . Ambrose."

"That's better. I like to hear you use my true name."

She looked discreetly at her watch and said, "I'm afraid I don't have a lotta time, Ambrose."

"Don't worry about the time, Blaze," he said. "I want the entire evening. You're going to get five hundred dollars tonight whether or not you accept my business proposition. Is that all right?"

"You own me," she said with a girlish grin that brought out the dusty freckles on her nose. "For the evening."

"First I'd like to tell you about myself. I'm a sailing enthusiast. Do you sail?"

"Never tried it."

"I used to have a thirty-three-foot sloop," Ambrose said. "Had to sell it when the real-estate market crashed. I'm also a realtor, you see."

For five hundred she could put up with it, so she unbuttoned her jacket and took another sip. At least the wine was good, better than she could afford.

•   •   •

Officer Rita Mason did a lot of damage to male libidos that Saturday evening. She bagged three motoring johns before she was out there an hour. It was a very busy evening on El Cajon Boulevard, and the horny Harrys were circling the hookers like little orbiting satellites. The more they orbited, the brighter they glowed. Not one of them guessed that the buxom babe in screaming-green shorts could be a member of the San Diego Police Department. And they were really shocked to learn later that cops were no longer writing citations for prostitution offenses but were taking johns to jail.

One of them got so horny while parked near the corner of Ohio Street trying to chisel down the price that he stuck his hand inside his pants. Rita figured him for one of those creeps who wanted to stiff the hooker by getting off in his own sweaty palm just from talking. He was still fondling himself when a blue Olds containing two mustachioed brigands squealed up beside his car.

His head swiveled toward the vice car, then back to Rita, and he exclaimed, "Are they carjackers?"

"Relax, honey," Rita told him. "They don't want your ride. And you can quit spanking little Sam. You're *busted.*"

After the vice team put the john in the backseat of their car, he cried and begged them just to write him a citation.

"No more coupons," Rita informed him. "It's slam city for you, hot pants."

When he cried and begged them not to call his wife, Rita said wickedly, "Doesn't your family have a right to know you're inviting AIDS?"

A blue Lexus stopped a block from Rita Mason while she was tormenting the blubbering john. She watched a string-bean blonde, in a skirt Rita couldn't have fit into when she was twelve years old, get out and thank the driver. The blonde sauntered to the street corner, held her purse down beside her thigh, and waited for the next one.

Rita spoke into her bra. "Letch, I think it's that girl you're interested in. Corner of Thirtieth."

Then she returned to the vice car, where the teary john screamed at her, "You can't arrest me! You lied to me!"

To which Rita replied, "I don't know where it says I have to tell you where I really work."

Then the john cried out, "You *can't* arrest me! I gotta go pick up my kids at Boy Scouts camp!"

To which Rita replied, "I'll phone your wife and tell her to get them. Should she stop for pizza on the way home?"

Letch Boggs watched Dawn Coyote pick up two dates that evening. Dawn was too streetwise to be tailed closely, but Letch watched her take them to the general vicinity of the Dream Scene Motel, owned and operated by an Iranian they'd arrested two months earlier.

That she was going to the expense of a motel room was suspicious in itself. Most of the street whores would just direct the john to someplace safe, like an apartment-house garage when a parking gate was left open.

The "strawberries," or rock whores, who worked farther east on the boulevard, would blow a guy in a doorway just for a taste of rock cocaine, but Dawn liked to take her tricks to a quiet church parking lot in North Park for the blow jobs. Sometimes they'd get to hear *another* organ being played in the church.

Referring to the Iranian motel owner, Letch said to his partner, "Some a those hanky-head dromedary rapers never learn."

His partner for the evening, a bearded, burly cop named Westbrook whose mother was a Lebanese Muslim, said nothing.

When Dawn Coyote emerged from the motel after turning her second date, she didn't return to the boulevard. Instead she walked directly from room number 4 downstairs to room number 13 upstairs. She was in number 13 for ten minutes before she came out and returned to work.

When Dawn was back on the boulevard, Letch and Westbrook entered the motel office, where the Iranian was watching *American Gladiators*. He was about Letch's age, but shorter, fatter, and his collar was littered with dandruff. Instead of rodent teeth, two of his were gold-capped, and the grease-clogged pore pattern on his fleshy nose and cheeks looked like a street map.

He recognized Letch at once and said, "Good evening, Officer! You have come to examine the register, yes? Please, you may help yourself! May I offer you a soda? Or a cup of tea? Or—"

"The key to number thirteen," Letch said.

"Number thirteen!" The Iranian blanched. "What is the problem? *What?*"

"Or you can wait till I talk to Dawn Coyote about how you rented her a hot bed tonight. *Again.* And failed to list her on the motel register, a violation of the municipal code."

"Officer!" The Iranian pressed his hands together in a prayerful gesture. "Please! I cannot be perfect. I was not present when the room was rented. I was gone to the mosque to pray for my mother. With great respect I must ask if you have a warrant to search?"

"You have the right to remain silent," Letch said. "You have the right to—"

"Wait! Wait!" the Iranian pleaded. "If I give you permission to enter number thirteen . . ."

"You can go back to *American Gladiators* and we'll forgive and forget. *This* time."

The Iranian reached under the counter and handed Letch a key.

"Allah ahkbar," Letch said to his partner. "God is *great*. Sometimes."

•   •   •

"I never liked selling real estate," Ambrose explained while Blaze stifled a yawn.

The third glass of wine had relaxed her to a snooze. She battled to keep her eyes open, smiling politely when he poured another from the second bottle.

He was careful to wipe the mouth of the bottle with a damask napkin. A drop plinked onto the old walnut coffee table and he quickly dabbed at it, then polished the spot with the dry half.

By now he'd removed his jacket and so had she. But he still hadn't loosened his old-boy tie, and he hadn't come close to stating his business. Blaze decided that she was going to earn the five hundred bucks one way or the other.

"Most of us have jobs we aren't fond of," she said.

"Of course," Ambrose said. "I'm sure you don't like yours."

"Sometimes I do," Blaze said, trying a coy smile even though her lids were at half-mast. "Like now."

"That's kind of you," he said, sipping his wine. "I know it must be hard for you to . . . offer relief to old duffers like me."

"You're not old, Ambrose," Blaze said. "What're you, fifty? No more than fifty-five."

"You'd be surprised," he said with a delighted chuckle. "I try to stay in decent shape by playing tennis and running on the beach twice a week."

"You're very fit," Blaze said. "I should know. I've handled your body often enough." Another coy smile and then, "Do you think we could talk about the business arrangement?"

"Of course. I just ramble sometimes when I'm with someone *simpática*. There isn't a woman in my life right now. I'm rather lonely, to tell you the truth."

"I can't believe that," Blaze said. "A fine-looking man like you?"

"One of my passions is cribbage. I belong to a cribbage club. Do you play?"

"No."

Suddenly he said, "What do you know about the America's Cup?"

Blaze looked blank. "It's about sailing, right?"

"The world's greatest regatta. And I . . . I'm the Keeper of the Cup."

The announcement had no effect.

Rambling again, he said, "I was just an ordinary member of the yacht club, and so was my father, a successful developer until he made some bad investments. It's feast or famine in that business. Probably why I never got into it. I'm just an agent in a local real-estate office."

"I'm sure you're a very good agent." The wine made her slur.

"When Dennis Conner won back the Cup from Australia in nineteen eighty-seven under the aegis of the San Diego Yacht Club, my life changed. Drastically. Dramatically."

Blaze kicked off her shoes, tucking her feet beneath her on the sofa, ready for a *long* evening. "Tell me about it, Ambrose."

"It's not easy to explain. I was living in an apartment at that time. Oh, I've lived in this house off and on over the years when my father was alive, and even later with my mother. And I've been in lots of little business deals. At the yacht club you hear about this and that, but nothing ever worked out for me. And then we got the Cup."

"Do you get paid a lot to be the . . ."

"Keeper of the Cup? Lord, no! I'm unpaid, except for a stipend when we travel together, the Cup and me."

"You make the Cup sound like a person," Blaze said.

He studied her, then said, "That's an interesting observation, Blaze. I think I've chosen the right girl to help me. You're very *simpática*."

•   •   •

Dawn Coyote was delighted that her third date of the evening was a premature ejaculator, saving a hell of a lot of work and time. She called them "preemies."

While he was in the bathroom cleaning up and apologizing, she was out the door, running upstairs to number 13. She unlocked the door, rushed into the room, and froze in her tracks. Leaning against the bathroom door was a bearded guy with a stud earring, a vice cop who'd busted her six months earlier. And sitting on the bed with her nine-month-old son, Billy, was Letch Boggs, grinning his rat-tooth grin and cootchy-cooing her baby.

"He *likes* Uncle Letch," the old vice cop said.

Ten minutes later it was Dawn who was on the bed, on her stomach, crying her eyes out. Letch sat beside her, still playing with the baby, who was getting cranky, no longer finding Letch's funny face so amusing.

"Atta girl, Dawn," Letch said. "Let it all out. You'll feel soooo much better."

When she sat up, her lips were black from mascara. She dashed into the bathroom and closed the door. The cops heard her retching a couple of times.

"Needs a pop," Westbrook said. "What's she do, heroin?"

"Speedballs," Letch said. "This little cub's gonna be an orphan before long."

When Dawn emerged, her makeup was gone, making her

look like an anorexic high-schooler. Her left eye was badly bruised underneath, and without the lipstick they could see she had a swollen upper lip.

"I jist left him here a few minutes ago," Dawn said, sobbing. "I jist couldn't find nobody to watch him tonight. My . . . roommate kicked me out all of a sudden."

"That's a pretty bad shiner," Letch said. "Oliver hit you with his fist or what?"

"Oliver who?" Dawn said.

"Any special instructions for the Polinsky Children's Center?" Letch asked.

"What's that?"

"The place we're gonna take Baby Snooks to after we book you for child endangering."

"I only left him for a few minutes!" Dawn wailed.

"You can tell it to Child Protective Services," Westbrook said. "And we'll tell them how we saw you bring two johns into a hot-bed motel room. And how this pup was alone for thirty minutes one time and forty-five the next. Left all alone in a motel frequented by hose monsters."

Dawn Coyote sat on the floor beside the bed and sobbed so violently she could hardly breathe.

"You're hyperventilating," Westbrook said, worried by her honks of pain. "And I ain't about to give you mouth-to-mouth if you pass out."

Dawn pulled herself up on her knees and said, "I'll do anything! Want me to do *you*? I'll do you *both* right now!"

"Get real," Westbrook said, dragging a chair over by the window. "Even Letch ain't *that* horny." Letch showed his hamster grin and Westbrook added, "Maybe I spoke too soon."

"I'll do *anything*!" Dawn said to Letch, who put the gurgling baby on his stomach. The infant had large blue eyes like Dawn's, and he reached out to his mother with chubby little hands.

But Letch said, "Don't touch him till we deal."

"Anything!" she said. "Anything you want!"

"We're gonna make a report. It's gonna tell how Oliver Mantleberry's been working you for the past year, all about how he
takes your money and kicks ass when it's not enough. And you're
gonna have a telephone conversation with Oliver tomorrow that
we'll listen to so we can corroborate the pimping. And you're gonna
testify against him in court."

"He'll kill me!" Dawn said. "You don't understand! He'll *kill*
me!"

"That part's *your* problem," Letch said. "I'd advise you to
move someplace where he can't find you. Outta town'd be best.
Come back to testify. I'll see that nobody bothers you. You try to
stiff me and I go straight to Child Protective Services *and* I get a
warrant."

"Lemme give you somebody else!" Dawn said. She thought
for a moment and said, "I can give you this girl does outcall massage. Name's Blaze Duvall. Lives in Mission Valley up in the hills.
You don't know about her. I'll give *her* up! She keeps her answering
machine in my apartment. I'll let you listen to her calls anytime you
want. Lemme give *her* up instead of Oliver, okay?"

"You can give her up *and* Oliver," Westbrook said. "What's
her name? Blaze what?"

Letch said, "We gotta have Oliver Mantleberry. Period. I ain't
much concerned with outcall masseuses." Then he switched on his
laptop memory and said, "That apartment in the hills? She
wouldn't be in number Two-A, would she?"

"How do you *know*?" Dawn gasped. "How could you know
that?"

Letch giggled and nudged the anxious infant into the arms of
his mother.

Westbrook said, "Don't ask. The Shadow, he just knows
things. The Shadow *knows*."

•   •   •

"Can you imagine how my life changed?" Ambrose asked Blaze for
the third time, if she was counting.

"I can only guess," she said, deciding not to accept any more wine. She was getting shit-faced.

"I've traveled the world, not as a tourist but as the Keeper of the Cup. I've met *kings*. Sometime I'll tell you about Princess Anne. She was the loveliest person. Not regal, a real person. I found Prince Rainier to be regal, though."

She had just enough alcohol boiling in her belly that she was getting irritable, something she tried to avoid with clients. "Let's talk *business,* Ambrose. How about it?"

"I want to *remain* Keeper of the Cup," he said. "I don't want it to end yet. Not yet."

"That's talking business?"

She plumped up a throw pillow behind her back. A sofa spring was on the verge of breaking through the fabric. She wanted to go home.

"Pour yourself another glass," he said. "I'll be right back."

Against her better judgment she poured half a glass, emptying the second bottle. Blaze figured he'd gone to the can. Guys his age, they were *always* running to the can. Prostate problems, they said, as if she didn't know. She'd massaged a *lot* of prostates in her time. Blaze Duvall figured she could be a pretty fair urologist if handling prostates had anything to do with it. Most of her clients expressed admiration for her long, graceful fingers. Of course she kept her nails clipped short.

When Ambrose returned, he had a folder full of papers, photos, and clippings. He opened it on the coffee table.

"See this," he said, pointing to a newspaper photo of a sailboat crunched on the ground.

"Yeah?"

"That's an America's Cup boat. Belonged to the French, who also had problems with their backup boat. That other one lost a keel and rolled over like a harpooned whale."

"So?" Blaze looked at the photo, then back at Ambrose, who at last had loosened his tie.

"I don't know for sure who's going to be the defender, but I know for sure who's going to be the challenger: New Zealand. The Kiwis. And they're the opposite of the French syndicate. All business. Ruthlessly efficient and professional. They've got two fast boats. And no American defender is going to beat *one* of those boats."

"You don't say."

"The Kiwis have NZL thirty-two and NZL thirty-eight. In nineteen eighty-seven they won thirty-eight victories to only one defeat through the trials, yet they ended up losing four races to one to Dennis Conner in *Stars and Stripes.* In ninety-two the Kiwis were one win away from the challenger trophy, yet they lost four straight to the Italians. This time they're hungry and they vow it won't happen."

"Okay, Ambrose," Blaze said, her patience gone. "Our business deal has something to do with the America's Cup. What the hell is it?"

"It's this. The Kiwis' thirty-two boat is better, *much* better than their thirty-eight boat. The defender will have no chance against the thirty-two boat. But we'd have a chance, a good chance in my opinion, against the thirty-eight boat. I've done my homework. I'm well-enough connected to have gathered good intelligence. I feel in my gut that the thirty-eight boat can be beaten."

"And what do you expect me to do? Exactly what?"

"I want you to help me. It's not personally risky, mind you, but I want nothing less than the destruction of the thirty-two boat. They'll have to race the thirty-eight in the finals. I think our defender can beat the thirty-eight."

"And how would I be able to help you wreck a boat?" Blaze asked. The guy was loony! A loony old geek whose life revolved around a dumb trophy.

"The Kiwis have seven people in their syndicate who they call designers," Ambrose continued. "Sail and hull designers, appendage designers who crafted their keel, and analytical designers. They have a meteorologist. They stop at nothing to ensure that all the people in their syndicate are loyal, dependable, dedicated. They even brought their own crane operator with them."

Despite her cynicism, Blaze was getting slightly interested. He looked so serious, and he was cold sober, unlike her. "They must have security people guarding those boats," she said.

"The Italians had *fifteen* last time. And a dozen TV monitors. Even dogs. The Kiwis have only two men, but they're police officers. Real police officers. Brought them all the way from Auckland on leave from the New Zealand Police. They're well protected in their compound."

"I hope you're not going to say you think I can get to one of *them*?"

"Impossible," Ambrose said. "Those people have national pride in winning the Cup that Americans can't even imagine. Auckland's called the City of Sails because they have more sailboats than cars. There's half an hour of live coverage on their major television channel every night during the challenger trials alone. But there's a weak spot in their program. In every program. A boat can simply be dropped when it's being lifted in or out of the water, and the lifting happens almost every day. Their boat can be dropped just like the French boat was dropped. They're loaded into the water in basically the same fashion, either by crane or by travel-lift. A crane operator can make a mistake. It happened to the French, it can happen to the Kiwis."

"I'm not much at operating cranes," Blaze said. She felt like saying the only machines she could work were electric: a toothbrush and a dildo, which she used on her clients, not on herself. Instead she added, "You want to bribe the guy that does the lifting, is that it?"

Ambrose smiled. "You truly are a bright young woman, Blaze. You're on the right track."

"What? *Tell* me, Ambrose!"

"I want to . . . *incapacitate* the New Zealand crane operator who runs the travel-lift. I want it to happen on the last day of the challenger trials when they're racing the Aussies. When they're on the verge of finishing off the competition. They'll have to replace their man without notice. They'll be forced to turn to the boatyard they rent their space from."

Blaze tried to keep her mouth shut. This guy was so anal, he had to get around to everything in his own time, but she had to ask. "Do you *know* the boatyard guy?"

Ambrose nodded. "There're three crane operators working there, but one of them is the brother of an American woman who's married to a Kiwi sailor. He'll be the one they'll go to on such short notice because his brother-in-law's a New Zealander and because he's very experienced and worked for racing syndicates in the last America's Cup regatta. I used to be a client of that boatyard. He's hauled out my sailboat many times. I *know* that man will be the one who gets the job."

"You're saying that something's gonna happen to the New Zealand crane operator."

"Yes."

"Like what?"

"I'd like you to meet him. I know where he and all the Kiwis will be this Thursday evening. Where they are every Thursday evening: at the AC/DC party."

"What's that?"

"The America's Cup Drinking Club. A different bar in town hosts a party once a week. Nobody knows where it'll be until the morning of the party, when the organizer sends a fax to each syndicate. The crane operator will be there, and if you accept my proposition you'll be there, too. He'll leap at the chance to have a drink with a girl like you. Who wouldn't?"

"And then?"

"Nothing *yet*. You have drinks. You get acquainted. You become friends. The important thing is, you'll also be wherever he is the night before they're to clinch the challenger series."

"What would I do to . . . *incapacitate* him?"

"You'll put some medication in his Steinlager."

"In his what?"

"It's the New Zealand beer that sponsors them. Their holy water. They all drink it. The drug is something I've kept since my mother's last days. It won't do him any real harm, but he won't be in shape to go up on a travel-lift the next morning. The Kiwis will be panicked. They'll have to call for help."

"You plan to bribe the substitute crane guy, is that it?"

"I'm hoping *you'll* take care of that. That's what the business proposition is all about. Making a deal with Simon Cooke, the crane operator."

"Why me?"

"I know Simon Cooke. Loves women, loves to drink, loves to go to Tijuana and gamble on the jai alai. Loves to talk. He's a perfect candidate to make a deal with a beautiful girl. After he gets to trust you."

"Wait a minute!" Blaze said, more soberly. "You want me to get next to this guy Simon? And get to know him? I think I know what *that* means. And then ask if he'll drop the New Zealand boat? Drop it on the ground?" She sat up, staring at the picture of the French sloop with its keel poking through the hull.

"Yes," Ambrose said. "For ten thousand dollars. That's a lot of tax-free cash for a guy who makes fifteen dollars an hour. I know he'll do it."

"How many jobs can he get *after* he drops a boat?"

"He'll think of something to blame it on. An excuse as to why it wasn't his fault. Nobody can ever prove anything when things like that happen."

"Why don't *you* make the guy the offer?"

"I don't dare get anywhere near this. Do you know what would happen to me if I got connected to a plot to sabotage a challenger's boat?"

"Yeah," Blaze said. "Same thing that'd happen to me. You'd go to jail."

"That's the least of it," Ambrose said. "My reputation—my life—would be . . . *gone*. I don't like to think about it. No, I can't be directly linked to Simon Cooke. Nobody must ever know about me."

"And what do I get outta this . . . business proposition?"

"Just about everything I have in the world," Ambrose Lutterworth said. "Fifteen thousand dollars. My life savings. My annuity, you might say. You get it all, if you persuade Simon Cooke to do it. And *if* he does it."

"And you get . . ."

"The Cup. I get to be Keeper of the Cup for another four years at least. Who knows? Maybe for a lot longer."

"This is pretty nutty," Blaze said. "I gotta think about this."

"There isn't much time," Ambrose said. "The last race between the Kiwis and the Aussies is only three weeks away. There's a lot to do before then."

Blaze said, "Let's say I could give the New Zealand guy his sleeping pill. How do you know for sure they'd call Simon Cooke instead of somebody else? And what if he weasels out? What do I get for trying?"

"You'll get five thousand, whether or not Simon bites. Whether or not he does the job. You know all about me now. You can trust me just as I'll have to trust you. I know Simon won't turn you down. I've done my homework, Blaze. This will *work*!"

"Why'd you pick me, Ambrose?"

"I've been waiting," he said, "for misfortune to strike the Kiwis like it's struck everyone else. A boat has been dropped. Another sunk. A keel fell off after being hit by a rogue wave. A mini-tornado even struck one of the compounds. An aircraft carrier almost cruised into the racecourse one foggy day. But nothing happens to the goddamn New Zealand boats! I can't afford to wait any longer. Something has to be done. The idea came to me a few days ago."

"Why *me*?"

"Because," he said, "you're smart and beautiful and discreet. And you're the only person I know—the only person I've ever known in my entire life—who works outside the law."

"What I do is a misdemeanor if I'm caught," she said. "What you're suggesting is a heavy-duty felony."

"It's only a matter of degree," he said. "There's nobody else in my life who can do it."

"I'm going to sleep on it," she said. "And I get five hundred for tonight. Right?"

"Of course. But I was wondering."

"Wondering what?"

"If you could give me a quick . . . massage?"

"Okay," Blaze said. "In the bedroom?"

"Did you bring the warming cream?" Ambrose wanted to know.

Ten minutes later Ambrose Lutterworth was lying naked on the two large beach towels that Blaze Duvall had spread on his queen-size bed. She was standing beside the bed, squeezing some Icy Hot on her palms. She was naked except for black bikini panties. Blaze smiled professionally when she spread the cream over his buttocks, kneading the muscles gently.

"That's wonderful, Blaze!" he said. "Just wonderful! You have splendid hands!"

Blaze glanced into her bag, fearing she'd forgotten the condoms, but no, a package was lying there, along with the toys that clients requested: a feather for tickling their balls, a vibrating dildo for rectal stimulation. Toys.

"Turn over, darling," she said, trying to speed things up so she could go home and think.

"No, I don't need it this time," Ambrose said. "Just rub on some more cream, please."

So at least she wouldn't have to blow the crazy old bastard.

While she was rubbing in the Icy Hot, careful to avoid tender tissue, he said, "Blaze, move the lamp a bit to the right, please."

She did it and saw that he wanted light shining on a framed photo on his dresser. In the photo Ambrose was standing by a sunny foreign harbor with a young woman in a white dress.

"Cap d'Antibes," he explained. "She was just a girl I saw by the waterfront and I asked if she'd pose for a picture with me. Are you at all familiar with the South of France?"

"No," Blaze said, working his right buttock so strenuously that he grunted in delight, finding her as sultry as a cheetah—rubbing, purring, blowing her warm breath on him.

Then he said, "It's between Nice and Cannes. After I got the picture taken I went up to my hotel room and sunbathed nude on the balcony. No problem if the people across the courtyard could see me. In the South of France nobody worries about such things." Then he said, "Blaze, I'd like to turn on my side, but please don't stop."

She was working up a sweat from the wine. Beads of heat lay on her upper lip, her mouth brooding and sensual.

She paused to let him turn on his side and saw his watery blue eyes gaze up at the photo, his brows silver-flecked in the lamplight. When she began massaging again, he said, "The Cup was on the balcony with me as I sunbathed that day. I put it on a chair and watched it. The sun glinted off the silver and the sun's rays were hot, *very* hot, reflected onto my bare bottom. I didn't care if I got burned. I didn't care about anything. I don't think I've ever felt so at peace with myself. So contented with my life. So . . . blissfully happy."

Then Ambrose Lutterworth surprised Blaze Duvall by reaching down and slowly stroking his penis.

Blaze smiled encouragingly, but he never looked at her. Never stopped gazing at the picture. In just a moment he was erect, and he didn't take his eyes from the photo until he was through.

This takes the cake, Blaze thought, watching Ambrose Lutterworth reliving an extraordinary moment in his life: when he'd sunbathed on a hotel balcony in Cap d'Antibes, literally basking in the reflected glow of the oldest sporting trophy on earth: The America's Cup.

Or, as Blaze later explained it to Dawn Coyote, "I got five hundred scoots to watch this geek skipping down memory lane and slapping old Porky. While I set his ass on fire."

CHAPTER 4

ON THURSDAY MORNING, APRIL 6, THE VARIOUS SAILING SYNDICATES IN-volved in America's Cup XXIX received a fax telling them where the America's Cup Drinking Club would be meeting that evening, the weekly do for hardworking sailors who were to begin crucial water jousting come Monday morning. A series of twelve races beginning April 10 and ending April 22 would decide the winner of the Citizen Cup and the right to defend the America's Cup under the aegis (or "burgee," the triangular identification flag) of the San Diego Yacht Club.

Among those U.S.A. syndicates vying for the Citizen Cup were Team Dennis Conner in the boat *Stars and Stripes* and Amer-ica3, called "America Cubed," in the boat *Mighty Mary,* which had been sailed by an all-women crew for the first time in Cup history. That is, until syndicate head Bill Koch flinched, deciding that he needed bearded Dave Dellenbaugh as tactician, resulting in *Mighty Mary* being dubbed "Mostly Mary" by regatta observers. The third competing syndicate was Pact 95 in its boat *Young America*. All three were squaring off in the series, which awarded points for winning, bonus points for winning in the semifinals, and even a bonus point for placing second out of three. It was a perfect scoring system for an esoteric sport that was going to cost the three syndicates

ᅟ

$67 million. Nobody outside the sailing community could under-stand it, and much of the sailing community was baffled as well.

In the battle for the Louis Vuitton Challenger Cup in the best of nine races—and the right to challenge the ultimate de-fender—was Team oneAustralia in *AUS-31,* the only boat Australia had left after the sinking of *AUS-35* during the fourth round-robin. Their budget for the regatta was an estimated $33 million. The other challenger in the Louis Vuitton finals was Team New Zea-land, favored to win it all. Their 38 boat had won twenty-three straight round-robin matches, and the older 32 boat was the victor nine out of nine times when raced in the semifinals. Most observers believed that the hulls were equally fast, and equally unbeatable by any defender. The Kiwis referred to their fearsome sloop as *Black Magic.*

Of course, as soon as each syndicate received its fax on Thurs-day morning revealing the location of the AC/DC soiree—those supersecret faxes designed to ensure against interlopers and camp followers—the sailors telephoned every free-spending interloper and camp follower they knew, informing them in which gin mill to meet.

There were several waterfront restaurants, in the vicinity of the syndicate compounds, which hosted the weekly dos, and all were interchangeable. They were restaurant-saloons with dark pan-eling, nautical decor, fake fireplaces, and waiters trained at the Department of Motor Vehicles. All served acceptable fish and steaks, baked potatoes, Steinlager for Kiwis, and Foster's for Aussies. And you could bet your boat on it, the cooked vegetables consisted of zucchini, cauliflower, broccoli, or a combination thereof—cheap veggies offered everywhere in a town not known for cuisine. The other thing you could count on in a San Diego restaurant was Caesar salad, a dish created decades earlier by an Italian chef in Caesar's Hotel, Tijuana. In these parts it was as ubiquitous as mold, even though nobody made it correctly with coddled egg.

Fortney and Leeds had dropped by the Aussie compound in

Quivira Basin on Thursday morning and promised to join a hundred other sailing-stupids who were not supposed to know the location of the boozer bash. But Team New Zealand's compound was located in San Diego harbor on Shelter Island Drive, not far from the San Diego Yacht Club, where Keeper of the Cup Ambrose Lutterworth watched and waited. The Kiwis did not welcome visitors, with or without police badges.

By the time Fortney and Leeds got off duty that evening and arrived at the restaurant, the AC/DC was rollicking. Both cops were in jeans and tennis shoes. Fortney, who was conscious of his expanding belly, wore a faded unbuttoned sport shirt over a Speedo print tee. Leeds, who was buffed-out and proud of his pecs, wore a Sideout tank top even though it was a brisk evening. He got bummed when he saw the sign on the door: NO BARE FEET. NO TANK TOPS. Which meant that the place was about as formal as it gets on the San Diego waterfront.

Leeds had to go to his car for his black windbreaker and bitched all through their first round of drinks that San Diego was getting too haute couture for him—and that when he retired from the police department he was moving to Maui.

An Aussie standing next to him at the bar said, "Come to the land of Oz, mate. In Perth you can wear a bloody loincloth and nobody wants to know."

By eight-thirty that evening there were so many bodies jammed together it was hard to scratch, and the decibel level was only slightly lower than it was on the runway of nearby Lindbergh Field. The cuppies, many of whom were dressed in upscale sailing togs, outnumbered sailors and sailing wannabes by a wide margin.

A cheerful Canadian cuppie seated at the bar explained to the cops that if they gave up their barstool to go to the head, they could be sure it'd be occupied when they returned. If they asked for it back, they might get it if the occupant was a Kiwi. The Kiwis were more reserved, she said, something like Canadians. If the squatter was an Aussie, the seat might be foreclosed. Aussies were more like Yanks, was how she put it.

Of course, if a cuppie took your vacated seat, you just smiled and moved on down the bar. Cuppies got preferential treatment and all the drinks they could hold. If the cuppie was hot-looking she had pick of the litter at AC/DC. Not many of the sailors and sailing wannabes took wives and girlfriends to the Thursday-night do.

"Buy you a brew?" Fortney asked a pair of cuppies who'd just arrived. One of them was a moptop with hefty tits that rested on the bar top.

She checked him out and declined. He had nice curly hair, even if it was going gray, but he was a tad long in the tooth when one is surrounded by celebrated America's Cup sailors, the average age of whom was about thirty-three. Her younger girlfriend looked at Fortney like she'd found a dead mouse in her martini.

He gave up, saying to Leeds, "You doing any good?"

"You gotta sail in the Whitbread Round the World Race to get anywhere with these babes," Leeds complained. "Maybe we oughtta try an Aussie accent and start calling them 'sheila.' "

"They'd know we're bogus," Fortney said. "No calluses. And our suntans aren't salty enough."

"So let's take the boat out on the ocean tomorrow," Leeds suggested. "Cruise in the chop and get smacked in the face by gull shit and kelp. Next Thursday we can say we're grinders with Team Dennis Conner."

Fortney pointed across the teeming barroom and said, "Be still, my landlubber's heart!"

Leeds turned and said, "Oooooh, baby!"

A Kiwi with an albino-blond buzz-cut and shoulders wider than a Rolls-Royce grabbed a cuppie by the hips and lifted her up onto a corner of the bar. The cuppie wore a little candy-striped cotton tee with a blue anchor on the left sleeve, white shorts, and white sneakers. Her fiery, shoulder-length hair cascaded across one shoulder and then the other each time she tossed her head to josh with the sailors surrounding her. Freckles dusted her bare legs and nose, observable because she'd wisely positioned herself directly under an overhead bar light.

She shook hands with eager sailors, making each one tell her his name and what he did on the racing boats. She was not exactly beautiful, but she had the best body Fortney had seen in the month of April. And out there on Mission Bay he saw a lot of good ones.

"I hate sailing and sailors," Leeds said. "I don't even like boats in general. But I'd learn to sail and navigate. I'd take a Coast Guard course. Hell, I'd *join* the goddamn Coast Guard if that's what it takes. To get naked *one* time with *that* cuppie!"

"Forget it," Fortney said. "She's giving the big eye to the creature that lifted her up. The one with a beer mug in each paw. I don't think your nine can stop a lowland gorilla, can it?"

"I gotta get a closer look," Leeds said. "Save my seat."

"Sure," Fortney said. "Be careful. Only thing that big I ever saw hauling beer was a Clydesdale."

Fortney's younger partner squeezed through the sweating throng, nearly upsetting the tray, which held six Foster's straight up, of a frantic cocktail waitress who was shoving people out of the way with her free hand. When he got close to the end of the long bar he smiled dreamily. She was even better up close.

"Another white wine, love?" the huge Kiwi asked her. Up close he looked even bigger.

She smiled at the giant and said, "Wouldn't say no, mate!" in a passable New Zealand accent, and all the sailors murmured approvingly.

Leeds saw in her glance a combination of jaunty smile and mysterious grin, full of mischief, full of hell. He didn't have enough booze in him to be superbold, but he slipped off his wedding ring, switching it to his right ring finger. "A young widower," he usually said, as if the babes he met in Mission Bay gave a damn.

When the big Kiwi went for the wine, Leeds jumped into his space. "Oooops!" he said, purposely bumping that freckled thigh. "Sorry."

She turned the smile on him and tried the accent again: "No worries, mate. Which team're you with?"

"I'm not," he said. "But I *do* work on a boat."

Then an Aussie on the other side of her said, "Blaze! Blaze, love! Tell Robbie here what you say when your darts partner knocks yours out of the target."

"Fair dinkum, mate!" she replied, and the Aussie sailors roared their approval.

The huge Kiwi muscled his way back with Blaze's wine and a mug of draft for himself, saying, "Cheers, love!"

Leeds tried to think of an opening, but Blaze was playing to the sailors. She said, "See if I have it right. Robbie, you're a mainsail trimmer, right?"

A young Aussie with collar-length, sun-bleached hair said, "Right you are, Blaze!"

"That means you take a scissors and trim off the excess threads, right?"

After all the guffaws he said, "Hard to do with carbon-fiber sails, but never mind. Carry on!"

"Okay," Blaze said, uncrossing those splendid legs and re-crossing them in the other direction. "You, Matthew, you're a pit man, right? That means you take the pits out of the peaches?"

"Peaches, oh, yes!" Matthew cried, staring directly at Blaze's perky, candy-striped bosom. Boozy sailors whistled.

"How about me? Me, Blaze!" the youngest sailor yelled, hoisting a mug of Foster's.

"You?" Blaze shot him a sidelong grin. "You, young Wally? You're on the mainsheets. I guess that means you have to make the beds. Tell me, Wally, do you ever short-sheet the guys just for a lark?"

Everything Blaze said had the boozy Aussies and Kiwis in hysterics, and they started poking young Wally, who blushed when Blaze puckered her lips at him.

"Me, Blaze! Me!" sailors yelled.

The wine was fogging her usually reliable memory. "Let's

see," she said. "You're Charlie. And, let me think, you're a sewer man? That must mean you have to fix the garbage disposal on the boat whenever it gets clogged with Matthew's peach pits. Correct?"

"That's all he's *good* for, Blaze!" a sailor yelled. "Tidying up rubbish!"

She turned to him and said, "You, Tony, you're a grinder. That must mean you tend to the coffee beans? And serve the coffee and biscuits for lunch."

Blaze paused then and aimed one of her long, delicate fingers at a very athletic lad who was nearly as tall as the young one and equally smitten. "Kevin," she said. "Let me see . . ."

"I think I've stumped you," he said. "But have a go!"

She unfurrowed her brow, grinned, and said, "You're a . . . bowman, am I right?"

"But what's that *mean,* Blaze?" he asked. "What *job* do I do?"

"You take a bow, of course," Blaze said. "Every time you beat the Aussies you take a bow!"

The raucous laughter was interrupted by an Aussie grinder, who said, "They're *not* going to beat us, Blaze! No bows for these boys!"

"Can I bet my dingo on it?" Blaze wanted to know, and the Aussies cheered.

There was much debate over who got to buy her next glass of wine.

"My turn. I'm buying," one sailor said.

"Not bloody likely!" another said.

"Steady, lads," Blaze said. "You wouldn't wanna get me tipsy so you could take advantage, would you?"

That brought the loudest cheer yet.

Like flies on a dead dog. Hopeless. Leeds glumly returned to his partner.

When he got back, he said to Fortney, "A bit dicey over there, as they say Down Under. Those guys're more dangerous than fertilizer."

"That humongous Kiwi next to her could pick his teeth with the bones of human-size cops," Fortney added. "Stretch that guy's T-shirt from bulkhead to bulkhead and it could sleep three."

"What a babe!" Leeds took a last forlorn look over his shoulder at Blaze Duvall.

She turned to the massive Kiwi, saying, "And you, Miles, you don't really sail on a boat, but you have the most important job. If I remember correctly, you run the crane that puts the boat into the water, right?" Then she reached down and squeezed the Kiwi's massive shoulder. "Only thing that puzzles me is, why do you need a crane?"

"She got that right," Fortney said to his heartsick partner. "With those mitts the guy could go kayaking minus the paddles. And if he did a handstand, he'd leave tracks like a platypus."

•   •   •

Another crane operator, this one much smaller than the Kiwi who'd leave platypus tracks, was having a drink in a neighborhood tavern that advertised "semi-live entertainment." It was one of the last saloons in town where most of the people there smoked, and that's why he liked it.

Simon Cooke was thirty-eight years old and had been operating cranes and other heavy equipment since he'd dropped out of high school at the age of sixteen. He smoked like a British rock band and was at least as unhygienic. His fingernails were so filthy, they could only be called Dickensian. His mousy hair was worn in an Elvis pompadour, kept in place by a lube-gunful of gel. Simon drank half a quart of gin every night if he had enough money. He ate anything that could be considered deadly junk food but remained cadaverously thin.

Simon's youngest sister, Dab, was very unlike her brother, and had been wedded for the past six months to one of the afterguard sailors on the New Zealand team. She expected to move to Auckland at the conclusion of the America's Cup regatta and would be glad to see the last of Simon, who was always mooching money that she'd never see repaid.

After he'd drunk his second gin and tonic and smoked his sixth cigarette, Simon paid the bartender, left a fifty-cent tip, changed his mind, and picked it up again, deciding to make the two-minute drive to the Shelter Island bars, where all the cuppies hung out. Last time he was there one of his brother-in-law's drunken mates had shared a plate of potato skins and greasy onion rings, washed down by a gallon of Steinlager. Simon started salivating just thinking about a rerun.

When he got to Shelter Island, he did an eeny-meeny and decided on the joint that looked the least crowded. He parked his battered Ford Escort, entered the restaurant, and was lucky to find a seat at the bar. He looked around at a room full of yachting types and regatta hangers-on but there were no Kiwi sailors that he recognized.

Simon didn't notice the overdressed older guy with a neatly trimmed gray mustache who'd entered just behind him and headed for the restroom when Simon ordered a drink.

•   •   •

In a more crowded barroom directly across Shelter Island Drive, Blaze Duvall was telling the tenth joke of the evening to her assembled fans when her beeper went off. She reached in her purse and checked the number.

"Okay, mates!" she said to the sailors. "Make way for Doctor Blaze. I'm being paged by the hospital. Emergency surgery."

A sailor called out, "What is it, Blaze? Hemorrhoid flare-up?"

"No, Stewart," she said. "A circumcision. I'd do one for *you*, but they tell me there's not enough to work with!"

While all the sailors chortled and whacked Stewart on the back over that one, Blaze made her way through the crowd to the public phone and dialed the number on the beeper.

Ambrose answered on the first ring: "Hello?"

"It's me," she said. "Where are you?"

"Across the street. I've been following him since he left work. At first I was afraid he was going home, but he didn't. You better hurry, though. I'm not sure he'll be here long."

"Okay," she said. "I've met your Kiwi crane man. In fact, I'm pals with half of New Zealand and all of Australia. It's gonna be hard to get away."

"Find out where they'll be a week from Saturday night," Ambrose suggested. "That'll be a good time to cement your friendship with the Kiwi. But Simon Cooke's more important. He . . ."

Ambrose stopped and quickly turned his back as Simon Cooke walked into the hallway, unbuttoning the fly of his dirty jeans even before he opened the restroom door.

"What's happened?" Blaze asked. "What's going on?"

Silence. Then in a whisper: "It's him! He just passed me on his way to the restroom. He's wearing a filthy blue sweatshirt. On the short side and scrawny. Dirty hair with gel all over it. He'll be on the right end of the bar as you enter. Hurry!"

"How old is he?"

"Hard for me to judge anymore. About forty or so."

"Gimme a few minutes to make a Saturday date with my *other* crane operator," Blaze said. "Have the bartender give him a drink."

"I can't risk this man seeing me," Ambrose said. "If he leaves I'll follow him to his next stop and call your beeper again."

Ambrose was away from the telephone by the time Simon Cooke emerged from the restroom, a cigarette dangling from his lips. The crane operator reached in his pocket and pulled out a five-dollar bill. He looked at it sadly. His *last*.

It wasn't exactly a coincidence that Leeds and Fortney were leaving at the same time as Blaze Duvall. Leeds was still miffed by her lack of interest, but Fortney said they might as well go across the street to eat because there was no hope of getting a plateful of anything unfermented in this joint. Besides, he wanted to see if she looked as good when she was on her feet.

"She does," he said when he and Leeds followed her down the stairs.

"I'm still too steamed to look," Leeds said, but he did, even more intently than Fortney. "She ain't the *best* thing I've seen all year."

"You lie," Fortney said. "How you lie."

"Too many freckles."

"Yeah, of course. How could I have been so foolish not to notice."

When they got to the street, they were surprised to see that she didn't head for the parking lot. Walking across Shelter Island Drive, she had to dodge cars driven by guys who jumped on their brakes for the tall redhead in white shorts.

"She's going to the same place we are!" said Fortney. "Wanna try again or are you in too much of a snit?"

"My needs moved up my body," Leeds said. "I'd rather eat. Besides, she prefers slobs. That Kiwi was so fat you coulda shot him a whole bunch a times and never hit anything important."

"I'm glad you got over her," Fortney said. "I think she must have at least two grams of cellulite on her thighs. Did you notice it when you were giving her the twice-over?"

"Those sailors?" Leeds said. "They were handing out business cards like a bunch a Japs. Maybe I oughtta start handing out business cards."

The cops opened the door to the slightly less crowded Shelter Island restaurant. Fortney glanced around at the stained-glass windows, fake teak flooring, nautical artifacts, potted greenery, and teak veneer on wooden handrails. He said, "A person could OD on the teaky-tacky decor. Death by fern and colored glass. Let's sit down and sample their version of potato skins Gothic."

The cops had to wait ten minutes for a table and lost sight of Blaze Duvall when she squeezed through the crowd at the bar, getting next to a little guy in a blue sweatshirt. When they were being seated they couldn't see her initiate a conversation with the guy who suddenly looked like he'd just hit five straight Lotto picks. And they weren't paying attention at all when she and the guy got up from the bar.

They only spotted the redhead with the amazing body when she and the guy, who had all the markings of a lowlife wharf rat, passed their table on the way to a booth.

Leeds dropped his fork melodramatically when he overheard Blaze say, "So tell me, Simon, whadda you do for a living?"

"I don't believe it!" Leeds said to Fortney. "She prefers that dirtbag with moo goo gai pan on his hair?"

"Look at his nicotine fingers," Fortney said. "Guy smokes like a maternity-ward waiting room."

"This can't *be*!" Leeds said.

Fortney said, "Don't let it ruin your appetite, Junior. When you get to be my age, life is just food and drink and lots of bed rest. Everything else is footnotes."

"I don't get it!" Leeds said, after Simon Cooke and Blaze were seated. "Will you just *look* at the dude? He's dribbling and drooling on her shoulder! And . . . Holy shit!"

That made the older Aussie couple at the nearest table turn sharply toward the two cops, the man saying, "Steady on, mate."

"What'd he do, grope her?" Fortney asked.

"No, but *she* paid the waitress for their drinks!"

"Could be we're not dressed right," Fortney said, starting on his salad while Leeds continued gawking. "Sure, he looks like the troll that guards the bridge, but he's wearing socks under those run-over moccasins. You and me, we're stylin', so we don't wear socks. Maybe she likes guys in socks."

Leeds turned to Fortney and said, "Partner, he *ain't* wearing socks. His ankles're so filthy, they match his slimy sweatshirt!"

Fortney was truly more amazed by the redhead's choice than amused by his partner's response to it. He squinted across the room—he was too vain to wear glasses—and said, "Some babes love vinegar douches. Whatever floats your boat."

Leeds replied sadly, "A scuzzball like that gets to skizzle those freckles off? The babe's *gotta* be tacky as wet paint. I'm gonna put her outta my mind."

Fortney noticed the plates being brought to the couple at the next table and said, "This joint serves food you should send to our forensics lab."

Before Fortney and Leeds had finished their fish and chips, Blaze was bidding a fond farewell to Simon Cooke, who was crushed that she was going home after only two drinks. Drinks that she had bought.

"Can't you stay awhile longer, Blaze?" Simon begged. "Maybe you'd like to go across the street and meet my brother-in-law? He'll introduce you to the New Zealand sailing team."

"Been there, done that," Blaze said. "I've already met Auckland and Wellington. And a week from Saturday I expect to meet the rest of the island nation."

Simon Cooke just *knew* this was too good to be true. "You like sailors, huh?"

"I like *men*. Period," Blaze said with that grin again.

Simon's spirits soared. "Don't go home yet," he pleaded. "Me, I can sail *better* than my brother-in-law. You think just because a guy's sucked his way on to a sailing team he's a real sailor? All he knows is how to crank a winch. A goddamn organ grinder could do what he does. Listen, I can borrow my boss's boat on Sunday and take you sailing!"

"Tell you what, Simon," Blaze said. "Why don't you meet me a week from Saturday night? That'll be a lay day when they're not sailing."

"Where'll I find you?"

"Just look for the Kiwis. I promised the boys I'd hunt them down and challenge them to a darts game, and I always keep my promises."

Simon was getting cranky. He needed a smoke in the worst way, but it was another goddamn nonsmoking joint. The town was full of fascist smoke police. And he needed another drink. But at the moment he wanted Blaze more than both of his addictions. He'd never in his life had a woman like this come on to him.

"Blaze," he said bleakly, "you *sure* you're gonna be there that night? Where the Kiwis are?"

"Sure I'm sure," she said. "I'll tell you a secret. I'm hoping to write an article and sell it to *San Diego Magazine.* About what the challengers do on their off time. But when you see me a week from Saturday night, I don't want you to mention it to anyone, not even your brother-in-law. It might make them guarded around me."

Simon was ecstatic to be taken into her confidence. "Him? I can't stand the cocky bastard! You a freelancer?"

"You can say *that* again," she said.

"Does it pay good?" he asked. "Freelancing?"

"It's just part-time. I also do public relations for one of the defender syndicates."

"Yeah, which one?"

"I'd rather not say till I get to know you better."

"Yeah? Why the secrecy?"

"Can I really trust you, Simon?"

"Of course, Blaze!" Simon scooted closer and she hid a wince when a plume of stale sweat hit her.

"Well, my boss wouldn't mind if I learned a few of the Kiwis' secrets. You know, about their keel and tactics? Stuff like that. Intelligence, you might say."

"I'll be damned!" His grin exposed a row of small brown teeth. "You're kind of a spy for a syndicate!"

"Not a spy," she said. "But if I could learn a few *secrets* . . ."

"I'll find you a week from Saturday night!" he said. "If there's anything I can do to help, you can count on me. I'd *love* to see the Kiwis get beat so my sister'd stop crowing about how her husband's team's gonna kick ass and take names. I get *sick* a that shit!"

She stood. "A week from Saturday night, then? Can I buy you another round?" She dropped a five-dollar bill on the table.

"You shouldn't do that," he said, but he let her do that.

Blaze wiggled her fingers back at him while walking away. She wasn't halfway across the restaurant when he picked up the five and slipped it in his pocket.

When Blaze was passing the table where Fortney and Leeds were sitting, the boozy young cop couldn't contain himself. He said to her, "*Tell* me you know that guy from somewhere! He's your dog walker, am I right? You're just discussing his wages, am I right?"

Blaze paused and looked quizzically at Leeds, then remembered him from the other saloon as the nonsailor who had tried to put a move on her.

She eyed his hands wrapped around the beer glass. His left was deeply tanned except for a white band of flesh on his ring finger.

Blaze said to him, "You better put your wedding ring back on before you forget and go home like that. I'm sure you only married her to keep her from testifying, am I right?"

Then she grinned, winked at Fortney, and strolled toward the door in those white shorts and that candy-striped little tee.

Leeds was speechless, staring at his naked left ring finger.

Fortney said, "If that babe isn't a cop, she oughtta be. I'd ask her to become my third wife instantly. No prenuptials. Nothing. I'd give that girl my Jet Ski!"

•   •   •

The vice cops promised they wouldn't arrest Oliver Mantleberry until Dawn had time to settle her affairs and go. There was no question of her staying in San Diego, not after Oliver found out she'd agreed to work with the cops and had made a transcribed phone call where Oliver had reassured her that she was his top bitch but demanded to know why she couldn't catch as many dates as Alice, his bottom bitch. When she'd asked if she could cash her welfare check he'd said, Fuck, no. He'd cash it like he always did.

Listening to that had made Letch Boggs break into an extra-big rat-tooth grin.

Her baby. At least Billy was safe with her mom and sister in L.A., and the cops promised they'd keep her mom's address a secret. That's where she was going temporarily. Then she was going to get a job and clean herself up. She'd told that to the vice cops. They'd said sure.

And they said when she got her own apartment she should check in with her mother twice every day in case her subpoena arrived. Dawn had asked the vice cops, What do you take me for? I'll be going there every day to check up on the baby! The vice cops said, *Sure.*

Most of Dawn's belongings were boxed and ready to go even if she wasn't. Her clothes—except for those she used in her business—were already at her mother's house, where they'd remain until she found an apartment in West Hollywood. That'd be a good location for her, West Hollywood. Close to Sunset Boulevard, where she could turn a few dates until she found a straight job and cleaned herself up.

She couldn't just white-knuckle it, could she? She'd need to be in a neighborhood like West Hollywood where she could get speedballs. How could she turn dates without speedballs? But only until she got on her feet.

A knock at the door. Not Oliver's knock. He kind of scratched at the door like a dog. And he seldom stopped by, thinking it was safer to meet away from his place and hers. And he never came by this late. If it was Blaze, she'd knock four times, pause, and knock again. No, this knock sounded like somebody who expected, *demanded,* admittance. It was either her landlady or a cop.

When she looked through the peephole her heart went icy. She opened the door for Letch Boggs, who leered at her with those scary rat teeth.

God! Maybe he came expecting her to *do* him? A friendly little half-and-half before you go away, Dawn? For auld lang syne or something? God!

"Hi, Mister Boggs," she said warily. "Where's your sidekick?"

"Working alone tonight," he said. "I work alone whenever it ain't dangerous. You ain't dangerous, are you?"

He *did* want to get laid. She just *knew* it.

"I'm almost ready to call a mover," Dawn said. "Maybe in a week or ten days?"

"Won't need much of a truck. This all you got?"

"My clothes're already at my mom's. At the address in L.A. I gave you. You probably checked it out, huh?"

"Of course," he said. "We don't wanna lose you."

Letch Boggs was dressed pretty much like he always dressed, in one of those Hawaiian shirts—this one a bright yellow—which hung over his belly outside his pants so it would cover up the gun and handcuffs. Most of the vice cops she knew wore jeans or Dockers, but this old dork wore those wide-wale corduroy pants that her father had had on the last time she'd ever seen him, when he abandoned his wife and three kids and was never heard from again.

"I wouldn't try to burn *you,* Mister Boggs," she said.

"Sure," he said, "but I couldn't just turn you loose up there in that big bad city without knowing how to find little Billy. Love that kid. So cute, just like his mom."

Here it comes! Take your clothes off, *Mom.* And get on the bed for a quick one before the movers take it away, *Mom.*

But Letch Boggs only said, "You got money?"

"About enough for gas."

He handed her a fifty-dollar bill and said, "This is my personal money. Pay it back when you return for Oliver's court date."

"Thanks," she said, waiting for the other shoe to drop.

"While I'm here, you can do something for me."

"Uh-huh," she said, hoping he'd settle for a fast head job. She didn't want this smelly old creep inside her.

"Show me the answering machine that belongs to your pal, Blaze Duvall."

"I thought you said you weren't interested in Blaze."

"Never know when information like that might come in handy."

"You said you'd settle for Oliver," Dawn reminded him.

"I didn't say I was gonna try to make a case on Blaze, did I? I just wanna know who's working and who ain't. I just like to keep up."

"Well, that's her answering machine," Dawn said, pointing to the machine on the sink counter. "I pay both phone bills and she pays me back."

"How long you been knowing her?" Letch asked, walking over to the machine and pushing the message check. Blaze's voice came on and said, "Please leave a message after the beep." Nothing more.

"I got busted with her back in, let's see, about eight years ago when I first came to San Diego. I was a seventeen-year-old runaway. Blaze is five or six years older than me."

"Did she work the streets with you?"

"I wasn't on the streets then. We both worked in this massage parlor. Some old-time hooker named Serenity owned the place. She taught me how to give massages. Sort of."

"Serenity Jones?" Letch said. "I know her."

"Yeah, well, after Serenity got busted along with four of us girls, she went outta business. Like, I did outcall for a while, but then I started messing with crystal meth. Then I went to jail two more times. Then I started doing heroin. Then I went to jail for ninety days. Then I started working the streets. Then I started doing speedballs. Then I got knocked up and go, Fuck it! I'm having the baby. Then I met Oliver. And here I am."

"And Blaze?"

"I don't think she ever got busted after that first time. She's real smart. Just stuck with outcall massage."

"When she was booked with you that time, what name did she use? Blaze Duvall's gotta be a humbug name."

"I ain't sure," Dawn said. "Back then I was dumb enough to give my real name, Jane Kelly. I don't know what name Blaze used."

"I'll check your old arrest report," Letch said.

"I thought you said Oliver was enough for you? Why you gotta fuck-over Blaze?"

"Just wanna know what's what," Letch said. "I didn't say I was gonna fuck-over her."

"She's gonna come by next week and get her machine. And I'm gonna say good-bye to her. And, like, I'd hate to think you're gonna work a case on her. She's been good to me."

"Don't worry about it," he said.

"And, remember, I need ten days to close my business here. You can't arrest Oliver till then! Promise?"

"Give your papoose a kiss for Uncle Letch," the vice cop said, walking toward the door.

"That's all?" Dawn Coyote said. "That's it?"

"Yeah, that's it," Letch said. "What else you expect?"

"Nothing," Dawn said. It was the first time she ever smiled at him. "Thanks, Mister Boggs. Thanks for not busting me and taking my baby away. And thanks for the fifty bucks."

When she opened the door, the garden patio down below was dark and quiet. Even though there were eighty-three units in the building there was seldom any foot traffic after ten at night. Only the walk lights were on.

Letch stood on the second floor with his hand on the railing, facing the waiflike hooker. "I was you, Dawn," he said, "I'd go into treatment. You need at least sixty days in a drug facility." Then he started walking.

"I'm gonna clean up, Mister Boggs!" Dawn Coyote called after him. "You'll see!"

Letch Boggs descended the stairs and walked slowly toward his vice car parked on the street. He passed an alcove by the community swimming pool. Inside the alcove was a machine that dispensed candy, pretzels, and potato chips, and beside it were machines for soda pop and ice.

Stooped against the wall in the shadow cast by the soda machine was a tall black man. He wore a collarless long-sleeved jersey that hugged his muscular torso. His head was shaved, but he had a heavy, droopy black mustache, along with a toothbrush patch of hair under his lower lip. He stared up at Dawn Coyote's door.

He'd changed his mind about visiting her to see if her flu was better and she was ready to work, or if she was just shining him about the flu, the lazy bitch. Instead he walked directly to his white Jaguar parked in the alley.

He drove out to El Cajon Boulevard and asked the first hooker he saw if she'd ever come in contact with a dumpy old white guy named Mr. Boggs. She hadn't. He asked every girl on the boulevard the same question that night.

CHAPTER 5

EVEN WITH OLYMPIC CHAMPION ROD DAVIS AT THE HELM, THE AUSSIES SO far hadn't been able to beat Team New Zealand. The Kiwis were handling the Aussies as they'd handled everyone else, and giving bouts of anxiety to the Keeper of the Cup every night since the challenger races had begun.

Nine days had passed since Blaze met the Kiwi crane operator and Simon Cooke, yet she'd phoned Ambrose only once to say he shouldn't worry, that she was confident. That she shouldn't rush things.

She was confident? She shouldn't *rush* things? Was he insane to conspire with someone like Blaze Duvall? He wondered how many years he'd have to serve if the conspiracy failed? If he was exposed!

In his heart he knew the answer to that: *None.* He'd rather die than spend one day behind bars. Ambrose Lutterworth could never face exposure, let alone a prison term.

Blaze Duvall. A face on the darkened ceiling, grinning at him in that way of hers. Undeniably bright and charming, in the way that a street person is charming. Not that he'd ever associated with someone streetwise. In his life, in his world, the most savvy people

he'd ever known he'd met in an eight-month army stint during the
Korean War. That was before severe asthma had resulted in a
medical discharge. He hadn't even succeeded at being a soldier.
He'd overheard his mother tell his father that men with IQs of 85
could succeed at that.

During the months when he was a patient at the army hospital, he read unstated censure in his mother's letters, as though a
respiratory disease implied a lack of patriotism. He thought he'd
have been a good soldier if he'd had the chance.

Ambrose needed reassurance from Blaze Duvall. If nothing
else, he needed her *hands.* And at last, after nine days, she'd phoned
to say she'd see him on Saturday evening, the fifteenth of April.
That she'd be at his house sometime before midnight, hopefully
with good news.

When he'd asked how she felt about their chances, Blaze
would only say, "I can deal with them, Ambrose. They're men,
aren't they?"

Easy for her to be flippant, a woman like her. How could *she*
know, how could *anyone* know, what his life had been like before
the Cup? He'd always suffered from insomnia, and he raked emotional trash during the hour of regret, obsessively uncovering every
peccadillo, every humiliation, every failure he'd experienced in his
uneventful life. A former lady friend once told Ambrose that some
people were unable to dwell on past successes, only on failures. He
didn't tell her that there were so *few* successes.

Then, after he'd become Keeper of the Cup, after he'd dined
with *kings,* after he'd signed autographs for people in a dozen foreign countries, he'd lie in bed at night and go to sleep recollecting
triumphs.

So while Blaze Duvall kept him at bay, unable to fathom how
anxious he was, how fearful, he strove to forgive her insensitivity.
How could he expect a person like Blaze Duvall to even grasp the
concept of glory?

Ambrose got out of bed and took his second sedative. He

hated to do that, but at last he fell asleep, awakening at daybreak with a pounding headache.

·   ·   ·

On Saturday morning, after returning from aerobics, Blaze found an urgent message from Dawn Coyote on her machine. The younger woman said, "It's me. Phone right away!"

Blaze phoned twice, but Dawn didn't answer. She reached Dawn at two o'clock in the afternoon.

"What is it?" Blaze asked. "Don't tell me you got busted last night?"

"No," Dawn said, "but I wanted you to know I'm outta here!"

"Outta where?"

"Town. San Diego. I'm leaving and I ain't coming back."

"Where're you going?"

"I ain't sure yet, but I gotta get out."

"What happened?"

"It ain't happened yet, but it's gonna happen tomorrow."

"What is?"

"I can't say."

"Dawn!"

"Honest, Blaze, I can't say! It's better for you if you don't know! I'm scared!"

"Of what? Did you kill somebody?"

"No, but somebody's gonna kill *me* if I ain't outta here before Monday morning. That's my deadline."

"What deadline?"

"I can't say. But I gotta work hard tonight and catch as many dates as I can. It's my last night on these streets."

"If you can't tell me anything, why'd you call?"

"To say so long. And to tell you I'll drop off your answering machine this afternoon."

"You know I don't like you coming here, especially if you're in trouble."

"I ain't in trouble today," she said. "I'm gonna be in big trouble Monday if I'm still in town."

"I love a mystery." Blaze sighed. "Come by at five o'clock, but no later. I've got a big evening planned with a crew of sailors."

"You're doing *sailors,* Blaze?" Dawn exclaimed. "I can't believe it! Where do ya catch 'em? Down by the Thirty-second Street navy yard?"

•   •   •

A cormorant veered, a gull plunged, a pelican soared. Seabirds were gloriously happy on this cool and blustery April morning. Fortney was sitting on the boat seat, enjoying the show, with his hands in the pockets of his blue flotation jacket. Suddenly a shaft of sunlight flashed on a leaping fish. Stormlight on the water seemed to fill sea creatures with inexpressible joy. Fortney felt it; Leeds only felt cold.

Leeds, who always wanted to show off his muscular calves, was in shorts. He also wore his jacket, but he was shivering. "Sometimes I miss the good old days when I had Saturdays off," he said as he steered the Boston Whaler out onto Sail Bay.

"You can cure that by walking into the boss's office and saying you wanna go back to four-wheel patrol," Fortney reminded him. "Then you can get weekends off."

"You might get stuck with partners you don't like even more than you don't like me," Leeds said. "You ever liked anybody? Your ex-wives, for instance? Or your ex-cat?"

"I liked my ex-parakeet," Fortney said. "But he got eaten by my ex-cat, who my ex-wife accidentally ran over with my ex-car after her lawyer put me into poverty. Nowadays, people learn the word *sue* right after *momma.* And sue ain't a girl's name. For things that used to get you called moron, they now get you a lawyer's business card. You're not a moron, you're a plaintiff."

"No wonder you're so cranky and bitter," Leeds said. "You're lawyer-whipped."

"So when're you going?" Fortney wanted to know.

"I ain't going nowhere."

"Then why're you bitching about working Saturdays?"

"Sometimes I like to hear a voice. You ever notice you don't open your mouth till you have your third cup of coffee? I might as well bring a karaoke machine to work. I could get more conversation outta Marcel Marceau."

Fortney said nothing.

Leeds nodded at him. "My point *exactly*."

Fortney thought maybe he could bear idle conversation after his second cup of coffee. There was no point in responding to Leeds's bitching. He knew that his young partner enjoyed the benefits of "yachting," which is what dry-land cops called the Harbor Unit's water patrol. Leeds just liked to babble and bitch, but after twenty years of police work older cops tended to talk less, and Fortney was no exception.

On Sail Bay slanting light beaming through the low clouds had turned the bay into a glitter of silver spangles. Fortney started to call his partner's attention to it but gave up the idea when Leeds said, "It's dead out here. Let's go down to Coronado. See if that babe's still working lunch. What's her name, Lois Lane?"

"That's Superman's squeeze. This one's Linda Lantz."

"Yeah, that one. Wanna go see her?"

"Remember last time we went there for our afternoon tea and cookies?"

"Yeah," Leeds said. "I remember."

One winter afternoon they'd decided to take a cruise down to San Diego harbor. The ocean was glassy when they'd left Mission Bay, but it had soon turned choppy. Leeds had spun his blue cap around backward and opened her up, getting them out past the kelp beds in minutes. The vast meadows of kelp discouraged frequent runs back and forth between Mission Bay and San Diego harbor, but when the tide was high, small boats could cut their travel time by motoring between the shoreline and the kelp. On that day they'd had to circle it, cruising out on the ocean.

Cloud shadow and whitecaps. Shafts of light set the whitecaps aflame. Fortney watched low, swirling puffs of cloud tear apart and re-form in a thousand wispy shapes. He would *never* voluntarily return to the streets.

As they entered San Diego harbor a nuclear sub was cruising out from the sub base. A young officer on the conning tower gave the police boat a salute as they passed. Leeds, who'd never been in military service, returned it with a sharp, Bill Clinton–like gesture. Fortney just waved at the sub with his fingers.

One of the home-port aircraft carriers was docked at the North Island Naval Air Station quay that afternoon. Fortney wanted to cruise close to see if it was the *Constellation* or the *Kitty Hawk,* but Leeds said he needed to deliver his hungry body to a ham sandwich, coffee, and the size-forty bustline belonging to Linda Lantz, the smart-mouthed waitress who worked in an eatery by the ferry dock.

That day she managed to keep the cops entertained longer than anticipated, and it was after 5:00 P.M. when they said good-bye. The sun had already dropped behind Point Loma and darkness was falling on the bay. And with darkness the pleasure-boat traffic in San Diego harbor had vanished.

When the cops pulled away from the dock, they spotted boat activity under the Coronado bridge near one of the huge concrete piers. A pair of 32-foot boats belonging to the Harbor Police were up to something. The Harbor Police—called "Harbor Ducks" by the San Diego cops—was the port district force that patrolled San Diego harbor, but not Mission Bay.

Despite Fortney's protests about minding their own business, Leeds drove under the blue-steel span that soared almost two hundred and fifty feet straight up, linking San Diego with Coronado. Every year about a half-dozen wretched souls would ignore the suicide hotline number on top of the bridge and end their lives in the cold waters of San Diego Bay. And one had done it twenty minutes before Leeds and Fortney approached in the Whaler.

She had very long fair hair that fanned in the salt water, glinting in the glare of the police spotlight as the Harbor Police dragged her by the feet toward their boat. Even though she had reached terminal velocity before striking the water, she had not died on impact. Pink froth clogged her nose and mouth, caused by aspiration of air and salt water, the foam indicating pulmonary edema. That she'd lived for those few moments was extraordinary because when she'd struck the water she'd burst.

When the Harbor Police lifted her into the boat, Fortney and Leeds could see her intestines spilling through a tear in her cheap cotton dress, and Fortney, who'd always feared dying in dark water, said, "Thank you very much, partner. Just what I needed before the liver and onions I'd planned to cook tonight. But which is now going to the neighbor's Airedale."

Leeds looked around at the otherwise quiet harbor and said, "It's *creepy* out here at night. Let's go home."

But when they were halfway out of the harbor and still half a mile from the tip of Point Loma, they heard a thundering roar aft. A black cigarette boat pounded past them in a throbbing, chugging blast of water. Then the driver trimmed his out-drives up and kicked rooster tails fifty feet in the air, hitting the cops like water cannons.

Both cops got soaked, and Leeds turned on the blue light and throttled forward. But they had to give up the chase. The cigarette boat's twin 454 Chevy engines were doing sixty knots, and the Whaler's twin 120 Johnson outboards were no match. When the cigarette boat got past the jetty, it turned toward Imperial Beach and was gone.

"Like a dachshund chasing a whippet," Fortney said.

He got on the VHF to report the incident and make inquiries, later learning that the boat belonged to a daring drug smuggler who made five or six runs a year, usually much later at night. Sometimes he'd take his cigarette boat all the way into the Chula Vista marina. Twice the Harbor Police had pursued him, but their twin 455s couldn't keep up as he blasted across San Diego Bay. They thought he might be coming all the way from Mexican waters.

On one occasion the smuggler had been clearly seen after being lit by a police searchlight. The driver was a tall, middle-aged white man in a golf cap, with what was described as a "goofy grin."

Fortney had wondered why the hell the guy was so theatrical, using a cigarette boat to haul dope when he could just drive it across at the Tijuana port of entry like every other drug dealer in western America. But after hearing the description, he'd said to Leeds, "Wait a minute! Cigarette boat? Golf cap? Goofy grin? What's George Bush doing these days?"

On this Saturday afternoon Fortney clearly recalled that winter day and the cigarette boat. But mostly he remembered the lonely corpse in the dark water. He said to Leeds, "Let's stay here in our quiet little bay, okay?"

An hour later Fortney was knocked from the bow of another cigarette boat right into their quiet little bay.

It happened when the cigarette boat, this one red with yellow stripes, came throbbing past Vacation Isle. A thirtysomething bearded Saudi, wearing a marble-bag European bikini, was driving. And what a beard he had. Leeds, ever political, said it was dense enough to nest two pelicans and Clinton's diminutive adviser, George Stephanopoulos. And they figured the guy wasn't really rich by Saudi standards, which meant he could buy the Islandia hotel for cash but might have to get financing for the Hilton.

As could be expected, he had four very young American babes, in bikinis even skimpier than his, cruising with him. They'd been having their own version of a floating rave party involving an imaginative mix of ecstasy, the trendy hallucinogen costing thirty bucks a tablet on the current market, and peyote. The Saudi was very annoyed to be stopped for speeding.

Leeds rafted up to him and tied up to the cleat, asking for the guy's license and finding five pairs of eyeballs staring blankly at him.

Leeds glanced back at Fortney, who shrugged. Which meant: Give him the attitude test.

The Saudi flunked the test instantly. "I do not concern about your ticket!" he said to Leeds. "The peoples in my country receive more money in one day than you will have make in your life!"

"Choosing between Iraqis and Saudis was like choosing between lawyers and insurance companies, wasn't it?" Leeds said to one of the gorgeous zombies.

"I have not understood what you mean," the indignant Saudi said.

"He just asked if you've ever heard of Rodney King," Fortney replied, as Leeds wrote down the driver's-license information.

"Of course we have king!" The Saudi looked to his young companions for translation, but the soberest of the four was watching a weeping madonna in the boat's exhaust and she was smiling beatifically at the mother of God.

Leeds climbed onto the bow of the cigarette boat and waved his hand before the eyes of the leggiest bimbette, the one with a coppery ponytail. She was toasting herself on her tummy, a black thong deliciously lost in the crack of her suntanned buns.

"Don't that feel uncomfortable?" Leeds asked. "I mean, do you *like* giving yourself a Melvin all day long?"

Fortney said with a sigh, "Barefoot girl with cheeks of tan. You could take her pulse with an hourglass."

She couldn't care less what the cops said. She was scoping out a winged purple pony galloping across the Ingraham Street bridge. Waiting for the fucking horse to get sick of the car traffic and *fly*!

"Whadda you wanna do," Leeds asked Fortney, "with this boatload of living dead?"

"Ship of fools," Fortney said. "Brain-nuked. They'd need three weeks to come up with a message for an answering machine."

Leeds sensed that Fortney was as indifferent and lazy as he was. "Wanna let 'em skate?"

"Yeah, if Ali Baba here signs the ticket without further ado, he can put a Handi Wipe on his bean and offer thanks to Mecca."

The Saudi scrawled his name across the citation and jumped back behind the wheel, gunning the engines the moment the cops were reboarding the patrol boat.

Leeds made it. Fortney made it with one foot on the gunnel just as the hallucinating Arab dropped it into gear. The cigarette boat jerked the cleat right out.

Fortney stayed where he was, but the cigarette boat roared from under his right foot. Leeds watched in astonishment as Fortney dropped straight down like an anchor until nothing was visible but his floating blue hat. Then the flotation jacket popped him up like a cork.

An hour later the bimbettes were sobering up in the company of two happy lifeguards who came to the Harbor Unit's assistance. And the Saudi was on his way to jail for driving under the influence, with his boat impounded. Fortney eventually returned to the Harbor Unit office with blue lips, chattering teeth, and clammy underwear.

The lifeguards couldn't have been jollier if they'd been hanging ten on the Banzai Pipeline. They were sick and tired of the cops dissing them with old Beach Boy songs whenever they motored by, so after they helped rescue Fortney and assisted in wrapping up the deadheads on the cigarette boat, they just *had* to drop by the Harbor Unit to check out Fortney's goosebumps.

When the lifeguards entered, they found Fortney pushing a broom, wearing nothing but swimming trunks and a blanket. His dripping uniform was lying in a puddle on the floor and his holster and gun were draped over the back of a chair. He was sweeping up sand, seaweed, and assorted flotsam and jetsam that had oozed and slithered out of his clothes.

"Whatcha doin', dude?" the older lifeguard asked cheerfully.

"What's it look like?" Fortney croaked. "I'm practicing curling for the winter Olympics."

The younger lifeguard said to the other one, "Dude, I am just unstoked and unvibed."

"Whadda ya mean, dude?" his partner said with an evil eye aimed at the shivering cop.

"I mean, like, we thought we wanted to raise a cop of good cheer? And whadda we end up with? A frozen copsicle!"

"If my nine wasn't drying out," Fortney said to the lifeguards, "I'd blast you moondoggies right outta your flip-flops."

The older one said, "Gotta go, dude. Our boat's parked in a handicap zone."

•   •   •

Blaze hadn't begun to get ready for her evening yet. She'd just finished a workout on her exercise bike and was still in her leotard when Dawn arrived at 4:45, carrying the answering machine and looking more harrowed than ever.

"So, you gonna tell me what's going on?" Blaze asked.

"I been sleeping wherever I could for the past few days," Dawn said. "Moved outta my apartment on Wednesday."

"Why?"

"Oliver's looking for me."

"So? He's your old man, last I heard."

"I been avoiding him for more than a week. Finally he gets mad and phones me. He goes, Stay in your apartment till I get there! That was on Wednesday. I split."

"Why?"

Dawn took a half-eaten bag of M&M's from her purse and popped a few. "I think I know why he's looking for me."

"I know you want to tell me, Dawn, so just spit it out."

"I think he found out somehow that I made a police report."

"What kind of report?"

"Pimping. Naming him as my pimp."

"Kee-rist!" Blaze said. "Why'd you do that?"

"He beat me up."

"*Lots* of men have beaten you up! He's done it before, hasn't he? More than once."

"It's a long story. I got no choice. The cops put a twist on me. I had to do it to save my baby."

"You *are* leaving town, right?"

"Tomorrow," she said. "I jist need one more good Saturday night. I need a stake."

"You need more drugs, is what you mean."

"Whatever. But I ain't going up to El Cajon Boulevard. I'm gonna work down on Midway Drive. Oliver won't look for me down there."

"Where're you sleeping tonight?"

"Here?"

"Goddamn, Dawn!"

"Only tonight!" Dawn pleaded. "I won't even get here till maybe four A.M. Jist lemme sleep a few hours, then I'll be gone for good. I'm scared to sleep in motels. I been beat up and even stabbed in motel rooms. I couldn't ever sleep in one by myself!"

"I'd loan you a couple hundred if I had it," Blaze said, "and tell you to get your bony ass outta town. But I don't have it to spare. I haven't been doing much outcall lately, but I've got a deal I'm working with one of my old clients tonight."

"I wouldn't ask you, Blaze, if I wasn't desperate. You been too good to me already. Kin I stay?"

"Just till tomorrow morning," Blaze said. "I don't care how many speedballs you shoot up tonight, you're getting outta here tomorrow. I mean it. Trust me."

"I trust you, Blaze," Dawn said. "You're the only one in this miserable fucking town I *do* trust! I'm gonna find a new life in West Hollywood."

"Dawn, honey," Blaze said, "Richard Gere isn't out there. You're just gonna find a whole lot of Oliver Mantleberrys."

•   •   •

For the Saturday-evening cocktail party that he was obliged to attend, Ambrose chose a navy-blue tie with green and white diagonal stripes: the old rep tie of the Oxford University Sailing Club. His mother would have approved.

There was at least one significant party every few nights during the challenger and defender series, and it would get even more hectic during the finals. Ambrose was afraid he might be bedridden by then if his nerves got any worse.

He'd nicked his upper lip while trimming his gray mustache and had plastered tissue on the wound. He couldn't keep his hands steady and hadn't been able to do so since the first day he'd formulated the plan, repeatedly reminding himself that he owed Blaze Duvall five thousand dollars even if he were to call it off. But he was past the point of no return—he was sure of that much, even though he was more scared than ever. His hands could hardly manage a Windsor knot.

It was late enough in the spring to wear white trousers, he thought. He chose pleated doeskin flannels—cuffed, of course—with a knife crease so meticulously pressed that he felt obliged to sit on the bed and pull them on both legs at the same time. It made him think of the sports cliché: "We put our pants on one leg at a time." He'd heard a helmsman say it on ESPN in reference to the challenger series. But not Ambrose Lutterworth, not if one wanted creases sharp enough to cut a wedding cake. Once his sister had asked why he didn't get a block and tackle and just lower himself into his pants.

The single-breasted blazer with the patch pockets wouldn't do tonight, not at an America's Cup party in La Jolla, where everyone would be dressed nautical style. His double-breasted blazer with side vents was just the ticket for this party. He had six special brass buttons on that blazer, each with an America's Cup crest. He'd designed the buttons himself and had them made in London. Sadly, nobody at the San Diego Yacht Club had noticed the buttons until Ambrose called attention to them. That's the kind of yacht club it was.

But that's the kind of *city* it was. The nation's sixth-largest city, yes, but only its twenty-fourth-largest media market, with still just one daily nonstop flight from Kennedy airport. Ambrose's late father had always said that San Diego was a lovely place to live because everyone with big ideas had inevitably *failed.*

His mother had genuinely hated the San Diego Yacht Club. She thought it ridiculous when compared to the New York Yacht Club, repository of the Cup since Queen Victoria's reign. And, of course, she thought that the New York club was a pretender when compared to *any* sailing club in the British Isles.

The first time she'd entered the San Diego club she'd said, "Where do you buy the live bait?"

And she used to complain endlessly about people dining at the club in jeans and T-shirts. Even in second-rate San Diego restaurants (and they were *all* second-rate, she thought) people did not dine in jeans and T-shirts. His mother was from Boston and her family had summered on Nantucket Sound.

Ambrose's father had often advised his mother to learn to throw a Frisbee and just enjoy the wonderful climate. Inevitably adding, "It's not a city, my dear. It's a huge resort."

The shirt Ambrose chose was a blue cotton broadcloth with a white Windsor collar and white cuffs. He started to step into the slip-ons he'd laid out for himself but changed his mind. It was a regatta party, so he needn't be subtle. He decided to wear two-tone brogans made of linen and cordovan leather, purchased in London on New Bond Street.

He tied his brogans by resting each leg on the upholstered bench at the foot of his bed so as not to wrinkle his flannels, then stood in front of the full-length mirror for inspection. There was still a needle of dried blood on his lip, but it was almost invisible. Yes, he looked all right, but he fretted about the blazer crest he'd recently added to the ticket pocket. It was handwoven with twenty-four-karat thread, an anchor and a wreath. But was it . . . over the top?

His mother would say yes, that it was so . . . San Diego. So . . . American. As though her native Massachusetts was not in the continental United States.

Ambrose unbuttoned the blazer. Maybe it *was* over the top. Perhaps he should have had the crest sewn on to his single-breasted blazer. After all, that was a more casual coat and had a patch pocket. He wondered if anyone in the New York Yacht Club would apply a crest to a ticket pocket on a double-breasted blazer? Suddenly it seemed *way* over the top!

Then he realized he was breathing fast and gulping air. He sat on the bench seat and tried to control himself, determined to concentrate on his appearance rather than on old memories and fears.

Ambrose stood up and breathed slowly, expelling all the air before he took the next breath. Slow, measured breathing always calmed him. He rebuttoned the double-breasted blazer, posing for a moment. Then he stepped back, did a half-turn, and examined the entire ensemble.

Ambrose Lutterworth told himself he didn't give a *damn* what an old dead woman would have said. Nor any of the poseurs and prigs from an East Coast yacht club. Ambrose Lutterworth *knew* who he was: He was Keeper of the Cup!

But before he left home he put a white handkerchief in the ticket pocket, hoping it might somehow modulate the effect of the golden crest.

Ambrose arrived at the party thirty minutes after the cocktail hour had started. Like all San Diego parties, it was an early one, and sunset was still an hour away when he parked the old Cadillac in front of a minimansion on La Jolla's Gold Coast. Ambrose knew that during the regatta, when so many partygoers were working on the race committee, this would end very early, thank God.

A valet-parking girl, in a white shirt with a black bow tie and black trousers, took his car, saying, "You won't need a ticket, sir."

Which meant that the do wouldn't be as big as some he'd had to attend lately. Another small blessing.

He was met at the door by Madge Stoker, wife of Grant Stoker, who, like Ambrose, was a second-generation yacht club member, and would probably be the next commodore.

Madge was the daughter of an Imperial Valley farmer who'd become wealthy growing truck crops. She was overweight, loud, and so comfortable with herself that she made Ambrose nervous. Madge looked people right in the eye, something Ambrose found vaguely distasteful. And her fingernails were cracked and split from working alongside a pair of undocumented Mexican laborers whom she employed full-time, tending her gardens and trees. She jauntily

reported that she'd never contributed to their Social Security benefits, therefore could never be appointed to Clinton's cabinet.

"Hello, Ambrose, baby!" Madge said when he entered the
marble foyer underneath a thirty-foot ceiling.

The foyer and living room contained several rococo mirrors,
Queen Anne lacquered antiques, and eighteenth-century Japanese
screens. The doorways and windows and all of the upholstered
furniture were overscale, including a pair of wool damask sofas that
could seat half of La Jolla. The floor-to-ceiling glass patio doors
were framed with taffeta. Ambrose had never entered the Stoker
home without wanting to burn it to the ground.

Madge didn't turn her cheek and buss the air like most host-
esses on the party circuit. She planted one on him. Her lipstick was
already smeared and would be all over her face by the time the last
guests arrived. And if any lady discreetly called her attention to it,
Madge Stoker would usually reply, "As Clark Gable never quite
said, Frankly, m'duck, I don't *give* a fuck."

After greeting Madge, Ambrose got himself a glass of white
wine at one of the two bars that were set up and strolled onto the
terrace, where guests could watch the sun drop into the Pacific.

Chablis. He might have known. Drinkable, but only just. A
real vintner wouldn't use it to make salad dressing. Yet the scotch,
vodka, and gin were the best money could buy. *So* like Madge
Stoker.

Grant Stoker approached Ambrose on the terrace and shook
hands vigorously even though they'd seen each other at the club that
afternoon. "So glad you could make it, Ambrose," he said. "You
had me worried when you said you weren't sure. Wouldn't be a
party without you."

"I cleared my calendar for you," Ambrose said, realizing they
were both lying. Two boating bullshitters.

Grant Stoker was taller and younger-looking than Ambrose,
by virtue of being robust and athletic. Unlike Ambrose, he had all
of his hair, wearing it slicked back like a yuppie. It was rumored
that he'd had affairs with at least three yacht club wives over the

years but had always been discreet so it probably wouldn't hurt his chances of becoming commodore.

"Come on over and meet some of our friends from north county," he said.

North county meant Del Mar, Rancho Santa Fe, and Fairbanks Ranch, pricey bedroom communities where wealthy San Diegans lived whose hobbies were more likely horses and golf than boats.

About sixty guests had arrived by then, and most of the men were wearing blazers or poplin summer sport coats. There were plenty of Ferragamo neckties with nautical motifs, but Ambrose would never wear nautical neckties. They *were* over the top, no question about it.

"This is Ambrose Lutterworth, the Keeper of the America's Cup," Grant Stoker said to a cluster of seven people, four men and three women, in casual cocktail attire.

A middle-aged woman with a trim figure, in a mint-green St. John knit, put her hand out and Ambrose shook it.

She said, "My name's Sam. I saw you on television in Tokyo when you brought the Cup there."

"*Did* you?" Ambrose was delighted.

He knew these people weren't yachtsmen, but, after all, it *was* a regatta party. Though they might not be sailing enthusiasts, they were probably going to be on spectator boats at some time or another, watching the race on a television screen in the salon, thus having an excuse to get hammered at one o'clock in the afternoon.

"Well, I've taken the Cup to quite a few places in the past few years," he began, smiling shyly. "That's why I was on Japanese TV."

"What does the Keeper of the Cup actually do?" Sam asked.

"He travels with the America's Cup!" her husband said. "Whaddaya think? He takes it to . . ." Then he turned to Ambrose and said, "Where besides Tokyo?"

"I've been to a *lot* of places," Ambrose said, forcing himself to drink the chablis, fending off a sudden impulse to flee.

"We're all landlubbers," another man explained. He was younger than the rest, wearing a pale blue pinfeather sport coat that Ambrose admired. "Tell us some America's Cup *gossip*."

"What sort of gossip?" Ambrose asked.

"Excuse me, everyone," Grant Stoker said. "I'll run along and help Madge at the door so I don't have to hear Ambrose telling you where all the bodies are buried."

"They're buried at sea, of course," Ambrose said, and everyone laughed vigorously at the little joke. He realized they were already half smashed.

Ambrose really didn't have to answer a single inquiry. They provided their own America's Cup gossip, and his headache went from a dull throb to a painful thump.

Nobody understood what the Cup meant to real yachtsmen; not even all club members understood. How could he tell *these* people? How could he explain the honor? He excused himself and went out on the terrace. The sun was about to set and guests waited, hoping for the green flash.

It was caused when an atmospheric change in air density created a bending of the light when it crosses from cool to warm, as in a giant prism. Blue and green refract more than red and yellow, the blue scattering more vigorously, and if the green is properly positioned, the red fireball may permit a magnified rim of burning emerald as it drops into the sea. Hence, the green flash.

Ambrose had heard of the Scottish legend that promised love and eternal happiness to all who sighted the green flash. It was a lovely thought.

Madge Stoker startled him by whispering in his ear. "Know why all the broads at these parties stand so close to each other when they talk? Their eyesight's not up to checking out cosmetic surgery from a distance."

By the time he turned from Madge and looked out to sea, the sun had vanished. Without a green flash.

CHAPTER 6

BLAZE ARRIVED AT THE WATERFRONT RESTAURANT AT SIX O'CLOCK AND headed straight for the bar. There was already an assortment of Aussies and Kiwis present who outnumbered the Yanks and certainly outdrank them.

She was wearing an emerald tube top, white Bongo jeans, and boat sneakers. The tube top would slip an inch each time she waved at one of the sailors, and she made it a point to wave frequently as she pranced across the barroom.

In a moment they were circling like sharks on a blood slick.

"Blaze!" an Aussie called out.

"Here, Blaze!" This one was a Kiwi.

"Over here, Blaze!" said another. "You gave those blokes all the attention *last* time."

"White wine, Blaze?" an Aussie trimmer asked. "I anticipated your arrival and ordered a bottle chilled."

"Good on ya, Charlie!" Blaze said.

The restaurant was one of several with Polynesian decor, mostly bamboo veneer and floral design. And there were paintings on the walls that Gauguin might have done if he'd been dead drunk. But the dining area had a sweeping view of the harbor, including the skyline, the North Island Naval Air Station, and the Coronado bridge.

Not one of the professional sailors gave a shit about the view. They couldn't stop looking at Blaze Duvall and her green tube top. Her eyes a vivid green against the tube.

The restaurant manager got worried that competing sailors might come to blows over *this* cuppie, so he told his bartender to keep an eye on the action and let him know if things got ugly.

After Blaze perched herself on a bamboo barstool, she looked around and said, "Did Miles get a better deal this evening?"

"Still had a few loose ends back at the compound," a Kiwi told her. "Never fear, he hasn't walked past a boozer in ten years without popping in."

After lights went on in the high-rise buildings downtown and on the sweeping curve of the Coronado bridge studded by lamps, Simon Cooke showed up. Filled with high hopes that Blaze would keep her word, he was as well groomed as he ever got. Which meant he was wearing fresh blue jeans, sneakers that were not caked with grease, and a semiclean sweatshirt with a kamikaze surfer on the back who was hanging five and flipping the bird to the world. Simon Cooke had even washed his ankles.

Blaze said to the sailors, "Excuse me, lads. Keep my seat warm."

She slid off the stool, much to the distress of the sailors, who started moaning and mooing like cattle, and twisted through the mob to greet a beaming, semisober Simon Cooke.

"I can't believe it!" he said. "You're here! You really like me!"

"Easy, Simon," she said. "You sound like Sally Field at the Academy Awards."

Blaze selected one of the bamboo booths away from eavesdropping sailors and schmoozed Simon with America's Cup gossip until he'd finished his first drink. She waited for his second to arrive before she said, "Simon, I'm getting closer to finishing that article, but I need technical help. For example, remember the French boat that got dropped by the crane operator?"

"Sure," he said. "Everyone knows about that fiasco. I think the guy wasn't their regular operator."

"It can happen to any team, right?"

"Just about," he said. "Cranes can be tricky. It wouldn't happen to me. I'm the best in the business." Then he thought he'd gone too far and added, "At least around this town, I'm the best."

"What if I decide to write a scenario about the dropping of a boat?"

"Is that like a screenplay?"

"Let's say I decide to fictionalize my piece about the America's Cup. Maybe I'd like to create a plot where somebody wants to sabotage the New Zealand boat."

"Who?"

"Can't you think of someone?"

"Sure," he said. "Dennis Conner or Bill Koch, whichever one wins the defender series. I'd include the Pact Ninety-five team on *Young America,* but they ain't got a chance against Koch or Conner. The thing is, they'd all like to see the Kiwis get hit with a Scud missile."

"Everybody fears New Zealand, right?"

"The Kiwis have speed they don't even need," Simon said. "And everyone knows it. But the Kiwis got *two* boats. Why would Conner or Koch want to sabotage only one of 'em? See, that's the problem with your . . ."

"Scenario."

"Yeah."

"But what if one of the Kiwi boats is a lot *better* than the other?"

"I ain't heard that."

"I've heard it," Blaze said.

"Who from? Them?" Simon indicated the rowdy mob at the bar who'd grown more raucous after darkness fell on San Diego Bay.

"Two more," Blaze said to a bosomy waitress in a sarong. Then to Simon, "Let's just agree for purposes of my plot that one

New Zealand boat is better, and somebody wants to arrange for a crane operator to drop the fastest of the Kiwis' two black boats. How would he do it?"

"First of all, you got problems," Simon said, draining the last of the gin from his bucket glass.

"Why is that?"

"It can't happen like the French accident happened."

"Why?"

"It ain't even a crane, that's why. The Kiwis use a travel-lift. In fact, *I'm* the guy that taught their operator how to use it!"

"Anything can be sabotaged," Blaze said.

Simon gave Blaze a patronizing smile, revealing that he'd even brushed food out of his teeth. "It ain't the same. The travel-lift is a steel beam between two lifting blocks. There's this big eye-beam called a spreader bar, see? I could drive the damn thing right outta their yard and bring it next door and show you, except I'd probably get my nuts tore off. Pardon my French."

"You can't go in there?"

"No way," he said. "After the Kiwis leased that part of our boatyard, they closed it off with barbed wire. They got their own cops inside that fence. They're probably carrying Uzis or some fu—some damn thing."

"What if they need something from your boatyard?"

"Believe me, we get escorted over there. One time I had to lift their boat while I was teaching their guy how the travel-lift works and—"

Simon was interrupted when the waitress brought their drinks to the table. "No, don't!" he said, but Blaze took a twenty from her purse and handed it to the girl.

Simon didn't fight too hard. He had thirteen bucks in his pocket after paying off two gambling debts. Those fucking Padres couldn't beat the Taiwan Little Leaguers.

"So go ahead," Blaze said. "You were teaching them how to work the travel-lift?"

"Yeah, and I had to lift their boat *blind*. They hung a curtain between me and their boat so I couldn't see the fucking keel. Oops."

"So, are you saying somebody would have to have the cooperation of a Kiwi to drop that boat?"

"No, Blaze," Simon said. "You don't get it. You *can't* drop that boat with a travel-lift. It's more foolproof than a crane. See, a shackle is attached to the spreader bar, right? With this Kevlar sling that goes through the deck to the top a the keel. Get me?"

"No."

"Well, it's like . . . there's these two finger piers that go out. You lift from the center between two finger piers. See?"

"No."

"Well, see, the travel-lift is actually a vehicle. I could drive it to Mission Beach if the road was clear. There's like a big horseshoe. There's two lift points. There can't be operator failure. With the travel-lift you pull levers to operate a hydraulic motor. You need lots a common sense, but it ain't like a crane where if you take your foot off the brake the load goes in free-fall. You don't have to daug the winches on a travel-lift. The hydraulic motor's operated by pressure. Get it?"

"No, but I don't have to get it. Not for my story purposes."

"But you could change it to a crane in your story, then it's easy to drop a boat. There ain't a fail-safe for the brake. I mean it's just a story, right? A guy's foot could slip off the brake on a crane."

"Come on, Simon," Blaze coaxed, putting her hand on his bare forearm, rubbing it gently. "I need my scenario to work *my* way. I'll bet *you* could do it. I'll bet you could figure out a way to drop that boat from a travel-lift."

He felt a swelling in his throat. He'd never felt such a silky touch. He'd never *seen* eyes so green. He could feel her breath on his face when she moved closer. "Well," he said, "maybe I could if I thought about it."

"Think about it," she said, massaging his arm lightly. "Think."

"It's like . . ." Then he looked into the liquid green irises. "Well, it's like . . . hard to do!"

"There's always a weak point," she said. "In all of life you look for weak spots."

"The sling," he said, swallowing hard. Goddamn! His throat was swelling faster than his willie!

"The sling is the weakest point?"

"Uh-huh," he said, disappointed that she stopped the forearm massage.

"Tell me about the sling," she said.

"It's like a braided Kevlar thousand-mile strand," he said. "A continuous strand, like. And over that is this protective sleeve. A sort of loose cover like a sheath. And it's fixed like a hem on a pant leg."

"So why couldn't somebody *un*hem it?"

"You'd have to remove it and cut enough of the strands on the sling to weaken it."

"How could you be sure it'd break?"

"The operator could make a sudden stop. With a big load you should be in low speed. But if it was accidentally in high speed and you released the levers . . ."

"What would happen?"

"There'd be a jolt."

"How much weight're we talking about?"

"The keel weighs more than twenty-two tons. The rest a the boat weighs two and a half tons. A sudden jolt with a half-cut sling? I think it'd go. I think it'd go *down*."

"Would they know it was sabotage?"

"The operator could just say, Oh! I was in high speed? I thought I was in low speed. Good heavens, mates!"

"Could they prove the sling'd been cut?"

"No. It's like a spool of heavy-duty thread. It'd just be hanging like spaghetti."

"Then the operator in my *story* could get away with it?"

"If he had a gun. He'd need it to get outta the boatyard with his life. They'd kill him, those fucking—oops!—those damn Kiwis.

I don't like *any* of 'em, especially my brother-in-law. They're all pushy. They demand the world from our yard because my boss is the landlord. But if you ask them for *one* little thing, they shine you. Bunch a pricks. Pardon my French."

"When they leased your boatyard, why didn't they lease one of you guys? You, for instance? I mean, your own brother-in-law is on the team and they wouldn't hire you?"

"He wasn't my brother-in-law then. Anyways, they're too paranoid, the whole bunch. In ninety-two the Italians leased the travel-lift *and* an operator. Nice guys. Made pasta for us. I liked them. And I even liked the Japs. Whenever you waved to them they'd bow a little bit. When they came back from a practice run they'd yell, Banzai! They were very polite. The Kiwis're arrogant jerks."

"Would you cut the thread on the sling with a penknife?"

"No way! You'd need a saw. It'd take some time. Hard to cut Kevlar."

"Let me see if I understand. The sling would unravel like a loose spool of thread. But it's hidden from view by a cloth condom, right?"

"That's funny!" Simon giggled. "Yeah. A cloth condom."

"So somebody could do it on the morning of the last race with the Aussies, who it looks like the Kiwis're going to annihilate. Would that be a good time?"

"Nope. Can't be done then," Simon said. "How about another round?"

Without waiting, he held up two fingers to the saronged waitress while Blaze said in exasperation, "You just said it *could* be done, Simon!"

"How you gonna get your guy in the yard so he can do it? Those pri—those *guys* won't let my sister in there unless my brother-in-law's holding her hand. They probably make her wear a blindfold if their goddamn keel's exposed."

"You could climb over the fence from your part of the boatyard to theirs, couldn't you?"

"With barbed wire and security guards that'd tear your nu—head off? No way!"

That was it then. Blaze leaned against the backrest and scooted away a bit. It *couldn't* be done. She'd have to settle for five grand. It was a stupid idea in the first place.

Her thoughts were interrupted when he said, "You'd have to do it when they're out racing. Maybe like you said, on the day of the last race against the Aussies. *Everybody* would be glued to the TV set, even the security guys."

Blaze leaned forward again and this time she grabbed his arm. "Keep going, Simon," she said. "Don't stop."

Simon Cooke looked across the restaurant, straining his gin-fogged brain for her. "You'd do it at four-thirty in the afternoon," he said. "When they're back from the race. They're gonna kick Aussie ass, so they'll all be congratulating themselves. That's when you'd do it. The sling'd already be cut by then, by the guy in your story. And the spaghetti'd be unraveling."

"How did you get in the yard to do it when they were out racing?"

"I didn't. I couldn't. I'm a Yank. They don't trust *no* Yanks. They wouldn't trust the U.S. Supreme Court. In your story you gotta get the Kiwi operator to do it. The guy who puts the boat into the water in the morning is on standby in the yard all day. He sits in the travel-lift reading a book if it's quiet. And it'll be real quiet in the yard on that last day. They'll be huddled around the TV from one to four o'clock, that's for sure."

"So for my purposes I gotta get the Kiwi crane operator to do the sabotage on the sling *and* drop the boat himself?"

"That's about it."

"But what if . . . what if on the morning of the last race against the Aussies—the clinching race—their travel-lift operator couldn't come to work?"

"You kidding? That guy's making more'n he's ever made in his miserable life as a bottom painter, or whatever he was down in that shitty little country. I used to be a bottom painter myself. Worked my way up to cranes and travel-lifts. When I worked for the Italians, they paid me four times what I make now. He's *not* gonna—"

"Let's just say for story purposes he *can't* come to work. Who's gonna put the boat in the water? And be on standby all day? And take it *out* of the water? *Who?*"

Simon Cooke stared at Blaze for a moment. Then he tossed down his third gin and tonic, wiped his mouth on his sweatshirt, and said, "They'd have to come to us. We're the landlords. My boss is, I mean."

"*Who* would they get to run the travel-lift on that important day? On such short notice?"

"I guess . . . *me*," Simon Cooke said. "I guess you gotta put *me* in your story."

Blaze expelled a mighty breath, then said, "*Thank* you, Simon. Want another drink?"

•   •   •

Fortney's body temperature reached 98.6 degrees Fahrenheit sometime before their shift ended that Saturday. It was one of the worst days he'd experienced since wearing a badge. He was thankful their sergeant was an understanding old-timer, not one of those pimpled semi-adolescents with chevrons on their sleeves, computer cops with no military experience and little life experience, too young to be out after curfew.

He remembered one such sergeant at a jumper call on the Coronado bridge. The crazed jumper was himself an off-duty cop with a nine-millimeter in his hand, trying to get up the nerve to blast himself off the span.

The young sergeant ordered him to put down the gun. Why? "Because it was city property." Which made Fortney want to draw his own nine and use it on the kid sergeant who lived with a permanent hard-on, but only for the troops.

His partner's erection was obviously aimed in another direction. Before they got their reports finished, Leeds said, "Let's go trolling for cuppies tonight, whaddaya say?"

"I've had a very busy day, Junior," Fortney replied. "Didn't you happen to notice, I almost *drowned*?"

"Come on!" Leeds said. "I gotta test that stupid survey about married people having better sex lives than single people. Hear about that? Tonight I'm gonna be a single guy and find out the real truth."

"You've *always* been a single guy," Fortney said. "Trouble with you is, you've never been a married guy since you got married."

"So let's go blow that freaking survey right outta the water."

"Don't mention water," Fortney said.

He didn't mention to Leeds or anyone else how much panic he'd felt during that moment in the bay. Even though he was wearing a flotation jacket. Even though his partner was right there in the Whaler instantly reaching down for a handful of that jacket. Even though Fortney knew logically that he wasn't going to drown, it was *there,* worming its way from the back of his mind to the front: a morbid fear of drowning in dark water. If it had happened at night he might have died of fright. He wondered if he'd dream about it.

Suddenly he wanted a drink. "Okay," he said, "I'll go along. The experience will no doubt be more amusing than anything that gets my taxpayer dollars on PBS."

An hour later they were eating tough potato skins, rigid calamari strips, and limp French fries in a Shelter Island restaurant that was not only packed with race enthusiasts but also with tour groups ready for a San Diego weekend at Sea World and the zoo.

Fortney looked around and said, "Name of tonight's story is: Natural Fibers Takes a Holiday. This looks like Rush Limbaugh's TV audience."

"I never seen so many VFW poppies," Leeds said. "And I'm pretty sure a couple of the females ain't primates."

"I'm not feeling all that human myself," Fortney said, "after drinking mutant-making liquids from the bay. If I ever find a third wife young enough to have my baby, I'll have to warn her it won't look good in family photos. She'll give birth to a blob of slime mold or a patch of fungus."

As soon as Fortney finished the potato skins, he got bilious. He jumped up and ran to the restroom. When he returned five minutes later, he said, "It's starting already. I just hunked up something that looks like Ross Perot, only taller."

•   •   •

Midway Drive wasn't such a bad place to catch dates, Dawn told herself, except that a lot of them were U.S. Navy enlisted men. She hadn't really done a lot of swabbies before and thought they might not have enough money. They looked pretty young and scared to her, with those sidewall haircuts, driving those cheap little cars. How much money could they have?

At least there were a lot of close-by motels on Rosecrans Street. She'd learned that many of the sailors would rather pay the tariff at a motel than risk doing the date in parked cars, and they seemed to like having a place to sleep away from the navy barracks. Dawn didn't mind a motel room. It was their money, and this was her last night in San Diego.

She looked at her watch hoping to catch five more dates. Then she'd call her connection, score some speedball, go home to Blaze's apartment, and tomorrow? A *new* life! The thought was so exciting that for the first time in months she actually felt happy.

It had occurred to Dawn that she'd better take off the nipple and clit chains. They'd worked very well with older dates up on El Cajon Boulevard. In fact, one guy gave her a thirty-dollar tip just to shoot a Polaroid picture of the thing. But this evening when the first navy guy took her to a motel room he'd almost passed out when she stripped.

While removing the clit chain she'd accidentally pinched herself and cried out in genuine pain, which brought tears to her eyes.

The young sailor almost started crying, too. He said, "Nobody

in Deming, New Mexico, goes around looking like a walking scrap-
yard!"

She had a hell of a time getting him hard.

•   •   •

The moment he arrived home, Ambrose Lutterworth removed his
blazer and trousers and hung them on the cherrywood gentleman's
valet in the corner of his bedroom. The white flannels would have
to be cleaned if he couldn't remove the stain from the cocktail sauce
that one of those drunken fools had splashed on him when they
were out on the terrace at sundown.

He brushed his teeth and squirted a little cologne on his
cheeks and neck, anticipating Blaze's arrival. Then he put on taupe
cotton trousers and his monogrammed bedroom slippers. He
thought the shirt and tie he'd worn that evening would look all
right under his burgundy smoking jacket.

He loved the softness of the jacket, the shawl collar, the feel of
the satin piping and the satin waist sash. He often wore the jacket
when he was home alone in the evening. It made him consider
taking up cigars, but he never could stand the smell of burning
tobacco. He didn't have a single friend at the club who'd ever
spoken of the incomparable pleasure of removing one's coat and
slipping into a smoking jacket.

Ambrose sat in his Chippendale wing chair, upholstered in the
red and copper stripes of the Royal Temple Yacht Club. He'd spotted that chair in London on his second trip with the America's Cup,
bought it on the spot, and had it shipped to San Diego.

When he picked up the *Union Tribune,* he felt that sack of wet
sand in his belly just from reading about Peter Blake, the forty-
seven-year-old leader of the Team New Zealand syndicate. A man
with five hundred thousand miles of sailing experience! The master
of the Whitbread Round the World Race and the only man to race
in the first five Whitbreads, the toughest sailing event ever devised.
And he'd won two of them.

The article told how, in 1992, Blake sailed a 92-foot catamaran nonstop around the world in a record seventy-four days, twenty-two hours, seventeen-and-one-half minutes. Reading of such incredible sailing feats made Ambrose admit that few Americans would take on the Whitbread. It seemed that only Aussies and Kiwis were crazy enough and macho enough to do it, and Ambrose could recall only one American boat out of fourteen in the last race. He wondered if Yank sailors were no longer tough enough for what to a Kiwi like Peter Blake was a rite of passage.

One thing was certain, and Ambrose just had to keep reminding himself of it: Neither Peter Blake nor his helmsman and skipper, Russell Coutts, nor anybody else, could win this race in a boat that was not fast enough. Not when the boat that *was* fast enough lies broken in a heap in a Shelter Island boatyard.

Ambrose let the newspaper fall onto the floor by his feet, feeling a bit light-headed and drowsy. He closed his eyes, hoping for a refreshing little doze. He almost removed his tie but decided against it. For the elegance of a smoking jacket to have an effect, the shirt and tie had to be as neat as it was when one conducted important business.

•   •   •

It was hard to get rid of Simon Cooke, especially after Miles, the giant Kiwi, spotted them in the booth together. Miles strode across the barroom and the crowd fell back as crowds do for extremely large people. He was wearing a black T-shirt in honor of their boat, *Black Magic.* Below the too-short cuff of his jeans, red socks showed. Red socks were worn by Peter Blake for good luck, and had become the hottest apparel item in New Zealand. Everyone from politicians to nuns was wearing red socks, New Zealand television reported, and that included Border collies and sheep.

Emblazoned in crimson across the front and back of the T-shirt was: BLACK MAGIC RULES THE WAVES. DENNIS CONNER WAIVES THE RULES.

"Hi, Miles!" Blaze said when he reached the table.

"Evening, love," he replied. "Been out on the water to see our lads doing business?"

"Haven't had a chance," she said. "I guess you know Simon Cooke?"

"Taught me how to operate the travel-lift," Miles said, shaking hands halfheartedly with the little man.

"Taught him in less time than a guy'd need to take a sh—nap," Simon said. "How's it behaving?"

"Right as rain," Miles said. In his paw the beer mug looked like a whiskey glass.

"Well, it's good to see ya," Simon said to Miles, and turned to Blaze as though to resume their conversation.

Miles didn't take the hint. He continued to smile at Blaze, exposing a gap where an eyetooth was missing. His white-blond hair was as short as any boot camp swabbie's.

Blaze said, "Can I buy you a beer, Miles?"

Only then did he glance at Simon and say, "I better go join my mates at the bar. Have to keep them out of mischief. Why don't *you* join *us*?"

"In a bit," Blaze said with a smile that made Simon Cooke want to get up and kick that big ape in the balls.

But then of course he'd die on the spot when the leg that did the kicking was torn from his torso and thrown into San Diego harbor.

After Miles was gone, Simon said, "I *never* liked that guy. Of course I never liked any a the Kiwis, especially—"

"The one that married your sister," Blaze said in that way of hers that made Simon's heart flutter.

"Yeah," he said, "especially him."

"How bad has he treated you?" Blaze asked, and signaled to the cocktail waitress again with two fingers up.

"Real rude, the arrogant cocksucker!" Simon said. "Pardon my French. One time I says to him, 'When you and my sis go to

New Zealand and have your first kid, I'm gonna come down and visit.' Know what he says to me?"

"What?"

"He says, 'That's a terrifying thought.' I says, 'Why is it a terrifying thought?' He says, 'That you might use our *towels*.' The prick! No offense."

"Guys like that should get what's coming," Blaze said.

"I'll say."

"I wonder how he'd like to go back to New Zealand a loser?"

"He won't," Simon said. "They're gonna beat anybody the Yanks throw up against them."

"Not necessarily," Blaze said. "Just think about it. All the money they've spent? All the months of hard work and sacrifice? All the fame and goodies they *think* they're gonna get when they go home with the Cup? All of it down the drain if they lose."

"Yeah!" Simon said. "Works for me!"

"Could happen," Blaze said. "If they have to race in their thirty-eight boat. I tell you the thirty-eight just isn't as good as their thirty-two."

"Well, they're *gonna* race the thirty-two boat," he said, "if that's the fastest one."

"Not if it's outta the water lying on its back like a dead turtle."

"I don't get it."

"Not if it's dropped from a travel-lift!" Blaze said, then lowered her gaze.

Simon didn't respond. He stared at her, and when she looked up with those heart-stopping eyes, he said, "Miles? He's gonna drop the boat?"

"I didn't say that."

"Blaze!" Simon moved his arm away even though she was touching it with those satin fingers. "What's going on here? Are you *really* writing a story or what?"

"Yes," she said, "but while I've been working on it and doing the research, I've met lots of people. I know a man . . ." She put her hand back on his arm tentatively. He didn't move away, so she said, "Can I trust you? I mean, *completely* trust you?"

"Sure. Why?"

"I know a man who wants to see that thirty-two boat on the *ground*. And he's willing to pay for it."

"Who?"

"I can't say who. But I can tell you he's serious."

"But why's he telling this to you?"

"Because I told him that I know you. He understands how the Kiwis run their security. And about things like the travel-lift. He already knows about you."

"About *me*? What about me?"

"That you're the best crane operator in San Diego. That you taught the Kiwi operator everything he knows about the travel-lift. That you've been crapped on by the Kiwis even though you and your boatyard always treated them real good. I told him that I know you very well because I could see I was talking to a very serious player."

"Player in what?"

"In the America's Cup."

Then Simon's expression changed. His narrow lips widened to a blade and he said, "You were talking to Bill Koch, weren'tcha?"

"I can't say," Blaze replied with a cunning grin of her own.

"I *know* it was him!" Simon said.

"I really can't, Simon. Please don't ask."

"Or Dennis Conner? You coulda been talking to Dennis Conner?"

"I can't say."

"Anyways, it was one a the two," Simon said. "I hope it was Koch. I don't think he's got more balls than Conner, but he sure got more *money*."

"The point is, the man I talked to is serious."

"You must think I'm dumb," Simon said, and now the crafty look had vanished. He looked hurt.

"Of course I don't!"

"Now I see why you're friendly with that pus-gut Kiwi. You're gonna make him an offer, ain'tcha?"

"You've got it wrong, Simon," Blaze said, "but hold the thought."

The waitress set the drinks down on the table and picked up the empty glasses. When she was gone, Blaze said, "You've got it wrong. I could never trust Miles. I don't even like the Kiwis."

"I seen you playing up to them," Simon said. "You got yourself into something with Koch or Conner, whichever. You got yourself into the America's Cup spy game. That's what you done."

"Is it a mistake?"

"I knew guys around this harbor that did spy jobs during the last America's Cup. Some of 'em got paid good money, some of 'em didn't. It was to take pictures of the keel. I never heard a nobody getting paid to dump a boat out. And I don't think your pal Miles is gonna do it for you." Then he added, "No matter *what* you promised to do for him."

It was Blaze's turn to look hurt. And to pout. She said, "I can't believe you think I'd . . . *promise* something to that guy! Whadda you think I promised him? My body?"

"I didn't say that."

"I don't sell my body, Simon!"

"I didn't mean that. No offense!"

"What *did* you mean?"

"I think maybe you got yourself caught up in the spy game and you're gonna be a middleman and maybe offer some money to Miles. That's what I mean."

"To *you*," she said simply.

"What?"

"To *you*. I'm in a position to offer the man's money to *you*. If you do the job just the way you explained it to me—on the day of *Black Magic*'s last race with oneAustralia."

"This is screwy talk," Simon said. "You drunk or what?"

"Five thousand dollars," she said.

"Screwy talk."

"That's what I told him," Blaze said. "And then he said *ten* thousand. That's as high as he'll go. He said if you could do it just the way you told it to me, he'd pay ten thousand bucks."

"I told you it's impossible to even *get* in that yard, Blaze. Jesus, this is crazy!"

"Miles is not gonna be able to go to work on the day of the last race with the Aussies." Now she was *gripping* his arm, dead-staring him.

For a moment Simon felt afraid of this woman. Then he said, "Leapin' les-bos!" Too astonished to add, "Pardon my French."

"I don't think it'll be too hard," Blaze said. "Just a harmless little something in his beer the night before and he won't be going to work the next morning. Come to think of it, I might need an extra dose. He must go about three hundred pounds, wouldn't you say?"

"You got this idea jist from talking to people for a magazine article?"

"To be honest with you, Simon, I've known the anonymous gentleman for a few years. I have a part-time job with a public relations firm downtown, and we handle his account. I've actually dated the man a few times. Nothing serious, but he trusts me."

"Tell me this. It's all I wanna know. Is it Koch or is it Conner?"

"I really can't say."

"It's Koch," Simon said, satisfied. "Smaller balls but bigger bucks."

"Whadda you think, Simon? Interested?"

"I gotta think it over," Simon said. "Man, I never been to jail before except for drunk driving. I gotta think it over. This is heavy."

"You told me they'd never even know the sling was cut."

"I know, but . . ."

"Ten . . . thousand . . . dollars," Blaze said. "Tax free.

Cash. How long does it take you to earn that at fifteen bucks an hour?"

"How do you know what I make?"

"He told me what crane operators get paid."

Simon thought for a moment. Then he put on his game face and said, "I suppose you want *half* of it?"

"Nope," she said. "It's all yours."

"Whadda *you* get?"

"A chance to be in on something more exciting than anything I've ever done. Think of the story I'll write!"

"Not about *me* being in on it?"

"Of course not. We're in this together, you and me. But I'll have an angle for a story that won't have to end up in *San Diego Magazine*. My story'll be in a *national* magazine. How the Kiwis' bad luck hounds them. How they really lost the Cup due to a simple mechanical failure. The tragedy of New Zealand."

"My job? How about my job?"

"It'll look like an accident. Your boss isn't going to blame you. Does he *like* the Kiwis?"

"None of us like 'em."

"There you are, then."

"I gotta think it over," Simon Cooke said. "Maybe I oughtta stop drinking and go home and think."

"Good idea," Blaze said. "I'll give you my home phone number."

"You oughtta do some thinking, too," he said. "A kid like you? You don't *know* people like Koch and Conner. They'll use a kid like you and then they'll dump you."

"I promise," Blaze said, "to think it over, too. But you should think of something *else*."

"What's that?"

"Think of the excitement of it! Only three people in the world will know how the Kiwis lost their chance to win the America's

Cup. You, me, and Mister Moneybags. Think of how that'll bring us together. Secret sharers. You and me."

"You and me," Simon said. Her green eyes made him woozy.

"We'll be bonded," Blaze said. Then she paused. "Would you *like* that, Simon? If we were bonded?"

"Leapin' les-bos!" Simon Cooke blurted. "Pardon my French."

CHAPTER 7

AFTER A "DINNER" OF SHARK TACOS WHILE LISTENING TO A JUKEBOX
full of Jimmy Buffett at the little saloon in Quivira Basin, Fortney
and Leeds headed for Shelter Island in Leeds's Chevy Blazer. They
had no trouble figuring out which restaurant had most of the Satur-
day-night action—the parking lots told the story. You just looked
for the one where you couldn't park a moped and wait around for a
car to leave.

The moment they got inside, Fortney went to the view window, looked out at the dark water in San Diego harbor, and shiv-
ered. Then he headed for the bar, squirmed through the mob of
drinkers, and ordered a double scotch.

"Looks like every sailing-stupid in town's here tonight," Leeds
said, catching the eye of a saronged waitress with a plastic orchid in
her hair. He winked and she smiled.

Both cops wore windbreakers over T-shirts, and both felt like
taking their jackets off. The bar was steamy enough to grow
orchids from all of the overheated sailboat-sillies milling around a
few molecules apart. And the floor was like flypaper from the
spillage of sticky exotic drinks the Polynesian motif seemed to demand.

After the cops drank with the other customers for half an hour or so, Fortney said to Leeds, "This guy on the other side of me tells this cuppie next to him he's a good Christian. I said, Where'd you park *The Bounty,* Fletcher? He didn't get it."

"Neither do I," Leeds said. Then he pointed at a booth. "Ain't that the bulletproof redhead that dissed me last week?"

Fortney fanned away a cloud of cigarette smoke and squinted. You couldn't mistake her, not with that flaming hair tumbling down the way it did, and wearing a tube top as green as her eyes.

"Goddamn!" he muttered. "She's with that wharf rat again."

Leeds said, "This is unnatural. Who *is* that guy? And what's he *got* on her? Maybe she's got vision problems?"

"Maybe olfactory problems."

"What's that mean? I hate guys that read."

"He's a little bit cleaned up. Probably smells no worse than a cholera epidemic."

"I ain't a detective," Leeds said. "Just a patrolman that drives a boat. You need a detective to figure out this one, partner."

Fortney's eyes had adjusted by then. He studied Blaze and said, "If she comes to the bar I'm buying her a drink."

"You *like* being dissed by a razor-tongue scorpion?"

"I'll risk it," Fortney said. "But she'll probably get mobbed by sailors before I get a chance. That babe's better protected than the California condor."

"Forget her," Leeds said. "Whaddaya think of the cocktail waitress in the sarong? She's into archaeology. Digs my bones, unless I'm mistaken."

"That's what you youngsters got that boomers like me lost," Fortney said.

"What's that?"

"High apple-pie-in-the-sky hope."

"Lost it in Nam, huh?"

Fortney said, "All I lost in Nam was two hundred bucks in a crap game one time. I lost my hope for humanity when my first ex-wife got custody of the entire Roy Orbison collection and I got Sonny and Cher."

"Well, you just watch your pard operate," Leeds said, signaling the bartender for another round. "I'll be wearing that orchid behind *my* ear."

Before Fortney got the second drink down, he saw Blaze Duvall's cadaverous companion get up from the booth and head for the door. Blaze waited a moment, then sashayed toward the bar, through a crowd that still consisted of more wannabes than professional sailors.

But she was quickly approached by three America's Cup sailors whom Fortney recognized as the ones who'd hovered around her the first time. Then a very large guy ballooned through the crowd, the same giant Kiwi he'd seen the first night, the behemoth with the albino buzz-cut.

Leeds saw him, too. "Your competition ain't necessarily pretty," he said, "but he's pretty damn *big*. Give up?"

"That's the same guy from last week."

"Or it's a John Deere tractor wrapped in a black T-shirt."

"Notice something?" Fortney said. "She either hangs around the skanky little wharf rat or that big Kiwi. Even when she's got every guy in the joint swarming like honeybees. Lousy taste in men."

"Then maybe you *do* have a chance," Leeds said.

"Spread your pecs and save me a place at the bar," Fortney said.

"Where you going?"

"Down to the other end."

"She won't remember you."

"I'm counting on it. I'm gonna eavesdrop."

"You piss off that big Kiwi, make sure you got cab fare. I'm *outta* here!"

Fortney leisurely worked his way through the drinkers. When he got ten feet from Miles and Blaze, he turned his back to them, as though he was chatting up one of the many cuppies standing in clusters flirting with sailors. Then he moved right into a clutch of sailboat-sillies who were rehashing the day's surprise setback for Team New Zealand.

He overheard Miles say to Blaze, "We'll not lose another race. You can wager on us and fatten your purse."

"But you *did* lose today," Blaze said. "I was watching on ESPN and I almost cried."

"By fifteen bloody seconds!" he said. "Our first loss, but it was good for us. Perhaps we were starting to believe our press notices. That we're invincible."

"Okay, when can I place my bet? What day will you *win* the Louis Vuitton Cup?"

"Next Thursday, of course," the Kiwi responded. "That'll be our fifth win and we'll close them out. Bet on it."

"Okay, I will," Blaze said, and she made an audible note for herself, saying, "On April twentieth, *Black Magic* will dominate skipper John Bertrand of oneAustralia. Blaze wins a bet of . . . oh, I might risk seventy-five cents!"

"Wager a few dollars for me," Miles said. "I'll use it to buy you a drink when we celebrate on Thursday night."

Blaze said, "How about Wednesday night? What'll you be doing next Wednesday? The night *before* you trounce the Aussies?"

"I know what I should do. Go home early and get a good night's sleep so I'll be fit for Thursday's festivities."

"Don't do that!" Blaze said, too quickly.

"What?"

"Don't stay home on Wednesday evening."

The big Kiwi looked puzzled. "Why?"

"Because I'm busy all next week *except* Wednesday. It's the only night I'll be free."

"And?"

"And I wanted to be with all the lads and hoist a Steinlager or two since I won't be able to join you on Thursday."

"Well, I'll try to make myself available," Miles said. "But if I can't . . ."

Blaze put her hand on his arm then, and Fortney saw her stroking his massive bicep. She said, "Miles, *please*. I'll meet you across the street where we met the first time. Let's have a drink together, maybe a bite to eat. Just you and me. Whadda you say?"

He clearly couldn't believe it. "Just you and me?"

"I'll buy the steaks. You like steak, don't you?"

"Bloody well right I do!" He looked at her hand on his arm.

"I'll buy you the whole *cow*," she said. "Be there at eight o'clock, Wednesday night."

"Count on it, love," he said. "Count on it."

"See you then," she said, grabbing her purse.

"Steady on," he said. "Where're you going? It's early."

"It's my mother," Blaze said. "She fell and broke her hip last week. I told her I'd only be out for a couple of hours. My aunt's coming to stay at the end of next week, then I'll have more free time."

"But you're okay for Wednesday night?"

"Wednesday night," Blaze said. "I'll give you my pager number in case anything should make you late."

"I'll *be* there!" the Kiwi said, grinning like a sea monster.

Fortney battled his way back across the barroom and was next to Leeds when he saw the fiery hair disappear through the doorway. His partner was being lectured by a pair of earnest yupsters about the life-threatening danger of eating butter.

Leeds said to them, "I don't know if I can stop. I been doing it all my life. Maybe someday they'll come up with a patch for it?"

•   •   •

She rang his doorbell at 11:10 P.M., awakening him from a sound sleep in his Chippendale chair, snug in the smoking jacket. Ambrose felt spittle on his chin and hastily wiped it off. He inspected his shirtfront, but it was dry and unwrinkled. It made him feel like an old man. Snoozing with saliva running down his chin.

When he opened the door he said, "How'd it go?"

She didn't answer but shot him a teasing smile. She walked past him straight to the sofa, where she dropped her blue duffel in case he wanted a massage.

"How'd it go?" he repeated hopefully.

"May I have a glass of wine first?"

"Of course," he said, dashing to the kitchen to get a bottle of chardonnay. His hands shook when he manipulated the corkscrew. He came back into the living room with the wine in a bucket and two stemmed glasses.

He thought she looked lovely in that green tube top. Her body was so firm, her smile so dazzling. It made him feel sad. And old.

After pouring, he said, "Don't torment me, Blaze."

She chuckled and said, "It's been my experience that most men—*all* men—like a bit of torment from a woman. When they're in the mood."

"Please, Blaze!"

"He'll do it," she said.

"Thank God!" Ambrose sat down heavily in the Chippendale. "Are you *sure*?"

"As sure as I can be without having him *say* yes and sign a contract. He's taken the bait, the hook, all of it. And he's not gonna spit it out."

"Tell me about it. I want to hear it *all*!"

"It's so late, darling," Blaze said, stifling a yawn. "Can't I tell you in the bedroom? I brought everything with me. I thought you might need some relaxation. Some *relief.* I know how much tension you've been under. It must've been awful, just waiting. No control over any of it. Just awful for a man who needs order and control."

Then Ambrose Lutterworth's eyes swam with tears of relief. He turned away. This young woman—a *girl* really—understood him. She was sensitive to his feelings in a way that no one had ever been. If he'd met someone like Blaze when he was still young, he wouldn't have remained a bachelor. And bachelorhood was growing so heavy now in his sixty-fourth year. He pawed at his eyes clumsily.

Blaze stood up slowly, walked to the Chippendale, and knelt in front of him. "There, there," she said. "There, there, Ambrose."

She held his face in her hands and kissed him under both eyes, then pulled back and tasted the salty drops with the tip of her tongue. "It's going to be all right," she said. "You have my word."

He was too overcome to speak. She took his wineglass and put it on the coffee table. Then she held him by the hand, urging him to follow. She picked up her duffel, and, still holding his hand, led him like a child into his bedroom.

She insisted on undressing him and he didn't object. She carefully removed his smoking jacket, his rep necktie, and his shirt. She opened his closet and hung the necktie on the tie rack and the smoking jacket on a hanger. She folded the cotton shirt and placed it on a nearby chair. And then she nudged him and he sat down on the bed.

She dropped to her knees and removed his monogrammed slippers, placing them precisely side by side at the foot of his bed, just as he would have done. Then she unbuttoned his cotton trousers and carefully unzipped the fly and pulled them off his legs, hanging them upside down in the closet, on a clip hanger, by the cuffs. He couldn't have done it better.

Only after she'd slipped off his paisley cotton undershorts and deposited them on the chair with his shirt, did she undress herself.

Ambrose Lutterworth said nothing. He just lay naked on the silk bedspread, in the lamplight, and watched Blaze peel off the tight jeans and tube top. As usual, she didn't remove her black bikini panties unless requested.

Then Blaze reached into her duffel and began preparing her accoutrements, spreading the two large terry towels on the bed and gently rolling him over onto his stomach. She reached into the bag and said, "Powder or oil?"

"Powder, I think," Ambrose said.

"Powder, of course," Blaze said.

And in a moment he felt baby powder being sprinkled on his back and buttocks. Those hands, those magnificent hands, began slipping over him, sliding gently and silkily over the powdered flesh.

Blaze sat astride him and worked his buttocks and back, leaning down to whisper, "Powder is the *right* choice for tonight. You've been through so much this past week. But tonight you're *safe*. Blaze has fixed everything. The mere aroma of powder will unlock old memories, old sensations deep within you. You can be a baby again. Tonight, you can be *my* baby."

Her voice was hypnotic. He closed his eyes and whimpered when she leaned down to brush his cheeks with her lips. Ambrose could smell the sweet aroma of wine and the baby powder. She'd never been so tender with him. No one ever had. Ambrose Lutterworth thought he could *love* this young woman.

Then Blaze turned off the lamp because Ambrose was a client who had difficulty if a light was on. She said to him, "Should I tell you now what happened tonight or shall I tell you later?"

"Perhaps later," he said. "This is so . . . exquisite!"

But Blaze Duvall said, "Maybe I should give you the bottom line now. You might be too sleepy afterward."

"All right then," he said, "but please don't stop moving your hands."

She smiled. "I won't, my darling." Then she said, "It was just like you said it would be. Simon Cooke's a greedy little man. And he was very interested when I told him about my anonymous friend who was willing to pay ten thousand dollars to destroy the New Zealand boat."

"Is he sure he can get the job?"

"Of course. He claims he's the best crane operator in San Diego. He's certainly the most experienced in his boatyard. And, of course, there's the connection with his brother-in-law. They'll go straight to their landlord and he'll go to Simon. You were right."

He shuddered when she squeezed his shoulders and worked

them hard. Then he said, "Did he demand to know who your contact is?"

Blaze laughed and said, "He's convinced it's Bill Koch or Dennis Conner."

That made Ambrose laugh, too. "That's the first chuckle I've had in days."

"You're feeling better already, aren't you?" Blaze moved her fingers down his buttocks between his legs, then added, "I can *feel* you are."

"And was he scared?" Ambrose asked. "I mean, when it came to the business of drugging the New Zealand crane operator? Didn't it frighten him?"

"Not a bit," Blaze said. "You're a good judge of men, Ambrose. He's only interested in money."

Ambrose Lutterworth smiled dreamily when he felt her doing things down there. He said, "I'm a good judge of women, too. I chose you and you've saved me. I'm not going to forget what you've done for me, Blaze."

"I care for you, Ambrose," Blaze said. "And when the Kiwi boat is destroyed by Simon, I'd love to go to dinner with you. Someplace romantic."

"After the Cup has been successfully defended," Ambrose added. "We'll still have to beat their thirty-eight boat, won't we?"

"Yes, after that. After Dennis Conner or Bill Koch beats the Kiwis, we'll celebrate."

"I promise you an evening you won't forget. Do you like champagne? We'll have champagne the likes of which you've never tasted."

"It's a date," Blaze said. "Would you like to turn over now, darling?"

When Ambrose Lutterworth rolled over onto his back, Blaze said, "My, my! We *are* happy now, aren't we?"

And then Ambrose pleased her by saying, "Perhaps we should finish quickly, Blaze. We've both had such a stressful evening. I'm so sleepy."

"Good idea," Blaze said, thinking she might even be home in bed by 1:00 A.M. She wondered if Dawn would arrive before daybreak.

When she took the pack of condoms from her bag, Ambrose opened his eyes and said, "I've never asked you, but just this once? Just for me, can we *dispense* with that?"

Blaze said, "I think so."

"You're the only woman I've been intimate with for at least three years," he said. "I know you've got to be careful these days, but really I'm safe, and—"

"Hush!" Blaze said. "It's okay, Ambrose. I know I don't need a condom with you. We're . . . bonded now. We're . . . secret sharers. Would you like being *bonded* to me?"

"Yes, Blaze," he said. "Oh, yes!"

"We don't want *anything* to come between us," she whispered. "Not a layer of latex. Nothing."

"No, Blaze!" he said, his excitement growing.

"Now, Ambrose?" she asked. "Would you like it now?"

"Oh, yes," he said. "Without the condom I'll really feel your lips and your tongue. And will you . . . ?"

"Yes, I will, Ambrose," Blaze said. "Just lie back and relax."

Before she began the blowjob, she reached into the duffel to return the pack of condoms. And when she did, she pushed the pause button on the cassette recorder. She already had far more than she needed.

•   •   •

"I ain't quite sure I could ever be comfortable in a bed like that," Letch Boggs remarked to Westbrook.

The bearded vice cop was wearing a muscle tank top, but for eveningwear he'd changed his stud earring to a loop. "It'd be kinda hard to turn over," Westbrook said, agreeing with Letch's assessment.

The bed was a surplus army cot in the Normal Heights bedroom of a very abnormal hooker. There were metal eye-bolts on each side of the bed at the head and at the foot, and blue steel handcuffs dangled from each of the four bolts.

Two S&M hookers were sitting handcuffed together in the second bedroom, listlessly answering the questions of two other vice cops and Officer Rita Mason, who was still in hooker mufti. Rita had operated a john who'd introduced one of her undercover partners as his cousin from Bakersfield to the pair of S&M hookers. For that bit of cooperation the john, who'd been caught soliciting prostitution from Rita Mason, won a get-out-of-jail card. He got to go home with no record made of his naughty encounter.

Rita Mason was counting the days. Sixteen more and her tour in Vice was over, then she could take a long, hot bath—no, make that *two* baths—put on her uniform, and go back to patrol, where people might hate her and even scare her but didn't turn her stomach as horribly as those she'd met while in Vice.

She sauntered into the back bedroom, where Letch and Westbrook were examining the setup. There were two velvet paintings of naked women on the walls, a rusty cattle prod propped in the corner, and a Mexican bullwhip draped across a low-hanging iron chandelier that had surely been bought in Tijuana. The walls were painted red. The door and door frame were done in black lacquer.

"Look at all this," Letch said, when Rita entered the make-believe torture chamber.

What the Freudian implications might be, Rita couldn't imagine. Anyway, the three-inch heels on her plastic boots were killing her. Feet were all she could think about.

"My ankles hurt!" Rita said. "Why don't men like to score with women in sensible shoes?"

"You could wear anything with me, Rita," Letch said, leering at her. "Or you could—"

"Yeah, yeah," she said. Jesus! She could smell him across the room. Like tear gas! And his aloha shirt had a Day-Glo Rorschach pattern that could only be described as brutal. "Why don't you change the batteries in that goddamn shirt? It's so full of violence it oughtta be restricted to major motion pictures. And rated!"

"Look!" Westbrook said, picking up a Ping-Pong paddle and ball from the nightstand, where they lay next to a hot-water bottle and a catheter.

"They play Ping-Pong?" Rita asked.

"This is a *golf* ball!" Westbrook said.

"What do they do with a golf ball?" Rita asked. Then she noticed that Letch's disgusting leer turned even leerier and said, "Never mind."

"You notice there's only one paddle?" Letch said. "The johns never *return* the serve."

"Go wash your hands, Westbrook!" Rita said. "Kee-rist! Where that golf ball's been? You're as perverted as Letch!"

"If you can't pound it in his coal chute on the first two strokes, do you think it's considered a double fault?" Letch wanted to know.

"I *hate* this job!" Rita said. "Tonight a twelve-year-old on a skateboard propositioned me! I should've slapped him silly!"

Letch really didn't mind what Rita or any of the female cops thought of him, as long as they thought of him. He was really going to miss this buxom girl, that's for sure. Then he remembered something he'd been meaning to ask her.

He closed the door and said, "Remember that skinny hooker, Dawn Coyote? If you happen to see her out there tonight, lemme know. Come Monday morning she better have her bony ass outta town."

Rita said, "Yeah, I meant to tell you—a guy in a white Jag was asking about her tonight. Talked to two girls working my corner. They told him they hadn't seen her for days."

"A brother?" Letch asked. "Big dude with a shaved head and a Fu Manchu?"

"Yeah."

"She's probably left town already," Westbrook said to Letch.

"She better have," the old vice cop said. "Monday morning we serve the warrant."

Just then Westbrook's electronic beeper went off and Letch said to Rita, "Is that your diaphragm squeaking?"

"Catch you later," Rita said, eager to go back to the boulevard for air.

"We could meet for a cup of coffee after work," Letch suggested.

Rita said, "I'd rather swallow fish bones."

Letch said sadly, "Okay. See ya."

Rita said, "Only for two more weeks. After that, the only time I'll see *you* is if they're desperate for a pallbearer."

•   •   •

Dawn Coyote was tired, as tired as she'd ever been in her young life. Hiding out from Oliver Mantleberry had taken a toll and she needed some speedball *bad*. She wanted to go to Blaze's apartment and sleep for twelve hours, but she couldn't leave Midway Drive just yet. The girls were chumming and the johns were in a feeding frenzy. She'd already done four sailors and three older civilians at forty dollars a date, with no end in sight.

When Dawn was crossing Rosecrans at 10:50 P.M., she spotted a very likely john in a blue Lexus ogling as he made a quick turn onto Midway, planning to turn around and come back. Dawn was too busy smiling at the guy to notice the crack in the sidewalk. Her stiletto heel caught and she pitched forward.

She fell on her right hip, rolling over and grabbing her ankle. The pain shot straight to her knee and beyond, a very bad sprain. She'd committed a street whore's venial sin: Watching the potential date instead of where she was walking.

Painfully getting to her feet, she limped toward a phone stand and called her connection, Rudolph, scared he wouldn't answer this late.

He picked up. "Yeeeees?"

"It's Dawn. I gotta see you."

"It's too late. How about tomorrow?"

"No. *Now.* I'll pay an extra twenty."

"Where are you?"

"Midway and Rosecrans. But I ain't staying here. I hurt my ankle. I'll drive to you."

"No way. I'll come to *you,* but not on the street. You still living at the same place?"

"I moved," she said. "How about meeting me somewheres? Anywhere. There's this bar I know."

"No bar," he said. "No street corner. No public place. If you don't have an address, sorry. We can't do business tonight. Maybe tomorrow, Dawn."

"But we did business on the street lots a times!"

"No more," he said. "Not this late, anyways."

"Rudolph, wait!" she cried. "I got an address! Jist for tonight I'm staying with a girlfriend. I'll see you there in one hour. Got a pencil?"

Her connection wrote down the address and the number on the security gate, saying he'd be there in one hour. When he hung up, he dialed the beeper number of Oliver Mantleberry, who'd promised him a hundred bucks for the information.

What the fuck, Rudolph figured. Dawn was leaving town anyway, according to Oliver. She'd never be a customer again. What the fuck.

•   •   •

When Blaze Duvall pulled into her subterranean parking garage, it was nearly midnight and dead quiet. She didn't like coming home this late, especially to the parking garage. It was protected by a security gate, but still . . .

Yet she was sure it was probably safer than the courtyard gate one floor up. The courtyard accessed the entire apartment complex and the "security" consisted of an eight-foot metal fence and a walk-in gate. Not wrought iron, just black aluminum painted to look like iron.

One of her neighbors, who installed security equipment for

commercial buildings, told Blaze that before she moved in a tweaked-out Charger cheerleader had kicked that gate wide open when she came to see a linebacker whose wife had thrown him out. That was the kind of security the gate provided. And just thirty feet from the gate was a tall brick planter. Someone could pull himself up on it and climb over the fence without breaking *anything*. Some security.

But there was nobody coming or going from any of the units at that time of night. Blaze hadn't realized how beat she was until she climbed the stairs to the second floor. She'd even forgotten about Dawn Coyote until she got her key in the lock.

Then she remembered, calling, "Dawn? You home?"

No answer. She walked three steps along the balcony to a banana tree growing in a big pot. She felt for the key where she'd told Dawn it'd be hidden. It was there under the banana leaves.

Blaze entered her apartment, kicked off her shoes, opened the fridge, and poured a large glass of orange juice. After that she went into the bathroom and took a shower.

When she was toweling dry the phone rang. Dawn, no doubt. A flat tire, maybe? A problem of some kind? Well, Dawn wasn't going to get her out of the apartment, not if she was in a full body cast, dying at Mercy Hospital.

"Hello," Blaze said, wrapping a towel around her head.

"It's me," he said. "Simon."

"Simon! Why're you calling so late?"

"Sorry, Blaze," he said. "I know I shouldn't. I'm cold sober."

"That's a relief," she said. "Most people do things like this when they're dead drunk."

"No, it's, like, well, I can't sleep. I been thinking about it."

"Look, Simon," Blaze said. "Don't make a hasty decision tonight. Let's meet tomorrow and talk about it. I *know* we can make it work."

"That's jist it," he said. "I ain't weaseling out. I decided to do it. I need the ten grand, and I couldn't go to sleep till I let you know."

"Wonderful!" Blaze said. "That's wonderful, Simon!"

"I think it'll happen next Thursday," Simon said.

"I know," Blaze said. "I've been reading every article about the races. Thursday the Kiwis're gonna take it."

"So you'll have to do *your* thing Wednesday night."

"Let's not discuss it now," she said. "Are you on a cell phone?"

"No, I'm at home," he said. "There ain't nobody with me. My roommate's gone to Ensenada for the weekend."

"We'll talk tomorrow," Blaze said. "I'll call you before noon. Get yourself a good night's sleep."

"Blaze?"

"Yeah?"

"You wouldn't wanna . . . come over tonight, would ya?"

"Not tonight, Simon. I'm pooped."

"Okay," he said. "Let's talk tomorrow."

"Night, Simon," Blaze said.

"There's one thing, Blaze," Simon said. "Only way I'll go for this is if you get a little something for yourself. I was thinking five percent. I wanna give you five hundred bucks."

"You don't have to do that," Blaze said.

"But I *want* to."

"Okay," she said. "That's really sweet, Simon. Go to bed now. Sleep warm."

When she hung up, she thought she heard something out on the balcony.

"Dawn?" she called out.

Nothing.

Blaze went in the bedroom and put on her blue terry robe. With her hair still wrapped in the towel, she went to the door and peered through the peephole.

Nothing.

Blaze finished toweling her hair but was too tired to blow it dry. She pulled back the bedspread and folded it across the foot of her bed. She liked to sleep with her feet under it. Her feet were forever cold, always had been even when she was a child sharing a bed with two little sisters. When she got enough money to get out of the massage business, she was going to wear warm socks ninety percent of the time, and the hell with how they looked to men.

After getting in bed she heard it again. The scraping of a footstep? But this time it felt like someone had run a cold blade along her backbone. *Fear!*

She thought of calling the police but decided against it. What if it was her neighbor Charlie's cat? What if it was her neighbor, Charlie? An alcoholic who came home soused several times a month. He might be trying to find his keys. He might have fallen down.

She got out of bed and put on her robe and slippers. She went to the closet and reached up next to the ski cap, where she kept her mad money, and found the .32-caliber nickel-plated revolver she'd bought from the horny gas station owner who serviced her car.

She'd never fired it, but he'd told her that he had and that the ammunition was "fresh." She'd told him she thought of lettuce as fresh. And men. But never bullets.

•   •   •

As Letch was finishing up his shift that night, driving back to Central by way of the Gas Lamp District, his partner couldn't stop talking about the Simpson murder trial, which to Letch—as it was to most Americans who didn't need Prozac—was sickening.

"The Dream Team," Westbrook snorted, referring to the Simpson defense. "The Dweeb Team is more like it."

"Forget about it," Letch said. Then, "There goes four more Medal of Honor winners."

He pointed to a quartet of ragpicking bums whom cops now had to call "the homeless." Two of the ragpickers had a couple of tourists pinned against a restaurant window and were ready to reach into their pockets for buy-off money.

One of the "vets" yelled, "Got any spare change for a Vietnam vet, buddy? I can't work because a my wounds."

Letch rolled down the window, shouting to the tourists, "*Spare change* consists of anything with a string of U.S. Treasury serial numbers on it."

The other two ragpickers were pushing debris-laden shopping carts, causing Letch to say to Westbrook, "They're putting the cart before the hearse. Barely." Then he yelled to them, "How far you gotta go to your place of unemployment?"

When one of the ragpickers flipped him the bird, Letch said, "Didn't we share a croissant and café au lait at Club Med last summer?"

Letch thought Westbrook had abandoned his Simpson case obsessing, but the bearded cop said, "Wonder why O.J. used a blade? Why not a gun with a silencer? A guy like him could get any weapon he wanted. Why a blade?"

"Don't you know anything?" Letch said. "A knife is the most phallic of killing tools. When you wanna fuck your babe to *death,* you use a knife. You stick it in *all* the way!"

Letch Boggs would recall those very words when he took a telephone call the next day from a detective who worked the Homicide Unit.

CHAPTER 8

IT WAS SILLY, SHE FINALLY DECIDED, TO LET THE PROBLEMS OF SOMEONE like Dawn Coyote affect her life in any way. The Dawn Coyotes of this world were viruses, and the best way to escape infection was avoidance. Yet from back when they'd trained together in the massage parlor, she'd always pitied the little junkie—back when Dawn was a teenage runaway and Blaze had just bolted from a miserable marriage to a construction worker.

Her mother had had no right to bitch about Matt. Her mother had lived with construction workers, *and* a career marine, *and* a dishwasher before she turned into a really sick drunk. Her mother had had no right bitching about any of her three daughters who had lived for the day they could escape the tiny apartment in Escondido paid for by welfare checks and the kindness of virtual (but not virtuous) strangers.

Blaze was the oldest and the brightest, and had always wanted to learn a skill, maybe even go to college. But waitress jobs had kept a roof over her head for two years and then she had met Matt and got talked into marriage by a pipe fitter who had plenty of pipe but lacked thirty IQ points. After the divorce she'd seen the ad in a throwaway about applicants wanted at Fingers Divine, a massage parlor on El Cajon Boulevard.

Tomorrow she'd be rid of Dawn Coyote forever and there'd never be another Dawn in her life. Blaze wasn't sentimental, had never been burdened with emotional baggage. In a dog-eat-dog world—or a man-eat-woman world—she was not going to be devoured. No man was ever going to control her, and nobody of either gender was ever going to manipulate her again as Dawn had done.

Dawn. A pathetic loser with cornflower-blue eyes like those of Blaze's youngest sister, Rosie, who'd died in a flaming pickup truck driven by a Pine Valley cowboy whose blood alcohol level, the coroner had said, was .31. Or too drunk to be walking, let alone driving. Dawn had always reminded Blaze of Rosie, that dead little sister.

There was no sound on the balcony.

And here she was standing next to the door like a fool with a revolver in her hand and beads of sweat running down her face, stewing over a junkie and a dead sister. She was a fool. There was nobody out there. Nobody.

Dawn and her creepy lifestyle were diminishing Blaze's self-control, that was it. And Blaze, much like Ambrose Lutterworth, had to be in control or suffer grave consequences. She understood that, but unlike Ambrose, whose control was exercised by a choice of clothes or by meticulous housekeeping, hers extended further and deeper. That made her ponder the cassette.

It was her insurance policy. You never knew when insurance might pay off. Someday, when she had real money and a decent life, she was going to purchase all kinds of insurance. But for now that cassette was her policy. An annuity, if she needed it.

Blaze decided to put the gun away and go to bed. For all she knew, Dawn wouldn't even come back tonight. If she was lucky, Dawn would *never* come back.

She got into bed again and punched the button on the clock-radio, wanting to hear soft hits, sleepy music. She closed her eyes.

Then, of course, the phone rang.

Reaching out in the darkness: "Hello."

"It's me, Dawn."

"Goddamn it, Dawn!"

"I lost the code to your garage. Can you buzz me in the walk-in gate?"

Blaze didn't say anything. She pushed number eight on her telephone and heard the buzz. Then she sat up and turned on the bedside lamp.

Control yourself, she thought. Scream? Lecture? Complain? That would be silly. It had never worked on Rosie, had it? Dawn was a street whore and a junkie and she'd be dead within a few years of an OD or AIDS. So just maintain, Blaze Duvall told herself.

•   •   •

It was so dark. She wondered why there weren't more walk lights. You could fall and break your ankle, and hers hurt like hell already. Where was the moon?

With every step Dawn Coyote could feel the thick roll of bills she'd stuffed inside her panties. It was a good feeling. She knew Blaze would *really* be pissed off when Rudolph showed up at the gate later. Dawn worried about what she'd say to Blaze then, but she didn't worry all that much. She couldn't think about anything but slamming that speedball. Dawn closed her eyes, the better to imagine it.

Her eyes were open when she passed a large banana tree by the darkened stairwell that led up to the second floor. But her attention was caught by a tiny pale object on the ground. A white flower had pushed through a pavement crack, struggling for life out of the darkness. It was so touching and sweet that she closed her eyes again, imagining the smell of white roses.

And before she opened them, a powerful hand was on her mouth.

•   •   •

This time Blaze definitely heard a sound on the balcony or on the steps. A thump. She figured that Dawn had been doing speedballs and staggered against the wall. Or maybe she'd fallen down like Blaze's drunken neighbor, Charlie.

Fuck it! She got out of bed and put on the blue terry robe, then headed for the front door.

When she opened it, she heard what sounded like a far-off cry of a gull. They didn't fly into her part of Mission Valley all that much, unless they were scavenging around Jack Murphy Stadium. A gull was crying in the distance.

She saw that the stairwell light was out. That was unusual. Maybe Dawn *had* fallen down. It was very dark and very quiet. Then she heard the gull again.

It wasn't a gull. And it wasn't far away. It was down there. Down in the stairwell. She never sensed danger, not for an instant. All she could think was that Dawn had fallen down the stairs and was hurt. Moaning in agony, maybe from a broken . . .

She rounds the corner of the stairwell, eight feet above a looming silhouette with its arm upraised. Oliver Mantleberry doesn't even see Blaze as he plunges the buck knife into the pale, sunken belly of Dawn Coyote for the last time.

Blaze screams! Oliver Mantleberry rises up, raging. Blaze turns to run but hears him coming. Coming for her.

She reaches the balcony level and rounds the corner. But she can't move.

As in a nightmare, she tries to run but can't. Blaze falls to her knees. She realizes that he's clutching the hem of her robe.

She scrambles and crawls, crawls out of her robe. Then Blaze runs naked to the open door of her apartment. She hears his footsteps. His panting!

She reaches the apartment and slams the door just as he crashes into it.

He howls one word: "Bitch!"

Blaze ran to the telephone and dialed 911. She heard heavy footsteps running away, down the stairwell.

Blaze screamed the address of the apartment building at the 911 operator, along with the word "Murder!"

Then she hung up without giving her name or any further details, while the operator yelled, "Wait! Don't hang up!"

Blaze dashed into the bathroom and locked the door without knowing why she did it. She was surprised to feel sobs deep in her chest. She never heard herself cry but she *felt* the sobs. She looked at her reflection in the mirror and was shocked to see that her face was contorted and tear-streaked.

She opened the door and ran to her closet, taking down the nickel-plated revolver. Then, realizing that her telephone number had been automatically recorded and that soon the police would come knocking at her door, she pulled on jeans and a sweatshirt and waited for them.

•   •   •

They called her "Anne of a Thousand Names." That's the moniker her fellow detectives hung on her because during her police-department career she'd been Anne Zorn, Anne Bartlett, Anne Sullivan, Anne Minsky, and now Anne Zorn again. Which was her maiden name (and *forever* name!) because no way, under any circumstances—even if he looked like Kevin Costner—was she going to marry again.

The bad marriages had occurred because of her mother's religious background, Anne believed. Her mother should have been a nun. She made her children go to church three, four times a week: mass, confession, novenas, you name it. And her mother was still alive—was she ever! Every time Anne had even discussed living with a man not her husband, the old lady had threatened to die from a coronary, yet Anne Zorn did not doubt that her mother would survive her.

So, because of her mom and the way she'd raised her eldest daughter, Anne felt the need to marry every goddamn one of them, even though divorce and remarriage were also forbidden by the church unless you were rich and famous or a Kennedy.

You couldn't tell her mother that. Her mother would just say that being married the second and third times in civil ceremonies was better than "living in sin." Yet, at least in the eyes of the church, after each divorce Anne *was* living in sin with subsequent husbands. But you couldn't tell her mother anything, not then, not now.

So here she was, forty-six years old, with one grown daughter and three half-grown ex-husbands and a freaking moniker: Anne of a Thousand Names.

When the telephone rang, she was having a very sweet *Bridges of Madison County*–ish sort of fantasy, with herself as the country wife and Harrison Ford as the stranger. Clint Eastwood was just a little too old.

"Hello," she mumbled.

"We shagged one," the voice said. "Get those big brown peepers open, grab a pencil, and pay attention."

"Dope, gangs, robbery, or domestic?"

"None of the above. Somebody did an O.J. on a babe. Wear fishing boots. They say there's enough blood to overfeed every vampire in Romania."

"How delightful," Anne said.

•   •   •

When the uniformed cop knocked at her door, Blaze peeked through the viewer and was surprised to see that he looked so young, much younger than herself. She was glad somehow, even though she couldn't pinpoint why his age made a difference.

He was no taller than Blaze, and slender. His tan San Diego PD uniform was too large for him and the nine-millimeter riding high on his hip looked oversize, as did the big flashlight he carried. He was blond like Dawn Coyote.

"You the one who called nine-one-one?"

"I'm sorry I hung up," Blaze said. "I was shocked."

"Understandable," the cop said, looking around the apartment. "Anybody else here when it happened?"

"No, I live alone."

"You Ms. Singleton?" he asked, having gotten the name from the gate directory.

"Yes, Mary Ellen Singleton," Blaze said, giving her true name.

"What'd you see? What'd you hear?" The cop sat down on the chair by the door, his notebook ready.

"I just heard a cry," Blaze said. "Like . . . like a gull."

"A sea gull?"

"Yes," Blaze said. "I thought it was a sea gull."

"You said 'murder' to the nine-one-one operator. Did you see the woman being stabbed?"

"Not really," Blaze said. "I just heard something and went to the stairwell and saw . . . saw all the *blood*. So much blood."

"Did you look at the victim?" the cop asked.

"Not really," Blaze said. "Does she live here?"

"We don't know yet," the young cop said. "We're waiting for the detectives to arrive. I just wanna get a few facts."

"Yes."

"Did you hear anything? Somebody running away? Any voices?"

"No," Blaze said. "Only the gull. What I thought was a gull crying."

•   •   •

Somebody said at the morning briefing that they'd handled 2.3 homicides a week all last year, down from the year before. Anne asked, How do you kill .3 of a human being? She was one of four women of detective rank working the Homicide Unit, along with one female sergeant. A homicide team consisted of four detectives plus a working sergeant, and there were four teams on call, meaning on twenty-four-hour availability. Anne figured that she'd pulled about one on-call case a week since coming to Homicide four years earlier.

It took her twenty-five minutes to get her face presentable, one of the extra burdens for a female detective on a call-out. Her chestnut perm was hopeless given the time she had, so she'd have to go looking at slaughter wearing a boink-me hairdo.

Her favorite "blood suit" was at the cleaner's and all she had that was passable was a one-button gray blazer and a winter-white wool skirt. Not what she wanted to wear at the scene of a bloody homicide, where she might have to root around in bushes or in closets or even in an attic crawlspace. Once, when her flashlight failed, she'd accidentally knelt in a gooey blood puddle while helping an evidence tech look under a bed for blood evidence.

Anne wondered if the Indian pathologist would roll on this one. She was a canoemaker with a sense of humor, and Anne enjoyed her accent. It reminded her of TV shows about the days of the British Raj. *The Jewel in the Crown* was her favorite.

On one call-out Anne had told the pathologist that she wouldn't have had any problem at all with a first-date boinking of the actor who'd played Hari. What a *memsahib* she'd have been, Anne said to the Indian.

She often recalled the first postmortem she'd ever attended. A Mexican kid was Uzi-riddled in a drive-by. They'd used a dozen forceps on him, and it seemed like the pathologist would never stop pulling out the bandage-packing that paramedics had futilely stuffed inside to stem leakage.

She'd always found "posts" interesting, even though she hadn't been into biology in school. Morgue humor helped sometimes: "Okay, Anne, this is where babies come from!" as the croaker sliced a sliver from a dead guy's balls. But gallows humor didn't work when the corpse was a little kid. The jokes pretty much stopped during those postmortems.

Anne Zorn had always believed, and many of her male colleagues concurred, that people were often more apt to talk to a female detective. People were less intimidated by a female and were encouraged by a woman's ability to communicate emotion. But that was not the case when guys murdered hookers or wives. Using a female detective with those guys just didn't work.

While doing final touches with an eyebrow pencil, she recalled how it had been with her last husband, Phil. She'd get a call-out, work half the night on a homicide—or *all* night sometimes—then she'd have to go home, change, clean the house, wash clothes, go to the store, and pick up *his* kids at school. Kids who'd always mistakenly thought that Anne had broken up Daddy's perfect marriage to Mom.

Phil was history now, and so were his darling children, who'd never had a decent meal before their old man's brief marriage to Anne. Well, those kinds of mistakes were over.

She gave herself a quick appraisal. Not too bad, considering. At least her eyes weren't bagged since she hadn't been asleep long enough. One thing for sure, the client wouldn't care.

Anne figured that her sergeant and lieutenant would already be at the scene, and the civilian evidence tech would already be collecting. Detective Sal Maldonado was up for the job of "scene man." Since coming to Homicide he'd food-inflated, and if he started floor-crawling to help the tech, Anne might have to help raise up that buffalo.

The crime-scene man would have to go to the morgue in the morning along with the evidence tech to attend the post. Anne and the other two team members would be responsible for witness checks, victim's background, neighborhood canvass, and so forth.

But a call-out wasn't all bad: They got paid time-and-a-half. The average homicide dick and dickette earned an extra seven to ten grand a year, so there was definitely an upside.

Her company car was hard to start and flooded twice. It was a four-year-old Ford Crown Victoria, and according to the guys on her homicide team, it badly needed an overhaul. "That makes two of us," Anne had informed them.

And she wasn't kidding. At age forty-six she was due, *overdue,* for her first face-lift. Maybe if enough San Diego citizens kept shooting, stabbing, bashing, and strangling one another she could get enough time-and-a-half to afford one. At least an eye job, if not the whole cut-and-snip.

The Ford sputtered and almost stalled when she pulled off Friars Road, up toward the anthill of apartment buildings overlooking Mission Valley. Anne had her map book open on the seat and used her flashlight to check the streets. At least she could still read a map at night. A lot of her detective contemporaries couldn't even read a newspaper in broad daylight without bifocals, and the men were more vain about it than the women. She was always having to check the fine print for somebody.

Maybe her eyes were still young, but not the tissue around them. Anne glanced into the rearview mirror at sleepy brown eyes badly lit by the dashboard light. The lids were definitely starting to sag, and there was too much going on *underneath* the eyes. She wondered what an eye-lift would cost. But if they're going to do an eye-lift how much extra would it be for the goddamn chin? She could reach under there with her fingers and feel excess.

It was all so depressing. Boomers weren't supposed to get old. It sucked. There was nothing good about aging except what the years had taught her about men. What she'd learned is, you don't need them for much because they're not *good* for much. And her sainted mother could get rope burns from rosary beads, but Anne was never, *never* going to marry another guy no matter how good a squeeze he was. And if her mom told her she liked a guy Anne was dating, it was adios, Bunky. That meant he was a sure loser.

She figured that she'd never have trouble getting laid even if she couldn't afford the complete face-lift and ended up looking like Buster the bloodhound. She was proportioned like an athlete, and she literally worked her ass off keeping it that way. Four days a week at the aerobics studio, and not just so she could have a kiss and a cuddle when she wanted it. No, it was because of what she'd accomplished with that body as a young police officer.

She loved to recall the proudest achievement of her life. Anne Bartlett (her name in 1978) wanted to be the first San Diego PD female to make it on SWAT. She'd made her bones back in the days when there were still a lot of dinosaurs left on the job, guys who wanted women to fail. Back before sexual harassment and the fear those words now instilled. Back when a woman might be teamed on patrol with a male training officer who'd stop their patrol car in an alley and piss on a bush, just to see how she'd handle it.

And if the female partner later said she also had to pee, the training officer might drive straight back to the bush and say, "Your turn."

In those days she almost got urinary-tract infections just from holding it in.

When she was a rookie she could take it with teeth clenched and a tight smile. She remembered one sergeant in particular, who liked to read crimes at lineup and make comments to humiliate the women. He'd read them one about a forced oral copulation where the suspect beat the crap out of his victim because she wouldn't swallow. Then he'd turned to Anne and said, "Do *you* swallow, Officer?"

She'd been young and green and *shocked*. Her heart had started pounding. A dozen uniformed men had turned to look at her—and waited.

Finally she'd replied, "How do you think I got my creamy complexion?"

Some of the men had accepted her on the spot. But it had been a heavy price to pay. Many times since then she'd fantasized that she *had* said, "Swallow *this*." And thrown her coffee in his face.

Clever responses like that had later cost plenty in the regrets department. During those years, whenever she'd get teamed with a real harasser, she'd had to figure out ways to discourage the asshole without getting him fired, and it hadn't been easy.

When Anne had announced to her then husband—a patrol officer in Southern Division—that she was going to try for SWAT, he'd smiled condescendingly and said, "Sure you are."

Then he'd realized that she was dead serious, didn't smile at all, and said, "The fuck you are!"

But she *had* applied. During grueling tests she'd competed with men who'd puked their guts out on the dreaded "four-forty run," a quarter of a mile flat-out.

"And what's your time?" the SWAT trainer had always asked her after the run. Then, "Oh, how nice. Now gimme some pull-ups. All the way up. Dead man's pull-ups!"

Having a baby had altered her body for a year, but SWAT

training had brought it all back, hard as a lawyer's heart—to the point that her upper body even got a bit too well developed.

She'd beaten out a lot of SWAT applicants, guys who'd refused to train and practice the four-forty and the pull-ups. She'd practiced. Her hands had looked like chopped sirloin from all the training, until at last she could pump out twenty. All the way down. All the way up. Dead man's pull-ups.

The SWAT trainer, who she thought hadn't liked her, had paid her his ultimate compliment when she'd pulled number twenty. He'd pointed to a dozen men lying exhausted on the ground and said, "You're a better man than *they* are, Gunga Din."

By the time Anne arrived at the call-out scene, yellow tape had been strung across the walk-in gate. There were two patrol units and a patrol sergeant, along with an evidence tech, her team sergeant, and one of her team members. A young patrolman approached her car, saw the police badge hanging from the shoulder strap on her purse, and shone his flashlight beam on a vacant parking space behind a media van.

The media often got to major crime scenes before the detectives by monitoring the police frequency with scanners. Anne hated the sight of that periscope pole and satellite dish, but she preferred cub reporters with videocams to the prima donnas who'd steal it all away at air time. She called all cub reporters of either sex "Jimmy Olson" after the Superman character.

Sal Maldonado was standing inside the tape at the bottom of the stairwell and he pointed downward as she approached. A stream of clotting blood ran from the bottom of the steps to the seam in the pool decking and out into a planter full of hydrangeas near the swimming-pool gate.

Sal nodded his head in the direction of a patrol sergeant, who was knocking on doors at the far side of the swimming pool.

He said to Anne, "Yupster sergeant. Wants to help but thinks bite marks are things on a computer. I told him to knock on doors and find us a witness. Didn't have the heart to send him home."

"Where's the woman who called in?" Anne asked.

"Upstairs, right," he said. "The boss wants you to talk to her. Take the other staircase."

He shone his light onto the stairwell and lit up the body of Dawn Coyote. She lay halfway up the steps on her back, her little skirt hiked above her red lace panties. A coil of intestine, pink as bubble gum, lay on her thin milky thigh.

Sal moved the beam to her blue eyes, which were wide open. "Let's get a picture of her eyeballs, Eddie," he called to the evidence tech working gingerly on the stairwell. "The image of the killer's in them."

"Sure," said Eddie. "Why didn't I think of that?"

"The motive wasn't robbery," Sal Maldonado told Anne, playing his beam over the crotch of Dawn's panties. "When I first saw that bulge I thought she was a transvestite. Until I saw the face of Alexander Hamilton peeking out at me from inside her panty leg."

"The girl was a hooker, all right," Anne Zorn said.

The most pathetic thing about the murder scene was the victim's toenails. She'd lost one shoe and the red enamel on her toenails was chipped and cracked. Anne knew that she'd remember the girl's toenails long after she forgot the rest of it.

"So fill me in on what we know," she said.

•   •   •

Blaze had been alone for nearly an hour since the first cop had arrived on the scene and taken the preliminary report. A detective sergeant had appeared next and introduced himself, but he said he'd be sending another detective to talk to her. Since then she'd had three cups of coffee even though a cup and a half with her morning cereal was her daily limit. Well, she wouldn't be sleeping, anyway, not even after they took Dawn away. Not even after the cops were all gone.

She put a cardigan on over the sweatshirt, but she was still cold. It was after 3:00 A.M. when she heard a soft knock at the door.

Blaze opened it and was surprised to see a tall woman in a tailored jacket and skirt and low-heeled pumps. She was carrying a clipboard, and a badge was attached to the shoulder strap of her purse. She was rather attractive in a no-nonsense way, and Blaze could see at once that she was very fit for someone who was fortysomething.

The woman said, "Ms. Singleton? I'm Detective Anne Zorn. I have a few questions."

"Come in," Blaze said. "Sit there on the sofa. Can I get you some coffee?"

"If it's already made," Anne said. "Black, please."

"It is," Blaze said, going into the kitchenette while Anne did what all cops do. She looked around the room.

It was tidy, cheaply decorated but with some taste. There was a California impressionist lithograph hanging over the sofa. The furniture was a mixed bag of contemporary with one antique: a little hall tree so scaled down that it looked feminine. A nice, tidy little apartment.

When Blaze returned with the coffee, she said, "I can't tell you much."

"I know," Anne said, "I've already chatted with the patrol officer who responded to your call."

"Have they determined who the girl is yet?"

"She had no purse," Anne said. "Do you have any idea?"

"None at all," Blaze said.

"You saw her then? The body?"

"Well, no, but the second police officer said she was a young blond woman. We don't have any young blond women living on this floor."

"Do you have any young blond friends?"

"No."

"Acquaintances?"

"No."

"There're six units on this floor, on this side of the building. Ever seen a young blond woman visiting any of them?"

"No." Blaze said. "How's the coffee?"

"Fine," Anne said. "It'll keep me awake. If you snooze you lose in my business."

"I can imagine," Blaze said.

"The officer told me you thought you heard a bird cry?"

"A gull," Blaze said.

"And that was the only sound? No loud scream? No voices at all?"

"That was all," Blaze said. "How about the neighbors? Did anybody else hear anything?"

"Two aren't home. The others were dead asleep. *Sound* asleep, I guess I should say."

"Does that mean he killed her instantly? Or did he gag her mouth or something?"

"He?"

"It must've been a man. She *was* stabbed, wasn't she?"

"Oh, yes," Anne said. "She certainly was. Can I just get a little information, Ms. Singleton? You didn't give the other officer a business address or a business phone."

"No," Blaze said. "I'm between jobs right now."

"What kind of work do you do?" Anne asked, sipping the coffee.

"Want some more?" Blaze asked.

"No, thanks. What do you do when you're working?"

"I've done lots of things. I've been a cocktail waitress. I've done general office work."

"Where was your last job?"

"Oh, I wouldn't want my former boss to be bothered by all this."

"Bothered by all what?"

Blaze hesitated and said, "Well, he's an older man and he might be alarmed if the police called him."

"Why would we call him?"

"You asked where I last worked. So I thought . . . I thought . . ."

"Yeah?"

"Well, I thought you might have to . . . *verify* what I tell you about myself."

"No, I was just making conversation until I could think of another relevant question." Anne Zorn stared into Blaze Duvall's anxious green eyes.

"My last job was in L.A.," Blaze said quickly. "A little plastics business called . . . Brunswick Enterprises. I only worked there for eight months. I don't like L.A."

"Don't blame you," Anne said, scribbling in her notebook. "Part of our San Diego heritage. L.A. haters, one and all."

"It's possible," Blaze said, "that the murdered girl took the wrong stairs. The other staircase is just on the other side of the pool. People're always taking the wrong stairs to get to the second floor."

"We had considered that," Anne said. "It may be what happened. I wonder if it might help us for you to actually look at the girl to be sure you don't know her?"

"No!" Blaze said. "No. I couldn't do that. I don't know any young blond woman. I don't want to look at someone who's been stabbed. *No.* I'm sorry."

"Okay," Anne said. "I guess that's all for now, but I may have to phone you. Is this number good day or night?"

"Yes, it is," Blaze said. "I'll be looking for a job during the day, but I call my machine for messages."

"Right," Anne said, standing up.

Blaze said, "I'd like to be informed if you catch the person. If that's permitted, I'd like to be informed."

"You will be," Anne said. "You may be called to testify when we catch the person."

"But I didn't see anything," Blaze said.

"We're troubled by one detail," Anne said when Blaze opened the door.

"What's that?"

"Near the bottom of the steps we found a blue terry-cloth bathrobe."

"Do you think the girl might've been carrying it? The murdered girl?"

"Unlikely," Anne said. "It was found thirty feet from her body."

"The pool," Blaze said. "The pool's very close by, as you can see."

"Yes?"

"One of the tenants probably dropped it coming from the pool. Somebody's always dropping something."

"Even bathrobes?"

"They drop everything," Blaze said. "Trust me."

"But this bathrobe had bloodstains on the hem," Anne Zorn said.

The detective was staring at her again, with unblinking brown eyes, the irises flecked with yellow. Unnerving, like cat's eyes. Blaze was afraid of this woman's unblinking eyes. "Blood?" Blaze said. "I don't understand."

"It's a pretty fresh stain," Anne said. "I'll bet it's the victim's blood."

"I don't understand," Blaze said.

"Neither do we," Anne Zorn said to Blaze Duvall. "Yet."

CHAPTER 9

ON EASTER SUNDAY THEY WERE OUT THERE ON THE WATER: EVERY SAIL-ing-stupid and Jet Ski doofus. Every ski-boat beavis and fishing dweeb. Anyone who wasn't indulging in safer pursuits on Mission Bay's surprisingly extensive twenty-seven miles of coastline. Of course there were plenty of dirtbags, too, with bulgemobiles full of crystal meth, ready for a relaxing Sunday doing the same things on a boat they did on dry land—tweaking or fighting.

The cops figured on seventy or eighty accidents a year in Mission Bay as boaters ricocheted off one another. One or two of those would be fatal.

Leeds was into his campaign mode again, but this time he wasn't dumping on Washington Democrats. He was bitching about the San Diego mayor and the police department's ongoing salary disputes with the city council.

"How'd you like to be the chump who has to chauffeur Her Honor around?" Leeds wanted to know.

Fortney, who was driving the patrol boat that day, said nothing.

" 'Driving Miss Lazy,' I call it," Leeds said.

Fortney didn't reply.

Then Leeds berated her for crash-dieting at election time, calling her "the expandable mayor."

Fortney said, "Shut up a minute, we just got a call." He picked up the mike and said, "One eighty-three king, ten-four."

"I didn't hear it," Leeds said.

"How could you?" Fortney said, heading the patrol boat toward the jetty.

There was a lifeguard boat already there as well as several looky-loos. And within a very short time body snatchers from the coroner's office showed up.

Another floater. The water was warm enough for the bacteria to have cooked fast, and after several days methane gas had brought it bobbing to the surface, bobbing lazily against the rocks. Water cops claimed that floaters somehow smelled even worse than stinkers on dry land.

Fortney inched the boat as close as he could. Leeds looked down and said, "Crabs and lobsters had their Easter brunch early."

Fortney was relieved that the body snatchers already had the assistance of lifeguards, who were lowering a basket down the rocks to the water. They wouldn't be needing the cops to help scoop it in.

Fortney recognized one of the body snatchers, a thick, red-faced guy with a heavy unshaven jaw who looked like a coronary candidate.

This one specialized in brain teasers, and he yelled to Fortney, "We can tell he's a male from his clothes. But can you guess what *race* he is?"

Fortney and Leeds studied the faceless, gristle-stripped mass of bleached-white rotting tissue, and Leeds said, "No way. No way anybody can tell."

The body snatcher said, "Throw a can of Colt 45 in the water. If he grabs for it, he's a brother!"

The body snatcher giggled and snuffled and hacked up a loogie, while Fortney fired up the boat and drove away, wanting to be well clear if the floater should explode.

"That's the same snatcher," Leeds said. "The guy who one time last summer got this floater with his head all stove in. And the snatcher had the guy's brains in a plastic bag with a twist tie. And he shows it to me and shakes it around and says, 'Think it'll make him *dizzy*?' "

"Guys like him," Fortney said, "don't collect stamps, coins, or figurines. They collect suicide notes so they can relive fond memories when they look back in their scrapbooks."

As the cops motored past the bustling oneAustralia compound, they saw a lot of pleasure boats bobbing at a respectful distance.

"Worshipers at the altar of the America's Cup," Leeds noted.

"Boating bozos," Fortney said.

Then, as they motored past the Dana boat ramp, the two cops were so astounded that they sucked half the air from Mission Bay. There was a man walking on water!

"Holy Christ!" Leeds cried out, scaring a gull into flight, which added a Holy Ghost symbol to the incredible vision.

Fortney, who figured it out more quickly, said, "It *is* Easter Sunday, you know. He's allowed."

Actually, the guy *appeared* to be walking on water. In reality, he was walking on the roof of a forty-foot executive motor home that was completely submerged.

It wasn't the Second Coming. They heard the guy screaming at a woman on shore, "You fucking bitch! I told you to put it in gear!"

"Lots of divorces at boat ramps," Fortney observed. "Speaking of which, I wonder when we'll get to see my future former wife again."

"Who's that?" Leeds asked, shaky from the near-religious experience.

"The redheaded cuppie," Fortney said. "The one they call Blaze. I'm marrying her, but I just know she'll eventually divorce me. They all do."

•   •   •

Letch Boggs figured it was a solicitor calling him at 8:00 A.M. on Easter Sunday. In San Diego solicitors were as relentless and unstoppable as illegal border crossings, and even people with unlisted numbers got hassled.

He was delighted when the telephone voice said, "Boggs? It's Anne Zorn. You knew me as Anne Sullivan. Or maybe it was Anne Bartlett. Remember?"

"Annie!" Letch said. "Do I remember? I'm the guy that always called you Legs!"

"Yeah," Anne said. "I haven't forgotten *you* either."

"You still got 'em?" Letch wanted to know, wide awake now.

"What?"

"Gorgeous, buff, volleyball player's legs?"

"Haven't changed, have you?"

"So what's up? You need somebody to color Easter eggs? I'm your man. You divorced again?"

"Yeah, but that's not why I called."

"You wanna come back and work Vice with old Letch? Okay, I'll put in a word for—"

"Letch, gimme a break," Anne said. "I've been working all night. I pulled a call-out homicide and I'm too tired for patty-cake. I got a few questions."

"Yeah?"

"You know a hooker named Jane Kelly?"

She could almost hear the famous Letch Boggs memory computer clickety-clacking. Then he said, "You mean Dawn? Dawn Coyote? What happened?"

"She got stabbed to death, is what happened," Anne said. "Disemboweled."

Letch was thunderstruck. "Where? When? Who did it?"

"That's what we gotta find out," Anne said. "We identified her by faxing her prints to CII. She had no ID, no purse. Nothing but a wad of trick money in her underwear. Along with *your* business card."

"I can't believe it!" Letch said. "He *did* her."

"Who?"

"Her old man. Oliver Mantleberry."

"A pimp?"

"I was gonna serve a warrant on him tomorrow. She made a pimping report for me. He *did* her!"

"Aw-right!" Anne said. "Now we're cooking!"

"I'm coming down," Letch said. "See you in your office in an hour."

"I'll have Mantleberry's rap sheet by then. Know where he lives?"

"Oh, yeah. And I wanna *be* there." Then he added, "She wasn't a bad little babe, Dawn. I wanna take down Oliver Mantleberry. *Me.*"

"I'll be waiting here with coffee and Pepto-Bismol."

Before he hung up, Letch said, "Where'd it happen? Dawn's apartment?"

"No, on the steps of an apartment building in Fashion Hills. We don't know what she was doing up there."

Letch said, "What's the address?"

When she told him, Letch said, "Blaze Duvall."

"Who's that?"

"A friend of hers. That's who lives there."

"You got it wrong for once," Anne said. "There was nobody by that name in the building."

"Any witnesses?"

"Nope."

"Who called it in?"

"A tenant named Mary Ellen Singleton."

"What was her apartment number, this Mary Ellen Singleton?"

"Apartment Two-A."

"Hah!" Letch said.

He blew so much wind with the "Hah!" that Anne could almost smell the garlic right through the telephone.

•   •   •

Her apartment was no longer the neat and tidy scene that Detective Anne Zorn had admired. Blaze was working faster than she'd ever worked in her life.

It hadn't been easy rounding up cardboard boxes on Easter Sunday morning. Her clothes, enough of them, were already in her Mustang—on the floor, in the trunk, stacked on the backseat all the way to the convertible top.

She left her answering machine turned on, and it wasn't until she was nearly out the door that she decided where to go. The important thing was, she was getting out of there. Away from Oliver Mantleberry. That's who it had to have been.

She'd never forget how the light from the lower patio glinted off his huge round skull. She'd never forget the panic of running in place, a killer grabbing at the hem of her robe. She knew she'd dream about that. Maybe it would become the recurring nightmare of her life. That unbelievable powerlessness. Running from death, but getting nowhere. Running from *murder*.

She didn't doubt that the pimp would come for her. If he knew where Dawn was, he had a good idea who Blaze was, Dawn's old buddy from the massage parlor. Dawn would have shot off her mouth to her pimp, of course she would. When Dawn was slamming speedballs she'd run her mouth about anything.

But Dawn was dead now. As dead as Rosie. As dead as Blaze's mother. As dead as Blaze would be if she let herself fall into the hands of Oliver Mantleberry. He'd butchered Dawn for naming him as a pimp. What would he do to a woman who'd witnessed him commit *murder*?

She opened a suitcase on the bed and began packing undergarments and cosmetics. When she was nearly ready, she took Anne Zorn's business card from her purse and dialed the number, intending to leave a brief message on her voice mail or with an operator. It never occurred to Blaze that Anne would not be home in bed yet. Detectives had to sleep sometime.

She was stunned when Anne answered.

There was silence for a moment and then Blaze said, "It's Mary Ellen Singleton."

Anne, who was still waiting for Letch Boggs to arrive, said, "Yes?"

"I . . . I, uh, thought I should leave a message for you. For when you came to work tomorrow."

"I'm still working," Anne said. "You have some information for me?"

"No, but you said you might be wanting to talk to me further, and I wanted to tell you I'll be gone awhile."

"Gone? Where?"

"To visit my sister up in L.A."

"Where in L.A.?"

"Does it matter?"

"In case I need to talk to you, can I have the address and phone number?"

"She's got a new phone number. Unlisted. I lost it. I'll call you with it when I get there."

"What's her name?"

"Uh, Rosie. Rosie Singleton."

"Her address?"

The first Los Angeles street that came to mind: "Sunset Boulevard. One-seven-seven-nine Sunset."

"East or west?"

"West."

Anne Zorn didn't know diddly about Los Angeles geography, but knew when she was being shined. She said, "There's no such address."

"Well . . . I could be mistaken about the number. But I'll phone you when I get it."

"When're you leaving?"

"As soon as I hang up."

Goddamn! Anne was frantic. There was nothing else to do but *fire*. She said, "We'll protect you. Don't leave."

"What's that mean?"

"I know you were a friend of Dawn Coyote. Or did you know her as Jane Kelly?"

Blaze almost hung up.

"Are you there?" Anne asked. "We'll protect you. You saw him. You saw him kill her, didn't you?"

"I'm *outta* here!" Blaze screamed it into the phone.

"He can't get to you."

"Bullshit!" Blaze said. "Tell it to Dawn!"

"Don't go, Blaze," Anne said. "You owe this to Dawn. And to yourself."

"I'll call you later," Blaze said. "Good-bye, Detective Zorn."

The instant Blaze hung up, Anne called Communications, but by the time a Western Division patrol unit got to Blaze Duvall's address in Fashion Hills, she was gone. She'd fled so fast that she left some of her favorite cosmetics behind. But she didn't leave her tape recorder or her nickel-plated revolver.

•   •   •

Anne had already been given the bad news by the responding patrol officer by the time Letch Boggs entered her cubicle in the Homicide Unit.

He shook hands and sat down on her desk.

God, his hand was soft! She had to move back from his breath.

"Yeah, you still got 'em," he said. "Legs."

"You wanna catch Oliver Mantleberry or flirt?"

"Where's your team?"

"Having breakfast. Or is it lunch? I don't even know what time it is."

"It's Easter. They're having brunch."

"All I know is, I just got some bad news."

"What news?"

"Blaze Duvall's bailed. She called me and said she was outta here."

"Why?"

"Scared of Oliver Mantleberry. What do you think?"

"Could she be in on it? The murder, I mean?"

"Very doubtful," Anne said. "I think the bloody robe we found would fit her perfectly. I think she was with Dawn during or right after the attack and ran for her life. Right out of her robe."

"Imagine that!" Letch said, imagining it.

"Don't you *ever* stop?"

"Did you try to get her to stay?"

"Yeah, I told her we'd protect her."

"What'd she say?"

"In effect, Fuck you."

"You sure she's gone?"

"I sent a patrol unit to stall her."

"Shit."

"She said she'd call me and maybe she will. She's not your run-of-the-mill tweaked-out hooker. She's intelligent."

"A looker?"

"Not your type, Letch, but yeah, definitely a looker."

"Good body?"

"Come on, Letch!" Anne said.

"Okay, okay," Letch said. "Wish your partners'd hurry up."

"Me, too," Anne said. "Maybe we can get to Oliver before he gets rid of all the evidence. I sure hope the address you got is a good one."

"I sure hope he tries to run," Letch said. "I get to carry a shotgun, okay?"

When they heard the sound of male voices coming down the hall toward the office, Letch said, "I wouldn't wanna work here. I don't like this team concept, with one Spanish speaker, one female, one black. I suppose you got one Nazi and one skinhead? Your own little Rainbow Coalition, right?"

"An independent contractor. That's you, Letch."

"Yeah, I gotta work alone much as possible so I don't have to share my little secrets. Of course, I'd make an exception for you, Annie. Sure you don't wanna come back to Vice and pair up with old Letch? All the girls *love* to work with me."

"Remember Holly Doolittle?" Anne asked. "The tall one who worked the john detail with me?"

"Yeah, nice, healthy chest," Letch said, leering. "She was hot for my bod."

"We're still pals, all us girls that were street whores together. Holly, she used to wear a locket and in it was a picture of those Vegas magicians, Siegfried and Roy."

"So?"

"Every time she shagged a job working with you, she'd kiss that little gold charm and say, Please, Siegfried and Roy, make him disappear! *That's* how hot she was for your bod."

To change the subject, he looked around at the decor of the homicide office and said, "You know, you should have our puke-green walls and we should have your color. Mauve. More appropriate color for a vice office. Like a baboon's ass or rotten meat. Very erotic, but not too fruity."

•   •   •

It took some courage for a man to wear a straw boater, even on Easter Sunday, even to a colorful event like a yacht-club brunch. But Ambrose wore one every year, the only member who did. The hat had a navy-blue pin-dot silk band and nicely complemented his tomato-red nautical-print silk necktie, Easter being just about the only time he'd wear something with an anchor pattern. His pin-feather jacket was a traditional pale blue; it was worn with navy slacks and oxblood loafers.

He'd enjoyed the brunch in years past, but he knew today he'd hate it. All the defeatist talk about how *Black Magic* was going to demolish the competition, the most fearsome black vessel since the kidnapping of Helen of Troy launched a thousand black ships.

Well, one way or the other, it'd all be over soon. Until then he just had to put one foot in front of the other. He had to go to the office, attend real-estate open houses, participate in real-estate caravans, and otherwise strive to make a decent living in this bleak market. And not think about the coming week.

In short, he had to try to lead the same conservative, uneventful life that everyone thought he led. People were forever trying to marry him off to Sharon Downey, a sweet but needy widow he'd dated two years ago. And before her it had been Carolyn Wilberforce, whose husband had left her $10 million in high-yield bonds. He liked both women and enjoyed their company, but sex with them had been calamitous, even though each was patient and understanding. The truth was that only Blaze Duvall had restored the sexual potency he'd feared was gone forever.

When he arrived at the club, Ambrose walked into the trophy room, stood before the glass case, and was flooded with memories. Long ago he'd anthropomorphized that piece of hammered silver. He thought of the trophy as a living thing, and he wondered if others over the years—other Keepers of the Cup—had similar feelings.

Members of the club who'd never understood the significance of the world's oldest sporting trophy, nor of the honor and glory connected with it, liked to denigrate any reverence directed at the silver vessel.

"The Cup has no memories, no affinity," he'd heard one say.

But Ambrose didn't believe it. They hadn't been there in Portugal, hadn't felt the excitement everywhere. They hadn't seen fishermen come out in Nova Scotia, men of the sea squinting to read the names of ancient sailors who'd tamed the wind for this trophy.

They hadn't seen the young girl in Gothenburg who'd said to him in unaccented English, "Someday I shall be a sailor and challenge for the America's Cup!"

And in addition to those moments—those moving, unforgettable moments—there had been adventures. On their way to Marble House in Newport, Rhode Island, a huge snowstorm had diverted them to Hartford. And the America's Cup had had to spend the night in a city jail because there had not been sufficient security at the local inn.

They'd had the most fun, the Cup and he, on their last Ireland trip, spending four days at an old farm in Ulster from where they'd visited all of the Northern Ireland yacht clubs. And then they'd traveled by train to Dublin, to the Royal Irish Yacht Club. And on to the Royal Cork Yacht Club, founded in 1720, the oldest yacht club in the world. There had been 350 boats ocean-racing on the day they were there.

If the San Diego Yacht Club could successfully defend against New Zealand, Ambrose had ideas that he'd revealed to no one yet. Dazzling ideas. He dreamed of encouraging a challenge from a Baltic nation. He could envision challenges from Finland and Estonia, not to mention the Scandinavian countries. And Germany, of course. In 1992 Russia had made a try without sufficient resources behind it, and he had ideas that might persuade it to try again. He wanted to take the Cup to places it had never been, to drum up world interest. Airlines like SAS should commit to sponsorship. Participation in the Cup regatta would benefit each country's economy and lift the national pride. He hoped to convince them all.

Here in America people hadn't a clue. In Dallas, a customs officer checking them in from London had actually tried to make him take the Cup apart to search it for contraband! An American Airlines field representative had arrived on the scene to quell the ensuing disturbance. It was the closest Ambrose had ever come to engaging in physical violence. It had been an outrage.

Cynical San Diego Yacht Club members called the regatta a soap opera and gave it nicknames: "As the Anchor Drags" or "The Coma Off Point Loma." They despised Bill Koch, most of them, and many didn't even like Dennis Conner. "Ego, Fear and Greed" is the America's Cup motto, they liked to say.

Of course he knew the only reason they'd selected him as Keeper of the Cup was because nobody else had wanted it as badly as he had. And he was a local businessman, a man without a family who was willing to devote himself to it heart and soul. He had never been high in the yacht-club food chain, but he was safe and absolutely dependable. He didn't care anymore *why* he'd been chosen. All he knew was that the Cup was more alive to him than any human being he'd ever known.

Perhaps no one who hadn't been there could ever understand. You had to have been to the Isle of Wight, back with the Cup from whence it came. Back to visit the Royal Yacht Squadron, a quaint old club with a separate ladies' entrance and a members' room where no ladies were allowed. A club whose commodore was usually knighted. On that trip the Cup had stayed in the wine cellar of the castle with security provided by the British Army—and five thousand people had come to see the America's Cup!

The Cup had no memories? Ambrose Lutterworth thought it did. Yes, he'd anthropomorphized that silver trophy; of course he had. But as Keeper of the Cup, he was its sole protector. He was keeping it for *another* man, a man not yet alive, who would gaze at it a hundred years from now with as much love. Someone very like him, perhaps.

Ambrose had to reach into the breast pocket of his pinfeather jacket for the tomato-red silk handkerchief. He dabbed the tears furtively, but he needn't have worried. He was all alone in the room. Except for the America's Cup.

•   •   •

There was a group of young adults practicing self-defense on the beach in Crown Point that afternoon. Fortney had to stop the boat for Leeds because two of the girls wore damp T-shirts over bikini bottoms. Leeds had already worn panda grooves around his eyes watching a pair of honeymooners screwing their brains out on the fifth-floor balcony of the high-rise hotel in Quivira Basin.

"Alfred Hitchcock did movies about peepers like you," Fortney informed him. "And they all ended up in trouble."

"Look at the one in pink!" Leeds handed Fortney the glasses. "Legs all the way up to heaven!"

"To purgatory if your old lady ever gets wise to you," Fortney said.

"Wanna look for a while?"

"Naw, I'm sick of watching those mutant ninja guppies doing kung fu. Let's do something really different. Let's do some police work."

"Mellow out," Leeds said. "Open my bag and have some a my wife's tollhouse cookies."

"My first ex-wife made tollhouse cookies," Fortney informed him. "They could've killed a horse, especially if you chucked one at its head. That woman had no business in the kitchen. I hear she finally found something she *can* do. Runs around with a gang of geeks that throw chicken blood on abortion clinics. They better never let her *cook* the chicken, that's all I can say."

Leeds put down the binoculars and said, "Let's go. Now they're doing tai chi or something. No interesting muscle movement."

Fortney steered the patrol boat into Sail Bay, cruising along the shoreline, dodging all the boating bozos who had rented boats for the afternoon with no idea of what they were doing.

Fortney particularly liked the Mission Bay view of San Diego topography. Today the quixotic blue dome of the University of San Diego's Immaculata Church flashed Easter sunlight appropriately.

But after they nearly got broadsided by a particularly inept Catamaran Clifford in a rented cat with blue-striped sails, Leeds said, "These cretins're more dangerous than high-absorbency tampons. Let's boogie."

When they got safely back into Fiesta Bay, they saw an extraordinary sight. A rented motorboat had turtled and its sole occupant was clinging to the hull while two lifeguards struggled to get her into their rescue boat. She wore a white swimsuit with a purple orchid pattern—the largest swimsuit either cop had ever seen in the aquatic park. The woman, about Fortney's age, weighed 350 pounds minimum. She was doing everything she could to help, but it was no use.

Fortney saw that it was the two surfer-dude lifeguards who'd dissed him after the sheik dumped him into Mission Bay. He turned about and motored away before the lifeguards spotted them.

The cops watched through binoculars at a safe distance while the lifeguards sweated and strained. One of them fell down in the boat, and Fortney snickered. The other pulled off his jacket and got in the cold water, trying to boost her up, and Leeds chortled.

Both cops grabbed for the binoculars when the swimming lifeguard actually got the woman's enormous bottom an inch or two out of the water. But when she dropped back in and floundered, the cops became hysterical, almost rolling on the deck. Fortney was holding his stomach, tears streaming down his face. Leeds could hardly catch his breath.

Finally the lifeguards decided to tow her. They put a surfboard in the water, rolled her onto it, and towed the half-submerged woman toward shore.

Fortney throttled forward, heading in the direction of the home dock they shared with the lifeguards. The cops had to loiter in the channel for ten minutes until the rescue boat arrived, apparently having put the woman safely ashore. Both lifeguards were standing by the wheel, exhausted.

Leeds drove up to the rescue boat while Fortney stood on the bow, doing his best imitation of his least-favorite evening-news anchor. Fortney held his waterproof flashlight like a microphone and in his most booming TV anchor voice yelled across the water: "Stalwart lifeguards rescue stranded whale in Mission Bay! Film at eleven!"

The older lifeguard cupped his hand over his ear and said, "What's that, dude? What'd you say?"

Fortney was only too happy to oblige. He superboomed the encore: "Courageous Mission Bay lifeguards rescue stranded whale in—"

He stopped when she rose up over the gunnels of the rescue boat from where she had been lying on the deck. The whale!

"Oh, shit," Leeds muttered.

She glared at the cops, hanging onto the gunnels, spitting up bay water.

Fortney said to her, "Oh. I didn't see . . . Oh. Well, hell, I got room to talk? Look at this load I'm carrying." And he patted his tummy, a frozen smile pasted to his crimson kisser.

While the lifeguards grinned their evil surfer grins, the younger one said, "Dudes, you are the most unharmonious news anchors I've seen since Connie Chung worked with Dan Rather!"

"We just got a call!" Leeds cried. "Gotta go!"

He roared away so fast, their wake almost swamped the rescue boat. But the fat woman lying on the deck was too sick to care.

•   •   •

Ordinarily, with a dangerous murder suspect, they'd have asked SWAT to enter the little clapboard house in City Heights, a house occupied by a welfare recipient named Tamara Taylor. She was a former hooker who'd worked for Oliver Mantleberry one hundred pounds ago when she was young and childless but who now lived off the taxpayers of San Diego. Sometimes she received a bit of financial support from Oliver Mantleberry, who, in a burst of paternal sentimentality, had decided to take one of the two bedrooms in the little house, claiming he wanted to be with the three children he'd given her.

But actually he wanted to be closer to his girls on the boulevard and "consolidate business." Which to him meant whipping the living shit out of any girl he caught holding out on him. One of those who'd been whupped-on one too many times had told Letch Boggs about the pimp's living arrangements. That was how Letch knew where to find Oliver Mantleberry.

In that it was Easter Sunday and the cops didn't want to waste any more time than they already had, SWAT was not included. Instead there were Anne Zorn, Sal Maldonado, the other two team members, Randy Bulstrom and Zeke Calhoun, their sergeant, Bill Bowden, two patrol units, and a K-9 unit.

Letch asked for a shotgun of his own, but the homicide sergeant said he preferred that patrol officers handle the shotguns whenever possible. Letch then requested that they turn the dog loose on Oliver Mantleberry for, oh, no more than twenty minutes before they bothered with handcuffs. The dog, Reggie, was a 100-pound German shepherd with a bite pressure that could shred training sleeves. The sergeant said he preferred to take prisoners with attached limbs whenever possible.

The moment they drove down the street the cops could hear kids playing. It was broad daylight on a pleasant Easter Sunday, so there were lots of cars and people around in this neighborhood of single-family residences. The only way to play it was to *charge.*

They caravaned in and quickly unloaded in the street. One patrol unit and three detectives ran down each side of the house to the rear. The sergeant, Letch Boggs, Anne Zorn, and the K-9 unit went to the front.

Sergeant Bowden knocked and said, "Police officers! Open the door! *Now!*"

Ninety seconds later the little house was full of cops as well as a dog whose rumbling sounded like the Simba exhibit at the San Diego Zoo. Three kids under the age of six were crying their eyes out, and their momma sat on a kitchen chair not looking like she could ever have made much money on El Cajon Boulevard.

"This is my house!" she yelled. "You ain't got no warrant!"

"But we do," Letch informed her. "A felony warrant for pimping and pandering." He failed to mention that the complainant would not be appearing in court.

When she heard about the warrant for pimping, she stopped hollering. As an ex-hooker, she vaguely understood that pimping was a nonreducible felony that requires prison time. In the big joint, not the county jail. That quieted her down.

She also recognized Letch Boggs from the old days, that smelly, funky vice cop who made everybody's life miserable. She was afraid of him and said, "I ain't his momma. I don't know where he went to."

The homicide detectives were content to let Letch run the show and do the talking since his specialty was whores and pimps. Everybody knew he was good at what he did.

Letch said, "Tamara, I think you better not fuck with old Letch over this one. We wanna talk about something much bigger than a pimping case."

She looked at him suspiciously and said, "What is it you wanna talk about?"

"Murder," Letch said. "We wanna talk to him about murder."

She showed genuine astonishment. "What? Who?"

"A human being, that's what," Letch said. "Named Dawn Coyote, that's who."

"Don't know anyone with that name," Tamara Taylor said.

"I don't care if you do or don't," Letch said, "but you lie to us and you better get the kids all packed up for a ride. And you can forget about the chocolate bunnies and jelly beans."

"I ain't done nothin'!" she cried. "You can't hassle me on no humbug murder charge!"

"Watch us," he said. "You're lying to us now so that puts you in it."

Tamara Taylor's youngest came crawling over just then. His diaper was soaked and he started bawling, reaching up to his mother. She picked up the child and tried to hush him.

"This ain't right!" Tamara said. "You know I don't know nothin' about no murder! This ain't right, what you're doin'."

"Life jist ain't fair," Letch said. "Ask Dawn Coyote."

As if on cue, the dog started rumbling louder, and the K-9 cop jerked the choker and took the beast outside.

Then Tamara said, "He came home and packed up some of his things and left."

"What time did he come home?" Anne asked.

" 'Bout five o'clock this mornin'. I wasn't really awake very much."

"Where'd he go?" Sal Maldonado asked.

"I don't know," she said. "Maybe L.A."

"Why's everybody in San Diego leaving town to run to L.A.?" Letch asked rhetorically.

"Can't go south," Tamara pointed out. "Bunch a fuckin' Mexicans down that way." Then she looked at Sal Maldonado and said, "But I ain't got nothin' against 'em, you unnerstand."

"Where in L.A.?" Anne asked.

"You think that man tells me where he goes?" Tamara asked. "All he ever give me is these three kids and enough money to pay the light bill once in a while. You think he tells me what he does in his life? Shit, you don't know Oliver Mantleberry, you think that."

When Sal Maldonado pulled open the drawer of the bedroom dresser, Tamara said, "He's taller than that."

"Where's his clothes?" Anne Zorn asked. "The clothes he wore when he came home this morning?"

"I don't know," she said. "I heard him change. But he didn't leave the soiled ones for me like he usually do. Musta took 'em with him. Maybe he found some other woman stupid enough to do his washin' and ironin'."

"Where'd he change clothes? In your bedroom?" Anne asked.

"In the bathroom," she said.

"You don't mind if I have a look in there, do you?"

"Anythin' you find in that bathroom you kin have," Tamara said.

Anne disappeared into the bathroom for a moment and returned grinning at Sal Maldonado. She said to Tamara, "Have you had an accident lately? Where you bled?"

"No."

"You having your period?"

"No."

"Any of the kids have an accident?"

"No."

"How'd your washcloth get like this?" Anne held up a damp grayish washcloth by the corner. There were wine-dark stains on it.

"Where'd that come from?" Tamara asked.

"The bathtub," Anne said. "Somebody dropped it in the tub."

"Not me," Tamara said. "That's my washrag, but I didn't use it."

"I believe you," Anne Zorn said.

"What's on that washrag?" Tamara Taylor wanted to know.

"The genetic signature," Letch Boggs said, "of a girl named Jane Kelly. The story of her whole life is written right there on that old washcloth."

CHAPTER 10

FOR TWO DAYS AFTER THE TERROR ON EASTER SUNDAY, BLAZE DUVALL left her Shelter Island hotel room only to visit one of the fast-food joints on Rosecrans. She avoided the hotel dining room, never used the hotel's gym equipment, and didn't go jogging on the island even though she needed a workout. She settled for a daily swim in the hotel pool but only after dark.

On the second night she awoke screaming. In her dream she'd seen a dark shape rising. A mask of indefinable menace leaped at her, howling, teeth bared. In the dream she was trapped in a sinister web of gold chain, like the terrible chains Dawn had worn.

On Wednesday morning, Blaze got up refreshed, having had her first dreamless sleep since checking in. The isolation had enabled her to examine every detail of her plans, and her fear was subsiding. If everything went the way it should, she'd soon have the fifteen thousand plus the five hundred finder's fee from Simon Cooke. The thought forced a smile, her first in three days.

If it didn't go according to plan, if anything went wrong, she had other ideas. She needed money, and soon, to reestablish herself away from cops and away from Oliver Mantleberry. Blaze had important phone calls to make.

She called Simon Cooke at the boatyard, telling his boss that she was Simon's sister and could he please come to the phone for an important message?

When Simon picked up, she said, "Simon, this is your sister, Blaze. Don't say my name if you're not alone."

"Hi!" he said. "I been calling your number for two days."

"Don't say any more than you have to. I'm calling to make sure you're ready to go tomorrow."

"I'm ready," he said.

"I'm just checking to make sure nothing's changed."

"Okay. Nothing's changed."

"Be ready to go to work tomorrow with whatever you think you'll need in the way of . . . tools. Tonight I'll be doing *my* job. Tomorrow you'll do *yours*."

"Where'll you be tonight?"

"Wherever our friend is."

"Kin I see you later maybe?"

"After tomorrow we'll have plenty of time to see each other, okay?"

"Okay," Simon said.

Blaze hung up, pleasantly surprised that he hadn't slipped and blabbed her name. Maybe he wasn't quite as stupid as she thought.

She dialed the home number of Ambrose Lutterworth, and when he answered she said, "My lucky day. I was afraid you'd be at work."

"I thought you'd be checking in with me every day," he said. "I've called your number, but I just keep getting that damned machine."

"I've been out of town. Family emergency. I'm back now."

"Is everything . . ."

"From my end it's a go. All I'll need from you is the medication."

"Where shall we meet?"

"I'll drop by your house at seven o'clock. And, Ambrose, I

hope you understand that all payments *must* be made at the close of business tomorrow. By then you'll have proof that all parties have performed."

"Of course, I expected that. Cash, as agreed. I've already moved the funds. I'll withdraw them this afternoon."

"Fine," Blaze said.

"And then we're going to have that romantic dinner, aren't we?"

"Why not?" Blaze said. "There'll be a lot to celebrate."

After she hung up, Blaze put on her swimsuit and went down to the hotel pool for a workout. She thought she might learn to enjoy swimming as an alternative to aerobics. Maybe soon she'd buy a little house with a swimming pool. This was the first day she felt secure enough to swim laps in broad daylight.

When Blaze got back to her room, she dressed in jeans, a T-shirt, and sneakers and drove away from the hotel to make another call, this one from a pay phone on Rosecrans. Anne Zorn was not in her office, but she reached Detective Sal Maldonado.

"This is Mary Ellen Singleton and I'd like to speak to Detective Zorn sometime today."

"Give me your number, Ms. Singleton," he said. "I'll have her call you as soon as she gets back."

"Just take down my name and tell her I'll call later. If she wants to talk to me, she'll have to be there."

"Just a minute," he said, "can't I have your—"

He was still talking when she hung up.

Blaze was ravenous now that she was settling down. She drove back to the hotel and headed straight for the dining room for a proper lunch: spinach salad, grilled swordfish, baked potato, asparagus, and iced tea. She permitted herself a glass of wine even though she seldom drank alcohol before the dinner hour.

When she was finished, she started back up to her room to nap but changed her mind and drove to a pay phone. A different phone, just in case.

Blaze wished she had a lawyer. She needed answers, wondering if she was a material witness in the eyes of the law, and if so,
could she be compelled by subpoena to appear at a criminal trial?
Assuming they ever arrested the guy.

Well, they couldn't compel anything if she hadn't seen anything. She took the card from her purse and dropped a quarter into
the phone.

This time Anne was there.

"Detective Zorn."

"It's Mary Ellen Singleton."

"Thank you for calling!" Anne said. "I have to see you."

"Look," Blaze said. "You know my real name and you know
my work name. I'm sure you've discovered that I was arrested with
Dawn in a vice raid a long time ago. Okay, I stayed friends with her
over the years, but I didn't see her much. There's nothing I can tell
you that'd help."

"I think you saw her killer," Anne said. "I think you know
who it was."

"Listen, Detective, I saw nothing!"

"Dawn was coming to visit you or she was leaving your apartment. One or the other."

"She might've been coming to see me," Blaze said. "I don't
know. I was in bed sleeping."

"How'd she get in the gate?"

Cops! "Okay, she called me and I buzzed her in, but she
didn't make it to my door. Whoever it was got her on the stairs
where you found her. I don't know who it was!"

"How well do you know Oliver Mantleberry?"

"Who's that?"

"I think you know."

"I'm gonna hang up."

"Okay, wait! Maybe you don't know him. But Dawn must've
mentioned him at some time or another."

"I don't know what she did in her life. Her *miserable* life. She was a prostitute, I'm not. Okay, I worked in a massage parlor when I was younger, but I don't live like Dawn lived."

"How do you make a living now, Blaze?"

"Fuck this! I *am* gonna hang up!"

"I'm not a vice cop!" Anne said quickly. "I don't give a damn about your private life or your business life. But we're gonna stop this guy before he butchers another Dawn Coyote. I don't think you're the kind of person who wants that to happen."

"I didn't *see* him! I heard her cry. Now I know it was her, not a gull. I went out. I looked down. I ran to the phone—"

"Whose bathrobe did we find?"

"I told you it—"

"With blood on it? Dawn's blood on it?"

"You think it's mine."

"Isn't it?"

"Okay, so it's *mine*! She borrowed it from me. She was returning it."

"At that hour of the night?"

"She was a hooker! And a junkie! Her whole fucking life was topsy-turvy! I don't know *why* she was returning my robe at that time of night! I don't know why she did *any* of the things she did! I just felt sorry for her and now I wish I'd never laid eyes on the dumb little—"

"If I guaranteed we'd protect you, wouldn't you consider doing what's right?"

"Why do you think I'm on the phone? I'm *trying* to do what's right. I like San Diego. I don't wanna run away. But I don't want cops giving me subpoenas and trying to make me say things I can't say!"

"We have some excellent evidence already. Evidence against Oliver Mantleberry. With your testimony, your *truthful* testimony about what you saw that night, he might even get the gas chamber."

"Oh, sure," Blaze said. "How many people in this state been executed in the last thirty years? One, maybe? Two? Get real!"

"Think it over. If you won't give me your number, then call me tomorrow."

"I'll think it over."

"Same time tomorrow?"

"Okay."

"She'd do it for you, wouldn't she?"

"Who?"

"Dawn."

"Detective Zorn," Blaze said, "Dawn Coyote would've sold me out, and her mother, and her own baby, when she needed something to jam in her arm."

"You *will* call me tomorrow?"

"I said I would, didn't I?"

•   •   •

Fortney did something so stupid on Wednesday afternoon that he promised himself he'd never tell a soul about it, not even Leeds. *Especially* not Leeds, since his partner was the only one who knew the source of that stupidity. Fortney, who'd been keeping up with the regatta, knew that the Citizen Cup trials to decide the defender boat were still in doubt, but the Kiwis would probably wrap up the Louis Vuitton Cup tomorrow afternoon in *Black Magic,* thus earning the right to challenge next month for the America's Cup.

He had some interest in all this because by the time the marathon regatta finally ended in May, the city would have realized a $300-million economic boost. Anything that helped the city's budgetary woes might indirectly forestall the threatened shutdown of the Harbor Unit. He had good reason to pay more than passing notice to the America's Cup regatta.

But not enough to justify the incredibly stupid decision he'd made at five that afternoon. Fortney had decided to join the sailors, and the sailing-stupids, and the cuppies, all of whom would be out there in the gin mills for sure. Because if past history meant anything, *she'd* be out there with them. The ultimate cuppie: the fiery redhead named Blaze whom he couldn't get out of his mind. If Leeds ever heard about this bit of middle-aged angst, this baby-boomer madness or whatever it was, he'd never hear the end of it.

Fortney shaved closer than usual that afternoon. He even splashed on a little foo-foo cologne. He combed his graying hair with the help of a rearview mirror to arrange strands over the balding crown, but his curls wouldn't cooperate. He wore jeans he'd taken right from the dryer, checking to see if his butt was still holding up. He even wore a long-sleeved shirt.

•   •   •

Simon Cooke thought, Fuck it! She was shining him! Okay, the deal *sounded* good and she talked a convincing game, but what guarantee did he have that he'd get paid after it was over? When you came right down to it, he didn't know Blaze Duvall. All he had was a phone number. And she hadn't answered that for the past few days, not until she'd called him today. How did he know she was for real?

Simon dismissed the thought almost as fast as it popped in his mind. Blaze was too straight, too honest. The way she looked at him with those big green eyes of hers. But maybe she was *too* straight, too naive? Maybe she was being used by Mr. Moneybags. Simon still figured it was millionaire Bill Koch, boss of the mostly all-woman team. Yeah, Koch was the guy. Just the kind of rich asshole who'd take advantage of a decent kid like Blaze.

He made a decision that afternoon identical to Fortney's. Simon Cooke was going out that night to hunt for Blaze Duvall.

•   •   •

Ambrose Lutterworth didn't have to go hunting for Blaze Duvall. She showed up on his doorstep at 7:10 P.M., dressed not in the tailored look he preferred for their encounters and not in the sexy sailboat-casual she'd affected for her cuppie appearances. Blaze was wearing a green, hip-belted leather miniskirt, a short-sleeved, black wool turtleneck sweater, and low-heeled black Gucci boots.

For once she was dressed the way *she* wanted to dress rather than being costumed for men who, in one way or another, were all just clients.

Ambrose pecked her on the cheek and said, "My, you look . . . different."

"Not your style, I know. But I felt like wearing it."

"No! I mean, you look beautiful. You always look beautiful."

"I'll wear a longer skirt for our dinner date," Blaze reassured him.

"No, you look wonderful. Really."

"Do you have the drug?"

"Yes, let's sit down for a minute."

Ambrose led the way into the living room, where he and Blaze sat side by side on the old sofa. Two bindles wrapped in notebook paper were on the coffee table. He opened one of them carefully and showed her the powder.

"It took me a while to mash the tablets," he said. "If you empty one of these into his drink . . . By the way, what does he drink?"

"Beer. What else would those guys drink?"

"Okay, one of these will do it. You said he's a very big man?"

"Very."

"I've done some discreet checking with my pharmacist and my late mother's doctor. I think a gram of this will guarantee that even a big man won't be ready to run machinery the next day."

"What is it?"

"Phenobarbital."

"We don't wanna kill him."

"It won't kill him, but he'll have the mother of all hangovers."

"But he'll be okay, right?"

"Do I look like a murderer?"

Blaze hesitated, then said, "No, you don't look anything at all like any murderer I've seen lately."

"Actually it's a little more than a gram," Ambrose said. "I crushed eleven of the hundred-milligram tablets."

"What's in the other paper?"

"Same thing. Just in case something goes wrong with the first one. But, for God's sake, don't give him *both*!"

"Don't worry."

"And you have no fears about Simon Cooke?"

"None at all. I own him."

"You didn't have to . . . *do* anything with him, did you?"

"Don't be silly, Ambrose. Can you imagine me in bed with someone like that?"

"No, of course not."

"Okay, I guess I'm ready."

"I'll have the money tomorrow afternoon. Twenty-five thousand. You know, I'm surprised Simon didn't make a demand of good faith. Didn't he ever ask for some money up front to prove our reliability?"

"I wouldn't have given him any front money. I don't trust him *that* much. But don't worry. I told you, I own him."

"You could own a lot of men, Blaze," Ambrose said.

"Wait up tonight, darling," Blaze said. "I'll phone you with a detailed report as soon as I get back to my hotel."

"Hotel?"

"Oh, didn't I tell you? Termites. Thirteen hundred bucks a month and I have to cope with termites. We've all had to move out for two days while they fumigate."

"Which hotel are you in?"

"That darling little place on Shelter Island. I selected it so I could be close to the sailor hangouts." Then she added, "And close to you. I like being close to you, Ambrose."

He was touched. He smiled and kissed her lightly, not wanting to smudge her lipstick. But he couldn't resist just touching her lips with the tip of his tongue. Blaze Duvall even *tasted* young.

·   ·   ·

There was more smoke than usual in the Kiwis' favorite barroom. That meant there were more foreigners boozing it up on victory eve. Blaze could hardly breathe until she got past a group in the doorway, all of whom were puffing away. One man was even smoking a cigar, something a Californian rarely saw being done in public these days.

Very few of the America's Cup sailors had arrived yet, but there were plenty of regatta fans, those who went out on the pricey spectator boats as well as the big cattle boats that didn't offer all the amenities but could haul a lot of sponsor pals to the racecourse off Point Loma. The nonsailing tourists were actually dressed more like photo-op weekend sailors than real weekend sailors. Many wore Polo shirts, longish shorts, and belts patterned with signal flags. Most wore Top-Siders, no socks. Several had sweaters thrown over their shoulders. All very preppie.

And very few, if any of them, failed to notice the tall girl in the green leather mini when she made her way through the crowd, heading for the bar.

It was so easy: Blaze just bumped against a burly sailing-stupid sitting on a barstool. When he turned around, she said, "Oh! Sorry. Just trying to get the bartender's attention."

"Let me help," the man said. He yelled, "Bart! Over here!"

Blaze said, "White wine, please."

The man said, "White wine, Bart. On my tab."

"Thank you," Blaze said. "That wasn't necessary."

"It's nothing," he said. "By the time tonight's over, I'll be buying drinks for half of New Zealand. One more won't matter. You a Kiwi by any chance?"

"Afraid not." Blaze smiled.

"Here, take my stool," he said, getting to his feet.

"Thank you," Blaze said.

Men. It was just that easy.

•   •   •

Fortney finally found her at 8:10 P.M., sitting at the bar, her hair glowing like fire under a taste of overhead light filtered through cigarette smoke. She didn't have the usual Cup sailors swarming her, but Fortney realized that was only because they hadn't arrived yet. The crowd was composed of regatta enthusiasts and hangers-on.

He didn't go directly to her end of the bar. Instead he got himself a draft beer, then saw he'd waited too long. A mob of twenty sailors came in with half that many cuppies in tow.

People started yelling greetings from all over the barroom and the place came alive, the crowd swirling and swarming like so many sea snakes. In no time at all the sailors spotted Blaze.

"Blaze!"

"Charlie!"

"Blaze!"

"Matthew!"

"Blaze!"

"Robbie! I saw you on ESPN. Who did your TV makeup?"

And so it went. Fortney was crestfallen. Blaze was surrounded by ebullient Kiwis as well as several Aussies, who were keeping up a brave front. The Aussies were probably resigned to annihilation tomorrow, but the dueling sailors usually talked about anything but the race.

Fortney wondered if the regatta was on their minds, or if the same thing was on their minds as was on his: Blaze Duvall. By the time he had another brew, ten of the sailors and Blaze were wedged in a booth designed for six. She was pressed between a huge Aussie and an equally large Kiwi. Fortney noticed that as usual she chatted with everyone, but she often glanced anxiously toward the entrance.

When he ordered his third pint of draft, Fortney felt more than stupid. This was midlife angst, nothing else could explain it. He had about as much chance with this babe as the Aussies had against *Black Magic.* He was embarrassed. He felt like getting drunk. This kind of childish behavior could lead to another bad marriage if any decent female human being was halfway kind to him.

He realized how pathetically lonely he'd become since his last divorce, and he felt humiliated. He often wished he'd fathered a kid somewhere along the way, somebody he could be with on lonely evenings like this. Now it was too late.

When he next looked over at the booth, the huge Kiwi with the albino buzz-cut was moving toward his mates, blocking out Fortney's view of Blaze Duvall and half of the sailors. Fortney decided to have one more beer and go home.

•   •   •

"Miles!" Blaze cried as the behemoth cruised through the crowd like the *Kitty Hawk*.

"Blaze, my love!" He grinned, looming over the table, baring the space where an eyetooth should have been.

"Aren't we gonna make room for a working man?" Blaze asked the sailors who had her sandwiched.

They weren't about to move. "We're the bloody galley slaves!" a Kiwi said. "That bloke only has to put the slave ship in the water!"

"Come on, guys!" Blaze said. "Let's play musical seats and give poor Miles a chance to take a load off. After all, he has the biggest load, doesn't he?"

After some grumbling and debates about whose turn it was to buy a round, two sailors got up and Miles wedged his wide-body into the booth next to Blaze. He'd just left the boatyard, was only half washed, and reeked.

But Blaze smiled warmly and said, "How about a drink, big boy?"

"My usual," he said to a frazzled barmaid with rivers of sweat running down her face.

The only reason Fortney wasn't off the stool and out of there was that four beers and one tequila shooter on an empty stomach had severely unbalanced his body chemistry. What the hell, he figured, you go this far, might as well stick it in all the way. But while nursing his second tequila shooter he realized that the only one he was screwing was himself.

Fortney used to work with a black cop named Sleepy Simpson

who, every time he figured the world was sticking it to him, would go out and finish the screwing by getting himself shit-faced. Poor old Sleepy suffered from an on-duty head injury he'd got by chasing a Corvette on a police motorcycle, ending up like a pancaked roadkill with half his scalp flapping in the backwash of freeway commuters whizzing by on their way to work.

Sleepy would go narcoleptic when he'd been boozing it, and if Fortney didn't watch over him, he'd fall asleep behind the wheel. One time Sleepy even left the shotgun on the roof of the patrol unit and drove off. To make matters worse, he never got enough rest because he owned property in Logan Heights and was up half the night doing slumlord collecting. When he finally got so sleepy that he dropped his uniform off at the cleaner's with $350 in the pocket, Sleepy figured that was it. Time to call it quits and apply for a medical pension from the old head injury.

Well, Fortney didn't have an old injury, wasn't a slumlord, and had about enough cash in his bank account to feed himself and his goldfish as long as they didn't need gourmet fish food. Yet here he was getting even with the world by screwing *himself,* just like old Sleepy Simpson. Over a woman. A fantasy woman at that. A woman who preferred a big kahuna Kiwi who looked like he ought to be taken to a carwash and bathed.

If only Blaze hadn't stopped at his table and insulted Leeds with that sassy little grin. If only she hadn't given that wicked slant-eyed glance at Fortney, a glance that had promised a heavenly battery charge to an over-the-hill cop whose future consisted of cruising around Mission Bay for five more years, watching the sun soar overhead and drop into the ocean beyond the south jetty. Five more years before retirement. *Then* what?

Fortney was rescued from a riptide of self-pity, but not by surfer lifeguards. By the unlikeliest lifesaver of all: Simon Cooke.

Simon squeezed himself between the last patron at the bar and the ersatz teak paneling and yelled, "Hey, barkeep! Bring me a double gin and tonic, hold the tonic!"

He was already hammered, but no worse than Fortney, who looked at him and thought: She drinks with you and that Kiwi. Why? Fortney wasn't leaving until he could explain the mystery, craving a solution to the puzzle that was Blaze Duvall. He picked up his bar change, leaving thirty-five cents for the bartender, the smallest tip he'd get from a Yank that evening, and made his way through the smoke clouds until he was against the wall, just behind Simon Cooke.

Fortney reached his arm between Simon and the drinker next to him as though to put his empty tequila glass on the bar. He bumped Simon's elbow.

"Hey!" Half of Simon's gin sloshed over the rim of his glass. He didn't bother to look around at the clumsy bastard but quickly licked his own hand, preventing catastrophic loss.

"Real sorry, man," Fortney said. "Whatcha drinking? I owe you one."

That made Simon do a half-turn and grumble, "Gin. Double."

Fortney said, "Another double gin for my friend. And a tequila shooter for me." Then he put his last twenty on the bar.

Simon Cooke offered a minismile and said, "Okay, dude. No problem."

"This place is rocking out," Fortney said to him.

"Yeah."

"You come here often?"

"No. Fuckin' drinks cost more'n a down payment on a used pickup."

"I don't come too often either," Fortney said. "It ain't even a good place for chicks."

"It sucks," Simon said, finishing the half-spilled drink and reaching for the fresh one.

"I'll be glad when all these sailboat tourists beat feet," Fortney said.

Simon Cooke didn't bother to respond.

"You work around here?"

"Yeah."

"You into any of this America's Cup stuff?"

"No."

"That's all there is around here these days," Fortney said. "Sailing types. May as well have another drink. My liver ain't quite big enough to eat me yet. Wanna join me?"

"Sure," Simon said, figuring the guy was probably a faggot even though he didn't look faggoty. Well, if he wanted to buy double gins, Simon could string him along for a while.

But Simon got confused about the guy's sexual identity when the next round was poured. Because he said to Simon, "You see that hot babe in the corner with all those sailors? I've seen her every time I been in this joint."

Simon didn't say anything, but his crafty little grin got craftier.

"You know her?"

"Why would you say that?" sly old Simon asked, slurring his consonants.

"I dunno. Just the way you're smiling, I guess."

Simon said, "Yeah, I know her."

"You do?"

"Sure. Her name's Blaze."

"I guess there ain't a chance, huh? I mean, for somebody to take her away from that big, ugly Kiwi."

"I know that prick, too," Simon said. "I know most of 'em. All pricks. Every one a them."

"What's she see in him?" Fortney wanted to know. "A slick-looking chick like that?" Now he was slurring his own consonants.

"I wouldn't know. Whatever floats your boat. I wouldn't know."

"I sure wish I knew."

"Why?"

"I'd like to come on to her."

"Forget it. You ain't her type."

"No offense, but how do you know?"

"She's a straight-up babe. She ain't no saloon floozy."

"She's a cuppie, ain't she? I mean, she's always with those sailors."

"She has her reasons, man," Simon said boozily, pushing his face close to Fortney's. "She don't give a fuck about that big piece a shit next to her! And she ain't the type that appreciates somebody comin' on to her in a bar. Know what I mean, dude?"

Simon was shooting Fortney his surliest sneer, and Fortney was debating whether to kick the stool out from under him or buy another drink with the last of his bucks.

He bought the drinks, and Simon seemed to forgive his lusting after Blaze Duvall.

After waiting for Simon to guzzle the next double shot, Fortney said, "I don't mean offense of any kind, but the way you're talking? I get the feeling maybe she's sort of . . . your girlfriend? If she is, I'll keep my oar in the boat."

"I know her real good, put it that way," Simon said.

"You ever . . . date her?"

"Dude, you sure ask a lotta personal questions!" Simon's elbow slipped off the bar.

Fortney grabbed him before he fell from the stool, saying, "I don't mean disrespect. I'm interested in her, is all."

"In her or me?"

"Come again?"

"I figured you for a sissy," Simon said, "when you started buyin' the drinks. I figured you smoked the pink cigar. Now I don't know *what* the fuck to think. You a rump rider or what?"

"The man has charm," Fortney said to a stuffed sailfish hanging high on the wall. "You have to say that for him."

"Who?" Simon demanded, looking up at the fish.

"Never mind. No, I ain't horny enough to chase guys. Yet."

"Well, you got no chance with Blaze," Simon said. "So forget it, understand me?"

That did it. Regardless of how pathetically obsessed he'd become with a cuppie named Blaze, Fortney had had it up to here with this little maggot.

He picked up his bar change and started to leave, but suddenly he whirled, saying to Simon Cooke, "I gotta ask you one thing, man. I bought enough drinks to deserve an answer."

"Yeah?" Simon muttered. "What's that?"

Fortney said, "Why the fuck would a woman like *that* waste even a nanosecond on a little gob of mucus that smells like nerve gas in a Japanese subway? That's all I wanna know!"

Simon Cooke pushed close again, saying, "You callin' me a Jap or what?"

Fortney didn't answer. He just hooked his sneaker around Simon's stool and jerked it sideways, sending the little boatyard gypsy tumbling across the beer-soaked floor.

While staggering past Blaze's booth on his way to the exit, Fortney stopped and warbled a lyric at her: "Wild thing! You make my heart siiiing!"

She never even noticed the crooning drunk.

·   ·   ·

Fortney wasn't San Diego PD's only multiple-marriage victim who was lonely that evening. Anne Zorn had gone to bed early after trying unsuccessfully to get interested in an issue of *Vanity Fair* that was all about Hollywood and movie stars. The trouble was, she couldn't concentrate. Not when she was working on a hot homicide and had herself a suspect she wanted badly.

She wondered if it was because of her own early experiences in the Vice Unit. The first time out she'd been so young, so green. She'd never forget how exciting it had been getting plucked from patrol for a vice assignment. Those were the days when the females were still called "policewomen" rather than "police officers." When they had to wear horrible tunic uniforms with no belt loops, so when you'd run after people your gun'd go sliding around to the front and you'd lose your handcuffs. When their hair wasn't allowed to ever touch their collars, and they had to wear stupid hats like U.S. Navy Waves. Someone had stolen Anne's hat, God bless the thief.

In those days salty male cops would say things like "Your zipper should be in the crotch. Tell me, Officer, what kinda cop doesn't have a zipper in the crotch?"

She'd dropped her Handie-Talkie radio in the toilet more than once, trying to unwrap herself from that stupid uniform. The antennas were always bent from being dropped by women.

A police academy classmate, one of the few females who'd survived with her, had had enormous breasts and every time she'd put pens in her breast pocket they'd point straight out. The male cops used to say, "I'm intimidated by torpedoes pointing at me." They had *lots* of fun with the women back before sexual harassment. And in those days they'd still call women "chrome-plated" if they ever dared to date a black cop.

But there was something they'd done *for* her back when she was between marriages. Her rented house had burned down with everything in it, and those old cops had taken over, buying clothes and toys for her daughter, Frannie, as well as clothes for her. Then they'd passed the hat and found her a place to live. They'd been supergenerous, those old misogynists.

Anne wondered if the reason she was so emotionally involved with this case was because she'd been a make-believe street whore herself. Sometimes when she'd been out there on Midway Drive or El Cajon Boulevard, an Oliver Mantleberry had hit on her and tried to cajole or scare her into becoming his old lady. And in those days she'd had no wire, only a backup team that she'd hoped watched through binoculars, waiting for the signal when she got a violation from a john.

She remembered a guy who'd offered her $35 for an *entire* night. She'd given the signal for Code Two Cover.

When her backup rushed in and grabbed the guy, she'd said to him, "Whadda you take me for? Thirty-five bucks for all night? I'm *insulted*!"

Then there was the British Airways pilot who'd stopped her on Midway Drive one night. He'd had wavy blond locks, dreamy brown eyes, a trim body, and an accent like Roger Moore's.

When he made the offer, she'd said, "You're a doll! I'll go with you for *nothing*!"

"What?" he'd said. "Beg your pardon?"

"Forget it," she'd said with a sigh. "Get outta here before my partners nail you."

The Brit had looked thoroughly confused, but he'd sped away from the bonkers streetwalker just before a minibus full of college kids had pulled up and asked for a group rate.

Then there was the time one of the johns had turned out to be a serial rapist, one who liked to drive up to a hooker and get out of the car to talk business. If the girl didn't go for his action, he'd force her into his car at gunpoint, take her to a remote location, rape her, then beat her half to death to consummate the act, rape being more about violence than sex.

Anne was wearing a wire the night she'd encountered him, and when she was about halfway through her spiel about what he expected for his money, he'd whipped out a cheap foreign .380 pistol. At ten yards it'd be about as accurate as a can of whipped cream, but he'd been only two feet away.

He said, "Get your ass in the car!"

And she said, "Oh! I see you have a *gun*!" for the benefit of her cover team, who were *supposed* to be listening but had left their van after a drunk rear-ended it.

He said, "Get in *now*!"

Anne looked frantically both ways on Midway but the team wasn't there. So she said, "Man, I have a filthy case of herpes and you wouldn't—"

"Now! Or you're dead!"

"Okay, okay," she said. "That's real, isn't it? That *gun*! It's real, isn't it? That *gun*!"

Luckily, the cover team had just gotten back to the van in time to hear, "That *gun*."

They forced his car to the curb as he was driving away, his right hand on the wheel, his left hand in his lap with the .380 pointed at young Anne Zorn.

During the ensuing investigation, they'd tied him to fourteen rapes in San Diego and twelve in Houston. Along with a rape-murder in Phoenix, when he'd let his fun get out of hand.

She'd later married Arnie, one of the vice cops on that cover team. Arnie was a love except that he couldn't handle serious domestic conflict such as who got the inside seat in a restaurant, thereby being able to take the gun off. Crises like that made Arnie flame out. The marriage had lasted eight and a half months, the worst of her bad choices.

It was during her second tour on the john detail that she'd worked with Letch Boggs and got sent to massage school. The one thing her bosses stressed after teaching her to be a bogus masseuse was that you get your violation of law without ever touching it. Don't touch *it* or there goes your case.

As Anne lay in bed with *Vanity Fair* lying open on her stomach, she thought of Blaze Duvall. Who undoubtedly had to touch it *every* time she gave a massage.

CHAPTER 11

AMBROSE KNEW HE'D NOT SLEEP A WINK UNTIL BLAZE CALLED WITH updates, so he tried to read the latest issue of *Cruising World*. But it was hard to get into the sailing articles when all he could think of was what might go wrong tomorrow. Oddly enough, he wasn't worried so much about the personal risk but about what a waste it would be if their plan succeeded and *still* the Kiwis' backup boat went on to beat the American defender. Next month he'd be out there on the water for every leg of that 18.55-mile race—praying.

If Dennis Conner's team became the defender, they'd prevail over New Zealand, he was sure of it. Conner had too much experience, had too many times snatched victory from defeat, was too clever and too *lucky* to be beaten. Conner was Mr. America's Cup, and his helmsman, Paul Cayard, was one of the best in the world.

Observers said that Conner and Cayard would certainly win a strange-bedfellows trophy. Rumor had it that Conner had blackballed Cayard when he'd first applied for membership in the San Diego Yacht Club, and people blamed Conner for commercializing the great regatta. But his defenders, like Ambrose Lutterworth, stoutly maintained that the Australian multimillionaire, Alan Bond, had been the first to turn the regatta into a commercial venture when he won the Cup from Conner and the New York Yacht Club in 1983 with his famed winged keel. That victory had paved the way for Conner's Holy Grail comeback in 1987 off Fremantle in Western Australia.

One thing for sure, ever since Alan Bond won with his innovative design, the America's Cup keels were more closely guarded than stealth bombers. Tens of millions of dollars were poured into keel design, hull design, sail design. Every syndicate needed one more sail, one more hull, forever begging the question with: "Don't you *want* to win?"

Ambrose yearned for a return to a better time, when it was still a yacht race, when there were no computers calculating everything from wind to speed. When human beings reckoned things like westerly swell and southerly chop. When sailors, not aeronautical engineers, decided if a boat should be wide-body stable or narrow and slippery—sailors who lived or died by seat-of-the-pants decisions. When yachtsmen could just go out onto the ocean and *race.*

But now, famous moguls—Australia's Alan Bond, New Zealand's Michael Faye, America's Bill Koch, and the wiliest of all, Dennis Conner—had determined the future of America's Cup racing. And computerized boats were floated on a sea of greenbacks vaster than the kelp beds off Point Loma. Boats had become sailing billboards plastered with sponsor logos. When the FCC forbade cigarette commercials on TV, Dennis Conner turned his spinnaker into a huge, ballooning Marlboro ad. He could always find a way.

All Ambrose could hope for was that Conner would find a way against the Kiwis, and there'd be four more years with the Cup in San Diego to put things *right,* to regain the goodwill that had been so foolishly squandered by rampant egos and the commercial exploitation of what should be the purest sport of them all.

Ambrose longed for a return of daring amateur sportsmen, like the first winning Americans who'd sailed to the Isle of Wight in 1851 when Queen Victoria hosted her world's fair regatta to celebrate Britain's mastery of the sea. The upstart American boat, a lightning-quick schooner, not only demolished all British competition but did it so convincingly that when Queen Victoria asked who'd placed second, she was told, "Your Majesty, there *is* no second!"

That was the sort of yacht racing Ambrose dreamed of resuscitating. To that end he would dedicate himself, if the American defender, whoever it might be, could thwart the New Zealand challenge next month.

It could be done, he knew, if by nightfall tomorrow the 32 boat, called *Black Magic,* lay in the Kiwis' boatyard with its back broken beyond repair.

•   •   •

She could tell that Miles was getting drunk extrafast because he was growing anxious about a possible sexual encounter. It had always amused her how insecure they were, especially the giants like Miles. He was the kind she'd always had to mother. They practically needed burping. The bigger they come, the softer they fall, Blaze always said.

But when his kind got drunk, they got handsy in order to compensate. He kept reaching under the table, where she sat crammed into a booth with seven boozy sailors, so sloshed they'd begun discussing race strategy in the presence of enemy sailors. That is, when they weren't on the subject of women. The Aussies were cruder than the Kiwis, but *her* Kiwi made up for his reticent mates.

"Not now, Miles," she whispered in his ear when the paw crept a bit too far up her thigh.

"When, then?" he whispered back, hot breath soured by beer and the dozen raw oysters he'd devoured, probably as much for potency myths as for a love of bivalve mollusks.

A middle-aged Kiwi tourist sitting at a nearby table observed Blaze's dilemma and leaned toward her, saying, "That's what Jessica Lange had to contend with in *King Kong.*"

The giant said, "Who invited your opinion, mate?"

Ignoring him, the tourist said to Blaze, "He's a right eager lad, he is. Just tell him to sod off."

"You're a right pain in the arse, you are!" Miles retorted. Then he raised up, his massive thighs taking the table with him.

Drinks spilled, and everyone started yelling.

"Steady on!"

"Ease off!"

"Goddamn it!"

Miles said, "It ain't me! It's that old fool over there. Won't tend to his own affairs."

"Tell you what, boys," Blaze said. "I'm going for a pee, and when I get back everybody's gonna be wearing a happy face. Whaddaya say?"

Blaze slid out of the booth and headed for the ladies' room. When she got there, she locked the door, took both paper bindles from her change purse, and transferred one of them to the currency compartment in her wallet. She tidied up her hair and lipstick, then returned to the noisy barroom with one bindle in her palm. Instead of going back to the booth, she headed for the bar, jostling through the hordes of boozers.

The drinkers made way, and she said to the bartender, "A mug of Steinlager, please."

"A pint?"

"If that's the big one."

"You got it," the bartender said with a flirty smile.

Blaze rejected three drink offers in the sixty seconds it took him to draw the New Zealand beer. She paid with a twenty and put the coins into the compartment next to the spare bindle, never noticing the blurry-eyed little drunk at the other end of the bar who was watching her with growing jealousy.

When Blaze returned to the table, she started to sit but appeared to change her mind, saying, "I'm not gonna get turned into a ham sandwich again until I'm sure everybody's all through jumping up and down."

"Sit down," Miles said gruffly, showing off for his mates. "You're the finest morsel of ham I've seen since I came to this bloody country!"

"Nope," she said. "Auntie Blaze says everybody who has to pee should get up now and go do it. Especially you, Miles. When you raise up, the table goes with you, as we've noticed. So hurry before I sit down and settle in."

One of the sailors said, "Never mind the table. The whole bloody *room* shifts when Miles gets up."

"Okay," Miles said. "I reckon I'll go in the gent's and drain Dennis Conner."

That made them roar, Aussies as well as Kiwis. All were enemies of the famous Yank and feared his bag of tricks.

When the big man was gone, Blaze forced herself to gulp down some of his beer, and while one of the sailors was telling a joke she peered across the smoky barroom and said, "Speak of the devil! Isn't that Dennis himself?"

All eyes jerked toward the door. And Blaze emptied one bindle of powder into the mug of Steinlager, quickly stirring it with her finger.

"That's not Dennis Conner! Blaze, you're getting pissed!" a Kiwi grinder said. "Go easy on the wine. Switch to beer."

"Speaking of beer," she said, "let me borrow some of yours. A big boy like Miles needs his full to the brim." She grabbed a mug belonging to a Kiwi trimmer and poured some of its contents on top of the Steinlager.

"Hey!" he said. "I need it more than that big horse."

"Hush!" Blaze said. "Auntie Blaze'll buy you a new one when you're ready."

When Miles came rumbling like a forklift across the barroom, an Aussie yelled, "Did you give Dennis a right good choking?"

"Had Dirty Den squealing like a hog," Miles said, and everyone laughed.

Blaze said to Miles, "Here you are, mate! A nice fresh pint of Steinlager! New Zealand's finest brew!"

But Miles curled his lip and said, "That's worse than the 'roo piss they serve in Australia. I wouldn't wash my socks in it."

Blaze was speechless for a moment. Then, "You're joking! *All* Kiwis drink Steinlager. That's one of your sponsors. The name's on your hull. It's on your sail."

"If it was on my bleedin' arse I still wouldn't touch that swill," Miles said. "Here, Charlie, *you* drink it."

"No!" Blaze said, pulling the mug toward her. "I'll drink it."

"That's the good girl," the grinder said. "You drink it."

"So whadda you want, then?" Blaze asked Miles. "I'm buying."

"Any North American beer," he said. "It's all mediocre. Maybe a Samuel Adams."

"One Sam Adams coming up," Blaze said. "Move over and let me out."

"What for? They've got barmaids to serve us."

"I have to make a phone call," Blaze said. "Be right back."

The big Kiwi sighed, got up, and let Blaze slide out once more. She took the mug with her and headed in the direction of the public phones by the ladies' restroom.

When Blaze went inside the restroom, two cuppies were combing their hair and discussing which one was going to seduce the Australian pit man and who was going to try for the bowman.

After they'd gone, Blaze leaned on the sink and stared at her reflection. Jesus Christ! She'd never considered the possibility that he wouldn't drink their sponsor's beer! She poured it down the sink, palmed the second and last bindle of phenobarbital, and walked very anxiously toward the bar.

This time she looked so grim that the flirtatious bartender didn't flirt. He just took her order and drew the mug of Samuel Adams, then watched her curiously while she gulped down four big swallows, grimacing like the brew hater she was.

Then she strolled toward the window as though to look down at the parking lot, and holding the mug pressed against her black turtleneck, she emptied the bindle, then stirred the beer with her finger.

When she returned to the bar, she said, "Can you top this off, please? I spilled some on the floor."

"Sure," the bartender said, happy that she was smiling again. He held the mug under the tap and filled it to the brim.

When she got back to the table, Miles said, "I was getting ready to send out a searching party."

"Got you your beer," Blaze said. "That's what took so long."

"You drink it," he said. "I've already got one coming from the barmaid."

"Goddamn it, Miles!" Blaze said. "You don't like Steinlager, so I went over there and fought through the mob to get you one you *do* like! Now drink it before I pour it on your noodle!"

"That's telling him, Blaze!" a drunken Aussie said, giggling.

"He needs a firm hand!" a boozy Kiwi concurred.

"Okay, love, I'll drink it. Keep your knickers on," Miles said.

"At least for the moment!" a Kiwi cried, and all the drunks roared.

And then an incident took place that to Blaze Duvall played itself out more dreamlike than real. Later, when she tried to replay it in her mind, she couldn't. Like a faulty video, it just wouldn't track.

Her mouth fell open when a cadaverous little man appeared at the table.

"Evening, Blaze," Simon Cooke said. "There's somebody here I want you to meet."

She was jolted, startled, astonished. She couldn't believe it. Not only was he there, but he was falling-down drunk. Smashed. Hammered. His bloodred eyes were swimming, and his fly was unzipped. He grinned stupidly at all the curious sailors.

When she was finally able to talk, Blaze asked, "What're *you* doing here?"

"I got somebody I want you to meet!" he repeated, tottering backward until a guy caught him and propped him up.

"Hello, Blaze!" a handsome young sailor said. "I'm Gordon. The lads've talked about you quite a bit."

"Gordon!" one of the Kiwis cried. "Buy us a drink or I'll tell your bride you're here!"

"Get out of here, you sod! You're a married man!" another said.

"He's a bloody newlywed!" a third piped up. "Ignore his advances, Blaze!"

"This is the brother-in-law I told you about," Simon said, keeping himself upright by holding on to the table with both hands.

"Very pleased to meet you, Gordon," Blaze said. "But don't you think your brother-in-law's had too much for one night?"

"Too much for a bloody year," Gordon said, looking down at his wife's disgusting older brother.

"I'll decide when I've had enough!" Simon announced to all of San Diego.

"Go home, mate," Miles said. "Gordon, *you* better take him. He can't drive."

"Hey, asshole!" Simon said to the giant. "*I'll* decide if I can drive or not! You couldn't even drive a fucking travel-lift till I taught you!" Then to Blaze, "This asshole couldn't even drive a travel-lift till I taught him!" To Miles again, "Call yourself a crane operator? You couldn't operate a weed whacker!"

His brother-in-law grabbed the crane operator by his skinny bicep, saying, "That's all, Simon! You're going home now!"

"The fuck I am!" Simon yelled, jerking away. Then he pointed to Miles and screamed, "The average length of a gorilla's cock is one and a quarter inches!"

"Get him out!" Miles roared, slamming his beer mug down and jumping up.

That's when the entire scene, as Blaze remembered it later, went out of focus.

The little crane operator took a swing at the big one and had his bony fist stopped in midflight by a paw bigger than his head.

But Simon Cooke, ever game, swung with his other fist,

missed, and knocked the mug of Sam Adams onto Blaze Duvall's chest.

Then everybody started yelling and cursing and hollering. And two waitresses scampered to the bartender, who jumped over the bar and ran toward the fracas.

Gordon, Miles, and a Kiwi grinder lifted Simon Cooke by the arms and one leg and hauled him out as he flailed at anyone in sight with his free foot, all the while yelling, "You can't trust *any* of 'em, Blaze! Bunch a wallaby fuckers!"

Blaze Duvall sat, stunned, the front of her turtleneck drenched with the full pint of drug-laced beer. She was still sitting, staring into space, when Miles and the grinder returned without Simon or his brother-in-law.

The grinder said, "Do you know what the little beggar said when we threw him into Gordon's car? He said, 'You'll need me one of these days to put your boat in the water.' "

"I wouldn't let that lunatic put my bum into bathwater," Miles said.

"If he ever comes near our compound I'll feed him to the crabs," a bowman said.

"Excuse me," Blaze said to Miles. "I gotta go home. My sweater's ruined."

"Don't go, Blaze!" the big man begged. "It'll dry. Please don't go."

"I gotta," she said, still dazed.

"Change and come back," the Kiwi pleaded. "I'll wait."

"We'll all wait!" the grinder promised.

Blaze said nothing. And when she was walking away, she heard Miles say to his mates, "Poor Gordon. Any child of his is going to have that *thing* for an uncle."

"A great pity," the grinder agreed. "I fear there's a lot of algae in the family gene pool."

•   •   •

Sometimes it was just as luxurious to wear the smoking jacket over silk pajamas. Of course it wasn't proper, and he'd hate to have anyone who knew better see him like this. Nevertheless, it was cozier than wearing his soft wool bathrobe, or even the silk one with his monogram on it.

There was just something about that smoking jacket. On his trips to Britain he'd discussed smoking jackets with the commodores of various yacht clubs. Virtually every one of them had agreed that a smoking jacket was an irreplaceable item of a gentleman's apparel—for a true gentleman.

Ambrose was listening to a compact disk, Beethoven's *Eróica,* when the telephone call came. He jumped up from the Chippendale wing chair and ran to the bookcase to switch off the music. His hand trembled when he picked up the telephone.

"Hello?"

"It's me."

"Yes."

"Got the money?"

"I told you I'd have it."

"I mean *now.* Do you have the money at your house *now?*"

"Why do you ask? Is anything . . . wrong?"

"Everything's gonna be fine," she said, "but Simon's making a fuss. He may need *some* money tonight."

"Simon! What're you doing with Simon tonight? Didn't you—"

"I can't explain now," she said. "Things're still happening. But if I should need some front money for Simon, I need to know it's available. That you have the money tonight."

"I have it," he said. "But I don't want you to give him anything until he performs tomorrow. I thought we agreed on that?"

"I'm working on him, Ambrose. I gotta know the bottom line in case he starts turning weird on me."

"How about your friend? Your very large friend? Did you make the delivery to him?"

"Soon," she said. "It'll all be done soon. Don't worry. I'll call you later."

"God! I was hoping it'd be done by now. I can't sleep. I can hardly think about anything else."

"I know," she said. "Try to relax. I'll call."

When she hung up the phone in her hotel room, she lay back on the pillow and stared out the window at the tall masts in the Shelter Island channel. There was no sense torturing herself with might-have-beens. It was pointless to look for another way out because there was no other way out.

She was alone in a hotel, hiding from a vicious killer who wanted her dead. Running from the police who wanted to expose her to the killer or to one of his friends if they should get lucky and arrest him. Well, no thanks!

She'd worked for the fifteen thousand and where had her hard work gone? Into the toilet. Or the harbor. Or wherever it was that drunken scum like Simon Cooke puked their guts out.

She had the five grand coming, but it wasn't enough, not the way things were going in her life. As a matter of fact, fifteen wasn't enough. Blaze wondered if that was why she'd taped the last encounter with Ambrose Lutterworth. Maybe she'd always known she'd need *more,* that he'd provide if it came down to it.

But at least she'd *tried* to keep her end of the agreement. It wasn't her fault the way things had turned out. She took two deep breaths, got up, and went into the bathroom to see how she looked. Not wonderful, but she didn't redo her lipstick, didn't run a comb through her flaming mane, merely tied it back in a ponytail. Somehow it didn't seem right to primp, given the job she had to do tonight.

Blaze put on an oversize green sweatshirt, blue jeans, and white sneakers. She rummaged in her suitcase for her audiocassette player with the tape still in it. She'd considered duplicating the tape, but asked herself why she'd need it. As long as Ambrose believed her, he'd come across. But if he played hardball—though she couldn't even imagine it—she'd decided just to throw the tape away and give up. She wasn't an extortionist at heart, and she actually liked the old guy.

Before leaving the room, Blaze shoved the nickel-plated revolver inside the waist of her jeans and pulled the green sweatshirt down over the gun butt, thinking: Sometimes a girl's gotta do what a girl's gotta . . .

●   ●   ●

Ambrose Lutterworth was sitting motionless in his wing chair when the doorbell rang. It startled him and yet it didn't. Tonight he was expecting everything and nothing. This was a very strange night.

He went to the door and switched on the porch light, seeing the swirling flame of hair through the frosted door panel. He switched off the light and opened the door.

"So, Simon must be demanding some earnest money," Ambrose said to her.

"Got any of that good chardonnay?"

"Please!" he said. "I can't stand it! Did it happen or not?"

"Pour me some wine." Her voice sounded dead. "And pour yourself something."

"Oh, God!" He turned and trudged into the kitchen, fearing that it was over, that something bad had happened.

Ambrose returned with two glasses of wine, but with no ice bucket this time. He handed her a glass and sat down heavily in the wing back. Exhausted and feeling old.

Blaze sipped the wine and didn't speak for a moment.

Ambrose said, "Is there any good news, or is it all bad?"

"Bad," Blaze said. "Simon Cooke crashed my party just as I'd managed to drug Miles's beer. I won't bore you with what I went through up to that point. Simon was absolutely blotto and fucked up the whole deal."

"Look!" Ambrose said. "Okay, so it went wrong tonight. But we can try again! During the America's Cup race when New Zealand's facing our defender, we can—"

"If Simon Cooke so much as sets foot in their boatyard, they'll keelhaul him," Blaze said. "If they still keelhaul people. He's poison. He's finished. He's finished *us*. You should've been there."

"No," Ambrose said sorrowfully. "No. I'm glad I wasn't. Very glad I wasn't."

"You picked our man," she reminded him. "He wasn't my choice. He was yours."

"I know," Ambrose said. "There was no one else who could've done it for us. Maybe he wanted out. Maybe he got drunk and ruined everything because deep down he didn't have the stomach for it."

"So that's that," Blaze said.

"He'll keep his mouth shut, I assume." Ambrose's voice was even more lifeless than hers.

"What's he gonna say? Who's he gonna tell? He doesn't know me. I'm just a sailing groupie named Blaze he met in a bar."

"I think this is the most depressing night of my life," Ambrose said.

"Maybe your American team'll win anyway," Blaze said. "Maybe you didn't really need the edge you tried to buy."

"No," Ambrose said. "It's becoming more hopeless every day. New Zealand will win big tomorrow over the Aussies and the Cup will be gone forever next month. Gone forever."

"That's a shame, Ambrose," Blaze said. "I'm sorry for you."

"Do you want your five thousand now? Is that why you came in person?"

"I would like it now," Blaze said.

He nodded and pushed himself up from the wing chair, using both hands on the rep-striped arms. He was too distraught to care that he must look foolish in a smoking jacket and pajamas. He felt ancient, shuffling into the bedroom in his monogrammed slippers. He felt as old as the Cup.

The twenty-five thousand was in two packets in his underwear drawer under his polka-dot boxers. He removed the smaller packet and counted out fifty one-hundred-dollar bills. It took him a few minutes. He was so distracted that he lost count twice.

When Ambrose returned to the living room, he was surprised to see her purse lying open on the coffee table with a small cassette player beside it.

Blaze didn't look when he dropped the packet onto the coffee table. She just said, "Sit down, Ambrose."

When he did, she punched the play button.

Ambrose had picked up the glass of wine but put it down on the lamp table beside him when he heard Blaze's recorded voice ask, "Powder or oil?"

He froze when he heard his own voice say, "Powder, I think."

He closed his eyes and didn't open them when he heard Blaze's recorded voice say, "It was just like you said it would be. Simon Cooke's a greedy little man. And he was very interested when I told him about my anonymous friend who was willing to pay ten thousand dollars to destroy the New Zealand boat."

Then he heard himself say, "Is he sure he can get the job?"

Ambrose Lutterworth didn't hear much more after that. He kept his eyes closed ever more tightly now as the cassette droned on. A cassette full of criminal conspiracy mixed with erotic suggestions.

It was very peculiar, but he started thinking of his mother then. And his sister, but mostly his mother. He almost felt that if he opened his eyes he'd see her sitting where Blaze was sitting. Looking at him with her relentless disapproval.

Then he heard Blaze's recorded voice say, "It's okay, Ambrose. I know I don't need a condom with you. We're . . . bonded now. We're . . . secret sharers. Would you like being *bonded* to me?"

Ambrose Lutterworth opened his eyes and said, "Turn it off, Blaze."

"It's not quite over yet."

He said, "Turn it off."

Blaze reached over and switched off the machine. Then she

said, "I've made copies for the district attorney, your yacht club, the New Zealand syndicate, and the *San Diego Union Tribune*. I hope I never have to send them."

"I see," Ambrose said quietly. "And now you want to sell them to me, is that it?"

"Yes," she said. "For five thousand apiece. Along with the five thousand you owe me already."

"You want twenty-five thousand," he said. "You want it all."

"Not all, Ambrose," Blaze said. "Not *all*." Only what you allowed for a caper that didn't come off. "My God, you have this house! What's it worth? Seven figures, right? Compared to me you're a rich man. I *need* that money, Ambrose. Something's happened and I need money real bad. I'm in serious trouble."

"Were you in this trouble when you made that recording?" He spoke so quietly, she could hardly hear him.

"I was just protecting myself," she said. "If Simon hadn't blown us out of the water, I wouldn't be doing this. I'm sorry."

"And you came here absolutely certain that I'd give you the twenty-five thousand?"

"It's up to you, Ambrose," she said. "I told you what I'll do if I have to. I hope you won't make me do it."

"If I'm guilty of a criminal conspiracy, so are you," he said.

She said, "I've already consulted my lawyer about it. Since our little arrangement never went anywhere, neither of us will be prosecuted. But it's all down there on the tape for your friends and associates to hear about. The plan, the money, the drugging of a Kiwi crane operator. All so you could keep your precious Cup. The notoriety won't hurt me. Hell, it might even get me on a talk show. Maybe a lonely old rich guy who likes massages might propose marriage. But what'll the notoriety do to *you*, Ambrose? Can you handle the disgrace?"

"I always said that you're a very smart girl."

"Look at it this way," Blaze said. "What if Simon had gone ahead and fucked things up like he probably would've done? Maybe got himself caught? Then we'd have to worry that it'd come back on us. If it did, we *would* be guilty of a felony and go to jail for it. Forget the America's Cup. It's over. It's worth twenty-five grand to avoid scandal and humiliation, isn't it?"

Ambrose said nothing. He just pushed himself up again and, with his head bowed, shuffled into the bedroom. He couldn't stop thinking of her—his mother. He opened the underwear drawer and took out the money. He put it in the pocket of his smoking jacket. When he did that, he looked at the band of his satin sash. He couldn't take his eyes off that wine-red sash, just as he couldn't stop thinking of his mother. She'd always implied that he was a failure for lack of fortitude. She'd always used words like *backbone*.

When Ambrose came back into the living room, Blaze had already put the cassette player in her purse. Ambrose took the stack of bills from his pocket and tossed it onto the coffee table.

She was very pale and didn't look at him, but she couldn't stop looking at the money. All that money. All those fresh new bills. As fresh as the bullets in her gun.

Ambrose walked around the sofa toward the front door as though to open it. He stood staring at the door. He could see his mother as clearly as he could see Blaze in the reflection of the frosted glass. He could see her milky-blue eyes and papery skin, loose and ill-fitting. She'd never come right out with it, but she'd thought he was a *coward*.

He reached down and quietly threw the dead bolt on the door, locking it. Blaze had her back to him, bending over the coffee table, trying to stuff the stack of bills into the small purse. Ambrose Lutterworth untied his sash and removed it.

Blaze heard a rustle of silk behind her. Her first instinct did not involve the gun. She'd never carried a gun before. No, she grabbed for the *purse* and pulled it to her with both hands.

Ambrose vaults over the back of the sofa and loops the sash down over her head to her throat. He roars.

She can hear him screaming one word as her body is jerked backward. They both tumble over the sofa and crash to the floor.

The word he screams is: "No!" And not just to Blaze.

Blaze also screams, or tries to. She drops the purse and reaches up, grabbing at the satin-piped cuffs of the smoking jacket. Then she claws at the sash, but it's drawn even tighter. She can't breathe.

Blaze thinks: But he's just a harmless old man!

She rolls and lunges and kicks the back of the sofa. But still Ambrose Lutterworth holds on. And the sash grows tighter.

She can't breathe.

Then she thinks of the gun and gets her hand on it. But it slips down, down to the crotch of her jeans. Blaze rips at the button, then at the zipper. But the sash gets tighter.

Breath! She needs breath!

The ceiling turns to pink Jell-O. The lamp on the table crashes to the floor and the pieces explode in pink shards of Jell-O. The walls are undulating Jell-O.

Blaze gets the gun free, but she needs a breath. Just one. And can't get it.

The gun sails from her hand. The gun is no longer a gun, it's a Frisbee. It sails away like a Frisbee in pink Jell-O.

A whirl of shimmering color. The lamp rained down kaleidoscopic glass, as from the Episcopal church windows of his youth. Ambrose wasn't roaring anymore. He was panting, wheezing, whimpering. He was trapped inside a kaleidoscope of stained glass. Still, he pulled tighter on the garroting sash. He was not a coward after all.

CHAPTER 12

AMBROSE SAT FOR A LONG TIME IN THE WING BACK. THE SMOKING JACKET was torn at one shoulder seam and was hanging open; the buttons were ripped from his pajama top. There were lacerations on the back of his right hand from Blaze's fingernails.

The wine-dark satin sash was loosely coiled around her neck, no longer biting into her flesh. She lay in a fetal position.

Ambrose hadn't looked at her since he'd sat down. He stared at his wineglass and for a moment thought about drinking it. It seemed an insane idea, drinking the wine. The thing that kept drawing his eyes was the nickel-plated revolver on the floor among the broken ceramic shards. Wherever his gaze roamed, it would always come back to that revolver.

He expected his Omega gold chronograph to be broken, but it wasn't, showing the time as 1:45 A.M. In the past, whenever he'd look at that chronograph, he'd think of the Barcelona boat show, but this time he didn't. His treasured chronograph had turned into an ordinary wristwatch.

And his burgundy smoking jacket? Suddenly he needed to take it off. When they'd crashed to the floor, blood had gushed from her nose and his sleeve had become sticky, glistening with her blood. The bloodstain was similar to the color of the sash: wine-dark.

He stood up and the smoking jacket fell from his body. He kicked it over by the broken lamp next to Blaze Duvall, whose lifeless body would soon begin the process of livor mortis: the obedience of blood to gravity's law.

In the end it was not fear or hope—not remorse or atonement—that powered his decision. It was that Ambrose Willis Lutterworth, Jr., could not bear for the world, his little world—but primarily the greater world of the America's Cup—to know him as a base, contemptible murderer.

He must not let that happen. He owed it to the Cup.

•   •   •

Jesse Bledsoe, toll sergeant at the Coronado bridge administration building, was dozing. Who *wouldn't* at two-thirty in the morning? What was he supposed to do, sit up and stare at the dark grainy images on the monitors to see if any sea gulls were crapping on the guardrails? Or maybe run up there and stop jumpers if one was crazy enough to come out on a foggy night like this when he could just drive up there in warm sunshine tomorrow and kill himself in comfort?

Jesse Bledsoe never even glanced at the monitors when the old Cadillac sedan slowly made its way through the fog blanket and stopped at the top of the bridge.

That was the first time that Ambrose Lutterworth—who'd lived in San Diego all his life—realized that video cameras had been installed at strategic locations near the suicide hotline numbers on the very crown of the Coronado bridge.

The cry of a lost and lonely heron made Ambrose look up at the foggy night sky, where he spotted a camera mounted high on a stanchion, looking down at him. Then, fog bank or not, Ambrose mashed on the accelerator and drove dangerously fast over the bridge through the tollbooth. Then he proceeded to Orange Avenue, turned around, and got back on the bridge for a return to San Diego with the body of Blaze Duvall in the trunk.

She was wrapped in an old blanket from his mother's bed, and her right ankle was tied to a concrete block with the satin sash that had strangled her. He didn't know why he'd used the sash. Perhaps an unconscious need to give them a clue? Tying her ankle to the concrete block with the sash was as senseless as the entire episode had been.

The smoking jacket would end up in his trash can along with any peace of mind that should have been his at this stage of life. Ambrose Lutterworth was now certain that he'd kill himself in the near future. It only remained to decide when and how and to assure that it could never be linked to his sordid relationship with Blaze Duvall.

When he was back on the freeway heading north, he thought of Mission Bay. Yes, she didn't have to be in San Diego harbor. Mission Bay was deep enough to hold her, at least long enough for nature to dispose of the dozens of clues he'd probably left. Like most people who commit only one crime in their lives, Ambrose Lutterworth believed the authorities had omnipotent detection skills.

Thirty minutes later he was driving slowly through mist and darkness along Ingraham Street in Mission Bay. The fog had lifted somewhat and there was almost no traffic this early in the morning, but he was so distracted that he overshot the south bridge, a better and more remote drop site.

When Ambrose was on the north bridge between Vacation Isle and Crown Point, he stopped the Cadillac and got out, shivering. He was wearing a windbreaker over his pajamas and was still in his bedroom slippers.

Ambrose was walking around to the trunk when suddenly he heard an engine behind him. A vehicle had pulled out onto Ingraham from Vacation Road and was coming his way in the fog, moving very fast.

Police! He knew it was the police. Who else would it be?

He ran back to the driver's door but couldn't get it open. He realized he'd locked it by reflex when he got out. He couldn't find his keys and the vehicle was coming closer!

Then he found the keys. They were in his hand.

Ambrose unlocked the door, leaped inside, and flooded the engine while pumping the accelerator in panic. Terror stabbed his belly like a hot dagger.

He had the nickel-plated revolver—Blaze's revolver—beside him. He picked it up with both hands. He hoped he had the courage to pull the trigger before the officers got out of their car. He raised it to his face.

The car sped by too fast considering the weather conditions. It was a bread truck making an early delivery to the hotel.

Ambrose sat for a moment with the gun in his quaking hands before putting it down on the car seat. He got back out of the car, but his legs were so weak that he was afraid they'd cave when he lifted her. When he opened the trunk, her blanket-wrapped body was illuminated by the compartment light.

She was staring at him. He slammed the trunk shut. The blanket had come partially undone and she was *staring* at him.

Ambrose started to sob and, with eyes closed, reached down and unlocked the trunk again. He raised it up and grabbed the blanket, rolling her onto her front, eyes down. Then he reached under her stomach and legs and lifted.

His back was struck by a spasm and he almost cried out. She'd been so fit that her flesh was all muscle, and heavy. She seemed heavier than when he'd put her into the trunk.

Wheezing, he lifted her and the block of concrete up over the pedestrian barrier. He dragged her to the metal guardrail, but dropped her, falling on his knees beside her body. Then he hauled himself up and, with all he had left, hoisted Blaze Duvall's corpse to the top of the railing. And shoved it over.

But he forgot the concrete block tied to her ankle. It tried to follow her, clanging on the rail when she dropped, but the satin sash broke loose from her leg. The body splashed down into Fisherman's Channel, still half wrapped in the blanket, and the concrete block smashed down onto his slippered foot.

Pain shot clear to his crotch. Moaning, Ambrose picked up the concrete block still fastened by the sash and limped to the car, then heaved it into the trunk.

Through tears of pain and horror he began to drive home but found himself almost in La Jolla before realizing he was going the wrong way. He cried out in utter frustration.

When Ambrose finally found his way home, he drove into the garage and sat in the darkness for several minutes. He got out of the car and hefted the gun again, but at last shoved it into the pocket of his windbreaker. He tried to open the trunk to dispose of the concrete block and satin sash but couldn't.

He was afraid of the satin sash. He was terrified to open the trunk. What if she was still in there staring at him? Not Blaze. She was down in the cold, dark waters of Mission Bay. No, not Blaze. She wasn't what he feared.

When he'd opened the trunk of the Cadillac to take her out, it *hadn't been* Blaze staring at him. Those eyes hadn't been green. They were blue. They were the milky-blue, censorious eyes he'd known all his life!

·   ·   ·

When Leeds tried to discover the origin of Fortney's hellish hangover, he was told to shut up and drive the boat.

When Leeds tried gallows humor by suggesting they take the boat out onto the ocean and try to jump it in board-breaking surf, Fortney patted his nine-millimeter and said, "We jump, you die."

"Wanna attempt some police work?" Leeds asked finally. "Down in the big harbor there's a lotta smugglers on Jet Skis with cocaine in their backpacks. Wanna check some Mission Bay backpacks?"

Fortney merely said, "Can't you drive more steady?"

"This ain't a freeway," Leeds grumbled. "Damn, you even *smell* boozy. Like a Dumpster diver. Eau de Thunderbird."

No response. Fortney sat holding his aching head, sucking in sea air to drive away evil spirits. He was holding up his head because his neck didn't seem strong enough for the job.

A 31-foot Sea Ray cruised past, the engine noise depositing a load of pain into Fortney's skull. Two guys on the boat were playing a Grateful Dead tape at a jaw-breaking decibel level. It sounded to Fortney like Jerry Garcia was strumming on a plate-glass window with a brick.

After an interval his bored partner said, "You read about the Coast Guard catching those poachers with lobsters and scallops squirreled away in their diving tanks? We oughtta check dive tanks for lobsters and scallops."

"Not . . . today," Fortney croaked.

A family of four putted by in a rented 16-foot Bayliner and a five-year-old boy waved exuberantly, yelling, "Hi, Officers!"

"Hello, citizen," Leeds said with a little salute.

Fortney looked up at him questioningly. "I've decided to say 'Hello, citizen' to kids from now on," Leeds said. "You know, like Batman used to do on TV?"

Fortney said, "I feel grotesque enough to play the Joker. What color am I? Rust-Oleum green?"

"Maybe you oughtta quit drinking so much," Leeds said. "You might remember something we could share. I could get more communication outta Lonny, the bomb-squad robot."

"If I quit drinking so much there'd be nothing worth sharing," Fortney said. "My life's that boring."

The patrol boat was on the north side of Fiesta Bay just beyond Ski Island when Leeds, scanning with binoculars, saw some people standing on the north Ingraham Street bridge, looking down at the water.

"Something's happening on the bridge," Leeds said. "Let's mosey."

Fortney said, "I wonder, if I poured more coffee into my tormented body, would it hurt or help?"

"Maybe it's a desperate jumper," Leeds said. "You ready for lifesaving?"

"Very humorous," Fortney said, in that the bridge was only twenty-five feet higher than the tide.

"You hear about the jumper that dove off the Coronado bridge *twice*?" Leeds asked. "Didn't die the first time, so he had to try again a month later. Wore a weighted belt the second time and sunk like the Mexican peso."

Fortney murmured, "I wouldn't wanna look for him at night in that dark water."

"Every dive is a night dive in that muck," Leeds said.

The people on the bridge spotted the approaching police boat and started waving and yelling.

Leeds said, "Hang on!" and turned on the blue light, throttling forward while Fortney tried to keep from tossing his cookies.

Beneath the bridge over Fisherman's Channel was a Filipino fisherman, standing on the bank as if he had a great white shark on the line and didn't know what to do with it.

He had hooked something large, all right, but it wasn't Jaws. He'd snagged the jeans of a female floater partially wrapped in a blanket. She was half submerged, and her hair trailed like fiery seaweed.

The Flip was terrified and jabbered something in Tagalog, but Fortney wouldn't have understood him if he'd held up Sesame Street flash cards. Fortney was gaping in horror at that ghostly trail of familiar flaming tresses.

When they got next to her, Leeds grabbed the radio mike, but Fortney didn't have to turn her over. He knew who it was facedown in that cold murky water.

•   •   •

Ambrose was stunned when he opened his eyes and realized he'd actually slept. He still had the same thundering headache he'd had at daybreak when he'd gone to bed. That was after he'd taken a bath and disposed of his silk pajamas and the burgundy smoking jacket by slashing them to pieces and burying them in his trash container. They were just rags now, waiting for a pick-up.

He dreaded what he had to do. He was terrified of doing it, but he knew he had to pull himself together and go to the hotel on Shelter Island. On the bed beside him was Blaze Duvall's purse and its contents included her room key.

Ambrose didn't dare put it off. For all he knew she might have told them that she was checking out today, so he'd have to search the room before the maid went in to clean. He assumed that checkout time was around noon, so he had to get it done now. He had to search for four cassette tapes worth five thousand dollars each.

But what made him think they'd be in the room? They could easily be at her apartment in Mission Valley, the address on her driver's license. He was looking for an excuse not to go to that hotel.

Ambrose sat up in bed and once again opened the leather wallet. It wasn't the kind he'd seen most women carry. His sister had always had a red leather wallet fat as a kidney, crammed with credit cards and photos. Blaze's contained only a driver's license, a Visa card, and ninety-seven dollars, with thirty-seven cents in the change purse. There was one photograph: a high school girl who bore a resemblance to Blaze. On the back of the photo was written: "To Mary Ellen. Love, Rosie."

Going through the wallet the first time had left him enormously upset. Even now he had to wipe tears when he read her name on the license: Mary Ellen Singleton. He'd always guessed that Blaze Duvall was only a name for her massage clients, but he hadn't figured on her having such a nice name: Mary Ellen Singleton.

Suddenly Ambrose Lutterworth started to sob.

•   •   •

There'd been very little news coverage concerning the murder of Dawn Coyote, aka Jane Kelly, but Anne Zorn hadn't expected much. The location of the murder, a nice middle-class apartment building in Fashion Hills, should have warranted reporters, but as soon as the press found out that Dawn Coyote was a hooker—and a street whore at that—they lost interest. There were lots and lots of unsolved hooker murders. It went with the territory, everyone said. N.H.I. murders they were called: No Humans Involved. Who cared when another hooker got murdered?

Letch Boggs cared. He'd been phoning so frequently, it made Anne think of her mother. Letch was full of suggestions about where Oliver Mantleberry might be hiding out, but none of them had paid off. At first Anne had thought the horny old vice cop was just trying to hit on her, but she came to understand how badly he wanted the pimp who'd murdered Dawn Coyote.

Misplaced guilt. She'd seen it before. Letch Boggs probably felt that if he hadn't coerced her into making the report, she'd still be alive. He was right, of course, but Anne figured that Dawn Coyote wouldn't have lived long in any case. She'd have OD'd, or the pimp would have killed her for some other reason. Or, even more likely, a sexual psychopath would have murdered her. There were enough of them out there, that's for sure.

Anne had to admit that she felt a twinge for the old lecher. As a Catholic, even a lapsed Catholic, heavyweight guilt always touched her heart, so when Letch called five minutes after she got to the office Thursday morning, she didn't get annoyed at him.

She just said, "We don't have any fresh ideas today, Letch. Except we're sending a criminalist back out there to make sure no blood evidence was missed. Just in case Oliver Mantleberry cut himself when he was carving on Dawn Coyote."

"Did you request a rush on the DNA testing of the wash-cloth?"

"Yes, Letch, yes," Anne said, rolling her eyes at Sal Maldonado. "But it takes time for genetic fingerprinting. Don't worry, that's Dawn's blood. We *know* it is."

"A clincher would be if some of Oliver's blood was there. You oughtta have them check by the security gate."

"We're going to take another look," Anne said, "but we'll still have a good case when the washcloth tests positive."

"Lemme meet you there," Letch said. "I got eyes like a pelican. I'll find Oliver's blood if it's there."

"Okay, Letch," Anne said, sighing. "The criminalist told me he'd get there about ten o'clock. Be there and you can watch, but stay out of his way, okay?"

After she hung up, Anne said to Sal Maldonado, "It doesn't seem fair when Internal Affairs puts a cop on a polygraph. We're such a guilt-ridden breed it's too easy to make us blow a needle off the chart. Poor old Letch."

•   •   •

Ambrose drove Blaze's car down the winding streets to Shelter Island but made a stop at the pharmacy to buy pancake makeup for his lacerated hand and some rubber gloves.

After parking her car in the hotel lot, he wiped off the steering wheel and door handle and then entered the lobby, where guests were queuing for checkout. All through the regatta the little hotel had been well booked, and it was full of guests coming and going. Ambrose worried that someone from the yacht club might be in the dining room having breakfast.

He put on his sunglasses and kept his chin lowered to his chest, using the staircase in order to avoid people in the elevator. He encountered an elderly couple in the second-floor corridor arguing about whether to visit Sea World or the zoo. Ambrose walked past them as though he knew where he was going.

But he didn't. He discovered that Blaze's room was in the other direction, so he stopped and looked at his watch as though he'd forgotten something. Then he turned and proceeded past the battling couple until he found the room. He unlocked it and went inside.

Wearing the rubber gloves, he began in the closet. She'd

brought a lot of clothes for such a short visit, but why should he believe that her apartment was being fumigated? Why should he believe anything she'd said?

Maybe there *were* no tapes! Maybe he was being a fool once again! Maybe . . . He had to get ahold of himself. He had to *assume* she'd made copies. He had to begin a methodical search.

After he finished running his hands over an item of clothing, he'd drop it on the floor by the bed. And when he was finished searching the closet, he searched the drawers.

Nothing but women's things.

He pulled the drawers out and looked under each one. In the movies people taped things to the bottoms of drawers. Then he tore the bed apart and looked under the mattress. He checked the bathroom, even behind the toilet and under the sink.

Nothing.

Ambrose was astonished at the jumble he'd made and started to put things back. But then he thought, No, better to leave it. Better if they find the room ransacked and a guest missing. They'd think she met a man who robbed and killed her, perhaps a man she'd picked up and taken to her room. Yes, better this way.

Ambrose left the room. As he was walking down the hall, he saw a Mexican housekeeper pushing a cleaning cart in his direction. She didn't look at him, but he rushed past her. He got to the staircase and was struck with panic.

The doorknob! He hadn't put on the gloves until he got inside. Would his fingerprints be on the doorknob? Or would the housekeeper destroy the fingerprints when she opened the door? He couldn't risk it.

And then he couldn't remember if he'd wiped the steering wheel of the car. His mind wasn't working properly. He couldn't remember what he'd done twenty minutes ago!

It was hard not to run back down the hall, straight to the door. He walked. He purposely dropped his key when he was abreast of the door, and when he stooped to pick it up, he pulled a silk handkerchief from his coat pocket and wiped the doorknob.

When he turned around, he was terrified that the woman would challenge him. That she'd look at him suspiciously and ask if it was his room. That she would demand to see his key.

Ambrose was afraid to make eye contact, but when he finally looked at her, he saw that she was munching a candy bar and reading the funnies. She didn't give a shit about a frantic old gringo.

·   ·   ·

By the time Anne arrived, Letch Boggs was already parked in front of Blaze's apartment building in Fashion Hills. The moment she saw him she knew she'd guessed right: Letch had the guilts.

"A lotta people walking around here since Saturday night," he said when she walked up.

"And good morning to you," Anne said.

He was wearing the most ungodly aloha shirt she'd ever seen. It was mostly yellow, but all of the primary colors writhed around, making the basic hue hard to call. "That shirt could cause permanent squints," she said.

"I think Oliver's gotta come home soon," Letch said. "Gonna have to make the rounds and muscle his girls for some quick green."

"Letch, everybody's seen his mug shot and everybody has his license number."

"He ain't gonna be in the Jag no more," Letch said.

"Maybe not."

"I think you oughtta tell patrol to watch for a blue Beemer convertible," Letch said. "This whore I know, she used to run with a whore that worked for Oliver. Told me he had a bro that drives a blue Beemer. Look for a blue Beemer."

"We'll get him, Letch," Anne Zorn said, patting his shoulder, the first time in her life she'd actually touched the vice cop.

"You don't think I'm becoming obsessive about this, do you?"

"No, Letch," Anne said. "Of course not."

·   ·   ·

By the time the old red Cadillac was driving slowly down the street, pausing to check addresses, Letch Boggs and Anne Zorn were inside near the swimming pool. A criminalist was complaining to Anne that it was a wild-goose chase. That nobody could expect to find any more blood evidence.

"How 'bout the O. J. Simpson case?" Letch Boggs said to the criminalist. "They found blood *weeks* later."

"Yeah, and I remember the defense claiming it was planted," the criminalist retorted. "You want a loudmouth lawyer like Flea Bailey yapping at you?"

Ambrose Lutterworth held Blaze's driver's license in his hand as he checked the facades of each apartment building. When he saw her address, he pulled to the curb half a block down the street so that nobody in the building would see his car.

He was still exhausted from having walked all the way home from Shelter Island, afraid to call a cab from her hotel. And his foot was throbbing, possibly from a toe fracture. He dragged himself out of the Cadillac, banking that one of her keys was for the security gate.

When he got to the staircase, he let out a gasp and stopped. Yellow San Diego Police Department tape was temporarily blocking the walkway by the swimming pool.

They'd found her already! And they'd found her residence even though she'd had no identification on her. They were already in the midst of a full-blown murder investigation.

When Ambrose was limping back to his Cadillac, he fully expected to be arrested before day's end. He was convinced: The police had *incredible* investigative powers.

•   •   •

After their futile search for more blood evidence, Anne Zorn was still feeling sorry for poor old Letch Boggs. She coaxed him to an Italian restaurant on India Street with an offer to buy lunch. When they got there, they took a sidewalk table and ordered linguine for her and a veal chop with roasted garlic for Letch.

The waiter raised an eyebrow when Letch said, "Bring extra garlic cloves. Maybe six or eight. They don't gotta be cooked."

After the waiter left, Anne said, "Garlic doesn't really have anything to do with potency, Letch."

"Oh, yeah?" he said with his notorious leer. "I could prove you're wrong."

"Glad to see you're back to normal," Anne said. "Which means anything *but*."

"We oughtta go out on a date sometime," Letch said. "And get better acquainted."

"I'm not much for slam dancing," Anne replied. "It wouldn't work out."

Just then her beeper went off and Letch said, "Snapped your garter belt? I have that effect on women."

She looked at the number and said, "The office. I better call."

While she was gone, Letch passed the time by ogling the downtown office girls who lunched on India Street. He wished that skirts were shorter. Anne was wearing a nice white blazer that didn't hide her bustline, but her blue skirt wasn't short enough. Legs like hers should be flaunted, Letch thought.

When Anne came back, she had a dazed look. She sat down and said, "You *aren't* gonna believe this!"

"They *got* him!" Letch said. "They got Oliver Mantleberry!"

"No, Oliver Mantleberry got Blaze Duvall! And dumped her in Mission Bay!"

"*What?*"

Letch Boggs yelled it loud enough to stampede the pigeons. The cops canceled their lunch order and sped downtown.

•   •   •

The team was assembled in the cubicle by the time Anne and Letch arrived. Everybody said hello to Letch, already having accepted his involvement, and Anne asked, "What happened?"

Sal Maldonado replied, "So far, all we know is there were

ligature marks on her neck and maybe a crushed trachea. And you can bet there's no water in the lungs. No ID on her. Fully clothed."

"Did you ID her from prints?" Letch asked.

"Yeah," the detective said, "but we pretty well knew who she was."

"How'd you find out?" Anne asked.

"Lucky break. One of the water cops had seen her around the Shelter Island bars. Called us saying he found a floater in Mission Bay by the name of Blaze. And I go, bingo!"

"Good thing she had that one arrest for prostitution or there wouldn't be prints on file," the sergeant said.

"Good thing we have Letch," Anne reminded her boss. "We wouldn't've put *any* of it together if Letch hadn't told us about Blaze's connection to Dawn Coyote."

The sergeant said to Letch, "Oliver Mantleberry's obviously still in business. We may need more of your help before we're through. I'll clear it with your boss."

"This is curiouser and curiouser," Anne said. "Why would a City Heights pimp dump a body clear down in Mission Bay?"

"Why would anybody?" Sal Maldonado said. "To get rid of it. To feed it to the fish."

"It was a dumb place to drop it," Anne said, "if the guy's got any brains at all."

"He ain't a Phi Beta Kappa," Letch said. "He strangled her and dumped her and now we want his ass a little bit more than we wanted it yesterday."

The lieutenant entered the cubicle and said, "Okay, the skipper says these two homicides are yin and yang, so your team gets this one, too. Randy, you go to Blaze Duvall's apartment. Get ahold of the landlady. Search it for anything that'll link the victim to Dawn Coyote or Oliver Mantleberry. *After* it's dusted for prints. We might find Mantleberry's prints inside, you never know."

"We won't," Anne said. "She didn't know him."

"We'll do it anyway," the lieutenant said. "Zeke, you find out what she drives. We gotta locate her car. Sal, find out when they're posting her and get to the morgue with an evidence tech."

"I'd like to interview the Harbor Unit officer," Anne said. "He might be able to place Blaze with somebody that knows Mister Mantleberry."

"I never heard of hookers hanging around Shelter Island," Letch said. "Farther down on Rosecrans, sure. But I guess it's possible."

"She wasn't a real hooker," Anne said.

"She's real dead," Letch said. "Lemme go with you, Annie. If there's any hookers working around Shelter Island, I'll spot 'em."

•   •   •

By the time Ambrose got home from his frightening experience at Blaze Duvall's apartment building, the sailboat race was on ESPN. In order to keep from going utterly mad, he forced himself to turn on the TV and watch.

Ambrose Lutterworth needed all 100 billion neurons to even concentrate enough to learn that *AUS-31* had got a terrific wind lift on the first leg and had actually led into the wind on the first mark. But then as *AUS-31* rounded the leeward mark, their gennaker wasn't retrieved fast enough and the sail fell into the water, wrapping around the keel.

As *AUS-31*'s skipper ordered his crew to cut away a sail that cost $35,000, *Black Magic* cruised to victory and the Louis Vuitton Cup. Ninety-six days after their initial race, the Kiwis were the first to qualify for the America's Cup regatta next month.

So that's it, Ambrose thought. They even have *luck* when they need it. How is Dennis Conner going to defeat that? How could any defender defeat that? Black-magic luck.

Ambrose called his office, half expecting to receive a message to phone the San Diego Police Department. But there were just three calls from potential clients who'd received his flyer and wanted a preliminary home appraisal. Ambrose didn't bother jotting down their numbers.

He took a bath, swallowed four aspirin with orange juice, and went to bed. He didn't bother to put on pajamas. He slept naked and dreamed terrifying dreams.

CHAPTER 13

FORTNEY HAD A PRETTY GOOD IDEA WHAT IT WAS ABOUT WHEN THEY received the radio call to go to the office. After they docked their boat, they found their sergeant waiting by his car. He said to them, "A homicide dickette's in there waiting for you guys. And there's a vice cop with her. Name of Boggs."

"Letch Boggs," Fortney said. "I can smell him from here."

When Fortney and Leeds entered their office, the woman stood up, saying, "I'm Anne Zorn. I think one of you knows Letch?"

"Worked together for a while," Fortney said, shaking hands with the vice cop. "How's it going, Letch?"

"I miss those good old days, Mick," Letch said. "Kick a door, bust a whore."

"I'm Leeds," the young cop said, shaking hands with the two detectives.

Everybody sat down and Anne opened a notebook. Fortney liked the way she looked in that blazer. She had a great shape for a woman her age. He figured she was a couple years his senior.

Anne thought Leeds was a stud muffin, especially in those cute khaki shorts and sneakers. She thought Fortney looked better when he took off his baseball cap. His curly hair was attractive even if it was a washed-out gray. He had a good chin and a nice suntan. She figured he was a few years older than she was, but that was no excuse for his spare tire. His butt was okay, though.

"Tell us what you know about Blaze Duvall," she said.

Leeds said, "We saw her one night, oh, a couple weeks ago at a joint on Shelter Island. Then we saw her last Saturday night at the same place. It's where the America's Cup sailors hang out."

"And I saw her last night," Fortney said, "at the same place."

"You did?" Leeds said to Fortney. "You never said."

"I'm saying it now."

"That's why you got such a hangover," Leeds said.

"Wait a minute," Anne said. "Let's start from the start."

Fortney began, and Anne wrote down the dates, times, and locations of their saloon sightings of Blaze Duvall. Then she started asking specific questions.

"That first time," she said, "on Thursday. Who was she with?"

"Sailors," Leeds said. "Always America's Cup sailors. Mostly New Zealanders and a few Aussies."

"Anybody else?"

"A boatyard rat," Fortney said. "I don't know his name, but she drank with him every time."

"What's he look like?" Anne asked.

"A maggot," Fortney said. "I'll show him to you. I can meet you over there after I get off work and you can question him. I'd say he's gotta be a suspect. And there's this really big Kiwi named Miles. He could strangle somebody, no problem."

"Both times I saw her she was all over the big guy," Leeds said.

Drily, from Letch: "Weren't you guys informed that she was killed by a pimp named Oliver Mantleberry?"

"That's what Maldonado told me on the phone," Fortney said, "but it's a little hard to believe."

"Why do you say that?" Anne asked him.

"Why would a pimp like him bring her all the way down here

to Mission Bay and put her in the water? And whoever did it didn't even pick a good spot. The south bridge woulda been safer and better for body dumping."

Anne gave a "See there?" smile to Letch.

Letch shot her a look that said, "Everybody's a detective."

"Whether they're suspects or witnesses, we gotta talk to the big guy and the boatyard guy," Anne said.

"How do you know he's a boatyard guy?" Letch wanted to know. "He tell you where he works?"

"When you're around the water you get to know," Fortney said. "He looks like a boatyard worker to me. Anyway, he was there again last night and I talked to him."

Leeds looked hurt, saying to Fortney, "You never tell me nothing. Michael Jackson has more meaningful conversations with Bubbles the chimp."

"What'd you talk to him about?" Anne asked.

"About Blaze Duvall. Of course, I didn't know her last name then."

"Why'd you talk about her?"

"You ever seen her?"

"Once," Anne said.

"Then you know," Fortney said.

"I should've figured," Anne said. "So what did the guy have to say?"

"Claimed he knew her real well. Sort of hinted they were real tight, the lying dirtbag."

"You don't believe it?"

"When you see him you won't believe it either," Fortney said.

"My partner had a thing for her," Leeds explained to Anne. "But she was a freak-show fan. She liked big ugly Kiwis and smelly little wharf rats. Fortney can't handle it."

When Leeds said "smelly," he glanced at Letch Boggs. What Fortney had told him about the guy was true.

"So now I get it," Letch said. "Mick here has himself a crush on a murdered masseuse and figures he knows who killed her. I saw this once before in an old black-and-white movie called *Laura*. Well, sorry, folks, but a pimp named Oliver Mantleberry killed her. Just like he killed another hooker named Dawn Coyote."

"Not just like," Anne reminded him.

"So he didn't have his knife with him last night," Letch said. "He probably tossed it in the bay the night before."

"Don't get me wrong, Letch," Fortney said. "I'm not trying to tell her about homicides. And I'm not trying to tell you about hookers. What do I know? I just drive a boat."

"You're entitled to an opinion," Anne said.

"All I can say is, a streetwise pimp isn't gonna drop a body in a little channel under the north Ingraham Street bridge, seems to me."

"Who *would* drop a body there?" Anne Zorn wanted to know. "Got an opinion on that?"

Fortney said, "Someone not streetwise. A geek, not some brother that's already offed another babe before doing this one."

"Where do I find the New Zealand sailors?" Anne asked. "I don't know diddly about America's Cup sailboat racing."

"Nobody does," Leeds said. "The rules're harder to follow than a Mafia hit man."

"So where's New Zealand's headquarters?"

"Shelter Island," Fortney said, "but it's best to catch them at their unofficial headquarters. They'll be there for sure tonight because today they just sunk the Aussies and won the Louis Vuitton Cup. That means they get to challenge for the big one."

"I don't understand all that sailing crap," Letch said.

"Nobody does," Leeds said. "It's about as exciting as a cricket match between Argentina and Western Samoa."

Fortney said, "It means they'll be powering down the brews tonight. Meet me at seven o'clock and I guarantee we'll find you the big Kiwi and the little germ. You tell me if you can understand her taste in men."

"Got anything better to do tonight, Letch?" Anne Zorn asked the skeptical vice cop.

"This is a waste," Letch said. "Oliver Mantleberry could be in Hong Kong by now, getting measured for a cashmere sport coat."

•   •   •

By the time Ambrose woke up it was late afternoon. For a moment, a wonderful moment, he thought it had all been a dream. The moment didn't last.

He dragged himself out of bed and stumbled to the shower. He didn't want to look at his face in the mirror, but he had to shave. After showering he tried it, discovering that it was possible to shave without looking at one's own eyes. He held the little mustache trimmer in both hands, almost growing accustomed to the tremor. He was beginning to feel as if he'd never had steady hands.

There was a new, very startling change: He was numb. It wasn't the kind of numbness that one might associate with excessive drinking or drug use. He was truly numb. He felt as though his heart had stopped pumping. He actually put his hand there to reassure himself. And he wasn't frightened anymore, wasn't particularly sad or even depressed. He was just numb.

When he got up the courage to look at his eyes, he saw that they'd sunk. His cheekbones jutted under the lusterless eyes of a very old man.

Ambrose Lutterworth dressed by rote. He knew what to do. He'd been doing it properly all his life. But he took no pride, no satisfaction when he chose the correct necktie, a university stripe: navy and silver white. It'd look fine with a blue blazer, but any fool would know that. And he chose a blue pinpoint shirt with a straight collar. What could be simpler? Then gray slacks and oxblood loafers.

He wondered how long one could live in this numbed state. Would his taste buds be numb? Could he work? Could he do his job as a Point Loma realtor when everything about him was absolutely numb?

By the time he arrived at his office, there was only one other agent there, Helen Keys. He'd known Helen for ten years, when she'd started there right after her divorce. She'd had to begin working again, trying to earn a living along with an army of part-time local realtors in the same situation.

He'd even dated her a few times last year. She'd been a pleasant dinner companion and she was attractive, but he'd known at once that there could never be anything sexual between them. Today it seemed strange to think that he'd recently felt the need for sexual experience. He couldn't imagine it now. He couldn't imagine ever again wanting a sexual encounter.

When he thought of Blaze Duvall, he was not overcome with sadness or remorse. This was a great improvement. He was numb.

"Hello, stranger," Helen said to him.

"Hello, Helen," he said, thinking, Why do people call other people stranger when they haven't seen them for a while? Is it to instill guilt that you haven't been attentive enough? Guilt wouldn't work on him anymore. It didn't work on numb people.

"I haven't seen you around lately," she said. "You're okay, aren't you?"

"I'm fine," Ambrose said.

"Well, I guess there really isn't much point in coming around here," she said. "It's been dead."

"Dead," Ambrose said. "Yes. Dead."

"If business doesn't pick up soon, I'm going to have to hunt for a rich husband," Helen said, looking at Ambrose hopefully.

"Shouldn't be hard for you," he said, and he felt himself smile.

"You look a bit tired, Ambrose," Helen said. "Are you sure you're not catching something?"

"Possibly," he said. "There's a virus going around."

"You're probably keeping late hours with the ladies," Helen said coquettishly.

Ambrose knew that Helen had hoped their relationship would develop, but he'd never tried to encourage her. Today he didn't know what to say. He just smiled. He knew he was smiling now. He could feel his face muscles contract.

"You just look tired," she repeated.

"I'm fine," he said.

"Uh-oh," Helen said, when she spotted a pair of middle-aged looky-loos reading the real-estate ads in the window. "I've got floor time today, but I have to get home. My daughter's bringing the grandkids over. Would you be a doll and take care of them if they come in?"

"Sure," Ambrose said, knowing that he was still smiling. "You have a nice day."

Helen grabbed her purse and kissed her fingertips, patting them on his forehead. Then she ran out the back door to the parking lot.

Ambrose sat there and waited for the looky-loos. They opened the door diffidently. The man, who was dressed regatta-casual, popped his head in and said, "Still open?"

"Come in," Ambrose said.

The woman was wearing a new sweatshirt with AMERICA'S CUP '95 emblazoned across the back above a silk-screened racing sloop heeling in the wind.

"Hoping to find out if you have anything in our price range," the man said. "Down from Oregon. Here for the regatta. Fell in love with San Diego. Don't know if we can afford it, though."

"Love to have a condo here," his wife said.

She was an overweight redhead, but not with fiery hair like Blaze Duvall's. Of course, he'd seen Blaze naked and knew she wasn't a true redhead. Still, her beauty salon had always done a wonderful job with her hair. Yes, wonderful.

"Don't know if we came too late in the day for a look-see," the man said.

How curious, Ambrose thought. Their speech was utterly devoid of pronouns, just like that of former President Bush.

He tried it himself: "Love to show you a few condos. Don't know if you'll like them. Won't know till we look."

They didn't catch on. They didn't smile at all. Ambrose wondered if they were numb, too.

The man said, "Don't wanna see anything like the house we

heard about from friends on the spectator boat. Heard a big real-estate developer leased a house for thirty thousand a month just for the America's Cup races. Heard he spent a hundred thousand just to light his paintings."

"Heard they were museum quality," his wife said. "Wonder if you know the place?"

"Saw it after he moved in," Ambrose mimicked. "Had no taste, none at all. Horrible lighting. Made the Monets and Picassos look like a pile of shit."

Suddenly he wasn't numb anymore. He looked at their startled expressions and started to snicker. In a moment he was giggling. Then he was guffawing.

After that he was laughing hysterically. Tears streamed down his face. He had to fold his arms on his desk and bury his face. When he stopped, the looky-loos were gone.

Ambrose Lutterworth was struck with overwhelming sadness. He wasn't numb anymore.

•   •   •

When they finished up late that afternoon, Leeds said to Fortney, "You can handle this one on your own. I go to bars to drink and pick up women, not to look for murder suspects."

"You pissed off at me?"

"I think it's pretty weird you didn't mention you saw that woman last night. I mean, what'd you think I'd do? Suspect *you* killed her or something?"

"I was just shocked, is all," Fortney said. "Since I saw her down there in the water, I've been in a state of shock. I wasn't thinking about last night."

"You wouldn't even tell me where you were last night."

"That was the hangover. I felt miserable. I'm still miserable and my day isn't over yet."

"There's such a thing as being too tight-lipped. It's insulting, is what it is."

"I'm sorry," Fortney said. "You want the truth?"

"Wouldn't hurt."

"I was embarrassed to say I saw her last night. That I went out looking for her."

"You went *looking* for her?"

"Letch got it right without even trying. I *did* kinda have the hots for her. Sorta. But before she was dead, not afterwards like the cop in the movie. I was ashamed to tell you I actually went looking for her. Pretty sick, huh?"

Thinking it over, Leeds said, "Hell, I wish I had a dime for every bimbo I went looking for."

"Sure you don't wanna come tonight?"

"I better run along home," Leeds said. "That way I can get away with pub crawling *tomorrow* night. Anyways, I agree with Letch. That pimp's the one who strangled that babe." Then he added, "What a waste of pussy!"

•   •   •

Letch and Anne had a pretty good head start on Fortney, having consumed an order of potato skins and six oysters on the half shell by the time Fortney drove his Honda Civic into the parking lot. Letch was bummed that they didn't have any garlic cloves, but he was on his third mug of beer, and Anne had drunk two margaritas by the time Fortney walked in.

Letch waved when he saw Fortney looking for them in the growing crowd of Kiwi celebrants.

Anne checked him out: sweatshirt, jeans with the roomy fit, deck shoes, no socks. Predictable.

Fortney shot a peek at her legs before he sat. Her skirt had hiked up, but she caught him gawking and pulled it down.

"Place is filling up already," Fortney said. "I guarantee a full-moon crowd in less than an hour. Howling Kiwis."

"How's the food here?" Anne asked.

Fortney looked at the empty plates and said, "Looks like you found out."

"No, I mean in the dining room. Not pub grub."

"It's okay," Fortney said.

"I'm almost a vegetarian," Anne said. "And I can't find an affordable restaurant in San Diego that serves any veggies except cauliflower and broccoli. If I could ever get a side order of green beans or spinach I'd stand up and cheer."

"I agree," Letch said, belching. "You ever try eating garlic on cauliflower?"

"Far as I'm concerned, cauliflower's the Bob Dole of vegetables," Fortney said.

Letch chugalugged, wiped his mouth on his shoulder, and said, "Mick, remember that little cowboy joint where we used to get the ribs?"

"Yeah," Fortney said. "As charming as an ER. Made you wonder who hosed down all the blood and body parts on Sunday morning. Remember the time the drunken cook pulled a knife on his boss? I jump up and point my piece but he won't drop it. Then Letch sticks his fingers in his own ears. And the guy sees him and throws down the knife and puts his hands up."

"Works every time," Letch said. Then to Anne, "Mick worked Vice with me back in, was it seventy-nine?"

"Seventy-eight," Fortney said. "I was young and impressionable, but not enough to wear Hawaiian shirts and eat garlic."

"That's your first name?" Anne asked. "Mick?"

"Everybody calls me Fortney," he replied.

"Quick Mick!" Letch said with a boozy chuckle.

"Why's he call you Quick Mick?" Anne wanted to know.

Fortney laser-stared Letch, but the vice cop grinned and said, "One night we had young Mick working the massage joints. So he goes into this Korean massage parlor—"

"Is this necessary?" Fortney glared.

Anne had enough tequila in her to say, "I wanna hear!"

"So he goes in posing as a customer," Letch continued. "And he has this pocket wire. And we're listening out in the van. And Mick takes off his clothes and hangs them on a hook—"

"This is *not* necessary," Fortney said.

"—and the pocket wire's working real good for once," Letch said. "And we hear this little gook come in and say, 'Ooooooh, you wanneee rub?' And Mick here, he says, 'Sure.' And she says, 'Ooooooooooh, you wannee numbah *one* rub?' And Mick here says—"

"Somebody shoulda shot you a long time ago," Fortney said. "Any halfway compassionate juror would vote to acquit."

"Go on, Letch!" Anne cried, wearing a salt mustache from the margarita.

"And they agree on twenty bucks and she starts the massage. And we hear our boy here go, 'Ow wow wow!' And she says, 'You like?' And he says, 'Ow wow wow!' "

Fortney yelled to the cocktail waitress, "A double scotch! And bring my *pals* another round."

"Then what, Letch?" Anne asked eagerly.

"Then Mick here goes *'Wow! Wow! Wow!'* And the gook masseuse goes, 'Ooooooh, you quick! You velly quiiiiick!' Mick comes out hoping the pocket wire don't work. But we all grab the corners of our eyes and draw them up and say, 'Oooooooh! You quiiiiiick. You quick, Mick!' "

Letch collapsed onto the table and Anne had to put her hand over her mouth to suppress her own giggles. Fortney looked around the barroom hoping to spot the big Kiwi or the boatyard termite—anything to save him from further misery.

When they quieted down, Letch said to Fortney, "You ain't the only one with a handle. Know what they call *her*? Anne of a Thousand Names. She gets married every other payday."

Fortney grinned and said, "Tell me about it."

But Anne turned serious and said, "I gotta go to the john. Save my chair. Or *don't*."

While she was gone, Fortney bought a round for three young marines at a nearby table. They all had identifying whitewall haircuts and one wore a T-shirt that said: JOIN THE MARINES, SEE THE WORLD, MEET INTERESTING PEOPLE AND THEN KILL THEM.

Fortney said to Letch, "When I was in the corps our T-shirts used to say 'Kill a Commie for Mommy.' "

"Now we sell the commies Pepsi and multicolored condoms," Letch said. "It's a crazy world."

The waitress brought another round and Letch said to her, "Bring me a double scotch next time, honey. And you might put some garlic powder in it. What kind a kitchen don't have garlic cloves, I'd like to know."

The cocktail waitress replied, "Garlic makes gas. Ginseng root makes virility."

Shaken by the waitress's quick read, Letch said to Fortney, "You down to sleeping with anatomically correct inflatable bimbos these days?"

"There's a Warren Beatty inside me dying to get out," Fortney said. "But I'm still recovering financially from number-two divorce."

"Yeah, I know how it is," Letch said. "I was married to this flight stew for a while. Had a few too many air miles on her, but, oh, could she stir your beverage."

Anne returned then and was half impressed that Fortney sort of raised up in his chair. But then he looked at Letch to see if he was being a pussy. Just like every cop she'd dated or married—scared that acting like a gentleman was effeminate.

"I won't call you Anne of a Thousand Names," Fortney said, "if you don't call me Quick Mick."

"I won't call you anything," Anne said. "We're here to interview witnesses."

Well, fuck her! Fortney thought. She can dish it out, but she can't take it. No wonder everybody divorces her.

Letch said, "I'm glad my job don't take me around Mission Bay. I'd OD on all the Speedo and Sideout T-shirts with matching trunks. And all the Guess sunglasses. Don't you get sick of it, Mick? Everybody posing?"

"You wouldn't object to all the spandex bra-tops and little bike shorts," Anne noted. "And where do you get off being a fashion cop? That shirt you're wearing belongs at a cockfight. Anyone wearing a shirt like that would eat eels."

"Okay, lighten up. I'm sorry. I shouldn't a told him your monicker. But you shouldn't get a divorce every time somebody asks you to wash windows."

"Why's everybody so pissy?" Fortney asked. "We all passing eggs or what?"

When the Kiwi sailors came in, the saloon exploded. Everyone began cheering, whistling, clapping. There were fifteen of them, several with women companions, and the bar crowd patted each one on the back and shook hands all around. Steinlagers started appearing on the bar as fast as three bartenders could draw them. Sailing-sillies couldn't buy drinks fast enough for the conquering Kiwis.

But the one Fortney wanted wasn't among them. He said to Anne, "Damn! I was sure he'd be here. Where the hell is he?"

"Maybe I just should've contacted him more formally and gone to their headquarters like I wanted to," she said.

"I don't understand it," Fortney said. "He's always been . . ." Then he pointed to the doorway, where, filling it, was the largest human being in the room.

Miles held his hands up over his head, palms clasped, as soon as he recognized acquaintances at the bar, then cruised straight into a group of Kiwi fans who were toasting their heroes with mugs in both hands.

"Which one of us is gonna badge him?" Letch asked.

"I will," Anne said. "I'm gonna take him outside."

"One of us should go with you," Fortney said.

"No, you stay here and watch for the boatyard guy," Anne said. "I think it'll be better if I break the news alone."

Fortney said, "Of course, you've considered that you might not be breaking any *news*?"

"I've considered it," Anne said. "Letch, you stay at the front

window and watch us. If I scratch behind my neck, you and Fortney come running with your nines ready."

"How many rounds we got altogether?" Letch asked. "I think
we might need 'em all."

Letch got up and walked to the window by the entrance,
where he could survey the street in front of the restaurant. Fortney
stayed at the table, sipping his scotch. Anne jostled her way through
the crowd until she got behind the giant Kiwi.

She tapped him on the shoulder and said, "Excuse me? Could
I talk to you privately for a minute?"

Immediately, a half-dozen sailors started razzing Miles, who
looked at Anne with approval. "Sorry, mates," he said, "my public
is calling me."

Anne walked toward the entrance with Miles behind her, but
he touched the sleeve of her blazer and said, "What is it, love? Do
we know each other?"

Anne reached into her purse, removed her leather badge
holder, and said, "I'm Detective Zorn, San Diego Police Department. I need to talk to you for a few minutes."

The big man leaned over to examine the badge, then looked
her in the eyes, saying, "I should've paid that traffic ticket they left
on my car. I'm sorry. I can still pay for it, can't I?"

Anne could see that he wasn't joking. She said, "I'm not here
about a traffic ticket. Follow me outside where it's quiet. I've got a
few questions and then you can rejoin your friends."

The big man followed her obediently down the stairs and out
the door, where slow-moving cars were passing back and forth in
the America's Cup commercial basin, stopping to gawk at the compound of Team New Zealand.

Through the window Letch watched Anne say something to
the big man. Then he saw the Kiwi raise both hands to the top of
his buzz-cut, like it was a white beanie that might blow away.

Letch could see the guy's mouth going. He was in distress, for
sure.

Anne let Miles rave for a while, then she said, "How well did you know Blaze?"

"This is bloody unbelievable!" Miles cried. "I can't conceive of such a thing. Murdered? Good God!"

"It's true, believe me," Anne said. "First of all, what's your full name?"

"I just cannot *conceive* of this!" he repeated, dropping his hands to his sides.

Anne took a look at those hands and at his face and neck. There were no scratch marks. No contusions. Nothing.

"Your last name? Miles what?"

"Hargrave," he said. "Miles Robert Hargrave. But are you sure it was Blaze? The same Blaze who's been coming here lately?"

"How well did you know her?" Anne asked.

"Hardly at all!" he said. "I can't believe it. Dead. We've had drinks together two or three times, but she drank with many of the lads. You can ask them."

"I may do that," Anne said. "But you were with her last night."

"So were my mates!" Miles said. "They're upstairs, most of them. You can go ask them."

"Yes," Anne said. "But tell me, what happened last night? You drank together, then what? Did you leave with her?"

"No!" he roared. "Absolutely not! Everyone can tell you I stayed and closed the bleedin' bar!"

"Okay, calm down," Anne said. "I know you're upset."

"Upset? Here I am, a foreigner, not knowing my rights, and I'm being accused of murder!"

"Nobody's accusing you of anything. I'm just trying to discover what happened to Blaze Duvall from the time you had your last drink with her until she ended up in Mission Bay."

"Mission Bay?" he said. "When you said she was found in the bay, I thought you meant here. In the big bay."

"Do you know Mission Bay?"

"A bit. The other New Zealand syndicate had their compound there. And the French, and the Spanish, and the Aussies, for that matter."

"Did you ever see her outside of this bar?"

"Never!" he said. "I swear."

"Why did you think she'd been dumped in the big bay?"

"Well, I probably shouldn't say this—"

"Say it."

"There was a cock-up last night. You see, I was hoping to . . . you know, hoping to *be* with Blaze later. But this little bloke came in. His name's Simon Cooke. Works for the boatyard we lease our space from. He started a terrible row and had to be ejected. I was one of the ones who did the ejecting."

"What's that got to do with Blaze?"

"He was raving something or other at Blaze. They were obviously well acquainted. I'd seen them drinking together. He was jealous, that was plain to see."

"How do you know his name?"

"He's the one that taught me how to operate the travel-lift."

"What's that?"

"It's a kind of crane that we use to lift our boat in and out of the water. In fact, one of our team members married Simon Cooke's sister. A nice girl, but I fear for her children with a brother like that."

"Was Simon Cooke mad at Blaze?"

"He wasn't pleased, I can tell you. And he was absolutely pissed."

"By pissed you don't mean angry?"

"No. By pissed I mean he was drunk. Very drunk. And very belligerent."

"What happened after you tossed him out of the bar?"

Miles looked up at the entrance, then lowered his voice, saying, "That's just it! This morning when I asked Gordon—that's Simon's brother-in-law—what he did with Simon last night,

Gordon said that he refused to be driven home. He went off walking after Gordon took away his car keys."

"So he was on foot in the vicinity?"

"Yes! And Blaze left just after that. Simon had knocked a pint of beer on her when he started the row and she said she had to go home to change."

"I guess I'd better have a chat with Simon Cooke," Anne said.

"Absolutely!" the big Kiwi said. "If you ask me, he's capable of anything. He seemed insanely jealous about Blaze sitting and drinking with me."

Fortney waited impatiently until Letch rejoined him at the table. "Anything wrong?" he asked the vice cop.

"No, Anne's on her way back up."

"Where's the big guy?"

"Took off walking back toward the Kiwi headquarters."

When Anne rejoined them, she picked up her margarita glass, grimaced, and said, "Letch, order me a scotch, will you?"

"So what happened?" Fortney asked.

"I ruined his evening," Anne said. "He wanted to go home."

"And?"

"Unless he's a very good liar, I think he had a drink with Blaze last night and never saw her again."

Fortney was bursting. He said, "Damn it, was she a girlfriend of his or what?"

Anne looked at Fortney and said, "Your romantic crush has not been sullied. He said he never did more than drink with her. In fact, you probably saw it every time it happened."

Fortney was glad even though he knew the two detectives would probably laugh at him behind his back. "So what about the little puke? Find out anything about him?"

"A lot," Anne said. "His name's Simon Cooke and he's definitely worth talking to."

"All you'll get is the S.O.D. story," Letch Boggs said. "*Some Other Dude* did it. We can question half the town, but it's gotta come down to Oliver Mantleberry. You may as well face it, Annie.

You told Blaze Duvall you'd protect her from that pimp and you couldn't do it. Just like I told Dawn Coyote and couldn't do it. All this Cup crap ain't going nowhere. Well, I'm here to say that all the denial is gonna stop—the minute I get face-to-face with Oliver Mantleberry."

CHAPTER 14

NORMAL. HE WAS DETERMINED TO BEHAVE IN A NORMAL MANNER, SO HE went to the yacht club for dinner.

Business that evening was good. Team New Zealand's victory had brought out lots of people, all of whom were stunned by the ease with which the Kiwis had won the challenger trials. Ambrose had not consumed solid food for a day and a half and still wasn't hungry. He knew he had to eat, but first he needed a drink.

Several people in the barroom greeted him and he pretended to be interested in what they had to say. One group was discussing how the Kiwis were demolishing the competition with "only" a budget of $20 million.

Someone else said, "We've seemed to lose sight that twenty million dollars is a lot of money for a boat race."

Nobody paid attention. They were more interested in whether or not Dennis Conner could beat *Young America* and *Mighty Mary* and end up as the America's Cup defender.

The Citizen Cup defender trials still were not decided, mired in America's Cup politics and confusion. Everyone was complaining about how the three defending syndicates had cozied up to one another and agreed on a "compromise" at a time when Dennis Conner's boat, *Stars and Stripes,* was on the brink of elimination.

The compromise had allowed all three teams to compete in three-way finals, thus pleasing all their multimillion-dollar sponsors. This compromise allowed *Young America* two bonus wins it hadn't earned. *Mighty Mary* was awarded one bonus win it hadn't earned. And Dennis Conner, who would have been eliminated, was still alive.

Because nobody in the general public could understand any of it, the defense committee had done its job said the press sardonically, adding that the rational segment of the sailing world believed that any possible drama had degenerated into farce and sponsor stroking.

The more vocal yacht club members openly hoped that the Kiwis would win and take the Cup someplace where greed and ego and politics might not corrupt it. That kind of mutinous and idiotic talk was upsetting to Ambrose Lutterworth and added to his headache. Where could the Cup go and not find corruption?

Finally somebody spoke up loudly, saying that Bill Koch of *Mighty Mary* and Dennis Conner of *Stars and Stripes* were about as welcome in the club as secondhand smoke, and that they cared about sailing the way Captain Kidd and Blackbeard had cared about sailing.

The gripes got to Ambrose, who'd had enough about how his club had mishandled America's Cup XXIX. He entered the dining room and asked for a table in the far corner away from the hubbub. He ordered the harpoon special, chunks of bass and shrimp and scallops on a skewer, and was surprised to discover that food tasted pretty much as it always had. But he could only eat half of it.

As he was finishing his coffee, he heard a member at the next table say to his guests: "Did you hear that a woman was fished out of Mission Bay this morning?"

"Probably swallowed some of the water and died instantly," said a guest.

The member laughed. "Only thing that can survive in our polluted water is plankton and Dennis Conner. You can't kill either one, even with arsenic. They just survive."

Ambrose left his table without signing the check, drove straight home, pulled into his garage, and sat in the car for a few minutes. Then he got out and, for the first time since the horror had begun, opened the trunk of the Cadillac.

Ambrose hauled out the concrete block and put it on the floor of the garage. The satin sash was knotted so tightly that he couldn't untie it. Using pruning shears, he snipped it free and then just continued snipping, hacking the sash into a dozen pieces, sobbing as he thought of the shamrock-green eyes of Blaze Duvall.

Back in his house, he realized that he had stopped feeling suicidal and tried to focus on what he'd heard at the dinner table. Maybe Dennis Conner would win the defender trials after all. And if he did so, maybe he'd find a way to beat the Kiwis next month and keep the Cup in San Diego. After all, he was like plankton. You couldn't kill him with arsenic.

•   •   •

Tamara Taylor was trying to get the ironing done while the baby was yelling his head off. The two older ones were fighting over the TV and she hadn't even started supper and wouldn't you know it? Somebody was at the door, yelling, "Tamara! Tamara! You there, girl?"

It was her neighbor, Velma. Tamara put the iron on the kitchen counter and went to the door, using a dishtowel to wipe the sweat from her face.

"Come in, Velma," Tamara said. "Jist step over these kids. They ain't gonna stop fussin' nohow."

"You got a phone call."

"A phone call? At *your* house?"

"Yeah, it's Oliver. He said he gotta talk to you, but not on your phone. You better come over and talk to him."

"I don't never wanna talk to that man again!" Tamara said.

"You better talk to him," Velma said. "I'll stay with the kids."

Tamara heaved a big sigh and shook her head, then trudged next door to a little clapboard house very much like hers. The only

difference was that Velma's kids were older and had gone off somewhere. It was nice and quiet.

She picked up the phone.

"It's me," Oliver Mantleberry said.

"I know it's you," Tamara said. "Whadda you want?"

"Whadda I want? Gud-damn, woman! I'm your husband and
the father a your children and you ask me whadda I want?"

"I ain't never noticed no marriage license," Tamara reminded
him.

"One thing I want is, I wanna know if what I heard was true."

"What's that?"

"I heard that there was some white men in suits standing in
the front yard on Easter Sunday."

"That's right."

"Who were they?"

"They wasn't Jehovah's Witnesses."

"That's what I thought."

"And I don't appreciate you bringin' your po-lice business to
my house on Easter Sunday."

"I didn't bring 'em!"

"They say diff'rent."

"What did they want?"

"I think you know."

"Was it about Dawn?"

"Yeah. And it was in the papers and TV, too. Somebody stuck
her. They say it was you."

"That's a damn lie!"

"It ain't nothin' to me one way or the other who sticks some
white-trash whore. But nobody is bringin' the law to my home on
Easter Sunday, you hear me?"

"I need for you to bring me some things. I can't come home
till this blows over."

"Bring you what?"

"I need some clothes. And I need some money."

"Where am I gonna get money?"

"Harold. Go see Harold. He owes me five hundred."

"I'm all through collectin' your money," Tamara Taylor said. "I'm through with pimps, period. I ain't bringin' nothin'. You got your own self in this, you get your own self out."

"You do what I say, woman!"

"Fuck you."

"You could end up like Dawn Coyote, you bitch!"

"Yeah? I wonder how you gonna sneak up on me, past the two dogs I'm gonna git tomorrow. *And* the thirty-eight-caliber pistol that Velma said I can have anytime I want it. *And* the new locks on my doors that I already got."

He was silent for a moment, then said, "Listen to me. When this blows over, you're gonna need me to help with the kids. I'm gonna make me big money and you'll get some. Now you do what I tell you, okay?"

"No, *you* listen," Tamara said. "If I was you, I'd get my black ass outta town right now. Because they got a piece a very incriminatin' evidence against you."

"I knew it!" he said. "That bitch! Dawn's friend, name a Blaze Duvall. She told 'em I did it, didn't she?"

"I don't know nothin' about no Blaze," Tamara said. "They didn't discuss their case with me. But I saw them find a piece a evidence that you was stupid enough to leave behind."

"Yeah? What's that?"

"A washrag."

"Washrag? What washrag?"

"The one you used when you came home that mornin'. The one you dropped in the bathtub and the cops found. *That's* what washrag."

She could almost hear him thinking over the phone. Very quiet. Trying to remember. Then, "What *about* the washrag?"

"It had blood on it. Did you cut yourself shavin'?"

"No."

"Was it your blood?"

"I don't know 'bout no blood."

"You better pray it was your blood. Because if it wasn't your blood, it was the blood a that white whore."

"They can't prove that!"

"That's what you think. You ever hear about D-N-A?"

"Woman, what the fuck you talkin' about?"

"If you ever did somethin' besides wreck your brain with rock cocaine, you might unnerstand. If you ever did somethin' educational like watch TV, you might know that you in big trouble because a that washrag."

"All I got to worry about is that *bitch*," Oliver Mantleberry said.

"Yeah?" Tamara replied. "Well, I got news for *you*. That white whore's whole life is wrote on that washrag. Which you would know about if you watched the O.J. trial instead a causin' pain with rock cocaine. And chasin' bitches all over the boulevard. Well, I on'y got one more thing to say to you: Phone up Johnnie Cochran quick as you can."

"You don't bring me my clothes, I'm comin' to get 'em!" a frustrated Oliver Mantleberry shouted.

"You try it and you won't be needin' those pointy lizardskin shoes," Tamara Taylor informed him. "They won't fit good over top a the tags you're gonna be wearin' on your motherfuckin' toes!"

•   •   •

"Well, shit, I might as well get drunk," Letch Boggs said. "Just so this evening ain't a total waste."

"You *are* drunk," Anne Zorn informed him, although she didn't look any too sober herself.

Fortney, still not completely recovered from his hangover, was the soberest, and he kept his eyes riveted on the door when he wasn't trying to sneak a peek at Anne Zorn's legs.

"I still don't know why a cop would wanna be a boat driver," Letch said to Fortney. "Look at all these blond-haired boat nuts. Nothing about them's real, for chrissake. I never seen so much bleach outside a Chinese laundry."

"Working by the sea grows on you," Fortney said. "Sitting on the patrol boat and looking at the sunset, thinking how the sun changes from egg white to egg yolk to *fire*."

Anne studied Fortney then. The flesh around his eyes was smooth and tan, but when he smiled it shattered into white crinkles. She liked that. "You enjoy sunsets?"

"Yeah, I like to look for the green flash," he said.

"I heard about the green flash all my life," Letch said. "There ain't no green flash."

"I've seen it," Fortney said. "Right when the sun sinks in the ocean. If it's clear and the atmospheric conditions are right, the flash is greener than . . ."

Anne didn't know he was thinking of Blaze Duvall's eyes. She asked, "Greener than what?"

"Just green," he said.

"You aren't much of a talker, are you?" she observed.

"My partner says I got lalophobia," he said. "That's fear of talking."

"I've got gamophobia," Anne said. "That's fear of marriage. I should've gotten it a lot sooner. My marriages had the shelf life of buttermilk."

"You got kids?" he asked.

"One. She's a grown-up schoolteacher. You?"

"None. Lucky, considering the women I was married to."

"How about me?" Letch asked, belching. "Am I still in this conversation? I got a kid if anyone wants to know."

"You do?" Anne was genuinely surprised.

"Yeah. He's thirty years old. My first wife took him away when she ran off with the electrician that shortcircuited our marriage."

"You ever see him?" Anne asked.

"Naw," Letch said. "He lives in Oregon."

"How about your second wife?" Anne asked. "Did she boogie, too?"

"Yeah," Letch said. "She was a stable Mabel. I woulda stayed with that one till her pubic hair turned gray."

Anne was starting to feel sorry for Letch because he had the guilts about Dawn Coyote when a lot of other cops would have just said it was N.H.I. Now there was a kid he never saw and a woman he missed. He was starting to emerge as a human being in her eyes! She wondered if she was drunk or what?

Then Letch reverted to type by saying to Fortney, "You'll forget Blaze in no time. Once I fell for an outcall masseuse who was my snitch. I got so hung up on her I paid the cleaning deposit for an apartment she rented. Then I found out she did *all* kinds a rubs with honey, mayonnaise, you name it. I lost my two-hundred-dollar cleaning deposit because a that babe. And if you ain't careful, that kind'll get you on drugs, too, and a cop can't study for a random urine test."

"What happened to her?" Anne asked.

"She got all tweaked out one night and went along on a stick-up of a 7-Eleven with another tweak monster. They both got shot and killed. Her pal had a squirt gun and it wasn't even loaded."

"Lotta sadness in your life, Letch," Fortney said.

"Actually, she woulda cost me my career," Letch said. "The sergeant caught us in the back of the surveillance van one night. I tried to tell him she's only giving me information, except that my Velcro ankle holster's stuck in her hair. She had real big hair. Not to mention a nice ass and a savings account. All I ever wanted from a mate was someone to wax my carrot better than I can."

"You're just a sentimental sap, that's all," Anne said. "We oughtta go home before we all start getting weepy."

"I wanna catch my favorite talk show," said Letch. "I hear they're having a guest tonight who *hasn't* had an affair with a U.S. senator."

"Not yet," Fortney said. "We're not going home yet."

"Why not?" Anne asked.

"Because that little boatyard germ just walked in the door."

Simon Cooke was carrying half a load already, after having searched for Blaze in the other joints before ending up there. He didn't want to come there at all because this was the Kiwis' very favorite, and he didn't want any more contact with those assholes, especially asshole number one, his brother-in-law, and asshole number two, that big turd, Miles. But he hadn't found her anywhere else, so there he was.

Simon hoped he could make it up to Blaze about last night. After all, it wasn't his fault they picked a fight with him. He'd been ready and willing to do his job today and wreck the damn boat. Christ, he needed the money bad enough, didn't he?

He'd tell Blaze that they could still do the job during the finals, now that the Kiwis had clinched the challenger trials. Of course he knew his brother-in-law wouldn't so much as let him touch the barbed wire on their chain-link fence, but maybe he could convince Blaze that he could make it up with the Kiwi cocksuckers.

Anyway, he was down to his last five bucks and Blaze always bought him as many drinks as he could hold. Who knows? Maybe tonight was the night he'd take her home and show her what a little man could do, now that she had no more reason to be stringing along that big pile of Kiwi crap. He'd get her freckles sizzling, all right!

He didn't spot her in the barroom, but there were his brother-in-law's teammates swilling down the suds and bragging their asses off, the pricks.

And he didn't notice the middle-aged, funny-looking guy in a scary Hawaiian shirt until the guy said, "Simon Cooke? Someone wants to buy you a drink."

Simon looked over at the table the guy was pointing at and recognized the dickhead that had dumped him on his ass the other night, the one he'd thought was a sissy. He was sitting with a babe who was dressed up more businesslike than any of the sailing types.

"What's this all about?" Simon's nose twitched at a whiff of Letch's breath.

"That woman wants to meet you," Letch said. "And she's buying drinks."

Simon shot Letch a suspicious glance, but he was too curious and thirsty not to accept the invitation. At the table he said to Fortney, "Don't think I can't remember you. If I hadn't been drunk, you wouldn'ta got away with that cheap shot."

"Sorry, pal," Fortney said.

"Sit down, Mister Cooke," Anne Zorn said, showing him her badge. "I'm Detective Zorn. He's Detective Boggs. And this is Officer Fortney."

Simon Cooke gawked in disbelief, but Letch took his elbow and said, "Have a seat." Sounding like a cop, all right.

Anne said, "Did you hear about a girl who was found this morning floating in Mission Bay?"

"No."

"The news accounts identified her as Mary Ellen Singleton."

"So? What's that got to do with me?"

"I'm gonna tell you," Anne said. "Would you like a drink?"

"Yeah. He promised me a drink," Simon said, nodding at Letch.

"What'll it be?"

"Gin and tonic. Double."

"I'll get it," Fortney said. "We'd have to wait half an hour for a waitress."

"What time did you go to bed last night?" Anne asked.

"Me?"

Letch rolled his eyes and said, *"You."*

"Pretty late. Somebody took my car keys and I had to walk."

"Anybody walk with you?" Anne asked.

"No."

"Where do you live?"

"Ocean Beach."

"Pretty long walk."

"Yeah, well, I needed the air. I had a lot to drink."

"Didn't anybody offer you a ride?"

"No."

"How about Blaze?"

Then Simon put on his crafty face and said, "Oh, this has to do with Blaze? Now I see why that other guy . . . What's his name?"

"Officer Fortney."

"Yeah, he was pumping me about her last night. Now I dig. You're investigating her, right? Well, I don't know nothing about what she's up to. Whatever she's up to, I don't wanna know."

"Who said she was up to something?" Anne asked.

He licked his lips nervously. "That other cop was red-dogging me, wasn't he? Whatever she's up to got *nothing* to do with me, that's all I can say."

Anne looked at Letch, who said, "This conversation is like Roseanne in a chiffon teddy. It don't quite fit together."

"He sure seems nervous," Anne Zorn said to Letch for effect. "Maybe we should advise him of his rights?"

And just like that Simon Cooke's sullenness vanished. He looked like he might run, and he blurted out, "Okay, she asked me to drop the boat, but I said no! No way I wanted anything to do with sabotage!"

Fortney arrived just then with a round of drinks, and Letch stood up, whispering to him, "Annie's caught herself a secret agent. Tell him not to talk till I get back from the head. I just *love* spy thrillers!"

By the time Letch got back, the drinking had stopped. Anne had paid the bar tab, and Fortney had Simon by the arm and was leading him outside.

A few minutes later they were all seated in Anne's car in the dark parking lot. Simon was in the backseat with Fortney and Letch was in the front with Anne. Both Fortney and Anne had to open a window the second Letch got inside and breathed.

With his most cynical smirk Letch said to Simon, "So was she sabotaging for Muslim fundamentalists, or who?"

"Tell us about the sabotage," Anne said, "and about dropping a boat."

"Look," he said. "I *admit* she came to me and wanted me to sabotage New Zealand's travel-lift. But, honest, I didn't think she was serious. Tell you the truth, I thought it was just a joke!"

"Uh-huh," Anne said, shooting warning glances at Fortney and Letch that said: Shut the fuck up and let me handle this.

Letch just shook his head. Pathetic. This was all pathetic! He was glad he worked vice and not homicide. And he was glad he didn't work near the ocean. Your brain must get all salt-clogged or something. Sabotage!

"How much do you know?" Simon asked.

"The question is," Anne said, "how much do *you* know?"

"Not that much," Simon said. "I mean, I never saw the chick before a couple weeks ago. I thought she was coming on to me when she started buying me drinks. Now I ain't sure what was going on."

"What do you think was going on?" Anne asked, utterly bewildered.

"Okay, here's what I think now that I had a chance to work it out. I think Blaze had a deal all along with the guy she called Mister Moneybags. I think she was really serious about me taking over the travel-lift job for the Kiwi racing team."

"Travel-lift?" Anne said.

"Yeah, like a crane. She said I could get some big money if I got the job. Because today was the last race with the Aussies, and she wanted me to sabotage the sling and drop the boat today."

Fortney, who knew a good deal more about sailboat racing and the America's Cup, asked, "Why?"

"So the boat'd be destroyed, of course! The Kiwis got another one, but Blaze claimed this thirty-two boat is the fast one."

"How much did she offer you?"

"Ten grand," Simon said, "but I thought it was a joke. I wouldn'ta did it!"

"Tell us," Fortney said. "Did that big guy have something to do with it? The one they call Miles?"

"Don't you know?" Simon asked.

Then Simon looked at Anne, who said, "We gotta hear it from you before we can determine if you really aren't part of the conspiracy."

That satisfied Simon. "Okay, she was supposed to dope him like a goddamn racehorse. She was gonna make him sick last night and I was gonna take his job today because I work for the boatyard they lease from us. But I *never* woulda did it!"

"Did you tell Blaze you *were* going to do it?" Anne asked.

"No way!" Then he hesitated and said, "Maybe in a *jokey* way. Like, I go, 'Sure, baby, I'll toss that boat for you.' Something like that. A joke, is all!"

"Why didn't she drug the Kiwi?" Anne asked.

"I don't know what she did. Miles and my brother-in-law, Gordon, they threw me outta the bar after they picked a fight with me. Gordon's a floater on the Kiwi boat."

"What's a floater do?" Anne asked.

"Nothing specific," Simon answered. "He's *there* is all. Just in case."

"Sounds like a cop," Fortney said.

"Why'd they throw you out?" Anne asked.

"Because Miles was jealous. He wanted Blaze, but she liked me better." Then he looked at Anne and said, "Can I ask you one question?"

"Go ahead."

"Is Blaze in jail? Did you arrest her for this? Because I can tell you one thing: I never agreed to *nothing*. I never woulda did something like that no matter how much money she tried to pay me. Even if I thought she was on the level, which I didn't."

"Do you remember I asked you if you heard about the woman they fished outta the bay? Mary Ellen Singleton?"

"Yeah?"

Anne was silent, watching him carefully in the darkness. Simon looked at Fortney, then back to her. Then he got it. "No!"

"Yes," Anne said.

"Oh, my Lord!" Simon cried.

"You see," Anne said. "It's a lot more serious than wrecking a boat, isn't it?"

"You sure it wasn't a suicide?"

"Very sure."

"Oh, my Lord!"

"You were one of the last people to see her alive," Anne said. "And you're unaccounted for from the time she walked out of that bar alone."

"I walked home!" Simon said. "Christ, I couldn'ta killed nobody. I was too drunk to find my own cock." Then he paused and said, "Pardon my French."

"Maybe you were faking it," Fortney said. "Being drunk."

"Oh, yeah. You should know. You bought me enough drinks trying to pump me about Blaze!"

"How many times have you been with her?" Anne asked.

"Only three. Always in this joint or the one across the street."

"Ever alone?"

"No. Always in a crowded barroom."

"Did she give you any idea who Mister Moneybags was?" Fortney asked.

"No, but . . ."

"But what?" Anne asked.

"I mean, I know who it *had* to be."

"Who's that?"

"I think Bill Koch."

"Who?" Anne asked.

Fortney said, "The leader of an America's Cup syndicate. His boat's *Mighty Mary*."

"Or Dennis Conner," Simon added.

"Why do you say that?" Anne wanted to know.

"Because one a them's gonna be facing the Kiwis in the finals. Who else'd give a shit about wrecking *Black Magic*?"

"*Black Magic*?" Anne said.

"I'll explain the racing stuff later," Fortney said. Then to Simon, "How did you know it wasn't the Aussies she was working for?"

"Because she planned the deal for today! The day we knew the Aussies would be eliminated. And I was supposed to do it at the *end* of the day, so the Aussies wouldn't have no reason to do it. And *Young America*'s gonna be eliminated in the defender races going on now, so that leaves Koch or Conner. She wouldn't say which, but I figured Koch. Smaller balls but bigger bucks."

"Who do you think killed her?"

Simon sat quietly for a moment. "Please, ma'am," he asked, fear in his eyes, "how did you find out about me?"

"We're detectives, aren't we?"

"Well, since you already knew Blaze tried to involve me in her scheme, maybe *he* knows *you* know! Maybe he wants to shut me up like he shut Blaze up!"

"Who?" Anne asked.

"Dennis Conner!" Simon cried. "Bill Koch might pay for dirty tricks, but Dennis Conner's got the killer instinct! I might end up with my fucking throat cut, floating in the ocean off Point Loma!" Then Simon Cooke stared bug-eyed at Anne Zorn and said, "Pardon my French."

CHAPTER 15

NOW THAT THE BABE NEXT DOOR HAD GIVEN HER YAPPING POOCH TO the family across the street, Letch Boggs slept in on Friday morning. When he finally got up, he made coffee and read the article about the body found in Mission Bay, identified late yesterday as Mary Ellen Singleton of Mission Valley. It wasn't much of a story, and there was no mention of Dawn Coyote or Oliver Mantleberry, so the media hadn't caught on to the connection.

Well, he hoped Anne and Fortney had had a good night's sleep, but he didn't think so. Not with all that intrigue and espionage ricocheting around in their skulls. After they'd sent Simon Cooke off, they jabbered like monkeys about Dennis Conner and Bill Koch and murder on the water. Cup crap. A crazy conspiracy that belonged in an Oliver Stone movie.

He figured the real truth was they were probably hot for each other, and this sabotage stuff was an excuse to get together. They might not even realize it yet, just two more lonely middle-aged cops trying to climb aboard a boat passing in the night. Letch sort of liked that imagery. He was feeling poetic today.

Well, he was all through dicking around with the whole bunch of them. He was the Shadow. He was going to find Oliver Mantleberry and wrap up both murders. Let them chase their spy theories with a bunch of rich sailboat sissies who couldn't choke a gas lawn mower, let alone a human being.

But before he was completely finished with the homicide team he had a little more business to conduct, so Letch got dressed, choosing a black aloha shirt with green Day-Glo lizards crawling all over it, and headed downtown.

Anne Zorn had already been to the morning briefing and heard about everything that had been learned the day before. First, that Blaze Duvall had been garroted, possibly with a rope or a thick wire. That the search of her apartment had led them to her closest relative, a sister in Escondido who hadn't seen Blaze in more than a month. And finally, that they'd gotten a break from a hotel on Shelter Island that reported a missing guest named Mary Ellen Singleton and a ransacked room.

By now they'd thoroughly gone over her telephone diary, but most of the numbers seemed innocent. In addition to her sister's, there were the numbers of her beauty salon, her aerobics studio, and three men who turned out to be guys in her aerobics class. But there were a dozen other men's names with double digits beside them and no telephone numbers. One of the names was "Jeremy 63."

There was also a number they'd already linked to Dawn Coyote through the separate phone line in Dawn's apartment. In short, it was easy enough to connect Blaze to Dawn, and Dawn to Oliver Mantleberry, but they'd found nothing to link Blaze to Oliver Mantleberry. That seemed to confirm their guess that during the ambush of Dawn Coyote, Oliver Mantleberry had been seen by Blaze Duvall, but that was the extent of their linkage.

And the best news of all was that, although the DNA testing was not finished, the preliminary work on the bloodstained washcloth indicated that it was the blood of Dawn Coyote, aka Jane Kelly.

There was one thing that Anne Zorn did *not* discuss with any member of the team or with her sergeant and lieutenant. That was her interview with Simon Cooke and his claim that Blaze Duvall had been murdered by none other than the most famous sailor on the planet, Dennis Conner. Letch had dismissed it, and Anne and Fortney had agreed to keep that little theory to themselves for a while. Fortney said he had an idea of his own and would call her that afternoon.

Anne was in the team's cubicle with Sal Maldonado when Letch Boggs came in.

"Good day, sleuths," he said.

"It's ninety-percent positive on the bloodstained washcloth," she said. "We'll know for sure pretty soon."

"Good enough for a warrant," Letch said. "A *death* warrant."

"And about the other case," Anne said. "A patrol unit got a call from a hotel on Shelter Island. A room registered to Mary Ellen Singleton had been ransacked. Her clothes were there but not her wallet or car keys. Her car was in the hotel lot."

"Oliver Mantleberry," Letch said. "Just like a scum-sucking pimp to steal her purse after he killed her."

"Maybe I'm slow," Anne said, "but how'd he get her body out of the room?"

"Simple. He didn't. He ambushed her away from the hotel somewhere, took her hotel key, and went back to the room."

"Why?"

"He needs money. He's holed up and almost broke."

"Just what I told her," Sal Maldonado said.

"I'd like to see her trick book," Letch said to Anne.

Sal looked at Letch and said, "It isn't a trick book. There're a few names with numbers by them that could be a code. Might be her massage clients, but no phone numbers. We checked out most of them. Pretty legit stuff."

"Mind if I have a look?" Letch asked.

Sal flipped him the telephone diary and left the cubicle for a coffee run. Letch went straight to the *S*'s and *J*'s. There was nothing interesting under *J*, but under *S* there was a local telephone number. He jotted it down, then turned to Anne. "I guess you ain't really convinced," he said. "You and Fortney're still gonna look for a killer down there on the water, am I right?"

"I'm not totally convinced Oliver did Blaze."

"Suit yourself," Letch said. "When I get him, I'll make him confess to dumping Blaze before I cap him right between the god-damn horns."

"What're you looking for in Blaze's telephone book?" Anne asked.

"A connection to Dawn. Or to Oliver."

"We've already—"

"I know, I know," Letch said. "Did anybody check this phone number here under *S*?"

He pointed to the number he'd jotted down. Anne shrugged as Sal Maldonado returned. "Did anybody check this phone number?" Letch asked him. "Under the *S*'s?"

"Yeah," Sal said. "It's a pet shop."

"Did Blaze have a pet?"

"She lived in a no-pet building," Sal Maldonado said.

"Then why'd she have a pet shop's number?" Letch asked.

"Probably wrote down a wrong digit," Sal said.

"Then you don't know why it's under *S*?"

Sal said, "The pet shop's called Pet's Heaven."

"That don't begin with an *S*," Letch said. "Must be a mistake. Guess I'll go get me a bite to eat. I was you, I'd forget wussy little murder suspects. Blaze Duvall was ambushed by a big strong guy."

"You know the most dangerous words a woman can utter?" Anne said. "'I can handle myself if a guy gets rough.' Well, I learned way back in my police career that no matter how fit I got, an average guy could toss me all over the place."

"So?" Letch said.

"She could've been strangled by just about *any* guy she came in contact with. He didn't have to be a big strong guy like Oliver Mantleberry. Even a wussy little amateur could've pulled it off."

"Oliver Mantleberry is your guy," Letch said stubbornly. "Bye-bye, Annie."

The moment Letch left Homicide he *ran* up the stairs to the Vice Unit. Three of the day-shift guys were working in the office but weren't particularly surprised to see Letch this early. Nobody questioned the Shadow, not as long as he got things done that ordinary mortals could not.

Letch went to a telephone and started dialing all combinations with the first digit of the phone number that Sal Maldonado had said was a pet shop. When he got an answer, he'd just say, "Oops! Wrong number."

When he was finished, he did the same with the last digit of the telephone number. On the third phone call, when he'd changed the written number 4 to a 3, it took a little longer to start ringing.

When the call was picked up by an old babe with a whiskey voice, Letch said, "Oops! Wrong number." And hung up, grinning.

He'd never met a hooker yet who had the imagination to transpose anything but a first or last digit in a confidential trick-book number. The delay on the ring had told him he had a call-forwarding location, hence, something very fishy.

He picked up the phone and called his old pal Rudy at Pacific Bell. "It's Letch," he said. "How ya doing? I got a number I'd like you to run up on your computer."

When Rudy objected, Letch replied, "Warrant? No, but I can get two box seats when the Padres play the Dodgers. Interested? Here's the number, but it's gonna roll over to another number."

A short time later the phone rang and Letch picked it up, saying, "Rudy? A cell phone? That's what I figured. Okay, thanks."

Fifteen minutes later Letch had AirTouch's version of Rudy on the phone, and he said, "Billy, it's Letch. I need a favor. Yeah, I know, but this is important. I got a cell phone number and I gotta know the billing address right away."

•   •   •

She was really looking forward to the show today. She had a plate heaped with cheese and crackers and sardines and a half-gallon of pralines 'n cream from Thirty-One Flavors. And two quarts of high-octane Coca-Cola. The cat was as excited as she was. The sardines were driving him crazy.

The talk show's panel consisted of family members who had dirty little secrets about sexual encounters with other than humans. The teaser indicated that one person admitted to sex with a llama. Another claimed she had sex with an extraterrestrial, but Serenity found that boring. These days *everybody* claimed to have had sex with extraterrestrials.

The second Serenity Jones got cozy in her recliner, the goddamn doorbell rang.

She sighed, grumbled, pulled her enormous bulk out of the chair, and went to the door. There was a man out there in the apartment courtyard, his back to the peephole. He was balding, shaped like a piñata, and had on a shocking Hawaiian shirt. There was something about that shirt. . . .

She opened the door, saying, "Yessssss?"

He turned around, leering, and she recognized him at once.

"Been a few years, Serenity," he said.

"Oh, m'God!" She flattened her hands over her enormous chest, which was heaving inside the muumuu.

"Can I come in?"

"Mister Boggs!"

"Some things never change, Serenity," he said, walking past the old woman.

He looked her over. Same Dolly Parton hairdo. Same Tammy Faye Bakker eyelashes. She'd gained an extra fifty pounds or so, not that it made any difference. He figured she was over seventy by now, maybe seventy-five. With babes this fat, you could never tell for sure.

"Is this official?" Serenity asked.

"Why? You engaged in some illegal activity?" With the leery little grin she'd always hated.

"If it is, I gotta see your warrant," she said.

"Let's siddown," Letch said. "Unless you're printing fifty-dollar bills in the back bedroom, I ain't interested in what you're up to. I gotta talk to you about somebody you know."

Serenity led Letch into the kitchen. He sat and she took two cans of beer out of the refrigerator, popped the tabs, and put one in front of him.

"Now I gotta move out again," she said. "If you found me that easy."

"It wasn't that easy," he said.

"So what's it about?" Serenity asked. "I'm retired from the game."

"Semiretired," Letch corrected her. "I was talking about you to somebody. Girl by the name of Dawn Coyote. Remember her?"

Serenity licked the foam off her lip and said, "Dawn . . . yeah, a skinny little blonde? Ain't you the one that busted my massage parlor that time? When Dawn was working for me?"

"Your memory's not as good as it once was," Letch said. "No, it wasn't my case, but I looked up the paperwork. There was another girl working for you then. Blaze? Remember her?"

"Sorta," Serenity Jones said. "I can sorta picture her."

"Redhead. Tall. Green eyes."

"I sorta remember her."

"Never seen the girl myself," Letch said, "but I feel like I know her. Anyways, did you read where Dawn Coyote was murdered early Easter morning?"

"No!"

Letch could see that her surprise was genuine. "Yeah. There wasn't much about it in the papers."

"I don't read the papers no more," Serenity said. "And the only TV shows I watch is happy stuff. I'm too old to wanna know about all the pain out there. Who killed the poor girl?"

"A pimp named Oliver Mantleberry."

"A nigger?"

"Yeah. Big dude, bald, mustache. Drives a white Jag. Or did. He's hiding out now, but I think he's still in town. Where's he gonna go?"

"I feel awful about Dawn," Serenity said. "Poor little thing. She was a lost little girl when I hired her."

"She never got found," Letch said. "But I'm gonna find *him*."

"What brings you to me?"

"Dawn stayed friends all these years with Blaze Duvall. And I found your phone number in Blaze's telephone diary."

"My number?"

"Well, your number *after* I decoded it and traced it through the rollover at the answering service to the cell phone company."

"You always were a smart cop, Mister Boggs."

"Did you see on TV about a woman named Mary Ellen Singleton getting fished outta Mission Bay yesterday morning?"

Serenity Jones didn't answer. She didn't have to. She tried to set the can down and missed the table. It clunked to the floor and beer spurted out. Letch picked it up and put it in the sink.

Serenity Jones suddenly looked her age. Her red moon face burst in a huge bubble of a sob. Then the old woman started weeping. In a moment the mascara was all over her lips and chin and the front of her muumuu.

Letch sipped his beer silently until she was finished.

"The . . . lamb," Serenity said at last. "The poor, poor little lamb! I wondered where she'd been the past few days!"

"Sorry to break it to you, Serenity," Letch said.

"Who . . . who killed her?"

"Same guy," Letch said. "Oliver Mantleberry."

"A pimp?" Serenity said. "A nigger pimp killed my little lamb?"

"Yeah, we figure she happened to be there when he ambushed Dawn Coyote. She saw too much and he had to shut her up."

"I hope he tries to resist arrest," Serenity said grimly. "I hope you *kill* him."

"What I was hoping was maybe you had a lead for me. That maybe some time or other you stayed in touch with Dawn?"

Serenity wiped her eyes and said, "No, but I knew Blaze talked to her from time to time. I saw Blaze maybe once a month, but we'd talk on the phone. Sometimes she'd pick up Chinese and bring it over here and we'd have supper together. And I arranged for a few highly recommended outcall clients from my old business, just to help her out."

"I ain't concerned about your outcall business," Letch said. "She wasn't killed for giving a massage. She was ambushed by Oliver Mantleberry. But I don't know where it happened, and if I knew that, maybe I could find him easier. Can you think of any way he coulda located Blaze after she moved outta her apartment? We know she was running from Oliver when she checked into a hotel on Shelter Island. And that's as far as we got."

"Dawn Coyote would be her only connection to a nigger pimp," Serenity Jones said. "Maybe he followed her to the hotel. I once had vice cops follow me for a whole week and I never even knew they were there."

"Maybe," Letch said, finishing the beer and standing up. "Well, it was a long shot. Good to see you anyways."

"Sure," Serenity said. "This means I gotta move again and change my phone number."

"Don't bother," Letch said. "I don't hassle senior citizens."

"I appreciate that, Mister Boggs," Serenity said. "I'm too old to move around all the time."

Letch handed her a business card and said, "Call me if you think a something."

"I will," she said, adding, "There's a colored girl used to work for me. She's out on El Cajon Boulevard now, hooked on drugs. She knew Dawn. I'll see if she can find Oliver Mantleberry."

"So long," Letch said.

Before she'd closed the door behind him, he heard the old woman start sobbing again, harder than ever.

Letch wasn't back at his office five minutes before he received a phone call. "Mister Boggs?"

"Serenity? What's up?"

"I been thinking, Mister Boggs. I truly might be able to help you find him through that colored girl I told you about. But she's gonna need a starting point."

"I can give you his home-base address in City Heights if you don't mention where you got it from. His old lady lives there with his three kids. She's an ex-hooker by the name a Tamara Taylor."

"I got a pencil," Serenity said. "I'm ready."

•   •   •

Both Fortney and Anne Zorn had a pretty good idea why they were getting together at seven that evening. Partly to explore unfamiliar territory and partly to see each other again. Since both were veterans of police marriage wars, both understood the extra zap that opposite genders sometimes get when they share a stressful police experience and get through it. Like all cops who'd been burned by marrying other cops, each had vowed to only date civilians and never marry another badge-packer.

Yet Anne rushed home after work, bathed, shaved her legs and underarms, gave herself a hair treatment designed to turn chestnut frizz into smooth tousles, and dabbed on perfume. All—or at least in part—because Fortney had arranged for an invitation to an America's Cup soiree, where they were maybe going to have an opportunity to see Simon Cooke's suspects in the flesh.

Anne decided to wear her latest purchase, which she couldn't afford but couldn't resist: a two-piece cocktail outfit with a camel-colored jacket and what looked like a straight knee-length camel skirt. But with the jacket off she was actually wearing a waist-hugging, sexy strapless dress. It had cost nearly a month's take-home pay.

If anything, Fortney went even more overboard, at least by his standards. He got off work early, sped home, showered, shaved, trimmed his own hair, showered again because he couldn't stop sweating, and used a hint of Grecian Formula because his hair looked as dull gray as a bayonet.

He'd borrowed a linen plaid sportcoat in beige and neutral tones from Leeds. It looked good with the cocoa-colored slacks he'd bought for a Christmas party that he hadn't bothered to attend. He wore his best blue oxford shirt and a yellow silk tie printed with figures of Babar the elephant. He fretted that the tie was too whimsical, but he wanted Anne to realize that he was younger than he looked.

Fortney tried a shoulder holster underneath the coat, then took it off. He tried a belt holster but didn't like that either. Technically they were sailing into uncharted waters with possible murder suspects, but a gun ruined the shape of the coat, so he left it at home.

Later Fortney couldn't believe how nervous he was when he gave his name to the parking attendant at the kiosk entrance to the San Diego Yacht Club.

The attendant checked a roster and said, "You're a guest of Mister Page? Okay, sir. Park anywhere on the water side of the lot."

Fortney saw that he was right on time—seven o'clock on the nose—but Anne was already waiting for him on the veranda. He didn't bother locking the Honda Civic and jogged up to the steps.

She smiled shyly when he said, "You look fabulous!" and opened her jacket to show off the strapless dress.

"Wow!" Fortney said.

"Thank you, sir," Anne said. "You look very fetching as well."

"I think this evening was a good idea."

"I'm not putting in for overtime," Anne said. "I'm treating this as a date. No obligation on your part, mind you."

"Let's find Murray Page," he said, suddenly feeling cotton-mouthed and awkward.

It wasn't hard to locate the bar; they just followed the noise. Everybody was revved up at the prospect of a racing weekend that involved all three defender boats battling it out—it meant more parties.

A slender, good-looking fellow about Fortney's age, wearing a tailor-made teal blazer, approached and shook hands.

Fortney said, "This is Murray Page. Murray, Anne Zorn."

"Hi, Anne," the man said. "I worked Northern with Mick in eighty. Or was it eighty-one?"

"Eighty-one," Fortney said. "Murray's a personal-injury lawyer now."

"Traded an honest job for a less honest one," the lawyer said. "But now I have time to sail. More than a hobby—it's almost my life."

"Thanks for inviting us," Anne said.

"I couldn't say no to old Mick. Said you need a crash course on the America's Cup."

He took Anne's arm and led the two cops away from the barroom to a corridor lined with black-and-white photos of past commodores, then into the trophy room to the glass cube that housed the Cup.

"There it is," he said. "Ugly, isn't it?"

"In a cute sort of way," Anne said. "We're just nosing around tonight. Our murder victim was *possibly* connected with somebody in the sailing community. That's about all we know, but we're trying to learn."

"I don't need to know the details," the lawyer said. "I'm just glad to help my old gang members."

"We wanna see what this regatta's all about," Anne said.

"If you find out, let me know," Murray Page said. "Do you know how the defender races work?"

"Nope."

"Well, all three American defenders are racing one another over the weekend, and on Monday maybe. *Young America* races Bill Koch's *Mighty Mary.* Then *Young America* races Dennis Conner's *Stars and Stripes* on Sunday. *Stars and Stripes* races *Mighty Mary* on Monday if *Young America* beats Conner. If Conner loses both races, there's a three-way tie at the end. Dennis has the worst record in the semis, so the other two would have a sail-off. Get it?"

"Sure I get it," Anne said. "Sure."

"Let's party," the lawyer said. "I'll introduce you around."

Murray Page walked them past the bar and out onto the rear patio, which faced the marina and the channel. To Anne, the boats looked much larger up close like this. There were sailboats and motor yachts of every description.

The lawyer said, "We're going to a little party on one of the demitasse boats."

"What's that?" Fortney asked.

"They're huge sailing yachts. Demitasse, like fine china. Here for the regatta. Some came all the way from Europe through the Panama Canal. I've seen them with swimming pools and grand pianos, not to mention full-time crews that include a chef. They have their own demitasse races, these rich people, these *extremely* rich people. The kind of people that call their skipper and say, Take the boat to Monte Carlo for a party on July the third."

"Got any clients like that, Murray?" Fortney asked.

"I wish," the lawyer said. "All I get is Harley riders with skull fractures. But it pays the bills."

After leading his guests down to the boat docks and some huge yachts, Murray Page said, "*That* one is the scene of the crime for tonight."

Eyrun was the largest sailing yacht that Fortney had ever seen and he had to stop to take it in. The mast looked taller than downtown police headquarters. The hull was cherry red, and the sun setting beyond Point Loma reflected red light back up on the mainsail, which had been left up for effect.

"Spectacular," Fortney said.

Murray Page said, "State-of-the-art. About a hundred and forty feet. Electric winches, computer-operated sails of Kevlar and carbon fiber. Teak throughout. Twin diesel. How much? Maybe fifteen million. I've heard the master charters her out for fifty grand a day. That doesn't include the beer, of course."

"Maybe we oughtta consider having our next barbecue here instead of the police pistol range?" Anne joked, staring up at the floating fortune eater.

"A crew of ten brought her here from New York," the lawyer said, leading them toward the dockside steps. "People with vessels like this seldom really travel on them."

There were at least a hundred people already milling around on the deck. Fortney hated to see the leather soles marking up the gorgeous wood, but he figured the crew would just sand and varnish it tomorrow.

A clutch of guests stood on the bow accepting drinks served on trays by young women in strawberry Polo shirts, khaki shorts, and white deck shoes. Several of the guests stirred Bloody Marys with celery sticks.

One of them waved to Murray Page, who led Anne and Fortney over. "Greetings shipmates-for-tonight!" he announced. "I'd like you to meet Mick Fortney and Anne Zorn, friends of mine also in the business of the law."

Several in the party groaned. One said, "*More* lawyers!" And everyone shook hands, exchanging names that were instantly forgotten.

Anne thought she was better dressed than most of the women, some of whom looked like Hummel figurines—although there were a few little numbers that cost more than her car. She and Fortney ordered Bloody Marys and chatted with a trio of sailing enthusiasts from Bangor, Maine, who'd leased a waterfront home for the entire regatta. All you had to do at boozy yacht-club parties, Anne realized, was nod from time to time and everybody thought you understood racing jargon and Cup politics.

Murray eventually drifted away and Fortney signaled Anne to follow him belowdeck, where he was more bowled over than she was. He had a better idea of how much this seagoing splendor cost. There were four staterooms, two with king-size beds, two with queens. Three of them had adjoining heads with nickel-plated fixtures. The master stateroom had platinum-plated fixtures and a huge Jacuzzi tub.

The salon and dining area boasted a marble fireplace and a

dining table made of solid mahogany, plus a state-of-the-art entertainment center concealed behind a sliding antique tapestry. The
galley featured gourmet appliances and a work space that most
restaurants would envy, and the crew's quarters were as spacious as
the apartment Fortney presently occupied.

All he could keep saying to Anne was, "This is a boat! It
actually *floats*!"

Some people were already helping themselves from the serv-
ing table in the dining area. There were chateaubriand, roasted
pork, and grilled sea bass, served by crew members in chef hats.

Anne said, "I'm not hungry yet. Let's go back up for the
sunset."

"Can't see it from this channel," Fortney said. "Point Loma's
in the way."

She looked at him over the rim of her Bloody Mary and said,
"We can see the *sky*."

Fortney liked her eyes. They were brown and alert, with
flecks as golden as apricots. But they weren't sassy and mocking and
heartbreakingly green like *hers,* like Blaze Duvall's.

When they were up on deck again, Anne was surprised to see
how many more guests had arrived. She wondered whether the
boat would sink under the weight of all its human cargo. A group
of four men and three women stood at the stern talking to Murray
Page. They all looked half-bagged; for that matter, so did the lawyer.

As the cops joined them, Fortney whispered, "Murray used to
drink anything that didn't have a human skull on the label."

Anne whispered, "Alcohol has caused untold death and misery to cops. Not to mention the terror of guessing who's on the
pillow the morning after payday."

The lawyer said boozily, "These are my law partners, Anne
and Mick. Anne and Mick, these are my shipmates-for-tonight,
whatever their names are."

Once again everyone shook hands and traded names. Fortney

flagged down a steward carrying a tray loaded with tulips of champagne. He took Anne's empty cocktail glass and replaced it with champagne, touched her glass with his own, and whispered, "We're with people that when their kids call to complain about school lunches, they're calling from Switzerland."

Murray Page said, "My friends are enthusiastic, but the only boats they know are gravy boats. I want you to tell them all about this weekend's racing. Who's doing it to whom and so forth."

"We know who does it to whom on land and sea," a very thin woman in a black satin shirtdress said to Anne and Fortney. "We can verify that Koch is the bastard everybody around here says he is."

But an exceptionally tall man, who said he didn't want to go belowdeck because he'd be smacking his head on the ceiling, said diplomatically, "It takes chutzpah as well as millions to win the America's Cup. And Koch's the second most famous Kansan next to Bob Dole. Don't sell him short."

A guy who talked as though his dentures were loose said, "The guy's so arrogant, all he needs is a riding crop and a saber scar. He's suing family members, you know."

"No, no! They're suing him," the man's wife piped up. She wore a white pants suit with a hot-pink shell that Anne thought was garish. "What do you expect with a fortune like that? Relatives *always* sue each other, don't they?"

"Well, I think he was brave to choose an all-woman crew," Too Tall said.

"I think he was a *jerk* to chicken out and put a man in as tactician," his wife offered. "*Mighty Mary* was manned—make that womaned—by a game team of females."

"How about the helicopter wars?" Slippery Teeth interjected. "Koch's always spying on Dennis Conner, sending choppers over his boat to take photos of his keel."

"The keel's under water," interjected a man with a bad toupee.

"I know, but I read where they could electronically enhance the keel configuration on the video."

"I've heard spies earn up to five thousand a month during these races," the oldest woman said. She wore a dress with a side split to the top of her thigh, even though what it revealed was support hose.

"That's ridiculous!" said Ugly Rug. "They're just a couple of boating blowhards. You couldn't control either of them with an overdose of medication!"

Then they all began jabbering at once:

"How about ninja raids by kayak, with scuba gear and underwater cameras?"

"That's a myth!"

"The Kiwis caught some guys last time and beat the living crap out of them."

"I don't believe that!"

"Heard about when a trucker was delivering a new keel in a sealed container and two hookers waylaid him at a truck stop? While one hooker's showing him *her* keel, the other one broke open the container and started snapping pictures!"

"Koch's about as believable as a whiplash plaintiff."

"Does anybody but me ever notice that Dirty Den can't smile with his eyes? He's about as sincere as Uriah Heep."

"Does Mike Tyson smile with his eyes? How about Jack Nicklaus with his game face on?"

"Dennis implied that the *Mighty Mary* crew were a bunch of dykes. I'll never forgive him for that."

"Do you think he wants your forgiveness?"

"He's a whiner. All he does is appeal the rules. His sails ought to be yellow and lined, like a legal pad."

"Seen his new bride?" the bony woman asked. "What is she, twentysomething? Not bad for a fiftysomething tippler with multiple chins."

"How'd you like to have that portly sailor on top of you?" the old babe asked.

"About like my Harry," the bony woman said. "I just yell, Elbows! Elbows! Harry, get on your goddamn *elbows*! Right, Harry?"

Everybody roared, picturing Fat Harry on his elbows panting like a beagle.

"Why doesn't somebody put a stop to all the spying?" Anne asked.

Fat Harry's wife said, "I'll tell you why. It's because nobody in the sailing world has the guts to enforce disqualification for someone after he pours fifteen or twenty million dollars into a boat race. The rules enforcers have all the moxie of the Trial Lawyers Association, who wouldn't have disbarred Judge Roy Bean."

The tall man said, "The real cynics may be in the New York Yacht Club. I hear that their committee is lending moral support to the Kiwis."

"Why's that?" Anne asked.

He said, "Because they wrote the rules years ago so that any American defender had to defend under *their* burgee. It backfired when the Aussies won it from them and Dennis Conner won it back for the San Diego Yacht Club. Now the San Diego Yacht Club benefits from that unfair rule. Unless a foreign challenger wins it from an American sailing for the San Diego Yacht Club, the New York Yacht Club can't ever get it back. They're here to become the first challenger of record the second the Kiwis clinch it."

Ugly Rug said, "The bottom line is, both Koch and Conner are such assholes, everyone I know is rooting for the Kiwis. Period."

"They may be assholes," Slippery Teeth retorted, "but they're *our* assholes."

Fat Harry, veteran of two hemorrhoidectomies, said, "I can tell you for sure, we're stuck with the assholes we got!"

CHAPTER 16

WHILE FORTNEY AND ANNE ZORN WERE HAVING THE TIME OF THEIR LIVES on a palatial sailing yacht, Tamara Taylor wasn't enjoying herself at all. One of her kids had fallen off her tricycle and was screaming her head off while Tamara was trying to bathe the baby in the kitchen sink.

Tamara figured that about now one of those damn phone solicitors would call since it was nearly suppertime. But instead of a telephone solicitor, she got a doorbell.

She hauled the baby out of the sink, wrapped him in a towel, and put him in his playpen. Then she grabbed the .38 revolver she'd borrowed from her neighbor Velma and peeked out to see if Oliver Mantleberry actually had the balls to try what he said he'd try.

No, it was a good-looking black girl in a short skirt and a tight jersey, with a silk jacket on top. The girl sure looked like a hooker, and she ought to know.

Tamara opened the door a few inches and said, "Who you lookin' for?"

"Oliver," the young woman said.

She had a pretty smile, Tamara had to say that for her. And a cute little beauty mark on her left cheek. Tamara said, "Did that bastard give you this address?"

The woman said, "I'm an old acquaintance of his."

"Yeah, I bet you are," Tamara said. "Well, he don't stay here no more and I don't know where he's stayin'."

Tamara started to close the door, but the young woman held it open with her foot. Tamara said, "Girl, you better be takin' your foot outta my door!"

"I'm sorry," the young woman said, "but this is important. I hear Oliver's in trouble and I owe him some money. Maybe he can use it?"

That interested Tamara. She opened the door a few inches and said, "You give the money to *me*. I'll see he gets it."

"I'm here to give it to him personal," the young woman said. "You know how it is."

"I oughtta know," Tamara said. "I'm the mother of his kids. Don't you trust me with the money?"

"Yes, but I have to give it to him personal."

Tamara said, "Harold sent you, right? Oliver said Harold owed him five hundred. You got five hundred dollars, girl?"

"Harold?" the young woman said.

"Look, I ain't got time to play no games," Tamara said. "Harold sent you, am I right?"

"Harold who?"

Tamara said, "Harold the gud-damn dope-dealin' son of a bitch from the Market Street Bar and Grill! That's Harold who! Now don't fuck with me, girl!"

"I'm sorry," the young woman said. "I can't give the money to you."

"Then you tell Harold to take and put his five hundred dollars in his crack pipe and smoke it! Because that's all that motherfuckin' Oliver would do with it anyways!"

With that she slammed the door and a pane of glass fell out, shattering on the welcome mat.

•   •   •

The Market Street Bar and Grill was doing some business at eight o'clock that evening. There were two white hookers sitting with clients in the booths, but everybody else in the place was black. Living Color was detonating out of the jukebox with enough decibels to kill every cockroach in the ceiling. Four men were shooting a game of nine-ball on one of two tables at the far end of the room.

It was hard to see why *Grill* was attached to the name of the joint, because the only edibles in front of customers came out of junk-food bags. There were plenty of drinks, though, and the air looked like SWAT had lobbed in a few of their smoke grenades.

A very shapely black girl in a short skirt sashayed in with a warm and friendly smile for one and all.

The pool players stopped the games and gave her a lot of "Yo, momma!" and "Say, baby!"

But she went straight to the bartender. "Johnnie Black and water. Tall."

"Comin' up, sweet thing," he said.

He was grossly fat with a flat-faced buttery smile, and what hair he had was cocaine-white. When he brought the drink to the young woman, he said, "I love that spot on your cheek there. Is it real or do you paint it on?"

"It ain't real, baby," she said to him. "But I am."

He laughed heartily, and when she put a ten-dollar bill on the bar, he said, "First one's on the house for new customers."

She said to him, "I'm lookin' for Harold. Is he here?"

"You lookin' right at him."

That surprised her, but she didn't flinch. She just said bluntly, "Oliver needs the money you owe him."

The fat man's smile faded and he said, "Come on, girl, let's talk where it's private."

When they were in a ratty little office behind the men's room, Harold slammed the door and said, "Girl, who sent you here?"

"Oliver," she said, still smiling.

"That's a lie. I know he ain't around."

She never changed expressions. "Okay, you want the truth? Tamara and her kids needs the money you owe him. I'm here to help her."

"How do I know you ain't a cop?"

With that, the young woman took her left arm out of the silk jacket and held it out under the dangling light. There was a Y of scar tissue running from her inner elbow almost to her wrist. Many of the needle marks were fresh.

"Okay, so you're a junkie," he said. "But you could be *workin'* for the cops."

"I told you who I work for," she said. "Don't you got no heart? Those children need food and clothes."

"I'm a bidness man. I do bidness."

"I wanna talk to Oliver. I got a message from Tamara for you. If he'll take fifty cents on the dollar on what you owe him, Tamara says he oughtta do it. That is, if it goes to her and the kids."

"You mean I'd only owe two-fifty then?"

"Yes, that woman needs the money."

"He never said nothin' like that to me."

"Tamara wants me to talk him into it."

"Why don't *she* do it?"

"She don't dare go near him now. You know why."

The fat man obviously knew why. He was thinking it over. Then he said, "I don't have no phone number. He calls me when he needs somethin'."

"Well, how do you bring him what he needs?"

"Somebody delivers. I got an address."

"I'll deliver it," she said. "And I'll ask him to phone you and tell you it's okay. And then you give me the two-fifty and I'll take it to Tamara."

"What're you, her sister or somethin'?"

"We're pretty close friends," she said. "She knew my momma when she worked the streets."

Hesitating, "I don't know about this."

"Tell you what," she said. "I'll pay you for whatever he needs. Right now. You gimme thirty bucks' worth a whatever makes him happy. I'll take it on over to him and tell him what Tamara wants him to do."

The fat man said, "I don't know. I jist ain't sure about this." But he was looking her up and down, mostly at her tits, saying, "You built for lac-tation!"

Her smile widened and she said, "You're a businessman and I'm a businesswoman. You gimme what I want and I'll give you a sample a what I usually get forty dollars for. How's that sound?"

"Yeah?"

"Yeah."

And then she reached down under his huge belly and unzipped his fly.

"Good luck," he said. "I ain't seen that thing for a coupla years. Not without a mirror."

"If it's there, I'll find it," she said.

•   •   •

After Anne and Fortney had finished their dinner, they took a stroll along the yacht-club docks in the moonlight. Fortney was gazing at the silver reflection on the water, and with an offshore breeze came the aroma of grilling fish. Jupiter sparkled. Though he couldn't see the planet's moons, it was somehow reassuring to know they were there.

Anne said to him, "What're you thinking about?"

"To tell the truth, Blaze Duvall."

"She was a striking girl," Anne said, disappointed.

"No, what I was thinking was, I'm glad she was dead before he put her down in that cold dark water."

"She was," Anne said. "Very dead."

"What else I was thinking was, we're way outta our element here. This isn't the kind of place where people like you and me look for bad guys. This rich man's sport is more corrupt than Uganda."

Anne said, "It's probably a dumb idea anyway. Maybe Blaze really *was* killed by Oliver Mantleberry."

They were quiet for a moment and then Fortney said, "You don't believe that."

"No," she admitted. "I never will."

"If this means we're giving up on an America's Cup murder, does it mean you won't be calling me anymore?"

"Why would I call you?"

"Oh, you might wanna take a ride on our boat sometime. And hang out with me by the south jetty and watch for the green flash. Or we could wait for one of those lightning storms where dead things come to life in castles and then go looking for trouble. Those kind of storms're beautiful when they're out at sea."

Anne looked at the reflection of spangled moonlight on the water and said, "Doesn't sound like a bad idea. Not bad at all."

Fortney faced her then and said, "Wanna go home now? Or maybe have a nightcap?"

Anne said, "I'm not really sleepy. Let's have a nightcap. This has been exciting, being in a place like this. I'll never get another chance."

"Suppose they'll accept cash from nonmembers?" Fortney wondered.

Anne said, "All the stuff we've heard about America's Cup pirates? They probably want pieces of eight."

•   •   •

Oliver Mantleberry was trying to watch TV but couldn't concentrate on anything. The walls of the hotel room were sweating and closing in on him. There were rust scabs on the bathroom fixtures, and the sink and the tub were so stained they looked like one of those inkblot tests. He'd seen parking garages cozier than this. He didn't know how much longer he could live like a fugitive. The fucking roaches were big enough to take on a pit bull.

But somehow he had to bide his time until he could get to her.

With her out of the way, he'd return to the world and go about his business. Let the cops arrest him. Let them try to make a case with nothing more than a bloody washrag.

He was just about out of cigarettes and gin and was considering a quick run to the liquor store across the street when he heard a knock at his door, a soft little knock. He jumped up, went to the door, and listened. Nothing.

Then the knock again and a woman's voice. "Oliver. You there?"

"No," he said. "There ain't nobody here by that name."

"Please open the door," the voice said. "Harold sent me."

Harold! Maybe the chiseling motherfucker was finally going to pay him! He wished he had a gun, but he didn't. He opened the door and peeked.

A little schoolyard smile, then she said, "Can I come in?"

He said, "Yeah, you kin come in."

When she got inside, she took off her jacket and said, "I got you a present from Harold."

"How much?"

"Not money. Not yet. But he says you like this?" She showed him a little plastic bindle, saying, "Want me to cook up a hit for you?"

He looked at the rocks and said, "I ain't done no crack in three days."

"You give it up?"

"No, but I got me some serious work to do. I don't wanna fuck up my head."

"If you don't want it . . ."

"Nobody said that. Put it over on the dresser."

"Long as I'm here," she said, "I wonder if I can take a taste of the present he gave to me?"

"What's that?"

She took out a plump little toy balloon and said, "Speedball."

"I don't like speedballs," Oliver Mantleberry said.

"Really? I heard you did. Or your girlfriend did?"

"What girlfriend?"

"I don't know any of your girlfriends' names. Jist a girl-friend."

"Harold's got a real big mouth. I'm gonna have a talk with him."

"He don't mean no harm," she said. "He wants to get rid of the debt he owes you."

"Then why the fuck don't he send me some money?"

"He will, baby, he will," she said. "But for now he sent you the rock. And he sent *me*."

"You? And whadda you do?"

"Anything you like," she said. "Anything you can think of."

"Well," Oliver Mantleberry said, finally smiling. "Maybe I will have me some rock."

"First I wanna taste my present, okay? It ain't tar. I can't stand the vinegar smell of tar. This is quality Mexican brown. And fine cocaine. You oughtta try some with me."

"That girl he was talkin' about? She turned me away from speedballs. I see what they done to her."

"Oh, baby!" she said. "You don't know what good is till you try real quality. You think it over. I promise if you'll let me give you one little pop, you'll be comin' down the track like the Amtrak train!"

•   •   •

By the time that Murray Page left the yacht party, he was definitely a candidate for car-key confiscation. He reeled into the barroom and spotted Anne and Fortney sitting at a table. The lawyer wove his way around the tables, then plopped into a vacant chair.

"Having a good time, you two?" he asked.

"Terrific, Murray," Fortney said. "Thanks."

"No problem. Have you learned all you ever wanted to know about the America's Cup?"

Anne said, "What we learned is, America's Cup racing

rules're about as obscure as the faces of dead people on postage stamps."

"And about as wholesome as gangsta rap," Fortney added. "But we had a chance to meet some people rich enough to make Paula Barbieri leave O. J. Simpson."

Murray turned around in the chair and yelled, "Ambrose, come over here for a minute, will you?" Then he said to Anne, "Here's the man who knows all there is to know about the America's Cup. Ask him *anything.*"

Anne saw a man at the bar turn, hesitate, and then put his drink down and make his way to their table. He was a nattily dressed older man, trim and good-looking, but with a very sad face for so festive an occasion.

Ambrose stood before them and said, "Yes, Murray?"

"Ambrose Lutterworth, meet Mick. And this is Anne. They're my guests and they're trying to learn a few things about the Cup. You're the man to tell them."

When Anne shook hands she said, "Hello. I'm Anne Zorn."

Fortney just smiled and shook hands.

It was easy for the cops to see that Ambrose Lutterworth was embarrassed and distressed, but Murray Page was their host and they didn't know what to do except humor him.

"I don't want to impose on Mister Lutterworth," Anne said. "It's getting late and we should go home."

"Ask him!" the lawyer demanded. "Ask him *anything*!"

To mollify the boozy barrister, Anne said, "Well, we've heard lots of stories about the millions that're spent on these races. We've heard that people'll stop at nothing to win. So I was wondering, how could anyone *care* so much about a trophy?"

"Good question, Anne!" Murray Page bellowed. "Tell us, Ambrose, what does the Cup mean in existential terms?" Then he belched.

People at the adjoining tables were whispering to one another now. Everyone was looking at Murray Page, who was swaying in his chair and chortling.

Ambrose Lutterworth stared off toward the marina before saying, "The government spends more money trying to save the California gnatcatcher from extinction. Why would anyone care that much about a gnatcatcher?" Then he said, "Please excuse me," turned, and walked back to the bar.

The cops were relieved. Anne said, "Poor guy. We really embarrassed him."

"That's the trouble with people," Murray Page grumbled. "They embarrass too easily."

"I think we'd better be going," Fortney said to his host.

"Why so soon?" the lawyer complained. "Aren't you having fun?"

Ambrose was signing his bar check and preparing to leave when a woman on the next barstool said to her husband, "Murray's drunker than usual tonight. And that woman with him, I don't know *what* her story is."

"What do you mean?" her husband asked.

"When we were in the restroom together, she was putting on fresh lipstick and I happened to notice her open purse. She's carrying a gun!"

"What?"

"A pistol in a holster. I saw it."

"No telling who Murray Page might be running with these days," her husband observed. "He's been in and out of Betty Ford lately."

"So has Jerry," the woman said. "But maybe not *lately,* at his age."

•   •   •

While walking Anne to her car, Fortney said, "From our conversations I've figured out you're about a year older than me."

"We had to say that, did we?"

"You look a *lot* younger," Fortney said quickly. "You have a very athletic body."

"I can do twenty pull-ups," she said. "Dead man's pull-ups. All the way up, all the way down. Can you?"

"We had to say that, did we?"

Anne said, "Are you sure we've never been married to each other? I'm getting an uncomfortable feeling."

"I've enjoyed working the case with you," he said when they got to her car. "And I'm getting that feeling, too. You were serious, weren't you? About the boat ride?"

"Call me," she said, "and find out."

"Okay," Fortney said, putting his hands in his pockets awkwardly. Wondering if he should give her a peck on the cheek or what.

She said, "I'm glad you're not all lit up over a dead woman. Like the detective in that old movie."

"I definitely prefer live women. But I'm never going to marry one again."

"I couldn't survive another name change," she said. "So we really do have a lot in common."

Suddenly he said, "I wonder if our actions on the job ever make a difference? Are you ever *sure* you made something happen? Or do things happen by themselves and we take what's left over to court?"

"I can't say for sure that I've ever made a difference," Anne said. Then, "You know something? You even *think* like I do. We may have to test your DNA to make sure you're not my lost twin."

Fortney reached down and touched her fingertips, saying, "We could roll your prints sometime and compare them to mine. Do you believe in alter egos?"

"I'll call you," she said. "Maybe if we go out on the water often enough, we'll see the green flash."

"They say the green flash brings love and happiness," he said. Quickly adding, "Of course, that's just what they *say*."

"You can't make it happen," she said. "A green flash, I mean."

"Any more than these sailors can make the wind blow," he said. "You try to be there when it happens."

"You try to *be* there," she agreed. "That's about all you can do."

"You have to float and hope," Fortney said to her.

"We're *all* just floating," Anne Zorn said to him.

CHAPTER 17

EVEN AFTER DROPPING A SPINNAKER ON SATURDAY, *MIGHTY MARY* DE-feated *Young America* by sixty-eight seconds. The women's team was still alive, but it needed *Young America* to beat Dennis Conner's *Stars and Stripes* on Sunday. No one could yet say how it was all going to end.

Ambrose sat on his patio deck drinking his morning coffee and reading about the regatta. His weight had been dropping alarmingly fast, and his teeth and jaws ached from the bruxing he did in his fitful sleep. In the past he'd enjoyed the nocturnal barking of the caged sea lions that the U.S. Navy kept down in the channel, training them for underwater surveillance. But now the barks had come to sound like the sorrowful cries of prisoners, and they filled him with sadness.

Suddenly a flight of a dozen wild parrots burst from the flowering jacaranda tree next door, screaming like cats. The once tame birds had escaped domesticity one by one over the years and by now had formed a wild community in the greenery of Point Loma. The parrot explosion was like a church window shattering, raining down jeweled feathers like shards of stained glass on a skeletal hillside olive tree. It made Ambrose want to weep, but he could not indulge himself. He tried to concentrate on a phone call he had to make.

Ambrose had been waiting for the start of business hours, and almost convinced himself that his imagination was running amok. The woman had a gun in her purse, but what did that mean? Everyone knew that Murray Page was a former police officer, so it was possible, but by no means certain, that she was a police officer, too. That'd be natural. She was about Murray's age, so they may have been old colleagues. It was silly to read more into it.

He'd spent days waiting for the police to call, hadn't he? Waiting for them to come for him. Somehow he'd imagined it would happen at night, but it *hadn't* happened. That meant there were no other copies of the tape, only the one he'd destroyed. If the police had searched her apartment and found duplicate tapes, he'd have been arrested by now.

So a woman had a gun in her purse. What did it mean? Nothing. Still, he was going to make a call just to satisfy himself. And then he was going to go out and watch the regatta, to see if Dennis Conner could manage a victory over *Young America,* keeping his hope alive.

At 9:10 A.M. he made the call to the San Diego Police Department, the call he had to make just to convince himself how foolish and paranoid he was. He reached an operator and said, "I'd like to speak to one of your homicide detectives." He almost had to smile at himself when he'd said it.

She said, "They don't work on Saturday, sir. Is this an emergency?"

"No," he said. "How about a Detective Zorn? Could I leave a message for her?" He felt utterly ridiculous. *Of course* there would be no detective by the name of—

"I'll transfer you to her voice mail," the operator said.

And then Ambrose Lutterworth heard a recorded voice saying, "This is Detective Anne Zorn, San Diego Police Department, Homicide. I'm away from my desk, but if you'll just leave—"

And his life was over. That was *that*. Blaze Duvall *had* made a duplicate tape and the police possessed it. For some reason they were not ready to arrest him yet but were keeping him under surveillance, in his own club, with the conscious help of Murray Page. And they were probably watching his office. Certainly they were now outside watching his house.

That explained the man in the blue station wagon yesterday afternoon. The man who pretended to be looking in a map book and checking addresses. And it explained the telephone call late last night, pretending to be a wrong number. He wondered how many detectives were assigned to his case. Of course, the man with Anne Zorn at the yacht club was obviously a detective, too.

He remembered exactly what she'd asked: "We've heard that people'll stop at nothing to win. . . . How could anyone *care* so much about a trophy?"

He should have known immediately. She was toying with him. She wanted him to know that the noose was tightening. What an ironic image: a noose. It would be very ironic, very *fitting,* to hang himself from the railing of his balcony. To let his dead eyes look down on San Diego harbor, at Dennis Conner's *Stars and Stripes* when it sailed out of the channel, perhaps to victory. But he couldn't do that. He couldn't die like . . . like *she* had died.

He'd been an avid if mediocre sailor all his life, as was his father before him. He knew what he had to do now. But he was so exhausted, he hoped he could find the strength.

•   •   •

A bit later that morning, Serenity Jones received a visitor.

The old woman peeked out, then opened the door and embraced her visitor warmly, saying, "Thank you, darling! Thank you!"

Her visitor, a pretty young black woman with a painted beauty mark on her cheek, said, "Always glad to help an old friend. You did me lots of good turns when I worked for you."

"It's on the kitchen table," the old woman said, then waddled back to her recliner, where she had to battle the cat for the vacated seat.

When the young woman came back into the living room, she was putting the package of money into her purse.

"If I'd had more I'da paid it," Serenity said.

"This ain't chump change," the young woman said. "I'm satisfied."

"You oughtta come by and see me from time to time," Serenity said. "I get lonely."

"Maybe I'll do that."

"You like Chinese?" Serenity asked. "You gimme a call and I'll order Chinese for us. We can talk about the old massage-parlor days. You and Dawn and Blaze and me, we had good times together."

"I will," the young woman said. "I'll do that, Serenity."

"Fab, darling," Serenity Jones said, waving bye-bye. "That's simply *fab*!"

•   •   •

The fleet of spectator boats were out on the racecourse just after noon, when somebody who couldn't have cared less about sailboat racing received an urgent phone call at her City Heights home.

"Tamara!" the caller cried. "It's Harold!"

"Yeah?" Tamara Taylor said. "Whadda *you* want?"

"I gotta tell you somethin', Tamara! Somethin' terrible! I'm in a hotel room. And I jist found Oliver. He's *dead*!"

Tamara thought that one over for a moment, then said, "What happened? One a his bitches shoot him?"

"No!"

"Stab him?"

"No! He died from a hot shot. The damn needle's still hangin' out his arm."

"No shit?" Tamara Taylor said. "Well, I knew he'd either die from drugs or bitches. But I thought it'd be bitches."

"What should I do?"

"Why you askin' me?"

"Gud-damn, woman! He was your old man!"

"It ain't my problem."

"Ain't your problem? Is that all you kin say? I'm here with your old man and he's layin' out on the bed stiffer than your gud-damn ironin' board!"

"Tell you what," Tamara Taylor said. "Put him in the back of a pickup and take him to the Sixth Avenue Bridge. Chuck the motherfucker off onto the freeway and let a few cars run over him. *That'll* soften him up."

CHAPTER 18

ON WEDNESDAY, APRIL 26, DENNIS CONNER IN *STARS AND STRIPES* DE-
feated Bill Koch's *Mighty Mary* in what the sailing world called a
miracle comeback. Conner's team was down by a sailing eternity of
four minutes and eight seconds at the final mark, yet somehow
made up a deficit of forty-two boat lengths, the most memorable
last-leg rally in Cup history. No trailing boat had ever made up five
minutes in three miles and won going away. Dennis Conner's team
had at last earned the right to defend the America's Cup against
Team New Zealand.

International journalists flooded into the San Diego Yacht
Club, as overweening and surly as your average customs official,
knowing they were covering the high colonic of sports, primarily
fancied in America by Northeasterners who also enjoyed squash,
lacrosse, and arbitrage larceny. The journalists had so many wires,
cables, and electronic gimcracks dangling off them, they looked like
creatures you shoot at in a video arcade.

Ordinary San Diegans laughed at a "race" that proceeded at
the speed of basal-cell carcinoma. They said it was all a blur of
inactivity. They said that America's Cup racing was so slow that the
announcer's comments echoed.

In short, nobody outside the yachting circle gave a shit one way or the other if Team New Zealand whipped Dennis Conner like a strawberry margarita and sent him packing back to New York or wherever he was going to settle.

•   •   •

Officially, the murder of Dawn Coyote and, unofficially, the murder of Blaze Duvall were considered cleared by the demise of Oliver Mantleberry from an accidental overdose of unusually pure heroin. Homicide detectives, especially Anne Zorn, suspected that Letch Boggs knew more about the pimp's death, but Letch wasn't talking. His leering snicker added to his legend by implying that yes, the Shadow *knows*.

•   •   •

Nobody had seen Ambrose Lutterworth since the party on Friday night. His office had left numerous messages that he didn't answer until Monday, when he told them he'd been ill with the flu. Then on Thursday, after Dennis Conner's spectacular comeback victory, Ambrose Lutterworth shaved, showered, and laid out his double-breasted blazer, his white flannels, and his very best pinpoint oxford shirt. He chose the tie of the Royal Temple Yacht Club, and he wore deck shoes so that nothing would seem amiss.

Ambrose carefully packed a picnic lunch in a heavy-duty wicker basket that had cost him three hundred dollars in London. He put the Stilton in the cheese compartment and included a bottle of old Château Margaux and a loaf of French bread. He made sure he had a corkscrew, a cheese board, and a cheese knife. He almost forgot a china plate but then remembered, wrapping it carefully in a white linen napkin.

When he showed up at the club that afternoon, he went to the glass cube housing the America's Cup. He looked at the Cup for a long time. He was content now, convinced that it would *not* be going to New Zealand. Dennis Conner was still the greatest sailor in the world.

Then he went to the boat slip belonging to his longtime friend, Henry Roth, who was working on his 58-foot motor sailer. Henry was surprised when Ambrose asked if he could take out his 22-foot Catalina sloop for a sail.

Henry Roth told him to help himself but was very worried by the gaunt, almost ghostly appearance of his old friend.

"I've had a terrible bout of flu," Ambrose explained. "If I don't get out in the fresh sea air, I'm afraid I'll never recover."

•   •   •

There was wind and a low somber sky off Point Loma that day. Tattered cormorants and gulls veered toward his sloop, hoping for tidbits. Ambrose was a bit chilly, but the red wine helped to warm him. He sipped the Margaux and nibbled some cheese and bread while setting his course.

When he was half a mile past the mouth of the channel, he balanced the sails, trimming the jib sheet and the mainsheet to run downwind. He rigged a preventer and tied it to the rail to keep the mainsail from flopping if the boat headed up into the wind and prevented an accidental jibe when going downwind. Then he tied the tiller, centering the helm. He was sure that it would eventually run aground somewhere on Coronado strand and not suffer damage on the sandy beach.

Ambrose wished he could have at least seen the first race on May 6, but he dared not wait any longer. How close they must be by now, close to knocking on his door. How near he was to dishonor and disgrace, not just for himself but for the club and the regatta. And for the Cup itself. He couldn't face that, and he hoped that if he did the right thing the police would have no reason to reveal all that they'd learned about him.

Years ago he used to race with a man who played Bobby Darin's "Beyond the Sea" on his tape deck at the end of every regatta. Now Ambrose could hardly remember the man, but he could almost hear the upbeat song.

How happy we'll be beyond the sea
And never again I'll go sailing.
No more sailing. So long sailing. Bye-bye sailing . . .

Ambrose stood up gingerly so as not to tip the picnic basket. He removed his blazer, folded it carefully, and put it on the seat.

It would look like a boating accident. There were lots of accidents in these waters, even with experienced sailors. They'd think he'd rigged the boat so he could have a nice relaxing sail. Perhaps he'd stood up to take a pee and lost his balance. People intent on self-destruction would never take a picnic basket so carefully packed and arranged. Would never have tasted the Stilton and bread. Would not have sampled the Margaux.

He knew the water was very cold, so the best thing would be to swim straight out as hard and as fast as he could. He'd never been a strong swimmer. It wouldn't take long.

Now no one need ever know what a coward he was. What a coward he'd always been. His mother had always known, and she'd always been right.

A gull screamed then, hanging on the wind, drifting to and fro like a pendulum marking the time. Telling him it was *his* time.

The blue and green were gone from the sea. The water was as gray as a shark's fin. But then the sun broke through the ragged clouds and cast a golden glow on the Point Loma lighthouse and the sandstone cliffs.

•   •   •

Cloud shadow, dappled whitecaps, shimmering cliffs receding. Cold, dark water enveloping.

The beloved memory sustains him: A balcony in Cap d'Antibes with the sun roaring down. Basking in the glow of reflected silver sunlight from the America's Cup.

EPILOGUE

They called it "Slaughter on the Water." Dennis Conner had persuaded defeated rival Pact 95 to give him the use of their fast boat, *Young America,* but nevertheless his team was annihilated in five straight races by *Black Magic.* The Kiwis led at all thirty marks and gained time on twenty-five of the thirty legs, trailing less than a half hour in thirteen hours of sailing. It was one of the most lopsided defeats in Cup history.

The remains of Ambrose Lutterworth, apparent victim of a sailing mishap off Point Loma, were found entangled in the kelp beds by a fishing trawler on May 6, the date of the first Kiwi victory. After an autopsy revealed death by drowning, he was buried on May 14, the day of Team New Zealand's final victory, when they officially took the America's Cup, which was bound for Auckland.

Even Dennis Conner admitted that the Cup would probably enjoy its sojourn in the City of Sails. "The America's Cup will have a good life in New Zealand," Conner said, thus joining a legion of others who, over the span of a century and a half, had anthropomorphized the silver vessel.

That particular subject, of attributing human qualities to non-human objects, came up when one of the news cameras revealed cheering throngs in New Zealand pubs with banners that read: CONNER IS A GONER and BLACK BOAT. WHITEWASH. The announcer was gleeful and said that their archenemy had received the worst thrashing ever given outside of an English boarding school.

The television feature ended with a shot of a deliriously happy lifelong member of the Royal New Zealand Yacht Squadron, who said, "When the lads arrive home I hope to greet the Cup with a big kiss and an assurance that life will be good under my care."

When asked if it was normal and healthy to attribute human qualities to a trophy, the yachtsman said, "We do it with dogs, cats, horses, boats, lawyers. Why not a gloriously historic trophy?"

When the yachtsman was asked what assurance he had that the Cup would approve of his being its caretaker, the yachtsman said, "No one could love the Cup more. I shall be the most reverential caretaker the Cup has ever known. I fully understand the responsibility and honor of being Keeper of the Cup."

ABOUT THE AUTHOR

Joseph Wambaugh, formerly of the Los Angeles Police Department, is the author of fourteen previous books—*The New Centurions, The Blue Knight, The Onion Field, The Choirboys, The Black Marble, The Glitter Dome, The Delta Star, Lines and Shadows, The Secrets of Harry Bright, Echoes in the Darkness, The Blooding, The Golden Orange, Fugitive Nights,* and *Finnegan's Week*—all of them outstanding best-sellers. He lives in Southern California.